THE JOB

THE JOB

DOUGLAS KENNEDY

New York

Library of Congress Cataloging-in-Publication Data

Kennedy, Douglas, 1955–
The job / Douglas Kennedy.—1st ed.
p. cm.
ISBN 0-7868-6370-6
I. Title.
PR6061.E5956J63 1998
8139.54—dc21 98-11222
CIP

Designed by Nancy Singer

FIRST EDITION

10 9 8 7 6 5 4 3 2 1

For my father,
Thomas J. Kennedy,
and for my brother Roger

The true way leads along a tightrope, which is not stretched aloft but just above the ground. It seems more designed to trip one than to be walked upon.

Beyond a certain point there is no return. This point is to be reached.

—Franz Kafka

ONE

ONE

Business was good today. I wheeled, I dealed, I schmoozed, I *closed*.

By seven in the evening—before calling it quits for the night—I followed a piece of advice given to me by my first boss, and listed the major things accomplished in the past ten hours. There were three highlights: (1) I nailed down a double-page spread with Multi-Micro, (2) I finally managed to score a meeting next Friday with the head of marketing at Icon, and (3) Ivan Dolinsky, my main outside sales guy for the tristate area, called me from Stamford in a state of high excitement, saying that GBS was about to commit to a major multipage insert—a deal I'd been pressing him to conclude for weeks.

Like I said, not a bad day's work—and one which leaves me on target to hit my April quota a full nine weeks ahead of schedule. Of course, there are a lot of variables at work here. Will Ed Fisher, chief marketing god of Icon, finally buy my act and start throwing some serious business my way? Will Ivan really be able to wrap up this GBS sale—or is this going to be another of his also-rans? (He's had three back-to-back, and it's getting me worried.) And though I did talk AdTel into a premium position spread for their new SatPad DL notebook, I was a bit disappointed when their media sales honcho, Don Dowling, would only green-light a single display. Especially as most of our phone calls consisted of me dangling bait, incentives, sweeteners—anything to get him to agree to more space.

"Don, it's Ned Allen here."

"Bad timing, Ned," he answered in his thick Canarsie whine. "I'm heading out the door."

"Then I'll cut to the chase."

"I'm telling you, I'm running—"

"Don, you know that at ninety-five grand for a back-of-the-book double-pager we're still thirty percent cheaper than the competition. . . ."

"Yeah, yeah, yeah. But their circulation is thirty-five higher than yours."

"Only if you believe their figures. You see the ABC stats last month? Our circulation was up seven percent for the third straight month in a row. . . ."

"They still got one point two million versus your seven-eighty—which, for my money, is a sizable circulation gap."

"Look, Don, you know as well as I do that when it comes to niche marketing, numbers like that mean *nada*. I mean, so what if they've got one point two? For a high-end product like the SatPad DL, you need the sort of mid- to high-market site that we can offer. You just go it alone with them, you're strictly aiming for the bargain basement. Okay, okay, I know they've got the stats, but so do the Chinese. A billion people. Too bad only a thousand of them can afford to buy anything more than a bucket of rice. Same situation here."

Don Dowling sighed loudly and said, "Ned, you tried this song and dance on me last month. . . ."

"And last month you wouldn't bite. But now we're doing business. A double spreader. A great start to our relationship."

"How many times do I have to tell you—it's not a relationship . . . it's a one-night stand."

"I know, I know—but all relationships start as one-night stands. You finally talk her into bed, next thing you know, it's love and marriage. And when you see the results you get from the back of our book—"

"Then maybe we'll do another one. But I'm not committing us to anything more."

"Even with an offer of a twenty-five percent discount and a guaranteed premium position for the entire spring quarter?"

"We're covering old ground here. Your guy Ivan offered me the same deal last week."

"Ivan offered you twenty percent. But as his boss I can—"

"What? Flatter my ass with an additional five percent sweetener? Get a life."

"Do the math, Don. We're talking nearly twenty-two grand that you'll be saving on prime display space."

"I've done the math, Ned. I've made a decision."

"Tell you what: We'll throw in a four-color bleed for the April issue."

"Ned, this conversation's history."

"How 'bout lunch next week? You in the city?"

"Dallas."

"Week after?"

"Ned . . ."

"You like French, we can do Lutece . . ."

"Since when has CompuWorld been able to afford Lutece?"

"Since we became players."

"You're still in third place."

"We try harder, Don. So how about a week from next Friday?"

"You're a pain in the ass, Ned."

"But an effective one. Next Friday?"

Another elongated sigh from Don Dowling.

"Call my secretary," he said, and hung up.

Got 'em! Well, sort of. Like I said, we're talking variables here. "Call my secretary" is about the oldest kiss-off line in the book. But in the case of Don Dowling, I think it means he's finally willing to sit down with me. No doubt the prospect of stuffing his face at Lutece is also something of an incentive. After all, lunch at a hundred-buck-a-head restaurant—surrounded by the city's heaviest hitters—can't help but make a guy from Canarsie feel like he's finally hit the big leagues (hell, I'm a poster boy for upward mobility myself, having grown up in a shit-kicker corner of Maine). But Dowling also knows that there's a price attached to accepting my invitation. By agreeing to break overpriced bread with me, he's signaled the fact that a barrier has come down—and that a new game *could* be played between us. Whether he decides to play this game will depend entirely on the success of the lunch.

Selling, you see, all comes down to one word: *persuasion*. And by consenting to lunch, Dowling has also indicated that he's willing to sit through a display of my persuasiveness—and find out if I can talk him into an ongoing commercial commitment. He'll want to see how I schmooze him, check out my style. Am I the shrewd shark who gets him talking about everything but business until the coffee arrives? Or will I be the overanxious type who starts hustling him before the bread hits the table? He'll gauge whether I'm the sort of salesman who's willing to peddle his elderly mother to the Arabs if it means getting results . . . or some grace-and-favor merchant who's deigning to do business with a dweeb. Most tellingly, he'll be assessing the way I approach him. Too much deference and he'll hate me for overplaying my hand. Too little, and he'll think I consider him nothing more than a Brooklyn *nouveau*.

Again, it all comes down to a bunch of variables. Variables are what keep the game interesting. And variables are also what keep me awake at three in the morning, worried about whether tomorrow's the day when it all starts to implode—when my well-honed pitch would finally lose its kick, stopped dead in its tracks by the one word I dread most in life: *No*.

So far (and I've only been in this business for four years), I've managed to dodge that nightmare that every salesman fears: the loss of his persuasive powers. My boss, Chuck Zanussi, summed it all up beautifully:

"You know, Ned," he'd said to me over lunch around eighteen months ago, "every goddamn bookshop in this country is crammed with volume after volume about how to close that deal and be the biggest swinging dick in your division. But forget all the business-guru, 'channel-into-your-influence-zones' crap. At the end of the day, selling is about just one thing: getting someone else to say *yes*. That's it. That's the object of the exercise, the bottom fucking line. *Yes*. Success is *yes*; failure is *no*. It's that simple. In fact, the way I see it, everything in life comes down to talking people into giving you a yes. Unless you're into date rape, you don't get laid without a yes. You don't get married without a yes. You don't get a mortgage for a house without a yes. You don't get a job without a yes. And you certainly don't *keep* a job without a shitload of yesses.

"Y'see, that's what *you* do every day: You procure yesses for this company. And you do it pretty well, I might add . . . which is why I'm bumping you up a notch."

And that's when he offered me the job of Northeast regional sales manager for the third biggest computer magazine in America.

The magazine is called *CompuWorld,* and the only reason we're in third place is because we're the new kids in town. Just five years old, but without question the real comer in a crowded market. Don't take my word for it. Just consider these numbers: The two titles ahead of us—*PC Globe* and *Computer America*—have each shed a total of 34 percent market share since we showed up on the block in '92. Of course, back then, every industry analyst was predicting we'd be on our way to the morgue within eighteen months. *We're talking 2 million readers already for the established titles, who needs a third? No room for an upstart*—blah, blah, blah.

O ye of little faith. Look at us now. Circulation of seven-eighty, a mere fifty thousand behind the number-two boys, *Computer America*. Hell, two years ago, there was half a million separating us. Now they're bleeding faster than a hemophiliac, and we're the title in the ascendant. You see that story on us in *AdWeek,* "The *CompuWorld* Phenomenon"—the basic gist of which pointed to our magazine as the beneficiary of the biggest readership defection in the past ten years. Want to know why? Editorial quality and pure visual class. I mean, when it comes to the caliber of layout and graphics, we're the *Vanity Fair* of consumer magazines. Okay, I take Don Dowling's point: We're still a sizable distance behind *PC Globe* in terms of circulation. But, like I told him, they're Filene's Basement to our Saks Fifth Avenue. I mean, if you're only interested in low-end/mass market clientele, by all means blow most of your media budget on a couple of big *PC Globe* spreads. But if you're trying to reach the more sophisticated corporate and personal consumer . . . Well, let's face it, there's only one choice in the marketplace, and that's . . .

Sorry, sorry—I'm pushing a little too hard here. As my wife, Lizzie, likes to tell me, sometimes I forget that there are hours of the day when I don't have to be chasing a *yes*. It's kind of an obsessive business—sales—and one which demands nonstop results. Just consider my monthly and annual quotas. *CompuWorld* publishes twelve issues a year. The average size of the book is around

320 pages—of which I am responsible for seventy pages of advertising copy. On average, we sell a page for $35,000 (though premium positions, like the back cover, can cost up to 30 percent more). Now 35k times 70 equals $2.45 million. My monthly quota. Multiply that figure by twelve and you come up with $29.4 million—a figure that scares the shit out of me every time I think about it.

Thankfully, I'm not the only person in our office who lives in terror of that $29.4 million mountain. As regional sales manager for the Northeast, I'm in charge of a staff of ten, all of whom have to hit their own individual sales targets every month. There are a half dozen telesales operators who spend every day working the phones, trying to close small deals. They're my bread-and-butter people. They hustle small retailers, modest-size software companies, and all those penny-ante operators who fill the Classified section at the back of the book. A lot of the uppity schmucks in Editorial make fun of the outfits we snag for Classified—mom-and-pop businesses that peddle discount bar code scanners, or software pawnbrokers who offer "Cash for Your Old Memory." But, believe me, all those little eighth-of-a-pagers are an essential component of the overall sales strategy. And they account for 20 percent of the space we have to fill each month.

My Telesales team works closely with my four outside sales reps—Ivan Dolinsky in tristate, Phil Sirio in the five boroughs, Dave Maduro in Massachusetts (the Boston area is probably the key software manufacturing market in the Northeast), and Doug Bluehorn covering the rest of New England. The pressure is on these guys nonstop to score the big half- and full-pagers, and to network heavily with all the media sales and marketing people for the major players in our region: AdTel, Icon, InfoCom, and the monster GBS (Global Business Systems, the biggest computer hardware manufacturer on the planet—of which we all wanted a piece).

Strictly speaking, I don't have to sell a single page of advertising—though I do get involved when a guy like Don Dowling refuses to play ball with one of my reps. My job is to be the strategizer. I'm the coach, they're the players. I coordinate all the campaigns we run; I monitor the advances of my sales team. I encourage, galvanize, threaten. Because if they don't hit their quotas, then I take an even bigger hit. And I'm not just talking about getting my ear bent by Chuck Zanussi—I'm also talking about a financial hit, since my bonus is pegged to how much business my division brings in. My salary is a basic sixty thousand a year—near-poverty-line executive wages in New York. If my team scales that $29.4-million mountain, then I'm due another sixty at the end of the year (the members of the sales force also receive incentive bonuses for every dollar of business they bring in). However, if we achieve less than the designated annual quota, then the bonus figure shrinks accordingly.

But ever since I took over as regional sales manager eighteen months ago, we've yet to have a quota shortfall. And when the Christmas bonuses are handed out Friday, December 12 (a date I starred in my diary), I fully expect to see the words SIXTY THOUSAND DOLLARS written across the check . . . which will help me sleep better, as I'm currently living on hot air. I owe something like $20,000 on my five credit cards. I'm clocking up $325 a month interest on a $25,000 bridge loan I took out five months ago. I'm now a month overdue on my annual $795 membership at the New York Health and Racquet Club. I've just booked us on a seven-day Christmas-week package to the Four Seasons Hotel in Nevis (a staggering $5,600 for room and airfare only—but, as I keep telling Lizzie, it's the first vacation we've had in three years). And Barney Gordon, D.D.S., informed me last week that I'm looking at $3,200 to replace an old bridge that has finally overstayed its welcome after twenty-one years (the result of a bicycle accident at the age of eleven, which cost me my upper front tooth). Unfortunately, bridge work isn't covered under the company medical plan. And though three grand plus in dental work is, financially speaking, about the last thing I need right now, Doc Gordon says I have no choice but to get the new bridge (the old one is so dangerously loose it's bound to pop out at any moment—like in the middle of a Lutece lunch with Don Dowling).

In other words, I'm going to see little change from that sixty-grand bonus check. But at least I'll be in the clear for the first time in three years. And my one big New Year's resolution for 1998 is: *Never get your ass in such a bad financial position again.*

The phone on my desk buzzed. I looked up from my list of the day's accomplishments and hit the speaker button.

"Ned Allen here."

"How much money you make for me today, Allen?" It was my boss, Chuck Zanussi.

"Plenty, but I've blown it all."

"Oh yeah? On what?"

"Life's little essentials: a new Ferrari, a Learjet, courtside season tickets for the Knicks . . ."

"Do I get one of the tickets?" Chuck asked.

"I thought you were a Nets fan."

"You know, some bosses would fire you for that comment."

"But you've got a *great* sense of humor, Chuck."

"You need one in this business." He dropped the bantering tone. "So tell me . . ."

The line began to crackle. "Where are you?" I asked.

"Midair between Chicago and La Guardia."

"I didn't know you were hitting Chicago today. I thought you were flying straight back from Seattle."

"So did I—until I got a call asking me to stop by Chicago . . ."

"A call from whom?"

"We'll get to that. So tell me—"

"I think I might have finally convinced that Big Buddha, Don Dowling, to come to the table."

"Anything firm?"

"A single-pager for April."

"That's it?"

"But he's willing to do lunch the week after next."

"Guess that's something."

"It's more than something, Chuck. It's a real breakthrough. Ad-Tel's been dodging us ever since Dowling stepped into the job eight months ago. And Ivan's been chasing him like hell."

"But *you* closed it—not Ivan."

"Ivan's all right."

"He's worrying me. He hasn't scored anything in months."

"Two months, that's all."

"That's long enough," Chuck said.

"We're still hitting the quota."

"Only because everyone else is covering for him."

"Ivan's been a winner before, he'll be a winner again. And he's on the verge of closing a big spread with GBS. . . ."

"I'll believe it when I see the ink on the contract."

"Come on, you know what the guy's been through. . . ."

"Yeah, yeah, yeah."

"I love a compassionate publisher."

"I covered his ass when he went through a cold streak like this two years ago."

"And he pulled through then. Even surpassed his quota by twenty-two percent. The guy's going to pull through again."

"I'm touched by your faith in humanity, Ned. It's so fucking uplifting."

"So why the side trip to Chicago?"

"Tomorrow."

"What?"

"I'll tell you tomorrow. At breakfast. Eight A.M., the Waldorf."

"Something up?"

"Tomorrow."

"So something is up?"

"Maybe."

"What d'you mean, *maybe*?"

"*Maybe* means maybe, that's all."

"It's bad, right?"

"Ned, we'll deal with this—"

"It's got to be bad."

"It's *not* bad."

"Then what is it?"

"It's . . . *interesting*."

"Oh, great."

"All will be revealed at breakfast. Be there."

I put down the phone. I drummed my fingers on my desk. I chewed my lower lip. I craved a cigarette—and regretted having kicked the habit six months earlier. *Interesting*. I didn't like the sound of that. It could only mean one thing: change. And change—especially in a big multinational organization like this one—was usually a synonym for *trouble*.

You see, *CompuWorld* is just one of a dozen international titles owned by the Getz-Braun Group. They're an American-founded company who owns a string of audio, video, and computer magazines in Germany, the U.K., France, and Japan, as well as the U.S.

They also have a very successful division that plans and runs major computer trade shows around the globe. It's a lean, no-frills multinational—and intensely corporate. Once you join the "Getz-Braun Family," you're a protected member of the organization as long as you're a "producer."

"Let me give you the official and the unofficial schtick about Getz-Braun," Chuck Zanussi said during my job interview in 1993. "The official line is this: You're joining one of the most lucrative publishing companies in the world. You want to know how lucrative? Get this: Thirteen months ago, Bear-Stearns purchased the entire worldwide organization for one point seven billion, then, seven months later, sold it to our current Japanese owners, Yokimura, for two point three billion. Not a bad chunk of change for half a year's interim ownership.

"Now the unofficial line on this place, the way you either survive or die here comes down to two simple questions: Can you conform, and can you perform? You might be a loose cannon when it comes to schmoozing customers, but around the office you've got to be a team player. If you start playing 'my dick's bigger than yours,' you'll be out the door before you have time to zip up your fly. Point two: As long as you keep making the company money, your ass is secure. It all comes down to productivity and whether you can keep hitting the quota month after month."

Ever since I joined *CompuWorld*, I've always hit the quota—and have been rewarded with steady promotions through the ranks. Hell, during my first two years in Telesales, I was the magazine's number-one rainmaker, bringing in 18 percent more business than any other sales rep. And since being named a regional sales manager, my team had consistently outpaced all other regional divisions when it comes to generating advertising revenue.

So why should things suddenly be . . . *interesting*? And why was Chuck—Mr. Shoot from the Hip—being so goddamn cryptic about what went down in Chicago?

I stood up and looked through the glass walls of my office. It's not really an office—more of an eight-by-eight cubicle stuck in the rear of a charmless white brick 1960s office building on Third Avenue and Forty-sixth Street. At least I have a window, which affords me a panoramic view of a grimy transient hotel on Lexington Avenue (the sort of down-at-the-heels joint that attracts package tourists from eastern Europe). Through the glass walls of my office, I can keep an eye on the action: a tiny rabbit warren of cubicles, in which my Telesales people remain umbilically attached to the telephone for the prescribed eight hours a day. Except, of course, for the office achiever, Debbie Suarez, who was, as always, still there after 7:00 P.M., jabbering a mile a minute into her headset as she hustled some poor unsuspecting schmuck who'd made the mistake of letting her unleash her sales pitch.

Around *CompuWorld,* Debbie's known as "Tommy Gun" Suarez because of her ability to talk faster than anyone else on the planet. She's also a spy extraordinaire, who knows everything there is to know about everyone at the magazine. The fact that she's the size of a kewpie doll—around four foot ten, short, dark curly hair, big green eyes, the build of a flyweight boxer—makes her Niagara of words even more startling.

As I left my office and approached her cubicle, I could hear her going at full throttle.

"I know I know I know I know, but lookit, where do you think you gonna find a better outlet? Nah nah nah nah. They tell you that but then you end up with nothin'. And I'm talkin' nothin' *nothin'*. You think I'm telling you all this seven P.M. on a Tuesday night—I could be home with my kid—if I didn't think I could do something for you? Whadda I mean, *do something*? Six quarter-pagers for six months. I can give you the deal of the week. Fifty-two five. Sure sure sure, it's thirty-five a page. A *full* page. But quarters are ten a pop. Why? You ask *why*? Get outta here—you know why. No quarter-pagers are ever, *ever* one fourth the price of a full page. You're always gonna pay ten percent more . . . except right now, where I'm offering you six quarters for exactly what you're asking. That's eight seventy-five per issue—and you're saving . . . hey, you're fast with the calculations. But now hit 'times six' on that calculator of yours. . . . That's right, we're talking seven-five you still got in your pocket. I mean, is that a discount or what? Yeah, yeah, yeah, 'course we give you final approval on position. But lookit, this isn't an offer you can sleep on. I've got three other standbys for that page. . . . You what? I give you a promise, it's a promise. How d'you know it's a promise? Get outta here. . . ."

I hovered by an adjacent cubicle, listening with pleasure to this manic spiel. Debbie has been my great discovery—the undisputed *CompuWorld* sales star of the year. I hired her to fill the Telesales space vacated by me after I got the promotion. There were other suitable candidates, but what really sold me on Debbie was not just her explosive motor-mouth hunger for the position ("You give me the job, Mr. Allen, you'll have no regrets. And when I say no regrets, I mean, like, no no *no* regrets"). It was also her "backstory"—the darker details of her life that she didn't list on her resumé but that, with a little gentle probing from me, she divulged. Like how she grew up in an East New York project. And how her daddy did a permanent bunk back to San Juan when she was four. And how she was pregnant at seventeen and widowed at nineteen, after her low-life husband irritated his drug-dealing employers by pocketing the proceeds of a coke deal. And how she went back to high school and landed a secretarial job and finally found a way out of East New York, via a tiny one-bedroom in Stuyvesant Town where she now lived with her elderly mother and young son, Raul. And how she knew she could sell anybody anything—all she needed was someone like me to give her a shot.

". . . So are we doin' this or what? Like I said, it's seven-eighteen now, shop here's about to close. And come tomorrow . . . yeah, right, uh-huh, sure, sure, sure, no other competitors near you, copy approval, fifty-two five . . . We on the same page here?"

I watched as all the muscles in her face went taut and her eyes snapped shut, like someone unable to watch a lottery draw. Then, suddenly, her shoulders slackened, and her face slipped into an expression of weary relief.

"Okay, Mr. Godfrey, you got it. I'll call tomorrow, we'll deal with all the fine print then. Have a nice night."

She pulled off her headset and pressed her forehead into her palms.

"You close?" I asked.

"I closed," she said, sounding as exhausted as a sprinter who'd just hit the tape.

"Who was it?"

"DustBust: 'America's Favorite Computer Dustshield Equipment.' " She shook her head, then looked up and gave me a jaded smile. I knew what she was thinking. *I kill myself, I shred my vocal cords, I act as if this is a life-or-death matter. And what's the payoff? Landing a lousy quarter-page ad by some guy who makes slipcovers for computer screens.*

I shrugged back as if to say, Welcome to sales. But God, how I knew that post-closing feeling—the sense of depletion, of loss. You've won . . . and yet, what *have* you won? You're someone who sells space in a magazine. In the great spectrum of human endeavor, what you do is negligible, maybe even worthless. But, as I always tell any new sales staff I hire, the real object of the exercise—the reason you expend all that effort cajoling and flattering and wheedling the client—is self-validation. Because when you close—when you get that *yes*—there is a flicker of triumph. You've talked someone into something. Your point of view has prevailed. You've verified your worth. For that day, anyway.

"Nothing wrong with DustBust," I said. "They've been around for ten, twelve years. Good product, good distribution network, not much in the way of competition. They should be a nice steady customer for you. Way to go, Debbie."

She beamed at me. "Thanks, Mr. Allen."

"You ever going to call me Ned?"

"When you're not my boss anymore."

"You mean, when you're running the show around here."

"Not gonna happen in this life."

"Rule Number One of sales, Debbie: Don't shortchange yourself. How's your mom?"

"Up and down. The angina's been really bad for the last week. Still, if she can keep from having to go to the hospital until January fifth . . ."

January 5 was Debbie's first anniversary with *CompuWorld*—and also the day that, according to the rules of the company insurance policy, she could (in addition to any children and a spouse) add one more dependent family member to her health plan. I knew that she was ticking off the days until her uninsured mom (who'd been sick, off and on, for the past year) was finally protected by the company safety net.

"She still baby-sitting Raul after school?"

"We've got no choice," Debbie said. "I'm not going to be paying a nanny on my salary . . . and, at six, he's too old for day care. Y'know he's been accepted for the first grade at Faber Academy?" she said, mentioning one of the best private day schools in the city (and just a three-block walk from her apartment in Stuyvesant Town).

"Yeah, I'd heard. That's fantastic news. He must be a gifted kid."

"He's the best. They're even gonna let him enter this January instead of making him wait until September. Which is okay by me, 'cause that kindergarten he's in right now is *guano*. 'Course, first grade at Faber is nine thousand a year—and they haven't been able to get him a scholarship. So that bonus check's real necessary."

"You should have more than nine grand coming to you, shouldn't you?"

"Thirteen thousand, four hundred dollars," she said. "I worked it out the other day."

"No kidding?" We both laughed.

"They really gonna pay us the bonus next Friday?" she asked.

"Debbie, that's the third time you've asked me that."

"Sorry."

"No need to be. Just try to stop worrying about it. As I told you before, this is no nickel-and-dime operation, and Yokimura really does honor its commitments. *Especially* to its employees. They're Japanese, for Christ's sake. They'd rather disembowel themselves than fail to pay you your bonus. Trust me here."

"I do, Mr. Allen. It's just, like, it's my first year here, and that bonus, it's gonna make the difference . . ."

"Tell you what. When I see Chuck Zanussi for breakfast tomorrow, I'll ask him to verify that—what was the figure you mentioned again?"

"Thirteen-four."

"Right—that thirteen-four is the exact amount you'll be receiving on the twelfth. He usually has all the bonus figures for the sales divisions around now."

"You're having breakfast with Mr. Zanussi? I thought he was still in Seattle, clearing up that problem with Mr. Roland."

She really did deserve a job in the CIA. Word had been filtering back to Chuck that Bill Roland, regional sales director for the Pacific Northwest, had become excessively acquainted with a certain

Mr. Jack Daniel's. And there was an unsubstantiated rumor going around that, having finally secured a lunch meeting with the marketing director of Microcom, he drank himself into incoherence before dessert. Not a good sales strategy, especially in such a crucial market as Seattle—which is why Chuck had flown out there, though of course Chuck told everyone around the office that he was simply paying the Seattle office his usual quarterly visit. That was a typical bit of Chuck strategy: Act as if nothing is wrong, then deal with the "problem" before anyone finds out there *was* a real problem.

"You hear how things went in Seattle?" I asked.

Debbie regarded her nails, currently painted a shade that was probably called Drag Queen Pink.

"Bill Roland's history," she said.

I emitted a low whistle. "When did this happen?"

"Yesterday morning."

"He go quietly?"

"I think he was actually real relieved. Especially since Mr. Zanussi offered him six months' salary and eight weeks in some rehab place if he resigned on the spot. Which he did. Kind of real decent of Mr. Zanussi, don't you think? I mean, this drinking thing . . . seems it had been going on for months. Mr. Roland's marriage's supposed to have gone real bad, his daughter—think she's around sixteen—just ran off with this biker creep, and, y'know, the pressure's always on at the Seattle office. . . . So Mr. Roland started hitting the whiskey first thing in the morning, sneaking it into his coffee . . ."

I looked at her with amazement.

"How the hell do you know all this stuff?"

"I've got my sources."

"You wouldn't happen to have a mole in our Chicago office, would you?"

Another glance at those electric-pink nails. "I might," she said.

"Then how about giving them a ring now and finding out why Chuck Zanussi was called to a meeting there today."

Now it was Debbie's turn to look shocked.

"He was sent to Chicago?"

"Yep."

"But I thought he was flying straight back from Seattle . . ."

"So did I. But he called me midair between O'Hare and La Guardia, saying that he'd been asked to stop by the Chicago office for the afternoon. Wouldn't say why. Wouldn't say who called the meeting—but you can bet it's someone pretty upper echelon in Getz-Braun or Yokimura."

"Mr. Zanussi didn't say anything about what happened in the meeting?"

"Just that it was interesting."

"Mierda."

Debbie also understood that, in corporate life, *interesting* was a highly charged word—and one that never boded well for the future. Putting her headset back on, she nervously punched in a ten-digit number.

"Lemme talk to Maria Szabo, please," she said. While waiting to be transferred, Debbie chewed on the headset wire. "Maria . . . Debbie in New York. Howyadoin'? Yeah, yeah, yeah . . . business as usual. But listen, you see our publisher, Mr. Zanussi, around your office today? He *was*? . . . Who else was there? . . . You're kidding me, right? All of 'em? *Shit* . . . You're telling *me,* something's up . . . but nobody spilled nothing, huh? Not even his secretary? Okay, okay. But listen, you hear anything else you call me pronto. Ditto if I get some news here. Got me? Thanks, hon . . ."

She pulled off the headset and gave me one of her anxious looks.

"That was my friend Maria, Telesales Chicago. Mr. Zanussi arrived at their office around lunchtime today, went straight into a meeting with Mr. Hertzberg, Mr. Getz, Mr. Watanabe . . ."

"Jesus," I said. "Jesus Christ." Moss Hertzberg was Getz-Braun's CEO. Bob Getz was the chairman of the board. And Hideo Watanabe was head samurai at our parent company, Yokimura. You couldn't ask for a more formidable collection of corporate heavy hitters.

"Did your friend Maria mention if anyone else was there?"

"Yeah. Some Euro guy with two flunkies."

"What did she mean, 'a Euro guy'?"

"I dunno. Said he looked like, well, uh, *Euro*."

"You mean, not American."

"Guess so."

"Did Maria say if he spoke English?"

"Yeah . . . but with this kind of accent."

"A *European* accent?"

"Think so."

"And the two flunkies with him? Were they bodyguards?"

"She said they were carrying briefcases."

"Lawyers," I said.

"What's going on, Mr. Allen?"

I had a good idea, but I knew if I told her she might not sleep tonight. So instead I flashed her my best salesman's smile, that "don't-worry-you're-safe-with-me" smile that hopefully engenders trust yet masks the fact that, like everybody else you pass on the street these days, you really don't know if the ground beneath you is solid anymore.

"Put it this way, Debbie," I said. "It is going to be *interesting*."

TWO

By the time I left the office it was 7:30, an hour in New York when the sight of an available taxicab is about as commonplace as that of a stray moose on Third Avenue, when frantically late theatergoers and exhausted executives throw themselves in the path of any oncoming yellow car, begging all those off-duty drivers to make one final detour for them.

A light snow was falling, which meant that the prospect of finding a cab had been reduced from no chance to less than no chance. So, turning up the collar of my overcoat, I headed north on Third for nine blocks, then swung west on Fifty-fifth Street. On my way I managed to chase down Dave Maduro (outside sales—Massachusetts) on my cellular. He was somewhere on I-290 south of Worcester.

"My master calls," Maduro said when he heard my voice.

"Only because you didn't call me, Dave," I responded calmly.

"You knew I was in with Jack Drabble at InfoCom all afternoon."

"And?"

A long sigh. "We're not there yet."

"The problem?"

"He still won't commit to that multipage insert for June."

I immediately understood why Dave sounded so touchy. A multipage insert is a special six-page advertising section that we try to feature in every issue. As it was worth (at top whack) 210 thousand in advertising revenue, it was considered the ultimate score by our sales team—and Dave had been stalking InfoCom for months.

"What's making him balk?" I asked.

"He won't go above one-eighty . . ."

"We can live with that."

". . . and he's also demanding a four-color bleed on all pages."

"Thief. You want some help here?"

"I was so certain I was going to close the sonofabitch today. And then, he pulls this four-color-bleed shit . . ."

"Dave—DO YOU WANT SOME HELP HERE?"

A long, reluctant pause. "Yeah," Dave finally said.

"Give me his direct line," I said. After telling Dave I'd get back to him tomorrow, I immediately punched in Jack Drabble's number. Poor Dave—he always hated asking me for a favor, just as he also can't stand the fact that, at thirty-two, I was six years younger than him . . . and I was his boss. And, like any salesman, he oozed despair when he couldn't close.

The phone rang four times. I didn't want to speak directly to Jack Drabble right then—and I was gambling on the fact that he'd already gone home. I gambled right—I was connected to his voice mail.

"Jack, Ned Allen from *CompuWorld* here. Haven't seen you since the AmCom convention in October, but I hear great things. Listen, about this multipage insert—I've got GreenAp Computers vying for this spot. . . . You can check with your counterpart at GreenAp if you like . . . but I really, *truly* want to give it to you. Now, one-eighty is fine—and you know you're saving thirty off our rack rate. But a four-color bleed on every page? No can do. The math just doesn't work. But—and this is more than we were offering the GreenAp boys—we *will* do the bleed on the first and back pages of your insert. And, of course, you'll be getting the space that GreenAp wants. Then there's that little matter of our annual winter sales event. It's Vail this year, Jack. February thirteenth through sixteenth. We pay, you ski, and the wife comes, too. But I need an answer by nine A.M. tomorrow. See you on the slopes, Jack."

Pocketing the phone, I felt that narcotic buzz that always hits me after making a good pitch. *See you on the slopes, Jack.* "Structure every pitch like a movie script," Chuck Zanussi once advised me. "Hit them with some fast exposition, hook their interest, give them cause to worry about where things are heading, then nail 'em with a surprise ending. Remember: Like writing, it's a craft. Maybe even an art."

The snow was falling heavily as I reached Park Avenue. Having spent a good part of my adolescence in northern New England, I am happy trudging through the snow. I like the silence it imposes on Manhattan's usual snarl; the way it magically empties the streets of people and makes you feel as solitary as someone tramping through the Maine woods.

Don't get me wrong—I'm not nostalgic for those deep "down east" winters. I don't long for flannel shirts and L.L. Bean boots and a deerstalker hat with flaps. By the time I was sixteen, all I could think about was that road marked "South" out of Maine. It took another six years before I finally made it down that road. That was almost a decade ago—and never once since leaving have I felt an urge to return and heed some "Call of the Wild." I'm a city boy now—and after ten years in New York I still find myself addicted to its manic rhythms—its power, its arrogance, its air of lofty indifference.

Crossing Park Avenue, I stood in the middle of one of its little traffic islands and stared south at that epic canyon of office buildings—the Christmas cross in the Helmsley Building offering a silent benediction to all those who compete in this playpen of ambition. It was my favorite New York vista, this view down Park. Because it underscored the fact: I was finally where I wanted to be.

I continued west on Fifty-fifth, then ducked into the St. Regis Hotel and headed across a plushly carpeted lobby. At the cloakroom I handed over my overcoat and proceeded to the men's room, where an elderly attendant with hunched shoulders turned on the sink taps while I emptied my bladder. After I finished rinsing my hands, he ceremoniously handed me a towel. There was a tray of aftershaves and colognes between two sinks. I splashed on some Armani Pour Homme. I read somewhere once (probably *GQ*) that this aftershave "exudes an aura of sophisticated power." I know, I know—it's a real smarmy kind of sales pitch. But pitches like that move product. Especially if you're aiming at the aspiring-young-executive end of the market—in other words, guys like me.

The elderly attendant, an Italian immigrant with permanently rheumy eyes and a tiny turtlelike head tucked down between his shoulders, handed me a comb and a brush. I ran the comb through my hair (still damp from the melting snow), then turned around and craned my head in an attempt to inspect a tiny patch of thinning hair at the top of my skull. When I say tiny, I mean *tiny*—the bald patch is no bigger than a dime. Still, it serves as a reminder that I am beginning that ever-rapid descent toward middle age. Everybody tells me that I still look like a kid in his mid-twenties—possibly because I'm built like a reasonably healthy scarecrow (six foot two, 166 pounds, a thirty-four-inch waist). So far, I've displayed no visible signs of aging (except that minuscule patch of thinning hair). Compared to just about every other guy I know in sales, I'm a walking advertisement for clean living. Anytime the national *CompuWorld* sales team gets together for its biannual conference—or I attend one of the big international computer exhibitions that the Getz-Braun group stages—I am amazed at just how toxic and hyper-tense everyone else looks. The outside sales rep guys are inevitably thirty pounds overweight (from an on-the-road diet of fast food . . . and the discovery that a double-dip milkshake or a half dozen beers can provide temporary high-carbohydrate relief whenever you fail to make a deal). The Telesales women, on the other hand, appear to be dabbling in anorexia, or are the sort of fanatical keep-fit junkies who work off all their stress and disappointment in the health club—they sport biceps that would shame G.I. Joe. And the regional sales managers are either dedicated nicotine fiends, or compulsive pencil chewers, or PWNs (People Without Nails).

No doubt about it, the sales game can have a nasty impact on your health, unless you work out a strategy for coping with its burdens. Like playing tennis twice a week. And maintaining a low-fat, low-sodium diet. And never drinking during lunch (unless, of course, you're with one of several clients who will only throw six figures' worth of business your way if you get smashed with them). And learning how to shrug off stress—that "convert-it-into-positive-energy" crap you always read about in assorted "business empowerment" books . . . which essentially means landing a new deal whenever you're feeling excessively anxious.

In fact, I had most of the "excesses" in my life under control—with one big exception: I'd yet to figure out how to stop spending excessive amounts of money.

The bathroom attendant pulled out a little wooden box from beneath the sink. Sliding it next to me, he stepped on top and began to de-lint my pinstriped shoulders with a brush.

"Nice suit, sir," he said.

It certainly should be—considering that it's a $1,200 Cerutti. If you peeked into my closet, you'd assume that suits are a weakness of mine. I own close to a dozen—and they're all designer. I also buy top-of-the-line English shoes and the usual expensive accessories. But I'm not a style junkie, or the sort of go-getting executive who actually believes that an expensive suit turns you into a corporate warrior. To me, looking sharp is simply an intrinsic part of the sales game. It always gives you an edge with a client, and also gets you noticed by the senior management guys. But it's nothing more than that. I meet guys all the time who bragged about their accoutrements—pulling back their French cuffs to reveal their $5,000 Rolexes, or boring me about how they knew they had arrived on the day they bought themselves a Porsche 911. I act dutifully impressed, but secretly think: Winners aren't measured by their five-grand watches. Winners are measured by just one thing: their ability to close.

I handed the attendant ten bucks—a hefty tip, I know . . . but can you imagine working a toilet? I've always felt guilty about anyone who's been reduced to a menial position. Maybe that's because, deep down, I've always feared such lowly status—having spent two summers during college working at a fast-food joint; a brain-dead job in which I spent the day reiterating the question *You want fries with the shake?*

The attendant blinked with shock when he saw the ten bucks. Then, slipping it into his breast pocket, he said, "You have a real good night, sir."

I moved on to the bar. It was all black marble and large silver mirrors, with a long, curved, zinc counter and opulent deco chairs. The place was packed with suits—mostly men in their thirties and forties, members of the deal-making executive class, all immaculately groomed, poking the air with their cigars to make their points.

I found a quiet corner table and had just ordered a martini straight up when my phone rang. I answered it quickly.

"It's me." I could barely make out Lizzie's voice over the line's static. "You on your way?" I asked, glancing at my watch and noticing that she was late.

"Still stuck in a meeting at the Royalton."

"Who are you with?"

"A prospective client. Miller, Beadle, and Smart. Midsize Wall Street brokerage house, trying to raise their profile."

"Sounds fun."

"If you like dealing with aging preppies."

"Want me to walk down and meet you there? It's, what . . . only ten blocks."

"That's okay—I should have things wrapped up here in half an hour. And then . . ."

"Yeah?"

"Well, I have big news," she said in a mock-dramatic voice.

"How big?" I said, playing along.

"Earth-shatteringly big. Stop-the-presses big."

"The suspense is killing me."

She paused for effect.

"I managed to get us a table at Patroon."

"Isn't that the place I read about in *New York* last week?"

"No, that's the place *I* told you you should read about in *New York*. . . ."

"Some kind of hash house, right? With great cheeseburgers?"

" 'The new favorite watering hole of Manhattan's power brokers,' if you believe everything you read."

"I never believe anything I read in *New York*. But Geena does. Was this her idea?"

"You score an A for perceptiveness. Of course, according to Geena, Ian's also been *dying* to eat there, too."

Geena worked with Lizzie at Mosman & Keating, a midsize public relations firm. Her husband, Ian, wrote an "Around Town" column for the *Daily News*. They were also members of the New

York fast lane—and, much to our mutual amusement, liked to flash their glitzy credentials whenever possible.

"They're joining us at Patroon after dropping in at a gallery opening in SoHo of some *fabulous* show by this *fabulous* Aboriginal finger painter . . ."

"And I bet the gallery's going to be full of *fabulous* people. Lou Reed's going to be there, right?"

"Sure. Along with Tim Robbins and Susan Sarandon. And Gore Vidal might drop in."

"Not to mention John F. Kennedy, Jr. . . ."

"Sharon Stone . . ."

"And that old standby, the *fabulous* Dalai Lama."

We laughed.

"Anyway, Geena is in awe," Lizzie said. "Because Patroon ostensibly has a five-week waiting list for a table . . . which I just managed to circumvent thirty minutes ago."

"Dare I ask how?"

"I'm the cleverest PR woman in New York, that's how."

"Can't disagree with that."

"Listen, I've got to fly back into this meeting. Patroon is one-sixty East Forty-sixth. The table's reserved for nine-fifteen. Bye."

And she was gone.

Leave it to Lizzie to snag a table for four at the hottest restaurant in town. Then again, if Lizzie puts her mind to something, she inevitably achieves results. Because, like me, she is the sort of person for whom results mean everything.

She, too, is a hick from the sticks. Ever heard of the town of Utica, New York? Smack dab in the middle of the snowbelt. The sort of place where there's a virtual whiteout six months a year, and where the best civic amenity is the road out of town. Her dad was a sergeant on the local police force, a depressive prone to pitch-black moods that he drowned with cheap Utica Club beer. Her mom was the sort of Suzy Homemaker type who always had a smile on her face as she busied herself with a thousand and one domestic details, yet also chased Valium with Bailey's Irish Cream.

"We weren't exactly the happiest of families," she confessed shortly after we met. "Once I hit seventeen, all I could think about was getting the hell out of Dodge."

I certainly understood such sentiments—I hadn't been back home once since leaving Brunswick in the fall of '87. Not that there was any home to go back to. By then my dad was newly dead, my mom had remarried a golf pro and moved to Arizona, and my older brother Rob had lost his heart to a Filipina bar girl named Mamie while stationed with the navy at Subic Bay.

We weren't exactly the happiest of families. No—that really wasn't us. We were the sort of folks who seemed reasonably content, never acknowledging any difficulties on the homefront. My dad was a military lifer—a guy from Indianapolis who saw the navy as his way out of the landlocked Midwest. He enlisted at the age of eighteen—and until his death twenty-nine years later, the navy was his Great White Father, who provided him with direction and dealt with all his essential necessities. Having been something of a screwup in high school (as he was fond of telling us), he got "discipline" and "focus" and "pride" from the navy. He rose quickly to ensign, then spent four years in training as a mechanical engineer. Two years into his Uncle Sam–backed studies at San Jose State, he met my mom (she was an English major)—so, as he was also fond of telling us, the navy found him a wife as well. They were married a week after graduating in 1962. Rob arrived the next summer; I showed up in January of '65. Our childhood was a string of tract houses in assorted naval air stations around the country: San Diego, Key West, Pensacola, and finally eleven years in Brunswick, Maine, where my dad was in charge of maintenance for "airborne operations." It turned out to be his last posting. He died on January 2, 1987. He was only forty-seven, a victim of a lifelong attachment to cigarettes.

Just as I can't picture my father without a Winston gripped between his teeth, I can never recall my parents fighting with each other. You see, my dad really bought into the idea of living a "shipshape" life. "You play the game well, and the game will always treat you well"—another of his pet expressions, and one that summed up his belief that the team player, *the good guy,* was always rewarded for his loyalty and service. But besides being a good officer, he also worked hard at being a good father and provider. Of course, from the time I hit my teens I began to sense that there was a certain "going-through-the-motions" quality to my parents' marriage—that my mom wasn't exactly thrilled with her permanent housewife status, that she found base life confining, and that she and my dad had possibly fallen out of love with each other years ago. But my old man's "code of duty" meant that the family had to be held together. It also meant that he could never show favoritism toward any one son . . . though it was pretty clear to me that Rob was his golden boy, not only because he followed my dad into the navy right after leaving high school, but also because, unlike me, he didn't seem to be dreaming of a world far removed from the Kmart realities of naval-base life.

When I was sixteen, my dad came into my room one night and found me reading *Esquire* in bed.

"You want *Playboy* I'll get it for you at the PX," he said. "But, *Esquire* . . . Christ, it's nothing but fancy-assed writing and fancy-assed suits."

Which, of course, is why I loved it. It represented the metropolitan world to which I aspired. I saw myself living the New York life, eating in those designer restaurants that *Esquire* featured, dressing in those $600 suits that adorned their fashion pages, talking the urban buzz talk that seemed second nature to their writers. Not because I craved these actual things—but because they struck me as essential components of true success.

Of course my dad knew this—just as he also knew that my mom encouraged me to have ambitions beyond Brunswick and the U.S. Navy.

"Take it from me," she said when I was struggling through my college applications. "There's only one person in the whole wide world who will ever stop you from getting to where you want to be—and that's yourself."

And so, I aimed high and applied to Bowdoin, an elite liberal arts college located a mere mile down the road from the naval air station. Growing up in Brunswick, Bowdoin represented yet another select realm that I yearned to enter, but from which I was excluded.

"It's the waiting list," I said, showing my father the admissions letter from Bowdoin in the spring of 1983. He could hear the disappointment in my voice.

"The waiting list at Bowdoin's not too shabby, right?"

"It's still not an acceptance, Dad. And according to Mr. Challenor . . ."

"Who's this Mr. Challenor?"

"My college advisor. Anyway, he said I probably would've gotten in if I hadn't needed financial aid."

I instantly regretted my thoughtlessness. My father looked at me as if I'd inadvertently kneed him in the balls. *Discipline . . . focus . . . pride*—my dad's credo. And without realizing it, I had punctured that complex, defensive dignity—and his sense of duty to his son.

"How much is a year at Bowdoin?" he asked quietly.

"It doesn't matter, Dad."

"How much?"

"With room and board, around seventeen. . . ."

He emitted a low whistle and regarded the yellowing linoleum on our kitchen floor.

"That's a hell of a chunk of change," he finally said, lighting up a Winston.

"I know, Dad."

"But the math doesn't work, son. You understand that?"

"Of course I understand," I lied. "Like I said, it doesn't matter."

"That's bullshit, son," he said, his face suddenly a mask of defeat. "It matters. You know it, I know it. It *really* matters."

And that's how I ended up at a very affordable, very second-rate branch of the University of Maine at Presque Isle—where I was just about the only student on campus not majoring in agricultural science. Of course, I hated being stuck in this nowhere town, surrounded by people doing graduate work on brucellosis (believe me, after Presque Isle, Brunswick seemed downright cosmopolitan). Whenever I saw my dad, however, I never let on just how much I loathed that hick university, or how I continued to rue the fact that lack of money had essentially barred me from Bowdoin . . . and the world it represented.

But *he* knew. Any time I was home for the weekend and Mom raised the question, "How's school?" Dad would get that whipped look on his face and light another cigarette. In his mind, he had failed me—and his own convoluted sense of pride made it impossible for him to see that I didn't think less of him because he was on a navy man's pay. So a painful distance—a stiff reserve—began to creep into our relationship. Even after he was diagnosed with lung cancer (at the end of my junior year), he dodged my attempts to get close to him again.

"The hell you crying about, son?" he demanded one night toward the end of his illness. When my tears subsided, I tried to sound an optimistic note. It rang hollow.

"Listen, when you get better—"

He cut me off.

"Not gonna happen," he said, his tone deliberately "right stuff." "So let's not dwell on the inevitable, okay? Anyway, a couple of months from now, after you've graduated, you're gonna be so far gone out of Maine, it's not gonna matter if I'm alive or dead. . . ."

"That's not true. . . ."

"I know you, Ned. I know what you want . . . and what you think you gotta prove. And for that reason I also know that, unlike me, the math *is* gonna work for you."

He understood me better than I realized. Just as he also knew that *the math* defines us. Provides us with our sense of worth. Fuels our ambitions, Feeds our insecurities. Fucks us up. Forces us out of bed in the morning. Gives us a reason to fight our way through the day.

My martini arrived. I raised the glass, touched the frosty rim to my lips, and let the gin trickle down my throat. Just as it was numbing my vocal cords, my phone rang again.

"Ned Allen here."

"Do you ever stop working?" the voice on the line said.

"Jack Drabble?"

"Perhaps."

"As my father used to say, Only the winner goes to dinner. You still at the office, Jack?"

"Yep. Just stepped away from my desk when you called."

"Eight-fifteen. You are a credit to InfoCom."

"And you're trying to lick my rectum."

"No need, my man. I'm sitting here in the bar of the St. Regis, sipping a bone-dry martini, about to meet my very beautiful wife for dinner, and I have GreenAp ready to grab that multipage insert at nine-oh-five tomorrow morning if we don't get into bed before them. So—no offense, Jack—but who needs to even *look* at your rectum when life is so sweet?"

"One-seven-five."

"Now you insult my intelligence. One-eighty is the deal . . . and we throw in the two bleeds as a door prize."

"Plus the weekend at Vail, right?"

Got 'em! "Only at one-eighty."

"What's five grand?"

"The difference between you squinting at the Colorado sun or sitting on your can in beautiful downtown Worcester, Mass. One-eighty. Take it or leave it."

"I'll call you tomorrow."

"No sale. You called tonight, you deal tonight. One-eighty. Going, going . . ."

"Okay, okay, okay. I'm in."

"Smart move, Jack," I said, taking a long swig of the martini. And as I put the glass down, I found myself thinking, *You're right, Dad. The math has worked for me.*

And God, how I love to sell.

THREE

"Isn't that Ralph Lauren seated over there?" Lizzie asked.

"Good catch," Geena said.

"And do you see those two guys in the corner?" Ian said, motioning all of us forward and nodding toward a pair of well-dressed men schmoozing at a discreetly prominent table. "The substantial one in the chalk-stripe suit. That's Graydon Carter."

"*The* Graydon Carter?" Lizzie asked.

"The one and only," Ian said.

"Have you ever written for *Vanity Fair*?" I asked Ian.

"I wish," Ian said, then added, "And the guy with Graydon is the famous David Halberstam."

Geena nodded knowingly, but Lizzie looked puzzled.

"Who's David Halberstam?"

She instantly regretted her honesty, as Ian put on a mock-haughty voice.

"Lizzie, if you live in this city you've simply *got* to know who David Halberstam is."

My wife tugged on a lock of her hair—a dead giveaway (but only to me) that she was feeling self-conscious.

"I've heard his name," she said.

"He only happens to be one of the most important journalists of the last thirty years," Ian said, continuing to tease her. "Ex-*New York Times*, author of *The Best and the Brightest* and *The Fifties* . . ."

". . . and a *fabulous* guy," I said, flashing Ian a big smile. "Let me guess—you met him at a party at Tina Brown's weekend place in the Hamptons, where you were also talking foreign policy with Joan Didion. . . ."

"Actually," Ian said, "I was talking Middle East politics with Tony Robbins—who told me he was a very close personal friend of yours."

Even I laughed.

"How's life at the paper?" Lizzie asked.

"A bit like living through the French Revolution," Ian said. "Every day, the new editor sends someone else to the guillotine. Still, he doesn't seem to want my head. Yet."

"That's because you're one of their big stars," Geena said.

"You're biased," Ian said. "Anyone who can string a sentence together and schmooze celebs can write a gossip column."

"You feeling all right?" I asked. "I mean, these sudden attacks of modesty can be dangerous to your health. . . ."

Ian threw his eyes heavenward. "With friends like these . . ."

"Anyway, you're not going to be a gossip columnist for much longer," Geena said. Then turning to Lizzie and me, she added, "Did you hear that *GQ* offered Ian this *amazing* freelance contract?"

"How amazing?" I asked.

"It's not bad," Ian said.

"Not bad?" Geena said. "It's fifty thousand dollars for six profiles."

"Wow," Lizzie said.

"You humble bastard," I said, raising my glass to Ian. "That is fantastic news."

"Well, it's still not the *New Yorker*," Ian said.

"In time," Geena said, "in time."

"Who's your first subject?" Lizzie asked.

"The poet laureate of the Joint Chiefs of Staff—Tom Clancy."

"Very popular guy, Mr. Clancy," I said.

"Yeah, salesmen love him," Ian added with a wink.

"Not to mention tabloid journalists," I countered with a smile.

Geena looked at Lizzie and said, "Do you ever feel as if we're kind of superfluous here?"

"Boys will be boys," Lizzie said drily.

"Salesmen are *never* competitive," I said.

"Until you face them across a tennis court," Ian said. "I tell you, Lizzie, your husband's got a killer instinct."

"I guess that's because I honed my game on public courts, not Daddy's country club."

I instantly regretted the wisecrack. Lizzie shot me a look that said, "Apologize fast." Which is exactly what I did.

"Just joking, pal," I said.

But, of course, I wasn't totally joking. Because there was a part of me that did envy Ian's rich-kid credentials. Like his wife, he exuded an aura of supreme confidence—the sort of self-assurance that, at times, was borderline arrogance. Then again, Ian and Geena had both been raised in an elite Manhattan world. They went to schools like Chapin and Collegiate. They grew up using Mommy's charge card at Bloomingdale's and Saks Fifth Avenue. They were sent off to summer camps in Vermont and New Hampshire. They had daddies who were senior partners at white-shoe law firms or Wall Street brokerage houses, and could easily pay their tuition to Brown and Smith. They spent their junior years in Dublin and Florence. They returned to the city after college, fully secure in the knowledge that they would have a relatively easy entrée into any professional field they chose. Because not only did they have all the right connections, they also had that most prized of native Manhattanite possessions: an *entitlement complex*—the belief that they had been anointed as two of life's winners, and that success was their natural domain.

Let's face it: As much as Ian derided his status as a *Daily News* gossip hack, he landed that highly visible job at the precocious age of twenty-six. Now, at thirty, he was effortlessly making the move into magazine journalism. No doubt, he'd crack *Vanity Fair* and the *New Yorker* within a few years. Book deals would follow. He'd become a celebrated writer—a member of the literary establishment, profiled in the *New York Times*, interviewed by Charlie Rose, sharing that corner table with David Halberstam and Graydon Carter. Because, naturally, Ian saw such success as his due, his inalienable right—whereas I always felt as if the corner table, like success, had to be fought for. Just as I also found myself wondering: Once I finally made it to the table, would I ever feel secure enough to sit down?

That's the problem with being a small-town kid in New York: No matter how well you do in Gotham, deep down you always consider yourself a fraud. Still looking up in amazement at "all them tall buildings," desperately trying to exude high-gloss sophistication, constantly wondering if your urbane act is as transparent as Plexiglas.

"Look who's sitting in the left-hand corner," Geena said, in an attempt to move the conversation on after my impolitic comment.

Ian glanced over in that direction, then said, "Oh yeah. Him." Then shooting me an ironic grin, he added, "Now there's a guy who *owns* his own tennis court."

"Edgar Bronfman, Jr.?" Lizzie asked.

"You *are* good at this," Geena said.

"She's the best," I said.

Lizzie shrugged. "I just read the gossip columns, like everyone else."

I smiled—because that comment was pure Lizzie. Though she was an adept player of the Manhattan "in-the-know" game, it really didn't define her. She saw the game for what it was: nothing more than a basic component of her work. Information was the central currency she traded in.

Shortly after we first met, she explained her job to me.

"In public relations, only two things count: who you know . . . and who you know."

"Don't you have to land the deals as well?"

She ran her finger across the top of my hand and gave me a sly smile.

"You close," she said. "I influence."

Talk about a seductive sales pitch. No wonder I was instantly bewitched. And looking back on it now, meeting Lizzie came around the same time (spring of '93) when my New York luck finally began to change. Up until that point I was scratching out a living as a "recruitment executive" at a big commercial employment agency in midtown. It was one of a string of dead-end jobs I'd landed since first hitting the city six years earlier. Professionally speaking, I was starting to feel like a loser—unable to graduate beyond the sort of dreary career prospects offered in the back employment pages of the *New York Times*. At first, just getting myself established in the city seemed like a real triumph. I found a shabby, railroad-style one-bedroom apartment for $850 a month on Seventy-fifth between First and York (complete with that ultimate low-rent touch: a bathtub in the kitchen). Then I grabbed the first job I could land ("telephone sales associate" for Brooks Brothers—i.e., the guy who takes your chinos order on the phone). I didn't exactly have defined career objectives. I didn't know what I wanted to be when I grew up. All I did know was: New York was the center of the cosmos. A place that anyone like me (armed with both boundless ambition and boundless workaholism) could eventually conquer.

Boy, was I in for a kick up my Horatio Alger ass. As I quickly discovered, a kid from Maine with a degree from a third-rate state university and no connections didn't exactly take Manhattan overnight. Sure, I tried to make inroads on Wall Street—but the competition for jobs was brutal, and those "in the loop," or from the good schools, always won out. Guys like me, on the other hand, were trapped in mid-level employment hell.

Though I was desperate to find something "executive," I kept bouncing from lowly position to lowly position, always hoping that it might lead to a promotion. Even when I was taking phone orders for Brooks Brothers, I kept trying to find a way into the management division of the organization—only to be told that, given my piss-poor entry-level status, I would have to put in several years' service before being considered for advancement.

But I didn't want to spend three years wired to a headset, asking customers questions like, "And do you want the crew or the V-neck cream shetland?" I knew I had a skill, a talent—something that would eventually allow me to flourish in New York. The problem was, I still hadn't figured out what that talent might be.

So I continued to drift, exchanging that mind-numbing job for a series of others, including a lackluster post in the Saks Fifth Avenue publications department. After seven dull months writing lingerie copy, I moved on, becoming a "placement officer" at a midtown employment agency. About three months into this electrifying job, I met Chuck Zanussi. He'd asked the agency to find him a new secretary, I was assigned the task, and we spent about a week talking regularly on the phone as he vetted assorted candidates.

I must have impressed him with my go-getting style—because,

during our last call, he said, "What's a sharp guy like you doing working in such a no-hope job?"

"Looking for a way out. Fast."

"Do you think you could sell?"

"Believe me," I lied, "I can sell."

"Then come in and see me."

Within a week of joining *CompuWorld*, however, I came to realize that that absurdly cocky assertion was actually true. From the moment I tied up my first deal (an eighth-of-a-pager from a software privacy prevention company called Lock-It-Up), I knew I had found my "calling." Every sale, I discovered, was a small victory, an accomplishment (not to mention another couple of dollars in my pocket). The more space I peddled, the more I began to learn the nuances of salesmanship: how to schmooze, sweet-talk, snare.

"Think of every sale as a seduction," Chuck Zanussi advised me shortly after I joined *CompuWorld*. "The goal is to get the client into bed—but to do it in such a way that they don't realize they're having their clothes torn off. You get too heavy-handed, you start slobbering on their neck, they're gonna tell you to buzz off. Remember: The operative word in seduction is *finesse*."

I recalled that advice two weeks later when I was wandering around the Javits Convention Center. I was attending my first industry trade show—SOFTUS—the national schmoozeathon for the software industry. Cruising through the thousand or so stalls spread around the main convention floor, I noticed a stand for a company called MicroManage—which had been high on a hit list of companies that Chuck Zanussi assigned me shortly after I joined the company.

"These MicroManage guys have got a great product called the Disc Liberator," Chuck had said. "But they've also got a hesitancy problem when it comes to advertising with us. Read up as much as you can on the Disc Liberator and land the fuckers."

To date, MicroManage had refused to return my calls. Which is why I was so pleased to stumble upon their sales stand—and to notice that their representative was a knockout. Mid-twenties. Long legs. High cheekbones. Jet-black hair cut fashionably short. Decked out in a smart black suit. Very preoccupied with the phone as I approached her stand.

"Hi there," she said, ending the call and proffering her hand. "Lizzie Howard. How can I help?"

The handshake was firm, no-nonsense, the voice suggesting a slight hint of upstate New York behind the sophisticated veneer.

"Ned Allen, *CompuWorld*," I said. "You know our magazine?"

"Maybe," she said with a teasing glint in her eye.

"If you're in software, you've got to know us. We're one of the biggest computer magazines in America."

"The *third* biggest," she said.

"So you *do* know us?"

Another of her sharp, impish smiles.

"Maybe."

"Well, I certainly know all about you."

"Do you really?"

"Oh yes," I said, trying to ignore the tinge of sarcasm. "MicroManage: makers of the Disc Liberator. The no-sweat way to liberate your hard drive of unnecessary files."

"Very impressive," Lizzie said.

"In fact," I continued on, "Disc Liberator is safer than any other Windows cleanup utility. More thorough than an application's own de-installer. And faster than . . ."

"So, you really have read our advertising copy."

"Part of my job. And it's also my job to get you to advertise with *CompuWorld*."

"But *PC Globe* is the main player in the market—and we already have a relationship with them."

"You know, Lizzie, the problem with main players is that they always believe they're the only game in town—that they don't owe the customer a little respect. . . ."

"Just respect?"

"And, of course, a discount."

"What kind of a discount?"

"Put it this way, our rack rate for a full-pager, middle of the book, is thirty-five. But with a new customer like MicroManage, we'd be in a position to give it away at—"

"Thirty," she said.

"Wish I could, but I can't shave twelve percent off the—"

"Thirty-one-five."

"That's still a ten percent shave. Thirty-two-five, on the other hand—"

"Sold."

"What?" I asked, taken aback.

"Sold," she said.

"What's, uh, 'sold'?" I sputtered.

"The MicroManage ad. A full-pager. Your July issue, if that's possible. . . ."

"I'll personally ensure that it runs then."

"Good. Just one thing: Though we're not after a premium position, if you bury us near Classified, we don't talk again."

"That won't happen."

"Glad to hear it."

"Because, uh . . . well, it would be nice to talk again."

"Would it really?" she said, avoiding my gaze and straightening brochures.

"Yes. It would. If, uh, you were interested . . ."

"Maybe," she said, handing me her card before returning to the business of tidying up the stand.

"Mosman and Keating Public Relations," I said, studying the company name on the card. "What's your relationship with MicroManage?"

"I'm their PR representative."

"But who handles their advertising?"

"Bruce Halpern at Ogilvy and Mather. But he usually authorizes any advertising recommendation I give him. Of course, if you want to speak with him directly . . ."

"No, no, I wasn't suggesting—"

"I mean, if you're worried about dealing with a lowly press rep . . ."

"I've offended you, haven't I?"

She shrugged her shoulders. "I'll live."

"I'm sorry."

"Apology accepted. You're kind of new at this game, aren't you?"

"Is it that obvious?" I said.

"Rule Number One: Never overplay your hand. Especially when the other party has signaled that they've bought your spiel."

"So you will talk to me again?"

A slight arching of her eyebrows. "Maybe."

During the next week, I called her three times at her office. She was always "in a meeting." The fourth time around, she deigned to answer.

"You're kind of persistent, aren't you?" she said after taking the call.

"And you're very good at playing hard to get."

"Oh, I get it. If a woman doesn't call you right back, it must be some sort of flirty game she's playing. It has nothing to do with the fact that she might just have a high-pressure job."

"So I suppose dinner tomorrow is out of the question?"

"I guess I could spend an evening listening to your sales pitch."

Now that's what I call *attitude*—of the sort that most guys would find a little too hot to handle. But I was charmed by Lizzie's self-assurance. Behind the flirtatious bravado, I sensed that she was a fellow urban hopeful—someone who was also trying to gain a foothold in the big bad city.

"You close. I influence."

I remember the moment when she said that line and stroked my hand with her index finger. It was during that first dinner together. It was late, the plates had been cleared away, we'd polished off a martini each and a bottle of zinfandel, and had just asked the waiter for two more glasses of wine to keep the alcohol flowing. Maybe it was excess intake of booze, or maybe it was the soft lighting that made her seem even more radiant than when we first met. Or maybe it was the fact that, ever since sitting down together two hours earlier, there hadn't been a nanosecond's lull in the conversation. I knew that we had clicked. Whatever the reason, I suddenly looked up at her and blurted out:

"You know, I'm going to marry you."

After this dumb revelation, there was a very long silence—during which I really did pray for the floor beneath my feet to open up and swallow me whole. But Lizzie didn't seem even remotely nonplussed by my drunken proposal. Instead, she kept running her finger across the top of my hand, while working hard to control her laughter.

Finally she graced me with a tipsy smile and said, "You really do have a lot to learn about salesmanship."

"Sorry, sorry, sorry. That was the all-time stupidest comment in recorded history. . . ."

"Shut up and kiss me," she said.

Much later that night, at her tiny studio apartment on Nineteenth and Second, she turned to me in bed and said, "You see, persistence does pay off."

"So does playing hard to get."

"Wise guy," she said with a laugh.

"I give as good as I get."

"You mean, just like me."

"Old Irish saying: There's a pair of us in it."

"Oh, is there?"

I put my arms around her and drew her close.

"I think so," I said.

She snuggled against me. "We'll see."

It had been four and a half years since that first drunken night together, and there was still "a pair of us in it." Don't get me wrong—I've never been one of those smug clowns who waxes lyrical about how he has the "perfect partnership." We are, after all, different people. Lizzie has a very black-and-white view of the world, a belief that the line between right and wrong is a clearly defined one. And though I also like to consider myself an ethical guy, I tend to see several angles lurking behind every situation.

So, though we'd been all but inseparable since that initial dinner (and were married in 1994), we had hit the inevitable bouts of turbulence . . . and just the month before we had negotiated our way through a rough passage that (had it been allowed to fester) could have swamped us. But what marriage hasn't weathered bad weather, right? And, at heart, I knew we were in it for the long haul because . . . well, put it this way: Words like *don't* or *you can't* or *I won't allow it* had never passed between us. We don't compete professionally, or play mind-fuck games of one-upmanship. We actually like each other. More tellingly, we still have the capacity to amuse each other. And how many couples can say that after nearly five years together?

Of course, we do have differences of opinion. Like on the matter of Ian and Geena. I like Geena, and enjoy Ian in small doses. Of course, I like to banter with him. But whereas Lizzie takes his name-dropping in stride, I always find myself competing with the guy. Maybe that's because, at heart, I am secretly impressed by the fact that he went to the same school as John F. Kennedy, Jr., had recently written a lengthy profile of Peter Jennings for *Mirabella,* and seemed to know everybody of journalistic and literary importance in New York.

That's a fundamental difference between Lizzie and myself—she doesn't get overawed by everything *cutting edge*—that world, according to *New York* magazine, that dictates what you should be eating, drinking, watching, reading, or talking about. Of course, she thrives on "being in the know" and occupying the inside metropolitan track, which is such an elemental part of public relations work. But unlike me, she never fears the loss of her power to convince. Nor does she feel the need to prove her credentials as a heavy-hitter by always flashing the AMEX Gold Card.

"We'll take care of that," I offered as the check arrived.

Lizzie's lips tightened, but she said nothing.

"Ned, it's a fortune here," Geena said. "At least let us split it."

I fingered open the half-folded bill that the waiter had placed in front of me. Three hundred and eighteen dollars. Ouch.

"You guys can do the next one," I said, tossing my American Express card down on the little tray and praying hard that it would be accepted (I'd gotten a letter from AMEX earlier in the week, all but threatening me with grievous bodily harm if I didn't pay up my overdue bill).

"I must say," Geena said, "for once, all the hype was true. Those risotto cakes were truly amazing."

"And at least they didn't charge us for the high celeb quotient," Lizzie added.

"Speaking of which," Ian said, "look who's walking in right now."

Along with everyone else in the main dining room, we all briefly craned our heads to watch the entrance of an exceptionally tall, powerfully built man in his early fifties. Everything about him exuded authoritative ease. At six foot four, he towered over the room. There was not an ounce of flab on his domineering frame. His face was perma-tanned. His suit and shirt looked Savile Row. His blue-gray eyes were clear and hard. But what really struck me were his hands. They were as immense as bear paws. The grab-all hands of a grab-all man.

"Well, well," Ian said, "the Great Motivator arrives."

The Great Motivator. Better known as Jack Ballantine. If you've been alive and cognizant for the past twenty years, you've undoubtedly read all about the Jack Ballantine story. How he grew up as a steelworker's son in Harrisburg, Pennsylvania, discovered a talent for football in high school, won a full scholarship to Michigan State, became the most renowned college quarterback of the mid-sixties, then led the Dallas Cowboys to three Super Bowl victories during his high-profile professional career.

Jack Ballantine wasn't just an ace quarterback, however. He was also a glitz-freak, someone who drove 150 miles per hour in the fast lane. During his decade with the Cowboys, he cultivated a reputation as a full-fledged convert to the *Playboy* worldview. A string of Ferraris. A string of Hollywood actress girlfriends. A string of designer bachelor pads in New York, the Hollywood Hills, Vail, and Dallas. And a propensity for trouble—for picking fights in bars, punching out nosy journalists, and allegedly hanging out with guys whose names were well known to federal law enforcement agencies.

Everyone expected Ballantine to end up as an archetypal screwed-up jock, someone who, upon retiring from the NFL, would blow most of his fortune on nose candy, rapacious women, and bad investments. Instead, he surprised the world by moving to New York in 1975 and becoming a self-styled real-estate developer. The cynics laughed—and predicted he'd be in bankruptcy court within twelve months. But Ballantine turned out to be a shrewd businessman. Starting with a series of small property acquisitions in the outer boroughs, he gradually moved into the Manhattan marketplace, cutting a series of big-news deals in the early '80s that guaranteed him a multimillionaire lifestyle and the status of a player.

But Ballantine being Ballantine, he wasn't satisfied with the humdrum role of multimillionaire developer. Rather, he had to transform himself into the Master Builder—Mr. High-rise, who, during the height of Reaganomics, imprinted his very own stamp on the Manhattan cityscape. Big buildings. Big deals. Two heavily publicized marriages. Two heavily publicized divorces. A man who sold himself to the public as the great entrepreneurial patriot of his time: Capitalism's Great Quarterback.

Of course, there were endless rumors that much of Ballantine's empire was built on sand—that he was constantly on the brink of financial collapse. Just as there were loud whispers that he played fast and loose in business—that he was a man with a flexible set of scruples.

Then, in 1991, it finally all went wrong. A casino deal in Atlantic City fell apart. A huge high-rise development in Battery Park City spiraled way over budget. Ballantine's corporate cash flow dried up. He was $200 million in debt. His bankers decided that he was no longer worth the gamble. So they pulled the plug. And the Ballantine building empire crashed and burned.

It was a widely publicized downfall. And the public loved it. To many people, there was something deeply satisfying about watching the waterloo of such a towering testament to self-admiration. We may worship success in America, but we are also riveted by failure. Especially when the individual in question has committed the sin of hubris. Pride goeth before a fall, after all. Particularly in the City of New York.

Though his business may have gone to the wall, Ballantine wasn't exactly reduced to selling pencils in front of Bloomingdale's, as he managed to hang on to most of his substantial personal assets. But after filing for bankruptcy, he did slip out of the public gaze for around three years. The man whose face once dominated the New York media simply vanished from view—and all sorts of gossip began to fly about how he'd had a nervous breakdown, and had become a Howard Hughes–type recluse on some obscure Caribbean island.

As it turned out, Ballantine used his three-year sabbatical to kick back and consider his next move. Because when he emerged during 1994 and again found the spotlight it was under the guise of his newfound persona. Mr. High-rise had become the Great Motivator—and he started cleaning up on the lecture circuit, giving uplifting, preachy talks about his win-win philosophy of life, and how it had given him the strength to reinvent himself after watching his empire crumble.

He also started churning out personal empowerment books. To date, he'd written three. They were all national best-sellers. They had titles like *The Success Zone* and *The "You" Conquest*. They were brimming with gridiron metaphors, and they all trumpeted Ballantine's basic worldview: Though the skillful tactician may travel far down the playing field, the guy who hits hardest actually scores the touchdown.

So, having fallen from grace, Ballantine was now firmly back in the public eye—appearing regularly on talk shows, filling three-thousand-seat conference halls, his face staring out at you from every bookstore window you passed. Of course, there was still much derision among the metropolitan elite about his comeback. Regardless of his mixed press, the fact was, the guy could still walk into a heavy-hitting joint like Patroon and cause it to momentarily fall silent. And that, to me, was real power.

Ballantine arrived with two men in black suits. One carried a briefcase and looked as if he was the Great Motivator's personal assistant. The other was evidently some sort of security goon, his eyes scanning every diner in the room. Ballantine made a brief stop at Edgar Bronfman's table—the Seagram heir already on his feet by the time they arrived and greeting Ballantine with a two-handed shake.

"See the guy with the briefcase?" Ian said. "I bet Ballantine's going to make him go from table to table and hawk his motivational tapes."

"Ian, your voice," Geena said, whispering.

"What's he going to do? Come over here and rearrange my face?"

As if on cue, the black-suited man approached our table. Ian turned a chalky shade of white. But the guy wasn't interested in him. He was staring at me.

"Ned Allen?" he asked.

I nodded slowly. He was around my age, with a chiseled jaw. I was certain I had seen his face somewhere before. He proffered his hand.

"Jerry Schubert," he said. "Brunswick High, class of eighty-three."

"Jesus," I said, standing up and clasping his hand. "Jesus Christ. I don't believe this."

"Small world. How long you been in the city?"

"Since leaving college. You?"

"Ditto. I've been Mr. Ballantine's personal assistant for the past three years."

"You've done well."

Noticing that Lizzie had her hand on the back of my chair, he gave her an approving nod. "So have you."

"Sorry. My wife, Lizzie."

Lizzie smiled thinly.

"And Ian and Geena Deane."

"Hang on, are you the guy who writes that column in the *News*?"

Ian looked a little edgy. "Yeah, that's me."

"Mr. Ballantine really appreciated the mention you gave him last week."

Ian avoided Jerry's unamused gaze. "It was just a gag."

"You have an interesting sense of humor, Mr. Deane." His expression lightened. "But Mr. Ballantine knows how to take a joke."

He glanced over at his boss. Ballantine was just leaving Bronfman's table, and the security goon was making discreet little head motions, letting it be known Jerry was wanted, pronto.

"Listen, got to go," he said, reaching into the breast pocket of his jacket and handing me a card. "It would be great to catch up. Talk some Maine talk."

"You still playing hockey?" I asked, slipping him one of my business cards.

"Only in my dreams." He glanced at my card. "Regional sales director. Impressive. Listen, nice meeting everyone—even you, Mr. Deane. Call me, okay?"

"Okay," I said.

"I mean it."

As soon as he was out of earshot, Geena said, "Well, I'm impressed."

"What the hell did you say about Ballantine in your column?" I asked Ian.

"I just made a jokey little aside about Ballantine's new book, saying it was full of great tips about how to go bankrupt but still hold on to your yacht."

"A laugh a minute, my husband," Geena said.

"Hell, it was the truth," Ian said. "Ballantine's business collapsed like the Fall of Rome, but he kept on living like Donald Trump. And now he's risen from the dead again. The man's so indestructible he makes Rasputin look like a wimp."

"Did you know that Jerry guy well in high school?" Lizzie asked.

"We were in the same homeroom, we hung out a bit during sophomore year—but then Jerry got to be a big-deal player on the hockey team, so he became part of the jock crowd." Had Ian not been at the table, I would have also mentioned the fact that, besides being a killer on the ice, Jerry Schubert also had something of an infamous reputation at Brunswick High. Because, during his senior year, he was involved in a small local scandal, when he was accused (along with two other players) of helping throw a crucial statewide championship hockey game. Allegations flew that he had links to some local bookies who'd bet heavily on the game—but a police investigation turned up no hard evidence, and he was eventually exonerated. It was all ancient history now—but there's no such thing as an old story to a gossipmonger like Ian. He'd have the tale in print the next day ("Word around town has it that Jack Ballantine's personal assistant may have once been involved in a small-town betting scandal. . . ."). And I would rightfully stand accused of dredging up dirt about an old friend. So I said nothing, except, "I read in some local paper that Jerry tried out for the NHL after college. Guess he didn't make it."

"So now he carries the Great Motivator's briefcase," Ian said.

"You know what I love about you, darling?" Geena said. "Your warm, all-embracing love of humanity."

"How can you expect humanity from a journalist?" I said, flashing Ian a smile.

"Ned's right," Ian answered. "It's like expecting subtlety from a salesman."

I managed a hollow little laugh. Yet again, the bastard had gotten the last word.

In the taxi back to our apartment, Lizzie said, "I really wish you would stop trying to outdo Ian all the time."

"It's just banter."

"To him, yeah. But to you, it's serious."

"No, it's not. . . ."

"Ned, as I've told you again and again—you don't have to compete with anyone, or keep proving that you are a success. You *are* a success."

"I'm not trying to prove anything."

"Then why did you pick up the check tonight?"

"Don't worry about the cost of the dinner. . . ."

"I am worried about the cost of the dinner. We are incredibly overextended."

"No, we're not."

"Sixty grand in the red isn't overextended?"

"In two weeks, my bonus check rolls in and we'll be back in the black."

"Until you start spending again."

"So I'll stop spending," I said.

"No, you won't. Because you need to spend. It makes you feel on top of things."

I needed to end this conversation fast. "Spending is fun," I said. "Especially with you."

She took my face in her hands and gave me a wry smile. "That's what I call a romantic evasion."

Our apartment was located on Twentieth Street between Fifth and Sixth, the so-called Flatiron district—better known as "SoHo Nouveau," if you believe what you read in the magazines. New warehouse apartments. New restaurants and bars. Trendy shopping (Emporio Armani, Paul Smith, even the de rigueur outposts of the Gap, J. Crew, and Banana Republic). And staggeringly high rents. Our one-bedroom loft (bleached parquet floors, floor-to-ceiling windows, state-of-the-art kitchen) ran us $2,200 a month—with the landlord threatening a 15 percent increase when the lease ended in February.

The message light was blinking on our answering machine. I hit the "playback" button and heard the voice of Ivan Dolinsky. He'd applied a coat of upbeat confidence to his voice, but it couldn't mask the precarious shakiness—the aura of damaged goods—which had, of late, become his defining trait.

"Boss, Ivan here. Listen, sorry, real sorry to call you at home. Was gonna call you on your cellphone, but then thought, hey, the guy's got a life, right? Don't need to be hearing live from me in the late P.M. So that's why I decided to try your land line. Everything's great, just great, like *real* great with the GBS spread. Closing tomorrow, high noon—after which, *pardner*, I'm gonna feel like the biggest gunslinger in the West. But, listen, the point of bothering you at home . . . word on the street has it that Chuckie Zanussi made an unscheduled stopover in the 'Big C'. . . ."

Shit. Shit. Shit. The jungle drums were beating at *CompuWorld*. And I knew who was hitting the bongos the loudest. Debbie Suarez. Great hustler. Big mouth.

". . . Anyway, you know me, Mr. Heebie-jeebies. The glass isn't just half empty, it's also the last drop of water on earth. . . . What I'm saying here is: We got a problem? A little Jap problem, perhaps? Don't get me wrong: Yokimura's been good to me. But when a Jap wants to fuck you over . . ."

I hit the "pause" button. Lizzie rolled her eyes.

"Charming," she said.

"Well, he is a Vietnam vet."

"I didn't realize we were fighting the Japanese in Vietnam," Lizzie said, heading into the bedroom. I clicked the machine back on.

". . . So, boss, if you wouldn't mind, gimme a fast call when you get back tonight, just so I can sleep soundly and not worry about having my butt downsized. Ring me anytime. Doesn't matter how late it is—just please give me that call and help me put my anxieties on hold."

Great. Just great. Dealing with Ivan Dolinsky—my onetime numero-uno rainmaker, for Christ's sake—had become like Psych 101. *"Gimme a fast call when you get back tonight, just so I can sleep soundly . . ."* The poor bastard hadn't slept soundly in over two years—ever since his only child, Nancy, had died of meningitis. She was just three—and the center of Ivan's life. Especially as she was an in vitro baby—the miracle (as Ivan called her) who arrived after five long years of trying for a child. The fact that he was forty-six when she was born (and that it was his first child after two failed marriages) made Nancy's arrival all the more emotional . . . and her death a sorrow beyond comprehension. Within months of losing her, his marriage was history. His concentration went south. He started missing appointments. And he stopped closing.

Chuck had wanted to fire him a year ago, after he lost us a major TechWorld multipage insert that was essentially in the bag (until Ivan missed four straight meetings). But I successfully plea-bargained his case with Chuck, then forced Ivan to see a grief counselor and started feeding him some easy accounts to gently ease him back into selling mode. And, within the past couple of months, he had started to deliver the goods again—to the point where I'd trusted him to land a big GBS spread. But the guy still needed nonstop TLC. And he had developed this unfortunate habit of talking your ear off whenever he phoned—a straightforward business call turning into a twenty-minute monologue. Which is why I wasn't up for phoning him tonight. So, heading over to my desktop computer (which we keep in a little home-office alcove adjacent to our kitchen), I banged out a fast e-mail, short and sedate.

> *Ivan:*
>
> *No need to lose sleep over small potatoes. I'm not. Because nothing—repeat,* nothing*—sinister is in the air. Break a leg with GBS tomorrow. And do yourself a favor:* ***Chill.***
>
> *Ned*

I reread the message and thought: God, how I'd love to believe my own bullshit. Then I hit the "Send Now" button and went to bed.

Lizzie was already curled up in her corner of the bed, reading a copy of *Vanity Fair*. She put the magazine down and looked at me.

"Why didn't you tell me about Chuck Zanussi's trip to Chicago?" she asked.

"Never got around to it, that's all," I said.

"Something big going on?"

"Not that I know of."

"Then why was Ivan calling here, sounding like he was in need of Prozac?"

"Because he is in need of Prozac, all the time."

"You would tell me . . ."

"What?"

"If something was up at work."

No, frankly, I wouldn't. Because I was educated in the idea that fear or anxiety was something you didn't share with those nearest and dearest to you. As my dad used to tell me: Never let anyone know if you're about to shit in your pants. The fact that you're scared will spook your family and please the hell out of your enemies.

Instead, you were supposed to internalize fear. Keep it out of sight . . . and, in the process, out of mind. Or, at least, that was my dad's theory—and one which I'd tried to follow over the years—much to the profound exasperation of my wife, who, during very occasional moments of hostility, has accused me of refusing to admit that I might just have a vulnerable bone or two in my body.

"Of course I'd tell you," I said.

"Bullshit."

"It's not bullshit. It's just . . ."

"You don't want to worry me."

"Exactly."

"Which means there's something to worry about."

"There is nothing to worry about. Chuck got called to a meeting in Chicago, that's all."

"An *important* meeting?"

"I'm not worried."

"So something *is* going on."

"At this point, all I know is it was just a meeting. And over breakfast tomorrow—"

"Oh, boy. . . ."

"Lizzie . . ."

"Chuck's hauling you in for breakfast?"

"We have breakfast together a lot."

"No, you don't."

"Okay, you're right. It's the first time in, I don't know . . ."

"Try *ever*. Chuck hates 'doing' breakfast."

"How'd you know that?"

"*You* told me."

"I guess I did. But hey, it's just a breakfast, right?"

"I really wish you weren't so damn secretive."

"I'm not secretive. Just coy."

"You are impossible, you know that?"

I slid into bed next to her.

"But you love me all the same," I said.

"Unfortunately, yes."

I pulled her toward me. Immediately, she began to move away.

"Ned . . . no," she said.

An awkward silence.

"It's been almost three weeks," I said quietly.

"I know," she said, her voice barely a whisper. "But the doctor said it could take up to twenty-one days before . . ."

"Whatever. I'm not trying to push you . . ."

"I know you're not. And I do, *will* want to again soon. But just not . . ."

"Fine, fine," I said, stroking her hair. "There's no rush. But you are feeling, uh, okay about . . . ?"

"Sure," she said flatly.

Another awkward silence—one which we found difficult to fill. Recently, there had been too many of these silences. And they all related to the same thing: Lizzie's miscarriage three weeks earlier.

The pregnancy had been a total accident, a "mechanical failure," perpetrated (we discovered later) by a microscopic tear in Lizzie's diaphragm. As such, the news that we were parents to be came as a massive two-thousand-watt jolt. After the initial shock, Lizzie was delighted with the news. But when the home pregnancy test turned a bright shade of pink, I went gray.

"Come on, sweetheart," Lizzie said after registering my high anxiety. "We always knew we wanted children eventually. So this is just nature's way of saying that eventually has arrived sooner than expected."

"Nature had nothing to do with it," I said grimly.

"You're scared of this, aren't you?"

"Not scared—just worried."

"Don't you want this child?" she asked, absently touching her stomach.

"Of course I do," I lied. "It's just . . . well, it's not exactly the right moment, is it? Especially considering the professional pressure we're both under."

"It's never going to be 'the right moment.' There will always be some pressing deadline, some deal going down. That's how life works. Okay, a kid will make things a little more complicated. But he or she will also be the best thing that ever happened to us."

"I'm sure you're right," I said.

She withdrew her hand and looked at me with care. "I wish you were happier about this news."

"I wish I was, too."

To be straight about it, I was never comfortable with the idea of parenthood. In fact, it was an event I was hoping to indefinitely postpone. To me, the notion of children has always been terrifying, because I know I'd be the sort of father who would live in fear of getting it wrong, who would obsess endlessly about my children's welfare. And because I remembered that look of profound disappointment in my father's eyes whenever he felt he had failed me.

Anyway, I rationalized, why create unnecessary havoc in your life—especially at a time when you have, professionally speaking, hit your stride? Things were going far too well right now for us. One day we'd be ready for a third party. But only when we could afford to give the kid the best.

So, I panicked. Lizzie's dismay at my hesitation was obvious. And though I tried to make up for it by being extremely attentive when she was hit with morning sickness, she was a little wary. That's the thing about Lizzie—she's nobody's fool. She comes equipped with an extra-sensitive bullshit meter that can always discern whether what I'm saying is what I'm actually thinking.

Still, after around eight weeks, I began to convince myself that I should calm down and embrace the news. Lizzie was right: Having a child would be the best thing that ever happened to us. Because, after all, she was the best thing that ever happened to me.

And then, one afternoon I received a call at the office. It was Geena. Her tone of voice immediately disturbed me. It was so controlled, so steady.

"Ned," she said, "I don't want you to panic, but . . ."

I instantly panicked. "What's happened to Lizzie?"

"Lizzie is going to be just fine. But we had to rush her to New York Hospital, she had started to bleed heavily. . . ."

I gulped. "The baby?"

"Ned, I'm really sorry. . . ."

I was at New York Hospital fifteen minutes later. The attending E.R. resident told me that Lizzie had miscarried, and had been whisked up to surgery for a fast D&C.

"She's going to be very weak when she comes around, not to mention a little traumatized when the loss of the baby sinks in. But from what I could determine, the miscarriage was a very straightforward one—so there's no reason why she shouldn't conceive again."

It was over three hours before I was allowed to see her. She was tucked in bed, attached to a drip, her face ashen from the loss of blood. But what immediately struck me were her eyes. They were shell-shocked.

I sat down and clapsed her hand tightly.

"I suppose you're relieved," she said quietly.

I felt as if I had been slapped across the face. "You know that's not true."

Suddenly she leaned forward, buried her head in my shoulder, and began to sob uncontrollably. I held her until the crying subsided.

"It'll be fine next time," I finally said.

"I don't want to talk about this," she said.

So the subject was dropped for the night. The next day, when I returned to the hospital to take her home, I made the mistake of faking an upbeat tone.

"As soon as you're better, we really should try again."

She stared at the floor and said nothing. So I took the hint and didn't raise the subject of the miscarriage again. For the first week her anguish was palpable—yet so was her equally strong desire not to discuss the matter with me. As she tried to cope with her grief, she erected a temporary wall between us. And though I respected her need for that thing called "space," I couldn't help but fear that a distance had opened up between us—that, for the first time since we met, an aura of doubt about me had been raised. And I kept privately kicking myself for having greeted her pregnancy with gloom, for letting my own anxieties and self-doubt cloud what should have been a great moment between us.

But after that first week her mood seemed to lift, and with relief

I watched the gap between us begin to close. I didn't mention the failed pregnancy again. Nor did Lizzie—until tonight, when we had yet another of those silences that now seem to occasionally descend on us.

But hey—this is probably par for the course after a miscarriage. Most of the time neither of us is exactly taciturn. We're still happy as hell together. It's just a phase, something that we'll get beyond in time. By which I mean *soon*. Real soon.

"I'm going to try to sleep," Lizzie said, turning to kiss me.

"Don't worry about anything. That's my job."

She turned off her light, embraced her pillow, and was unconscious within seconds. I stared at the ceiling, waiting for sleep to arrive. And telling myself, *There really is nothing to worry about. Because you're a winner, right? And only the winner goes to dinner.*

FOUR

Dan Sugarman was serving for the set when he began to have doubts. Having broken my serve in the sixth game, he was now up five–three, thirty-love, just two more points to win in order to clinch the set. But then he double-faulted, slamming down a blistering second serve that went way east of the box.

Thirty–fifteen.

I glanced at my watch. 6:41 A.M. Nineteen minutes to go in our designated hour on court. Sixty-four minutes before my breakfast with Chuck Zanussi. *Don't think about it, don't think about it,* I told myself. *Just concentrate on the next point.*

Sugarman's first serve was another slam-dunk attempt at an ace—and one that I just managed to get my racket on, sending it airborne. It was a shallow lob and Dan came racing in, ready to perform the *coup de grace*. But taking his eye off the ball, he volleyed it right into the net.

Thirty–all.

Now he tried a change-of-pace serve: low velocity, yet with considerable topspin. But I managed to position myself properly and hit a clean forehand winner right down the line.

Thirty–forty.

As Dan returned to the baseline, he shook his head, muttering something inaudible. Then he glanced up quickly at me—a look of ambivalence and uncertainty, of hesitancy and lack of belief. The look only lasted a second—but it said it all. I knew that I was going to win the set.

A ferocious first serve, just wide of the center line. Then an ultra-cautious "shit-it's-break-point" second serve that plopped right down in the middle of the box. I moved forward, racket way back, ostensibly poised to hit a deep shot. But as Dan hovered behind the baseline, I switched tactics and chipped a little drop shot right over the net. Dan scrambled to reach it, but it was into its second bounce by the time he was within its vicinity.

"SONOFABITCH!" he screamed as ran straight into the net—but then he raised his hand in instant apology. Tennis is a gentleman's game, after all. Until you start having doubts and begin to make mistakes. Then it suddenly becomes a do-or-die battle. With yourself.

Dan Sugarman was always having this sort of battle with himself. From all accounts, he was an attack dog of a metals trader, a guy who gave nervous breakdowns to all his underlings and stalked the futures pits of the commodities exchange like a psychotic general. Or, at least that's what I'd heard around the locker room at the New York Health and Racquet Club, where Sugarman and I played at 6:00 A.M. twice a week. Having faced the guy over a net for the past three months (we were put together by the club's resident pro after I mentioned I was in the market for a regular early-morning game), I still knew nothing much about Sugarman's background—except that he was in his early forties, was worth big bucks, lived on Sutton Place, was married to a shopaholic named Mitzi whom he worked hard at rarely seeing . . . and had this habit of slamming his 375-dollar Wilson graphite racket into the court whenever he blew a point.

Yeah, Sugarman was a real type-A, I-gut-the-competition specimen—for whom life was an ongoing combat zone. And, of course, being five foot four, he also had his Napoleonic thing on constant auto-drive—a real little man's need to assert himself at all costs. That's the thing about tennis—after you've played against a guy a few times, you get to see all his limitations, his fears and self-doubt. Because winning on the court is only partially dependent upon your skill and your physical stamina. What ultimately determines the outcome of a match (especially when you and your opponent are evenly matched) is whether you can maintain the advantage when it comes your way. Can you convert it into success? Do you really want to win that badly? Or is there some nagging, latent uncertainty regarding your ability to pull it off?

This was Sugarman's problem. Every time we played, he'd grab an early advantage—and then inevitably screw it up by becoming agitated. Maybe that's because, on the court, he's so nakedly determined. I'm the sort of *competitive* player who simply worries about winning the next point—and, as such, looks upon a match as a string of little victories. Sugarman, on the other hand, is a maniacally *ambitious* player—for whom every match is a war in which he simply has to triumph. But whenever the guy has victory in his sights—*wham*—a couple of aggressive bad shots and he starts to fall apart.

Serving at four–five, I quickly won the game, thanks to his series of unforced errors. But at five–all, his first serve came back to life. He aced me twice, then placed a brilliantly executed lob that totally wrong-footed me. Suddenly he was up forty–love, serving for the game, smiling smugly at me. A smile that said, *And you think you're a winner*.

That's when I went on the offensive, punishing his tentative first serve by dropping it right at his feet. Then, on the next point, I hit a clean forehand straight down the line.

Thirty–forty.

His next serve arrived with plenty of topspin, but I managed a cross-court backhand that was unreachable.

Deuce.

He had an attack of nerves and double-faulted. And then, having delivered a shallow volley at the net, I was suddenly up six–five and serving for the set.

Sugarman was no longer smiling—because he knew I was determined to end this thing fast.

Two aces, followed by a vengeful overhead smash, and it was set point. I tossed the ball up and slammed a clean winner down the center line. Sugarman dived for the serve, but it shot past him and he stumbled across the court like a drunk.

"SHIT, SHIT, SHIT!" he screamed. With that, a bell chimed on the club's loudspeaker, announcing that our hour on the court was up. Sugarman wearily approached the net. I followed suit. We shook hands.

"My mind's elsewhere this morning," he said.

"Yeah, so's mine."

"Didn't look that way to me. You were judge, jury, and executioner out there. A comeback like that, you're set up for a good day, pal."

"Your lips to God's ear," I said.

Within fifteen minutes of leaving the court I was showered, suited, and barreling uptown in a cab. Just south of Forty-ninth Street we drove directly into a massive gridlock. For a quarter of an hour we sat there without moving a yard.

"Anything you can do?" I finally asked the driver.

"I ain't a helicopter," he said.

Seven-thirty-seven. There was no way I was going to make the Waldorf in fifteen minutes. So I tossed ten bucks at the driver, threw open the door, and said, "Thanks, I'm outta here." Then, to the accompaniment of three dozen wailing car horns, I started weaving my way through the bottleneck. Heading toward Fifty-first Street I charged across the overpass. Seven-forty-one. And Fifty-first going west was just as bad as the Drive: one long coronary occlusion of traffic. I began to jog, dodging pedestrians, bicyclists, dachshunds on leashes, and kamikaze D'Agostino delivery boys. First Avenue . . . Why are crosstown blocks so long? . . . Second. Third. "Watch where you're running, jerkoff," snapped an elderly woman after I nearly collided with her. Lexington. Park. Fast turning south. Seven-forty-eight. Look out for the guy with the takeout tray of Starbucks coffee. The Waldorf was now in sight. Five, four, three, two, one . . .

I burst through the front doors and leaned against a wall, panting. Though it was barely twenty degrees outside, my shirt was soaked and my face saturated with sweat. I wanted to retreat to the men's room and clean up, but I was already five minutes late. So I turned to the bellhop standing by the door and asked for a handkerchief.

He reached into his pocket and pulled out a packet of Kleenex. I ripped it open, grabbed the wad of tissues, and quickly mopped my face. Then I handed the empty plastic back to him, along with a dollar.

"Thanks—that should buy you another one," I said.

"You okay now, sir?"

I straightened myself out, unkinked my shoulders, and took a deep, steadying breath.

"I'm great. Just great."

Chuck Zanussi was sitting at a corner table that faced into an alcove. Anyone glancing into the Peacock Alley Restaurant would have noticed Chuckie right away. Because—at six foot three and two hundred and seventy pounds, and with a treble chin, two bear claws for hands, and the belly of a Sumo wrestler—he was a guy who, like Mount Rushmore, commanded attention. As I approached the table I noticed a steaming stack of pancakes at his place. They were drenched in a small reservoir of maple syrup.

"Sorry I'm a bit late," I said. "Traffic on the Drive was fucking impossible. . . ."

Chuck cleared his throat and nodded uncomfortably across the table at a man in his thirties, hidden from view in the alcove recess. Tall, rail thin, with slicked-back hair (jet black), dressed in a well-cut charcoal gray suit, white spread-collar shirt, and a discreet polka-dot tie. Definitely a "Euro." And from the way he was now pointedly studying his fingertips, a guy who could be instantly filed away under *Trouble.*

"Sorry, sorry," I said, still sounding breathless. "I didn't realize . . ."

The Euro gave me a nonchalant shrug, followed by an unctuous little smile.

Chuck said, "Ned, I want you to meet Klaus Kreplin."

"I have heard much about you," Kreplin said, his English frighteningly precise.

"Have you really?" I said, shooting Chuckie a look that essentially said, *Who is this joker?*

"Of course I have heard of Ned Allen," Kreplin said, motioning for me to sit down. "You ask anyone at *CompuWorld,* Who is the number one regional manager, the advertising wizard—and it is your name which they say."

"That's, uh, nice to know," I said, sliding into the chair and giving Chuck another bemused glance. But Chuckie kept his eyes firmly fixed on his plate of pancakes. Kreplin kept talking.

"Naturally, in our company, we are always keen to let talent prosper . . ."

Our company. My pulse jumped a notch or two.

". . . and we believe in rewarding the *supernormal* . . . sorry, sorry, my English . . . the cut above, the superior. Men like yourself."

I addressed the next question to Chuck Zanussi.

"He's bought the magazine?"

Kreplin led out a strained laugh. "No, no, no, it is not I who has bought *CompuWorld,* much as I would find such a prospect amusing. It is my company that has purchased your magazine."

"And every other title in the Getz-Braun group," Chuck added. "Klaus is with Klang-Sanderling."

"You have heard of us?" Kreplin asked.

They were only one of the biggest infotainment multinationals in Europe—and a major player in the expanding communications markets of Asia and South America.

"Who hasn't?" I said.

Another smarmy smile from Klaus Kreplin.

"We have been looking for a North American platform for some time," Kreplin said. "And we saw Getz-Braun as the perfect milieu in which to reside on this side of the Atlantic."

The perfect milieu. Klang-Sanderling probably gobbled up Getz-Braun for over $3 billion, but Kreplin made it sound as if they'd just changed interior decorators.

"And what's your role in this new milieu?" I asked.

"Klaus is our new publisher," Chuck said.

"No, no, no," Klaus said. "As I told you, Chuck—*you* are still the publisher of *CompuWorld*. I am simply the *uber*-publisher of all Getz-Braun audio and computer titles. But . . ."

He addressed me directly now.

". . . please let me assure you: The individual sovereignty of each magazine will be respected. This is what I told Chuck on the plane back from Chicago yesterday evening. . . ."

"When you called me," I said to Chuck. Kreplin jumped in again.

"When *I* asked Chuck to call you and set up this meeting. And the reason why I wanted to meet you without delay, Ned, is because

Klang-Sanderling puts great faith in the idea of ordered continuity. We have great experience of this sort of transitional corporate situation, and we pride ourselves on causing as little interference as possible in the ongoing affairs of a viable title such as your own."

"You mean, I can tell everybody on my team that their job is safe?" I asked.

"Without question. And, by the way, I admire a manager who is protective of his underlings."

"They are not underlings, Mr. Kreplin."

I felt a shoe hit my shin. Chuck's way of telling me to back off.

"Of course, of course. My English again. 'Colleagues,' yes?"

"You've got it. And the best sales team in the business."

"Well, again, let me assure you, your team will remain *your* team. And please—my name is Klaus, okay?"

"Sure," I said. "Mind if I get some coffee here?"

"My God," Kreplin said, "how rude of me." He snapped his fingers at the waiter. "Coffee and . . ."

"Just coffee," I said.

"Surely you must eat some breakfast?" Kreplin said.

"I'm not hungry."

"Chuck?"

He stared down at his stack of pancakes.

"I'm doing fine, Klaus."

Kreplin consulted his watch, then pulled a small cellular phone from his briefcase.

"I must call the head office in Hamburg. You will excuse me for a minute?"

We both nodded and he headed out to the lobby. There was a long silence, during which Chuck continued to stir his lagoon of maple syrup. After Kreplin was well out of sight, Chuck motioned me forward and whispered, "What sort of aggressive asshole behavior was that?"

"Asshole? Asshole?" I hissed back. "You're the total *asshole* here, Chuckie. Dropping me in this without a warning."

"You think I find this fun? I only got crash-landed with this scenario at five last night. 'Hey, Chuckie, how 'bout stopping by Chicago on your way back from Seattle for a little late lunch?' And then, *badda-bing, badda-boom,* here are a couple of heavy-hitting Krauts, announcing they're running the show now."

"You still should've called me . . ."

"Cut me some slack here, huh? I had Mr. 'Master Race' Kreplin baby-sitting me all the way back to La Guardia—and as soon as we land, he has to hit the town. All I want to do is catch the airport limo to Larchmont and call it a night, but the guy's insistent. And since he is suddenly my boss, what am I gonna do? Tell him to go blow a chicken? Sonofabitch keeps me out until one-thirty. Insists on dragging me to some strip joint on Seventh and Forty-ninth where the champagne's one-fifty a pop. Ever see a girl with a glass eye twirl a couple of tit tassles counterclockwise? Kreplin's idea of a good time. Didn't get home until nearly three, two and a half hours' sleep and I'm back into this crap again. Wondering whether Kreplin is leveling with us, or speaking with forked tongue."

"You think we're toast here?"

"Put it this way: I'm scared . . . but not shitless."

"Terrific."

"Look, Neddie—I want to believe the Klang-Sanderling line that we're gonna remain one big happy family . . . but, hey, when was the last time you ever believed any shit from a suit?"

" 'Transitional corporate situation . . . supernormal.' The guy's a goddamn Nazi."

"Lower the volume, huh? Kreplin hears you, you'll be shining shoes at Grand Central."

" 'Ve respect individual sovereignty.' Wasn't that the same line Hitler used on the Czechs in thirty-nine?"

"Neddie, Neddie, listen to me—we've got a situation here. A no-win situation—because, let's face it, Klang-Sanderling now holds all the cards. So getting all hot under the collar against Kreplin . . ."

"I wasn't getting hot under the collar."

"You were flirting with sarcasm—which is probably not the most politic of moves right now. Especially since we know that our new '*uber*-publisher' can toss us both on the street in a heartbeat."

He had a point. I shrugged in weary agreement.

"Listen, Neddie—you know you're our top guy on the sales front. You could charm the shit out of Saddam Hussein. Now all you have to do here is make Kreplin like you. I mean, he's heard all the good buzz about you around the company. And I think he's a smart enough cookie to realize that, by and large, *CompuWorld* is a lean, mean operation—so why install a new regime when this one delivers the goods? Just sell yourself to the asshole, okay?"

"All right, all right," I said. "The charm offensive starts now."

"Smart guy. And believe me, I'm in shock, too. I mean, with three kids to support, a mother of a mortgage, bills up the wazoo, and the annual Christmas spending spree about to kick in, this little turn of events is making me more than a little nervous."

"Does anyone else know about the change of ownership?"

"Not yet—but you can bet that the grapevine is already humming. So when we get back to the office, I want you to get on the horn and personally inform everyone on your team of what's happened—and try to reassure them that it's simply business as usual."

I thought about my late-night message from Ivan Dolinsky. The poor guy was going to be *mainlining* Prozac when he heard the news.

"Another thing you'll have to explain to them . . . ," Chuck said, his voice tense once again, ". . . is the way their bonuses are going to be paid out from now on."

"Oh, Jesus," I said, inadvertently raising my voice, "don't tell me they're going to fuck with our bonuses."

"We would never do such a thing."

I looked up. Klaus Kreplin was back at our table, beaming with pleasure at my gaffe.

"I do apologize, Mr. Kreplin," I said, attempting to sound contrite.

"Please, you *must* call me Klaus."

"I didn't mean any offense, Klaus."

"None taken, Ned."

"But please do understand . . ."

"I know, I know. You think you have just been landed in a danger zone. New management, a new corporate order. And you naturally worry, 'Will they terminate us all,' *ja*?"

I stopped myself from responding with a "*Ja*" (*kill the sarcasm, Ned*), and simply nodded.

"These concerns I understand," Kreplin continued, "and respect. Because they reflect wider concerns about the future of those who work with you. But, please—you have my assurance: As long as the productivity of your division remains high, there will be no terminations."

"I appreciate that," I said.

"And as to the matter of the Christmas bonus: Everyone will be paid *exactly* what they are entitled. Our problem—and it is not precisely a problem, more a small accounting detail—is that Klang-Sanderling's end of fiscal year is January thirty-first, and we never pay bonuses until this time. However, respecting the American tradition of the bonus before Christmas, what we propose is this: fifty percent of the bonus on the last Friday before Christmas, and the remaining fifty percent of the bonus on thirty-first January. A good arrangement, yes?"

No, it wasn't. Especially to someone as deep in debt as me. Or to Debbie Suarez, who was counting on all the bonus cash before the New Year to pay for her kid's tuition. Or to Dave Maduro, who was juggling two alimonies. Or to just about everyone else I could think of in Northeast sales, all of whom were paragons of fiscal irresponsibility (Well, you show me a salesman who lives within his means). So, sorry, Herr Kreplin—but this is a totally shitty arrangement.

I glanced over at Chuck. His eyes said it all: *Don't argue with the bastard. We have no leverage here.* I mustered a workmanlike smile.

"It sounds like a perfectly reasonable compromise to me."

"Wonderful," he said, happy to have "terminated" that piece of grim business. "Now, if your schedule will allow it, Ned, I would like you to accompany me to dinner tonight. And then, maybe you can show me this SoHo and Tribeca scene we have read so much about in the German press."

I felt Chuck's shoe rap my shin again.

"Sure, Klaus. I'll just have to call my wife and—"

"Excellent. I will make reservations at eight-thirty for this amusing new restaurant I have read about on Lafayette Street."

"You mean Pravda?" I asked.

"Most impressive," Kreplin said. "And do you also know what *pravda* means in English?"

"Yeah," I said. "Truth."

Kreplin excused himself to work the transatlantic phone lines in his suite upstairs at the Waldorf Towers. Chuck and I headed back to the office. It was only a five-minute walk. We said nothing until we reached Third Avenue and Forty-eighth, where a Salvation Army Santa was ringing his bell and shouting "Happy holidays" in a reedy voice.

"I think I've just lost my Christmas spirit," Chuck said.

"Like you said . . . Why should he waste us when he knows that we're more than meeting the bottom line?"

"I keep telling myself, Don't panic. And I'm finding it real hard to follow my own advice. But listen: When we get to the office, the two of us have got to break the news nice and calmly. It's business as usual. Right?"

However, when we walked into the office, calm was not exactly the order of the day. Chuck was immediately cornered by his secretary, Louise. She looked stricken.

"Mr. Zanussi, the phone hasn't stopped ringing. I've got about twenty urgent messages for you. You've gotta tell me: Do I still have a job here?"

"Louise, there is nothing, *nothing* to worry about," he said, shepherding her into his office and mouthing *Good luck* to me as he shut the door.

I turned and headed down the corridor toward Northeast sales. I didn't get very far. A frantic Debbie Suarez blocked my path.

"They're not paying us our bonus?" she said, raw fear in her voice.

Trust Debbie to be first with the late-breaking news.

"Debbie . . ."

"That's what they told me this morning. . . ."

"Who told you?"

"People."

"What people?"

"People in the know. And they said some Germans bought us, and that they're gonna throw us out on the street. And . . ."

"Hang on now . . ."

"They're gonna pocket my goddamn bonus, the assholes."

Everyone with an office along this corridor was now standing at the doorway, watching this outburst. They all looked apprehensive.

"Debbie, please. *Easy.*"

"I've got to have that money, Mr. Allen."

"I know you do," I said quietly as I steered her back toward her cubicle. "And you will get it."

She stopped and looked at me. "You're on the level here?"

"Believe me, I am. And your job's secure, too."

"You're not saying that just to shut me up?"

I managed a laugh. "Listen, why don't you get everyone from Telesales together now in my office, and I'll explain exactly what's going on."

"Mr. Dolinsky's in your office."

I glanced over at my little glass-fronted work space. There indeed was Ivan Dolinsky, standing by the window, gazing blankly out at the street.

"He say what was going on?"

"Nothing—except he said he had to see you, pronto. He looked real bad to me, Mr. Allen."

He was probably just as shaken as everybody else. Or, at least, that was my best case scenario. I needed Ivan right now like I needed a colostomy. So I asked Debbie to get him a cup of coffee (and three Valiums, if she had any handy) and say I'd be with him in ten minutes—after I briefed all the Telesales people in the conference room.

Eight very scared women filed into the windowless room that *CompuWorld* uses for meetings. They didn't sit down. They stood in a semicircle while I perched on the edge of the conference table and essentially did a song and dance to the tune of "We have nothing to fear but fear itself." Klang-Sanderling, I assured them, was no fly-by-night outfit. They wanted to play ball with the same team. No personnel changes. We're going to remain one big profitable family—*blah, blah, blah.*

Then I got to the business about the bonuses—and the conference room's decibel level suddenly went into the red zone.

"They can't do that to us, Mr. Allen," Debbie said.

"Yes, they can," I said. "It's their company now. They can do whatever they want."

"You think this is fair?" shouted Hildy Hyman, one of the *CompuWorld* oldtimers—sixty-three, never married, still living with her very geriatic mother in Kew Gardens, and just two years away from her pension.

"Of course it's not fair, Hildy," I said. "But we don't exactly live in a kind and gentle corporate world anymore. If someone has the cash to take you over, they're perfectly entitled to do so."

"Especially if they're Germans," Hildy said. "You should talk to my mother. Burned down her father's pharmacy in Munich in nineteen thirty-two . . ."

"Hildy," I said, "I know what happened to your mother. And it's terrible . . ."

"They destroyed my family's business then. They are destroying *our* business now."

"No, they are not. They're keeping us together, even though they don't have to. And yeah, I know waiting an extra month for half your bonus is lousy—but at least we'll be getting the bonus. I mean, they could have told us to take a hike. And, from what I can gather, there'll be no change in terms of health benefits, IRAs, the works. I really think they're trying to be honorable about this."

"Honorable Germans," Hildy said dismissively. "That is an oxymoron."

"What the fuck's an oxymoron?" Debbie Suarez asked.

By the end of this impromptu meeting, I'd managed to assuage most of my Telesales team's worst fears—though they were not exactly the happiest collection of campers as they returned to their desks. And who could blame them? A takeover is an invasion. You suddenly find yourself swallowed up by a superpower. They now make life-or-death decisions about your future. All you can hope for is that your new masters don't turn out to be graduates from the Joseph Stalin School of Management.

As I headed back to my office, I found Debbie loitering with intent in the corridor. She radiated stress.

"Look, Mr. Allen," she said, pulling me into a side hallway. "I gotta say something here. I'm still real worried about this bonus thing. I mean, I gotta pay Raul's tuition by January first. And they also make you pay a one-term deposit, which you don't get back till your kid graduates or leaves. That's three terms I gotta pay them: nine thousand bucks. But if I'm only gonna get sixty-seven hundred, how am I gonna make it? And then there's the heart drugs for my mamá, and the money I owe MasterCard, and all the stuff I gotta do for Christmas. I'm not gonna make it. . . ."

"Tell you what I'll do," I said. "Find out the name of the money guy at Raul's school and I'll talk to him. Explain what's going on, schmooze him into letting you pay half the money now, and the other half when the second bonus check arrives at the end of January. It's Faber Academy, right?"

"Yeah. Real nice Quaker school."

"Then they shouldn't be jerks about money."

"Thanks, Mr. Allen."

"Piece of advice: It's new management, not the street. So just get on with your job. Because—trust me—I think it's all going to work out just fine."

"I do trust you, Mr. Allen."

Then God help you—because, personally, I didn't believe a word I was uttering. But I was willing to say anything reassuring if it maintained calm among the troops.

With Debbie's fears now eased, it was on to the next personal crisis. Ivan Dolinsky. He was still standing by my window as I entered my office, and seemed so preoccupied that he didn't hear me until I spoke:

"I thought you were supposed to be up with GBS in Stamford this morning."

"Meeting's postponed," he said, not turning around to look at me.

"Till when?"

"Later."

"You okay, Ivan?"

He finally turned and faced me. Skin the color of paper. Deep shadows beneath his eyes. A drab navy blue suit with wide lapels, which—thanks to the drastic amount of weight that Ivan had lost—gave him a sort of scarecrow-mormon-missionary look. His nails were nonexistent, his cuticles red and scabbed. Though we spoke almost every day on the phone, he was always on the road, so I hadn't seen him in over two months. And I had to work hard at hiding how disturbed I was by his appearance. I wondered if he was still seeing the grief counselor I'd found for him.

"Guess you heard the news," I said.

He nodded and turned back toward the window.

"When I sent you that e-mail last night, I really didn't know what was going on. And I didn't want you to be worrying all—"

Ivan had started to cry. Softly at first—a strangled sob which he fought to control, yet which quickly escalated. I kicked my office door shut, quickly lowered the blinds on the glass-fronted wall that looked out on the Telesales cubicles, and eased Ivan into my chair. I grabbed the phone and told Lily at the switchboard to hold all calls. Then I sat down opposite Ivan and waited until his crying jag ended.

"Tell me," I said.

He stared down at the desk and said, "I just lost the GBS account."

FIVE

It was like a right to the jaw. I flinched. And Ivan saw me flinch.

"I'm sorry, I'm really sorry, you don't know how sorry . . ."

His voice started to get shaky again. I tried to sound very sedate, very composed.

"What exactly happened?"

"How should I know? The past two, three months I've been building a relationship with this Ted Peterson guy in their media sales department, we shake hands yesterday on this six-page insert for April, I'm heading north to Stamford on I-95 this morning, paperwork in my bag for Peterson to sign, somewhere near Rye he calls me: 'Listen, sorry, but we've changed marketing strategies for late winter. So, no sale right now.' Nearly ran my car off the road."

"And that was it?"

" 'Course it wasn't *it*, Ned. I mean, it's my balls on the chopping block here. I've invested three months romancing the cocksucker, WE HAD FUCKING CLOSED YESTERDAY . . . so do you really, really think I was just gonna go, 'Oh, hey, that's kind of disappointing . . . but into every life a little rain must fall?' "

He was yelling. I held both hands up.

"Ivan. Chill. I am not angry." (Lie.) "I am not upset." (Bigger lie.) "I just need to know the facts."

"Sorry, sorry . . . I'm really adrift here, Ned. It's just, like, with what's been going on, this bad news was . . ."

"I hear you." And I did. His kid. His marriage. His professional worth. Loss. Loss. And more loss. But though one side of my brain was sympathizing with his fragile state, the other sector was sending out red alert signals. Because, with the GBS multipage insert suddenly gone, there were now six empty pages in the April issue (due to go to press this Friday). And six blank pages meant $210,000 in lost advertising revenue. Talk about handing our heads to Klang-Sanderling on a platter. If they were looking for a way to ease a bunch of us out, this would give them the perfect excuse.

"What price was GBS paying for the multipage insert?" I asked.

"One-eighty-nine. The standard ten percent discount."

"Did he give you any hint about a possible budget squeeze? Or maybe one of the competition edging us out?"

"Ned, like I told you, he just said 'no dice' and hung up. I tried to call him back, I don't know, five, six times in the next hour. Driving back into the city, I must've called him every ten miles. The asshole was always 'in a meeting.'"

"Okay, look, it's a setback . . ."

"It's a fucking car crash, Ned. You know it, I know it. . . ."

I put a finger to my lips. "It's a situation. And we've got to deal with it—but in a way that won't have everyone in the company talking. Word gets out about this, and the situation turns into a *critical* situation—something we definitely don't want with new management looking over our shoulder. So the thing to do at the moment is examine our options here. You got anything else on the go?"

"I don't know . . . NMI was talking about a possible double-page spread for their Powerplan Desktop series in May."

"Can you talk them into jumping forward a month?"

"Worth a shot."

"Then do it now. Offer 'em twenty percent off, and tell 'em that the four-color bleeds are on the house. Meanwhile, I'm sure we can get the Telesales girls to cover the other four pages."

"It's gonna look like crap, though—a lot of shitty eighth-of-a-pagers in a prime location. And everyone's going to know it was my space. . . ."

"Ivan, the bottom line here is: If the pages are paid for, everybody's happy."

"It won't happen again, Ned. You've got my word. . . ."

"It's a bad hand, Ivan. The jerk dealt from the bottom of the deck. Don't blame yourself."

"Easier said—"

"You still going for your sessions with the counselor . . . what's-her-name?"

"Dr. Goldfarb. I stopped two weeks ago."

"She no good?"

"She was great. Really helpful. But the company health plan only covered a year. . . ."

"I'll make a few phone calls to Blue Cross, see what I can do."

"Thanks. I owe you."

He stood up, rubbing his eyes with his sleeve.

"You sure you're gonna be okay?" I asked.

"Not if I keep blowing it. . . ."

"You've been doing fine, Ivan," I lied. "Like I said: It's a bum deal, not Armageddon. Now go close NMI. And remember: You're good at this."

He nodded and headed out the door. As soon as it closed behind him, I put my head in my hands. Shit. Shit. Shit. This *was* Armageddon. *My* Armagedon. Unless . . .

Rule Number One in a crisis: Be systematic. Explore every option for burrowing your way out of the dead end into which you've been dropped. I picked up the phone and called Joel Schmidt, *CompuWorld*'s production manager. When I asked him if I could have a couple of extra days' grace on the GBS copy, he went ballistic.

"You nuts, Ned? Ten minutes ago some German ice maiden walks into the office, introduces herself as Utte something, says she's the production supervisor for all Klang-Sanderling titles, and wants to know everything about the way we work. She also said she knew the magazine was going to bed on Friday—which, according to her calculations, was four days behind schedule. Which, in turn, was costing the company, blah, blah, blah. Get the picture?"

"Kind of a chilly customer?"

"Chilly? This babe was without heat. And I can already tell that she's determined to *supervise* me into the ground. So there is absolutely no way I can cut you any slack. Final ad copy Friday, or it's your *cojones*."

So much for buying myself some more time. I picked up the phone and called Ted Peterson's office at GBS. His secretary was a real charmer. As soon as she heard the name *CompuWorld*, she informed me that Mr. Peterson was in a meeting and would probably remain in said meeting for the next five years. Or, at least, that's the sort of brush-off vibe I was getting from her.

"If I could just have five minutes of his time."

"He doesn't have five minutes today, Mr. Allen," she said crisply.

"Everyone has five minutes."

"I will tell him you called. I can do no more." And she hung up.

Ted Peterson. I'd met him last year at one of Getz-Braun's big sales shows. Your typical corporate stain. Age thirty-two and determined to snag that executive vice presidency by the time birthday number thirty-five rolls around. A real play-to-win type.

"I heard you're a helluva tennis player," he said at a cocktail party thrown by Brighton Technology Inc. ("Data storaging you can trust.")

"I played a little in college. But now . . . I'm just a serious amateur."

"What school you play for?"

"U. Maine, Presque Isle."

I could see his lips twitching into a little smile. "Don't think we ever played you."

"Where'd you go?"

"Princeton."

Having won that point, the conversation somehow drifted on to the subject of our all-time favorite players.

"Stefan Edberg, hands down," I said. "A gentleman on the court—but with a real deadly sting. And you?"

"Ivan Lendl. The living embodiment of ruthless efficiency."

No doubt Peterson thought he was being ruthlessly efficient when he dumped Ivan overboard . . . even though the bastard surely knew all about Ivan's ongoing series of tragedies. I love a Samaritan.

The five lights on my phone were flashing madly. I hit the speakerphone.

"A few messages, Lily?" I asked.

"You must have two dozen messages here, Mr. Allen."

"Great. Give me the big ones."

"All the outside sales reps. The media sales guys from AdTel, Icom, InfoCom, Microcom . . . It's a really long list."

Worse and worse. The word about the takeover had evidently spread through the industry like cancer—and every major *CompuWorld* advertiser had phoned in, obviously to find out if we were still in business.

"Would you mind e-mailing me the entire list of calls, Lily?"

"No problem, Mr. Allen. Oh—one last thing—your wife called, said she'd heard the news. She wanted to talk to you right away."

"Is she holding right now?"

"No—you got Mr. Maduro on line one, Mr. Sirio on line two, Mr. Bluehorn on line three . . ."

All my main guys in the field. All understandably worried about whether they still had a job.

"I'll talk to Sirio. Tell the others I'll call them right back."

"You got it, Mr. Allen. One last thing: Should I start looking in the want ads?"

"Put it this way, Lily: I'm not worried."

"I hear ya, Mr. Allen."

I punched button two on my phone.

"Yo, Phil," I said. "Sorry to keep you dangling like that."

"*Fugedaboudit*, Ned. Sounds like it's some kind of screwed-up day there."

Good old Phil. Mr. Laconic. And a rock-solid good guy. Of all my sales team, Phil was, without question, the easiest to deal with. Early forties, unapologetically fleshy, Queens born and bred, still a resident of the 'hood (Ozone Park, to be exact), a snappy dresser who liked mother-of-pearl-gray double-breasted suits, and had zero tolerance for bullshit. Ever since Ivan Dolinsky's eclipse, Phil had been our number-one man. I'd never seen a smoother operator in my life. All the guy had to do was pick up a phone, and he closed. His client list was watertight—no sudden jumping ship to the opposition (I often wondered if it was Phil's "Mr. Big" demeanor that kept his customers in line). And, unlike my other guys in the field, he never groaned, wept, or wailed about business. He got on with the job.

"So you heard the news?" I asked.

"Yeah. I heard. Germans. They gonna work with us?"

"That's what they say."

"Then that's okay. I heard about the bonus biz as well. Not exactly my idea of a good time."

"Nor mine."

"They gonna deliver the goods?"

"They've given me assurances . . ."

"Then that's okay, too."

I loved this guy. No angst. No crap.

"Listen, Phil. I've got to ask you a favor."

"Tell me."

So I explained about the GBS crisis—and how we were now looking at six blank pages in the April issue.

"That pig fucker Peterson pulled this stunt?" Phil asked.

"I'm afraid so."

"Guys like that, I wanna castrate 'em with a chain saw. You want me to talk to him?"

"He's not taking any phone calls. Believe me, I've tried."

"Yeah, but Peterson would take my call."

"Why's that?"

"Because I know stuff."

"What sort of stuff?"

"Stuff about Peterson."

"Such as . . . ?"

"Remember last year's winter sales event at Grand Cayman? Well, the final night we're there, I'm leaving the hotel, thinking about taking a little stroll down the beach, when all of a sudden Joan Glaston comes tearing down the street, looking spooked as shit, totally shook up. You know Joan, don't you?"

"Telesales Chicago?"

"Yeah, that's her. Hell of a sharp operator, and great legs. Anyway, she runs right into me outside the hotel, hysterical. I lead her inside, bring her to a quiet table in the bar, feed her a whiskey, calm her down a little. Turns out she had been at this GBS reception down the beach at the Grand Hyatt, and she got talking to Peterson. When she decided to leave, Ted, being such a nice guy, offered to escort her back to her hotel. Halfway there, they stopped to look at the water. Next thing Joan knew, Peterson was all over her. But when she told Mr. Family Values to back off, instead of taking the hint, Peterson pulled her down onto the sand and tried to spread her legs.

"That's when Joan caught him between *his* legs with her knee, and managed to hightail it outta there—which is when she ran into me."

"Jesus Christ," I said. "Did she report him to the police?"

"I wanted to march her down to the nearest precinct—but she was scared about Peterson inventing some bullshit story for the cops. So I said, 'Okay, to hell with the Cayman cops. Go directly to his superiors at GBS, tell them exactly what happened, and force them to sack the sick fuck.' But again, she got all frightened about how, even if GBS believed her, they would never deal with her again. And since she was dependent on GBS-related products for fifty percent of her monthly quota, she was terrified of blowing her relationship with the company.

"Anyway, I told her not to be intimidated by Peterson or by GBS. She said she'd sleep on it, give it all some thought. The next morning, I'm checking in at the airport, and who should I find standing behind me but Mr. Romantic himself. I say 'Howyadoin', Ted?' and he starts imitating my accent. Preppy sonofabitch thinks he's a comedian. Real hysterical stuff like 'I'm doin' good, Philie. How's the family—and I mean that with a capital *F*.'

"Now I've only met this clown maybe once or twice in my life—and I do not like being the object of fun. So I lean over and whisper into his ear, 'At least I wasn't trying to rape someone on the beach last night. The way I hear, the only way Joan could stop you was by kicking a field goal below your belt. Man, I'd love to see the look on your wife's face when she checks out your bruised equipment.'

"Well, the blood drained so fast from Peterson's face, it looked like he'd been bitten by Count Dracula."

"Did he say anything to you?"

"Bastard was too stunned to speak. Then, around two days later, I got a call from Joan. She was back in Chicago, and wanted to thank me for giving her a shoulder to cry on. But no, she wasn't going to be pressing charges against Peterson. Because the day after she got home from Grand Cayman, she got a call from one of Peterson's underlings, saying how his boss so liked meeting her in Grand Cayman he wanted to offer her a GBS full-pager for the next six months. Joan did her math, worked out the commission, and said yes . . . even though she knew she was taking the easy way out. But at least the sonofabitch knew that she now had something on him."

"I don't believe this," I said.

"Hang on—it gets better. Around an hour after I finish talking with Joan, I get a call from some GBS sales rep out in Queens, saying the company wants me to have one of their new top-of-the-line laptops. The 804FE. Street price: Fifty-three hundred."

I was speechless. GBS was such a conservative, play-it-by-the-book, now-wash-your-hands organization. If they knew one of their executives had tried to buy silence (after committing a sexual assault), they'd fire him in a heartbeat.

"You didn't take it, did you?" I said.

"Ned, Ned—you think I was born stupid? 'Course I didn't take it—though, I gotta tell ya, I was tempted for about a minute, 'cause that is one sexy laptop. But what I did do is this: I told the rep guy to personally thank Mr. Peterson for his generous offer, and to inform him that he was in my thoughts . . . all the time."

"Jesus," I said. "Jesus Christ."

"Lord's only son. So there you go. Ted Peterson now kind of owes me a favor. I pick up the phone. He does me the favor. You get your six-page multipage insert for April. Ivan gets to close this sucker. We all walk away happy."

I shut my eyes. I could feel my hands turn clammy—that same old sticky dampness that always hit whenever I became nervous. And I was really nervous now. Because . . . Oh God, how easy this would be. All I had to do was tell Phil, "Make the call" and the problem would be solved.

But. But. But. Once you've sanctioned a call like that, what next? A fiddle here, a fiddle there, wink-wink, nudge-nudge, *I'm lookin' the other way, pal*. And, of course, Phil would have something on me now. Not, of course, that Phil would ever dream of using that "something." Unless he needed to. Information is power, after all.

"Ned, you still there?" Phil asked.

"I'm here."

"So you want me to make the call?"

Another long silence. There is no thrill in doing the right thing, is there? Especially since there is something so enticing about the illicit, the deceitful. It's there in all of us, the need to toy with danger. The problem is, doing the wrong thing rarely has an escape clause. And you have to live with the consequences.

"I really appreciate your offer, Phil," I said. "And though it would solve a hell of a lot of problems . . ."

"I hear ya, pal."

"I just can't work that way."

"You sure you're not a Catholic?"

I laughed. "Just a guy from Maine."

"So what are you gonna do about the six pages?"

"Any chance you could sweet-talk a client or two of yours into buying some additional space, pronto?"

"When's the copy deadline?"

"First thing Friday morning."

"How 'bout I say a novena to Our Lady of Fatima while I'm at it?"

"You think it's gonna be that impossible?"

"Unless I offer the space at bargain-basement rates."

"Do it," I said. "We'll deal with the bottom line later."

"Okay, boss. I'll see what I can cook up."

After Phil hung up, I sat at my desk, drumming my fingers on the table, watching the dancing lights on my telephone. That was close. So close. *Make that call*. Three words. Say them and your hands are permanently dirty. Draw the line at saying them and you're an ethical jerk, still facing a major business crisis. Moral dilemmas are never black and white. They're always an ugly shade of gray.

I speed-dialed Dave Maduro's number. He did not sound happy.

"I must have left you four messages," he said. "Thanks for making me feel like the lowest asshole on the totem pole."

"Dave, sorry, all hell's been breaking loose this morning. But look—"

"No fancy bullshit, Ned. Just some straight talk: Do I still have a job?"

It was the question each of my outside sales guys asked first. And I spent most of the morning calming them down, stroking their egos, giving them the usual reassuring spiel, and begging them to somehow immediately cough up an extra page's worth of advertising. As planned, I also put the word out to the Telesales team that I needed some major space filled by the day after tomorrow. This was a high-risk strategy, insofar as news was bound to start leaking around the company that Northeast sales had a little "empty space crisis" on their hands. But I had no other option. There was no doubt that Chuck would hear about Ivan's disaster with GBS—but I was gambling on the fact that he was so preoccupied with the takeover that word of the emergency wouldn't reach him for at least thirty-six hours, by which time, Allah willing, the pages would be filled. I just hoped to God that Ivan closed something with NMI. Otherwise, Chuck really was going to demand his head this time.

The day evaporated around me. As soon as I finished soothing my sales guys, I had to deal with the eighteen or so calls from all our major advertisers. I treated them all to the same song and dance:

> *We're now even bigger and better thanks to our new owners, Klang-Sanderling. And, let's face it, those Germans aren't in the habit of backing losers. Just watch how we increase our market share in the next quarter.* Computer America *now knows its days as number two are numbered. Because it's Klang-Sanderling's avowed battle plan to blow them out of the water. And to inaugurate their new ownership, they want me to offer you a six-page multipage insert in our April issue at twenty-five percent off the usual rate. Now demand is so heavy for this space that we've set a deadline of five P.M. today. . . .*

Of course, there were no takers. Not that I expected anyone to bite. The big guns in the computer business always have their advertising strategy mapped out months beforehand—so the odds of someone agreeing to a last-minute multipage insert (and supplying us with the copy in less than thirty-six hours) were up there with my chances of flying on the NASA space shuttle next month.

Still, it was worth a shot. Anything right now was worth a shot.

By five I'd finished with the last name on my call list, and made my eighth (and, I decided, final) call to Ted Peterson's office. I hadn't eaten all day, hadn't moved from my desk, and was borderline brain-dead. Then Debbie popped her head in my office and said that the combined Telesales force had struck out on the last-minute advertising front.

"Everyone I call, they keep asking, 'Ya still in business?' So, like, it was kinda hard convincing them to do a last-minute eighth-of-a-pager. And, I've gotta tell ya this, Hildy and the others are worried that we're comin' across kinda desperate, scrambling for all this last-minute ad space. I mean, we're already working on May . . ."

"I hear ya, Debbie."

"Don't get me wrong, we're bustin' ass here. Especially 'cause we all know Mr. Dolinsky's job is on the line."

Unbelievable. My office must be bugged.

"So whatcha want us to do, Mr. Allen?"

I sighed. Loudly.

"Concentrate on the May issue. I'm sure one of the outside sales guys will come through."

But that didn't happen. Ten minutes later, as I was returning with my twelfth cup of coffee of the afternoon, the lights on my desk phone began to blaze again. First Dave Maduro, then Doug Bluehorn, followed by Phil Sirio. And they all had the same answer for me: None of their clients was in a position to commit to more space on such short notice.

"I don't have to tell you the name of the problem here," Phil Sirio said. "It's called Christmas. Everyone's budget is shot to shit and nobody's interested in complicating their life right now. Believe me, I pulled every hustle I could think of. No dice."

"Thanks anyway for trying, Phil."

"So how you gonna solve this?"

"Don't know what I can do—except ritually disembowel myself in front of the Germans."

"Boss, let me call Ted Peterson."

"It's blackmail."

"Get outta here. It's persuasion, nothing more. Like, the guy *told* Ivan he was gonna close the deal. All I'm gonna do is remind him that a verbal contract *is* worth the paper it's written on."

I leaned my head against my damp hand. Finally I said:

"I'll sleep on it."

Six-ten. I glanced at my fingernails. For the first time in about ten years, they were bitten to the quick. Just like Ivan's. Another day like this one and I'd start considering the medicinal benefits of cigarettes.

Another phone light was blinking. What next? I reluctantly punched it.

"Where the hell have you been?"

It was Lizzie. A very agitated Lizzie—and for good reason, as I hadn't returned one of the half dozen messages she'd left today.

"Lizzie, hon, sorry, sorry, I can't tell you what it's been like—"

"What were you thinking? You had me so worried. I mean, I walk into the office this morning, and everyone's running up to me, saying that Klang-Sanderling just bought Getz-Braun. And then, when I didn't hear from you . . ."

"Look, it's been crisis a-go-go around here. I didn't have a minute . . ."

"Everyone has a minute," she said, echoing my sarcastic exchange with Ted Peterson's secretary hours earlier. "Especially for their spouse."

"Lizzie, don't be angry. I didn't mean . . ."

"I'm *not* angry. Just a little hurt. And naturally worried. For you." Her voice softened. "You okay?"

"Not really."

"They showed you the door?"

"No—but by Friday morning, they most certainly will."

I told her everything that had happened since I'd walked into that breakfast with Chuck Zanussi. Everything except Phil Sirio's offer to blackmail Ted Peterson.

When I finished, she said, "Oh, sweetheart—that is one shitty day."

I managed a laugh. "The shittiest imaginable. And it ain't over yet. I mean, I really don't know how I'm going to fill those six pages—except with nude photos of Chuck Zanussi."

"Tell you what—give me an hour, and I'll take you out for a drunken dinner. . . ."

"No can do. That creep Kreplin's already snagged me for dinner."

"Terrific."

"Believe me, I'd cancel if I could. But there's no way out of this. Especially as Kreplin is the new *führer* around here."

"Understood, understood." But I could tell from her tone of voice that she was disappointed . . . and worried.

"You're upset."

"I'm just feeling a bit marginalized again. I mean, last night, you sort of knew a takeover was imminent—but you didn't want to say anything."

"Like I told you, why share the worry?"

"Because we're married, that's why. Because being married means we're supposed to share stuff like that. And because I feel a little patronized when you don't . . ."

"I would never, *ever* patronize you."

"Maybe not intentionally. But, to me, this 'don't-want-to-worry-your-little-head-dear' crap is definitely patronizing . . ."

"Lizzie, please . . ."

". . . and if the shoe had been on the other foot—if our company had been suddenly bought out—you would have been the first person I called."

I put my head in my hands. A little marital tension was just what I needed right now. Best to say nothing, except . . .

"Guilty as charged."

"I'm not accusing you of anything. And I'm not trying to give you grief—especially after what you've been through today. It's just . . . You don't have to keep playing the salesman with me. Always acting as if you're on a perpetual winning streak—"

She was stopped by Lily's voice on my speakerphone.

"Mr. Allen, really sorry to interrupt, but I've got Mr. Dolinsky on line two. He says it's urgent."

"Say I'll be with him in a sec."

"I'll let you go," Lizzie said.

"Sorry, but Ivan's heading up my intensive care list right now."

"Stop apologizing, Ned. I do appreciate what's going on."

"You're a star."

"Are you going to be late?"

"Very, I'm afraid. Kreplin's hinted he wants to hit the town, big-time."

"Then I won't wait up. And look—if it all falls apart, we'll still be just fine. Remember that."

"I will."

"Love you."

"You, too," I said, then punched line two. Over the static of his car phone, I heard the curiously buoyant voice of Ivan Dolinsky.

"Ned, have I got news for you . . ."

"You close NMI?"

"You bet I did. Not only that, they agreed to a full six-page multipage insert for their new Powerplan series."

"Fan-fucking-tastic," I said, punching the air with my fist. Crisis averted.

". . . and I even drove over to their headquarters in Paterson to make certain they signed the contract. Just got out of the meeting, heading back to the city right now."

"It's great news."

"There's only one small problem . . ."

Oh, God . . .

"They're adamant that it goes into the May issue."

I exhaled. Loudly.

"Ivan . . ."

"I know, I know—and, believe me, I was all but licking the guy's shoes, begging him to move it forward to April. But May's when they're launching the new Powerplan models. . . ."

Do you have any idea of the career-threatening shit you've dropped me in? I wanted to shout. But I knew such a temper tantrum was pointless. Phil was right: Having agreed to the multipage insert, then pulling out of the deal, Peterson had reamed Ivan. Okay, Ivan should've forced him to sign a contract there and then—but you expect a GBS executive to abide by his Scout's-honor word. It wasn't Ivan's fault. And he had just closed a biggie. Not the biggie I needed right now—but a biggie nonetheless. I tried to sound upbeat.

"You did great, Ivan," I said.

"What are we gonna do about April?"

"I think we might have sorted it out," I lied. "Go buy yourself a beer. You deserve it."

I hung up before my Mr. Nice act cracked. Fucking Ivan. I felt for the guy, but simultaneously wanted to punch out his lights. His timing for disaster was impeccable.

Six-forty. I stared at the phone, willing it to ring and to discover Ted Peterson on the line, with the news that—after a surprise late-afternoon visit by the Ghost of Christmas Future in the GBS executive washroom—he'd been wracked by conscience, and had not only decided to immediately green-light the April M.P.I., but was also setting up a soup kitchen for the homeless. . . .

Fat chance.

Six-forty-one. My gaze hadn't moved from the phone. It had always been my conduit out of any difficult business situations. When verbally cruising along at full throttle, I felt I could talk anybody into just about everything. But, for the first time in my life, I couldn't think of a single call that could save my ass. The phone was no longer my ally.

Six-forty-two. There was a sharp knock on my office door. Without waiting for me to shout "Come in," Chuck Zanussi entered, glowering. I knew immediately that he'd heard about Ivan's fiasco.

"Your first day here—what was it, four years ago?—and what did I say Rule Number One of working with me was?"

"Chuck, let me explain—"

"Rule Number One. I'm sure you remember it. . . ."

"I'm telling you, the situation's under control—"

"What was Rule Number-fucking-One, Ned?"

I swallowed hard and said, "If there's a problem, you want to know immediately."

"Very good. You have excellent powers of retention. Now, would you not agree that the loss of a GBS multipage insert—a mere two days before copy deadline—constitutes a problem?"

"There have been a lot of problems today, Chuck . . ."

"No shit, Sherlock."

". . . and that's why I didn't call you."

"Bullshit. The reason you didn't call me was because you were covering Ivan's ass. Trying to guarantee your canonization as the Patron Saint of Salesmen Who Fuck Up."

"I simply figured you had enough crap on your plate without—"

"You figured wrong."

"The situation's under control. . . ."

"More bullshit. From what I hear, you might as well have issued an all-points bulletin announcing the GBS debacle. So now—thanks to your brilliant strategy—not only is everyone in the industry speculating about whether Klang-Sanderling is going to vaporize the entire *CompuWorld* staff; they're also gossiping about how we're desperate to fill a handful of pages in the April issue. And desperation—as I've told you over and over again—is the cardinal sin of salesmanship. But you temporarily forgot that, Ned, so our credibility rating right is now subzero. Congratulations."

"I take full responsibility . . ."

"Damn right you do. Especially since those pages *must* be filled. Otherwise you're out of here. Understand?"

Ever been kicked in the stomach? As you gasp for breath, the world suddenly turns watery in front of your eyes. Everything blurs.

"You hearing me, Ned?" Chuck asked.

"I hear you," I muttered.

"You know, making this kind of threat—it gives me no pleasure. But it was your call to sit on this all day—so it's your neck the ax is gonna fall on. Believe me, I want you to get out of this . . ."

"I will get out of it."

"How? Through prayer?"

I shrugged. "I'll do it. Just watch."

"I will. Closely. Another thing you're gonna have to do . . ."

"Yeah?"

"Fire Dolinsky."

"Hang on now, Chuck . . ."

"No arguments here, Ned. He is the root cause of this major screwup."

"Ted Peterson is the real villain in this story. . . ."

"That may be, but Dolinsky delayed the contractual niceties, allowing that thief Peterson a way out of the deal. Look, you know I have cut Ivan one helluva lot of slack since Nancy's death. And, like you, I've covered his ass when he couldn't get it together—because I really, truly pity the bastard. But, let's face it, two years later and the guy still doesn't have his eye on the ball anymore. And now, his incompetence is threatening both our asses. . . ."

"Ivan is not incompetent. He just closed a major six-page insert with NMI this afternoon. The May issue. And he's got signed contracts to prove it."

"I'll make sure he gets the commission from the sale tagged on to his severance pay."

"Come on, Chuck. Be reasonable here."

"The decision's made. He's history."

The voice of Phil Sirio hummed in my head. *"It's persuasion, nothing more. . . . All I'm gonna do is remind him that a verbal contract is worth the paper it's written on."*

"Say I manage to get the multipage insert back from GBS. . . ."

"You won't. Dream on."

"But just say I did convince Ted Peterson to come around. . . ."

"I'd call you a miracle worker, and I'd still insist that Ivan goes."

"That's not fair. . . ."

"Fuck fair. The man's all over the place. Okay, he scored a big one with NMI. The first big one in two years . . ."

"It's a comeback."

"It's a lucky break. NMI are pushing their Powerplan series everywhere. Donald Duck could've closed that deal. And you know as well as I do that it's only a matter of time before Ivan drops us in deep doo-doo again. Sorry, Ned. He's out of here. And if you don't fire him by noon tomorrow, then I will."

"You mean, right before you fire me."

"If you solve the problem, you still have a job. That's the bottom line. Got it?"

I nodded. Chuck opened the door—and quietly said, "Don't make me fire you, Ned. Please."

I sat immobile in my desk chair for a very long time, staring out at the snow-filled night. There was only one solution to the problem, only one way of saving my skin. *"Boss, please let me call Ted Peterson."* Tomorrow morning, first thing, I'd instruct Phil Sirio to do just that. To hell with the consequences. This was now life or death.

Once again, the heavy snow meant that all New York City cabs had gone into hibernation. So I walked over to Grand Central and jumped the downtown six train. The subway car was empty and overheated. At Fourteenth Street I was joined by your typical urban punk: greasy skin, wispy moustache, zip-up hooded sweatshirt,

$200 Nikes, plenty of attitude. He plopped himself down opposite me and locked me in a malevolent stare. I eyeballed him right back. *Read my lips, jerkoff. I'm about to authorize a serious blackmailing. So who's the real badass here?*

"The fuck you looking at?" the punk said.

My stare hardened. "The fuck *you* looking at?" I shot back.

"You trying to make trouble?"

"Only if you are," I said, casually slipping my hand beneath my overcoat, as if I might be packing a gun. At that precise moment, he broke his stare.

"I ain't interested in no trouble," he said.

"That makes two of us," I said.

We rode on in silence. The train pulled into Lafayette Street and I stood up to leave.

"Yo," said the punk.

"What?" I said.

"Merry Christmas, man."

"You, too," I said and found myself smiling for the first time all day.

I trekked through now blizzard conditions down Lafayette Street to Pravda. Klaus Kreplin was already seated at a prominent table when I arrived. He greeted me with a snaky smile, motioned for me to sit down, then scooped a pack of Dunhill cigarettes up off the table and fired one up with an elegant silver lighter.

"Do you know why I chose this restaurant?" he asked. "Caviar and cigarettes. It is one of the few places left in this health-neurotic city where one can smoke and not risk arrest."

All the waitresses wore low-cut slinky black dresses. One of them was approaching our table, tray in hand. Kreplin watched her intently.

"And, of course, the *ambiance* is charming, would you not agree?"

The waitress lowered the tray, which held a block of ice and two small, exquisitely designed stainless steel racks. Each rack contained six small glasses, brimming with clear liquid. She placed one in front of each of us.

"I hope you do not mind," Kreplin said, "but I took the liberty of ordering for us both."

"Six shots of vodka?" I said.

"It is their special Vodka sampler. Accompanied by caviar, of course," he said as the waitress set the block of ice down between us. Embedded within was a hefty jar of Beluga. I dreaded to think of the cost.

Kreplin raised the first glass from the rack. I followed suit. "*Prost,*" he said, clicking my glass, then throwing his back in one gulp. I downed mine, the frozen vodka anesthetizing the back of my throat. Immediately I felt its tranquilizing benefits.

"You were in need of vodka, I think," Kreplin said.

"It has not been an easy day," I said. "But I think you know all about that, don't you?"

"I have heard you have found yourself in a dangerous predicament. Will you solve this?"

"Absolutely," I said.

"Then we must drink to this good news," Kreplin said. We both hoisted the second glass of vodka. *Click*. Down the hatch.

"Do you know why I knew we would work well together?" Kreplin said, spooning a dollop of caviar onto a blini, then devouring it in one gulp. "Because you were a bit cool to me when we first met. A bit confrontational. I like this style—a good company man, a good captain to his troops—sorry!—'colleagues'—but someone who does not immediately agree with everything his superiors say. I respect a man who can balance corporate allegiance with an independent outlook. Unlike Chuck Zanussi."

"Chuck's a good guy."

"Do you want my opinion on your boss? Chuck Zanussi is very fat. And scared to death of me. Which is one of the reasons I have no respect for him. That—and the fact that his physical grossness hints at a complete absence of discipline."

"He might eat too many doughnuts, but if the magazine's a success, it's due to Chuck. He's really a top-notch publisher, and he knows the computer business inside out."

"I am impressed, Edward. Such loyalty to the man who, just an hour ago, threatened to terminate you if you did not solve the GBS crisis."

"How did you know that?"

"Because I *instructed* Chuck Zanussi to terminate you if you didn't find a solution to this problem."

"Thanks."

Kreplin managed a muted chuckle. "It is a test. And one which I know you will pass. Brilliantly. So Chuck Zanussi will not be firing you, will he?"

Phil, make the call.

"No, Klaus. He won't."

"Excellent. Because after the crisis—and indeed after Christmas—has passed, I will be firing Chuck Zanussi. Personally."

I fingered the third glass of vodka—and tried to appear calm.

"You serious?" I asked.

"In business I am *always* serious, Edward."

"I'm sure you are," I said.

"So serious that I already know who Chuck's successor will be."

"And who's the lucky guy?"

"You."

I blinked. "Me?"

"Yes, you."

"No way."

"It is all decided. Come January second, if you want it, we will appoint you the new publisher of *CompuWorld*. Congratulations."

Without thinking, I raised the vodka glass and drained it.

"Uh . . . thanks."

SIX

I couldn't sleep. For an hour I stared up at the dancing shadows on our bedroom ceiling. The illuminated alarm clock by our bed said 3:12 A.M. I'd been home since two, having finally extracted myself from the clutches of Klaus Kreplin. After dropping that little bombshell about offering me Chuck's job, he then quizzed me about my ideas for the magazine. I attempted to rise to the occasion, explaining how we could strengthen editorial content through provocative consumer guides, innovative features, and also increase our advertising market share (especially in the crucial Pacific Northwest battleground).

Around the fifth shot of vodka, I'd found myself saying, "There is no reason why—with proper marketing strategy—we can't become number two in the business within twelve months. *Computer America* talks a good game, but they're neither as low-rent as *PC Globe* nor as upscale as us. My approach would be to keep the overall visual style of the magazine upmarket, but gradually broaden its appeal, focusing on the crucial home computing sector. And, of course, it wouldn't hurt to go for a more cutting-edge visual approach.

"I mean, I'm not spouting anything original here. Just good old common-sense salesmanship. And if I do take the job—"

"You *are* taking the job," Kreplin said.

By the sixth shot of vodka, I was saying, "I've got to tell you, Klaus, I'm kind of freaking a bit. . . ."

"Freaking?" he said, rolling the word around his tongue like some alien substance. "What is this 'freaking'?"

"Nervous. Scared. Guilty."

"Nervous and scared I can understand," he said. "It is a normal human reaction to any great career advancement. But 'guilty'? Edward, please. This is business."

"Chuck is my boss."

"And I am Chuck's boss. And Dietrich Sanderling is my boss. And the shareholders are, ultimately, Herr Sanderling's bosses. We all must answer to someone. And if that someone is displeased with us—"

"He brought me into the company, he gave me my start. . . ."

"As I said before, I greatly admire your belief in loyalty. But it is not you who are terminating him. And it is not as if you have schemed to provoke his downfall. I want him out because, to my mind, he is flabby. Flabby in weight, flabby in business. But if you think that by not taking this post you will save Chuck, you are wrong. He is finished here. *Kaput*."

After we had worked our way through dinner and a $55 bottle of cabernet sauvignon, Kreplin shifted the conversation back to business.

"You have not once asked me about the money," he said. "Why is that?"

"We've been eating."

"Very civil of you. Would you like to know the figure involved?"

"Absolutely."

Kreplin gave one of his low little chuckles. "Well, it is quite an attractive package. The basic salary is one hundred and fifty thousand dollars per annum, but you should be able to double that figure with profit participation and bonuses."

I gulped.

"Of course, in addition to the standard IRA and full medical insurance plans, we will also provide you with a company car—your choice of vehicle, worth up to, say, fifty thousand. And we will pay for all garage costs. And if you are a member of a sports club . . . You are a tennis player, no?"

"You've done your research."

"Naturally. Anyway, we will also cover the cost of the tennis club. Klang-Sanderling likes its executives to be—how do you say it?—lean and mean."

He called for the check, then said, "So . . . you approve of this package?"

I had hit the jackpot. Won the lottery. Broken the bank. Well, not exactly . . . but, Christ, three hundred grand a year? It was breathtaking. I was about to enter the major leagues.

"Klaus, I definitely approve." Though as soon as I said that, I thought, . . . *but I'm going to hate myself for betraying Chuck.*

As the snow was too heavy for a drinking tour of SoHo, he insisted that I return with him to his suite at the Waldorf Towers for a nightcap. In the cab uptown, he turned to me.

"I must ask one favor of you."

"Sure, Klaus."

"It's not a favor, actually. More of a mandate, I'm afraid. And it is this: You must not discuss this job offer with anyone."

"I assumed as much."

"By *anyone,* I mean you must not even raise the matter with your wife."

"Well, she's got to know. I mean, it *is* big news."

"Agreed. And she will know. On Friday, January second. The day you return from your holiday in the West Indies."

"Have you had someone tailing me, too?" I joked. Kreplin managed a smile.

"When we began considering the purchase of Getz-Braun a few months ago, I naturally began to examine the dossiers of the senior people in the titles I would be overseeing. And Chuck Zanussi was so enthusiastic in his praise of you, I began to investigate . . ."

I couldn't believe what I was hearing.

"Hang on," I said, "are you telling me that Chuck knew about you buying the company months ago?"

"No—all he knew was that we were interested in Getz-Braun, and that, in September, we engaged in a feasability study, which included meeting with its top executives and examining the records of existing personnel. But then he heard nothing more about the sale until yesterday, when he was asked to stop by Chicago. In a takeover situation, secrecy is crucial."

"He was certainly secretive about Klang-Sanderling's interest in us."

"That is because he was *instructed* to remain silent about our exploratory meetings. He didn't know if the takeover would happen—and he was kept out of the communication loop until it was a *fait accompli*. What he did know, however, was that if he informed anyone about our interest in Getz-Braun, his future in the company would be nonexistent. So he wisely decided to keep his lip buttoned."

"But now he's still getting fired."

"That, my friend, is the ebb and flow of corporate life. Do not fear—he will be handed a very handsome parachute before being pushed out of the plane. And we will not terminate him before Christmas—which, after all, would ruin his holiday. But there is an even more pressing reason why you must remain absolutely silent about your promotion. Our market surveyors fear that it might rattle *CompuWorld*'s advertisers, were word to get out before the New Year that we were installing a new publisher. At Klang-Sanderling, we are very systematic about such matters. We plan them meticulously to minimize potential commercial damage, and to ensure the smoothest transition of power."

"Understood—but, really, my wife won't talk . . ."

"She is in public relations? No offense, but it is the nature of PR people to talk. Maybe she tells, in confidence, her closest colleague about your promotion. The closest colleague then tells, in confidence, her husband, who just happens to be the lawyer for a client who is purchasing a major network system from GBS. He mentions in passing to the client that he hears *CompuWorld* is getting a new publisher, the client casually drops this information during his next meeting with GBS, and before we know it—"

"With due respect, Klaus—I really think you're being a little overcautious."

"With due respect, Edward—that is my prerogative, and one which I must ask you to honor. Because if word leaks out prior to your appointment, it may jeopardize things. Your wife will have a wonderful New Year's surprise when you are made publisher on the second of January. All you will have to do is call her from the office on that day and act as if you have just been given the news. You are, from all accounts, a brilliant salesman. Which means you are also an actor. Surely, you will be able to act astonished and overwhelmed."

"I suppose so. . . ."

"So I do have your word that you will share this with no one?"

"Because if word leaks out prior to your appointment, it may jeopardize things."

Three hundred grand. I nodded. Kreplin slapped me on the back.

"Excellent," he said. "The matter is settled."

He had a corner suite on the seventeenth floor of the Waldorf Towers. It commanded a formidable view of the midtown skyline. The living room was the size of a football field. There were two bedrooms and a full-size kitchen.

"Quite a space," I said.

"They like Klang-Sanderling at the Waldorf, so they always upgrade us. Champagne?"

"Why not?"

He picked up the phone, called room service, and ordered a bottle of Krug. If he was trying to impress me with his "money-is-no-object" attitude, he was succeeding. About a minute later there was a knock on the door.

"Our guests have arrived," Klaus said, moving toward the door.

"Guests?" I said. "I didn't know you were expecting . . ."

I didn't get to finish that sentence, as in walked two very tall, very blonde, very heavily madeup women. They were both in their mid-twenties. Handing Klaus their coats, they revealed near-matching little black dresses which fit them like surgical gloves. True escort agency material. I suddenly felt uneasy.

"Ladies," Kreplin said, ushering them into the living room, "I would like you to meet my associate, Mr. Allen. Edward, this is Angelica, and this is Monique."

"Howyadoin', hon?" said Monique, her strident vowels making it very clear that, despite her name, she was by no means French born and bred. They both arranged themselves on the sofa. Kreplin gave me one of his sharklike smiles—and I quickly understood that this was a test, a way for Kreplin to gauge my loyalty. If I played up my indignation about being set up with a couple of hookers (and this was definitely a well-planned set-up) he would dismiss me as self-righteous. If, however, I slept with Monique or Angelica, he'd have something on me . . . and he'd know that I was, at heart, weak—someone who was willing to compromise his marriage in order to advance his career.

As Monique and Angelica fired up their cigarettes, Kreplin sidled up to me and whispered, "I hope you don't mind this surprise."

I chose my words carefully. "It certainly *is* a surprise, Klaus."

"But an amusing one, yes? A little Christmas treat from Klang-Sanderling. Have you thoughts on which one you prefer?"

Angelica was chewing gum while puffing heavily on a Salem. Monique—God help her—looked like a slightly more upmarket version of those working girls you used to see on Eighth Avenue (but instead of wearing purple hotpants, she was squeezed into a tight black number).

"Tell you what," I whispered, "I'm going to take a leak. When I get back, we'll decide. Okay?"

"Excellent," he said.

The bathroom was massive—an acre of marble flooring, a sunken bathtub, gold taps. I sat on the edge of the tub, pondering my next move. The bastard had really dropped me into a tricky situation—to see how I'd react to its obvious pressures, no doubt. I couldn't simply up and leave—that would be considered tactless and clumsy. But there was no way I was going to stay for the fireworks. I stood and absently patted the breast pocket of my jacket, touching my cell phone in the process. Bingo. Turning on the taps, I punched in one—five—one, a digital answering service that also could be programmed to give you wake-up calls. I checked my watch. 1:17. I quickly tapped in 1:21 A.M., pressed the star key twice, and then repocketed the phone.

When I returned to the living room, the champagne had arrived. A room service waiter was popping the cork. Kreplin was sitting between Angelica and Monique, making small talk and trailing his left index finger up and down Angelica's black-stockinged thigh. The two women both seemed supremely bored. No doubt they just wanted to get on with the job, get their money, and get on home to bed. But Kreplin was determined to be festive. As soon as the champagne was poured, he saw the waiter off with a $10 tip, then handed a glass to each of the women.

"You are familiar with Krug, ladies?" he asked.

"It's got bubbles and it's French, right?" asked Angelica.

"You know your champagne," Kreplin said. Handing me a glass, he whispered in my ear, "Have you made your choice?"

I watched as Angelica spat her gum out into an ashtray before sipping the champagne. *Why hadn't the phone started ringing?* Stalling for time, I said, "I'm going to let you make that decision, Klaus."

"No, no, no. I am the host—so I must insist that you have first choice."

"Where did you find these girls?"

"An agency we often use for 'entertainment' whenever we are in New York. A very *reliable* agency, so there are never any worries about disease."

"That's nice to know."

"So, Edward, *please*—the meter is running. Your choice . . ."

I took a deep breath. "Well . . ."

And then, thank God, my cell phone rang. Kreplin and the two women looked startled. I had to work at masking my relief.

"Yeah?" I said as I answered it. A digitalized voice said: *"This is your one-twenty-one alarm clock call . . . This is your one-twenty-one alarm clock call."* I hugged the headset to my ear in an attempt to keep it inaudible to anyone but me.

"Oh, Lizzie," I said into the receiver, then covered it and mouthed to Kreplin, *my wife.* He rolled his eyes heavenward. I continued talking into the receiver. "Yeah, yeah . . . I'm up at Klaus Kreplin's suite at the Waldorf. . . . *What?* . . . Oh, Christ, no. When? . . . How bad does it look? . . . Okay, okay, I'll be right there. The E.R. at Roosevelt? Give me ten minutes."

I hung up and immediately grabbed my coat.

"There is a problem?" Kreplin asked.

"That was my wife, Lizzie. Her father, who's staying with us for a couple of days, is having severe chest pains. They've rushed him to Roosevelt Hospital. . . ."

I now had my overcoat on. "Listen, Klaus . . . sorry to do this, but . . ."

He shrugged. "You must do what you must do," he said.

"Thanks for a great evening," I said, pumping his hand. "We'll talk tomorrow." I waved a fast good-bye toward the two hookers. They didn't wave back.

As I opened the door, Kreplin said, in a voice dripping with sarcasm: "My best wishes to your lovely wife."

Thirty minutes later I was sliding into bed next to my lovely but very comatose wife. I leaned over for a kiss, to which she reacted with an incoherent groan before rolling away from me. I pulled a pillow toward me and shut my eyes in the futile hope that sleep would knock me out cold. I wanted to erase this day, to pull the plug on all that had transpired, and catch a five-hour vacation from assorted ethical dilemmas. Like, Could I look Chuck Zanussi in the eye tomorrow, knowing full well that he was, companywise, a condemned man—and that I would step over his corpse to take his job? And should I really keep silent on this entire matter with Lizzie—especially after the little stunt that Kreplin pulled tonight? Then again, might Kreplin now reconsider my promotion after I wangled out of his little Christmas festivities with the two hookers? And, of course, if Phil Sirio's strong-arm tactics with Ted Peterson ever became known, not only would I be permanently unemployable, but the Manhattan D.A. would probably be making my acquaintance. . . .

My eyes jumped open again. And for the next hour, I lay rigid with dread; a severe case of the middle-of-the-night willies. Only unlike the usual free-floating, four-in-the-morning fears, these were tangible, substantive, genuinely dangerous.

Eventually I succumbed to the inevitable and quietly snuck out of bed. Collapsing onto the deep white sofa in the living room, I stared out at the dim flicker of the sleeping city. *Make the call, Phil.* Five hours from now I'd utter that phrase. And then . . . ? No doubt we'd probably get away with it. Peterson would be so scared of exposure, he'd capitulate and authorize the multipage insert. My ass would be saved. Come the second of January I'd be the new publisher of *CompuWorld,* and rolling in the dough. End of story.

Except, of course, there'd be plenty more nights like this one—when I'd wake at three and wonder, Do you ever really get away with anything? Can you be involved in a moral car crash and actually walk away unscathed? Or will some little voice creep up on you at vulnerable moments like this one, and whisper, *There is no free lunch. . . . There is no zipless fuck. . . .*

My goddamn father. Mr. Ethical. Someone who rammed home,

again and again, his central credo of life: You always pay a price when you make a wrong call. But, sometimes, the wrong call is the only call, isn't it? Especially in a situation where there is no way out—except, of course, to fall graciously on your sword . . . and, in the process, blow the defining promotion of your career.

Ted Major Asshole Peterson. Probably sound asleep right now at home in Connecticut, unaware of the fact that his flippant decision to cancel one lousy ad had put careers on the line. Typical amoral yuppie. Fucks around in business, fucks around on his wife. Faithful to no one but his own penny-ante ambition. I remember that sales event in Grand Cayman—how the day before Ted had attacked Joan, he was at the bar of the Hyatt, showing off pictures of his new house in Connecticut. Right on the water in a town called Old Greenwich. $1.4 million worth of house, he had insisted on informing me. Big deck overlooking the Sound. Five minutes by car to the train station. Forty-five minutes to Grand Central. Great schools. And the only nonwhite face you ever saw belonged to domestic help.

Old Greenwich, Connecticut. You probably had to be called Brad or Chip or Ames or Edward Arlington Peterson, Jr., to live there.

Old Greenwich, Connecticut. Forty-five minutes by train. An hour by car. Probably less at this time of night.

I picked up the phone. I punched in the number for directory assistance for the Old Greenwich area code. The operator informed me that there were two listings under the name of E. Peterson in the area.

"It's the E. Peterson with the waterfront-sounding address," I said.

"You mean, Shore Road?"

"The very one. Number forty-four, isn't it?"

"Ninety-six Shore Road. Please wait for your number. . . ."

Having finagled Peterson's address, I now turned on my computer, went on-line, connected myself to the Yahoo search engine, and asked them to find a map of Old Greenwich, Connecticut. Within ten seconds, a prompt appeared on the screen, asking for the exact address in Old Greenwich. I typed *96 Shore Road,* hit

"Search," and . . . bingo: I downloaded a fully detailed map of Peterson's section of Old Greenwich.

As I printed out the map, I reached for the phone again and called Avis Rent-A-Car. Was there a twenty-four-hour agency in Manhattan? Forty-third between Second and Third? Perfect. And did they have a car they could rent me tonight? A Chevy Cutlass? That'll work. I glanced at my watch. 3:43. I told them I'd be there to pick it up at 4:30.

I showered, I shaved. I put on a suit and tie. I made myself a fast mug of instant coffee, popped five Raw Energy vitamins, and left Lizzie a note:

Sweetheart:

Couldn't sleep. And I need to make an early morning business trip to Connecticut. Call me when you get up, and I'll explain all.

You're the best . . .

I grabbed the map of Old Greenwich. I tossed my overcoat over my arm. I let myself out of the apartment as quietly as possible. I hailed a cab on the street and was at the Avis office within ten minutes. By 5:00 A.M., I was cruising north on the FDR Drive, veering right onto the Triboro Bridge, then following the signs for I-95 North to Connecticut.

I had decided to brave Peterson. Face-to-face, on his doorstep. It was the only way to force his hand. I was going to appeal to his decency—and *sell* him on the idea of doing the right thing. But if he refused, if he told me to drop dead, then I'd bring out the tactical nuclear weapons. I'd let Phil make that call.

I reached Old Greenwich by 5:50. Using the map, I easily found my way to Shore Road. It was still dark and I had to drive slowly down the narrow two-lane road, squinting at house numbers on mailboxes. Chez Peterson was located at the end of a long driveway. It was even more impressive than the photos Ted had shown me—a rambling Cape Codder on about a quarter acre of land. Peterson wasn't lying when he said it fronted the Sound; the house was equipped with a wraparound deck that jutted out over the water and even had its own boat dock. I now knew why it came with a $1.4 million price tag.

I cut my headlights and pulled into the driveway, parking right behind Ted's BMW and a Ford Explorer earmarked for the wife and kids. It was cold outside—around ten degrees Fahrenheit, according to the temperature gauge in the Chevy—so I kept the engine running. I wished to hell I had grabbed a newspaper and a cup of coffee en route. Now all I could do was play WINS 1010 and hope to hell that Ted wasn't a late riser. I tilted back the driver's seat, cranked up the heat (my toes were beginning to go numb), and tried to fight off a surge of fatigue by concentrating on the news.

"WINS ten-ten. All news, all the time. You give us twenty minutes, we'll give you the world."

I settled back into my seat and felt another ripple of exhaustion drift across my brain.

"WINS news time . . ."

Suddenly there was a sharp rapping sound—metal hitting glass. I blinked and found myself squinting into bright winter sunlight.

. . . is now seven-ten A.M.

Damn. Damn. Damn. Jolted awake, I found myself staring at a pert-nosed woman in her early thirties, dressed in a black down parka and white turtleneck, a black hairband holding her shiny blonde hair in place. Behind her stood two well-groomed children. They were both carrying school bags and looking bewildered as their mommy used her wedding ring to tap against the window of a car they'd never seen before—containing a sleeping man they'd also never seen before—which was now blocking their driveway.

"Sir, sir, *SIR*," shouted the woman. I jumped out of the car, the blast of cold air snapping me into instant alertness.

"Sorry. Really sorry," I said, rubbing my eyes. "Fell asleep . . ."

She took a step back from me in alarm. "You've been asleep in our driveway all night?"

"No, just over an hour. Does Ted Peterson live here?"

"I'm his wife, Meg."

"Good to meet you, Meg. I'm—"

"Ned Allen?" said a shocked voice.

I looked up. There was Ted at the front door—in his best charcoal gray Brooks Brothers overcoat and his shined wingtips and his black Coach briefcase and his unlined patrician face now taut with unease. He came walking slowly toward me.

"Well, this is a surprise," he said carefully as he shook my hand. Though he was understandably astounded to find me in his driveway at 7:10 A.M., he was also shrewdly maintaining a polite front until he knew why I was there. The guy was a consummate actor.

"Morning, Ted," I said, trying to remain very steady, very calm. "Sorry to drop in like this, but—"

"I know, I know," he said, now all friendly. "You're on a tight deadline, and you couldn't get through to me at the office yesterday about that multipage insert, right?"

"Absolutely right," I said, amazed by his affable tone. "And I really hate landing on your doorstep like this, but we do have a small crisis on our hands."

"I totally understand," he said, giving my shoulder a reassuring tap. "Hey, sorry, I haven't introduced you to my wife. Meg, this is Ned Allen from *CompuWorld* . . ."

"We've already met," Meg Peterson said.

"And my kids, Will and Sarah."

"Hi, guys," I said, but they both continued to regard me with suspicion.

"Meg, darling," Peterson said, "if you wouldn't mind . . . I just need to do three minutes of fast business with Ned. . . ."

"You know Sarah's got to be at school by seven forty-five this morning." Then, turning to me, she said, "It's her class field trip to Mystic Seaport today."

"Three minutes, tops," Ted assured her.

"No longer, please," Meg said, then herded the children back into the house. Ted motioned for me to follow him to the end of the driveway. Once we were safely away from the house, he turned toward me. His smile had vanished.

"You low-life piece of shit . . . ," he hissed.

"Ted, hear me out . . . ," I whispered back.

"How dare you pull a stunt like this . . ."

"I am only here because Ivan Dolinsky is going to be fired at noon today."

"That's not my problem. Now fuck off."

"It *is* your problem, Ted. Because you agreed to that ad. . . ."

"I agreed to shit. The deal was never finalized, and then we decided to switch marketing strategy for April. End of story."

"Ivan assures me you gave him your word. . . ."

"Ivan's a flake, a loser. He'd say anything to save his sorry ass."

"I've worked with the guy for four years. He's totally straight when it comes to business."

"The fact remains: There's no signed contract, so there's no deal. Case closed. Now you have one minute to clear out of my driveway."

"He'll lose his job because of this."

"Shit happens."

"You know what the guy has been through. And he really will go under if he's fired. So be a good guy. Approve the deal. It won't break the bank. It's Christmas, for God's sake."

"This conversation's finished," he said, and started walking back toward his house.

That's when I decided it was time to play my ace. Glancing up at his home, I shouted after him, "You know, it really is quite a piece of property, Ted. Even nicer than those photos you showed me and Phil Sirio at Grand Cayman last year."

He froze. After a moment, he turned back toward me. His eyes were filled with apprehension.

"Just get out of here," he said quietly.

As he marched toward his front door, I was about to shout *Joan Glaston sends her regards*. But I stopped myself and instead said:

"Noon today, Peterson."

Jumping into the Chevy, I slammed it into reverse and got the hell out of there.

Five minutes down the road my hands were shaking so hard I had to pull off. Had I just committed blackmail? Peterson certainly got a shock when I dropped that Phil Sirio/Grand Cayman mention. . . . but still, I hadn't made that blatant reference to the Joan Glaston business. So, though I did feel a little sleazy, I really couldn't be accused of coercion, could I?

But, given his shithead reaction to my appeal, I really didn't know if Peterson would budge on the Ivan issue. Which meant that, if I wanted to save my ass, I might still have to resort to blackmail before noon that day.

I got back on the road and pointed myself in the direction of I-95 South. When I was safely on the highway, my cellphone rang and I jumped. I hit the answer button.

"This had better be good," Lizzie said, "or I might not talk to you for a while."

I gave her a blow-by-blow account of the scene in Peterson's driveway, but didn't mention the Grand Cayman business. When I finished, she whistled.

"You are insane," she said.

"This is true. And probably out of a job."

"You don't know that."

"He's a ruthless operator. And I'm worried I might have overplayed my hand."

"Sounds like all you did was ask him to do the honorable—"

"The asshole has no honor."

"But the fact is, you do. And that's what counts."

If only you knew about your honorable husband's blackmail plans, Lizzie.

"Listen," she said, "I've got an eight o'clock breakfast meeting, so I better run. Are we still on for dinner tonight?"

"Definitely. Only, with me being out of a job, you're probably going to have to pick up the tab."

"Done deal. How was the evening with this Kreplin guy?"

It wasn't the moment to get into what had gone on last night. Because as much as I wanted to tell her, I kept hearing Kreplin's voice in my head, promising me a fatal dose of bad karma if word of my promotion leaked out before the second of January. And as to saying anything about that stage-managed encounter with the two hookers . . . to quote Phil Sirio: *Fugedaboudit*.

"It was just a getting-to-know-you thing."

"A kind of into-the-night getting-to-know-you thing."

"Tell me about it. The guy likes to booze. Late."

"As long as that's all he likes to do late."

Why do women always have this instinctual ability to sniff out the aroma of near or actual infidelity? Even when they're just talking to you on the phone?

"Put it this way," I said, "that's all *I* like to do late."

"Glad to hear it."

"Unless you're around, of course."

"Y'know, sometimes I think you have a Ph.D. in romantic bullshit. . . ."

"You've finally worked that one out."

"Later, toots. Keep your nerve. And call me as soon as you have some news from GBS."

"I promise," I said.

Thanks to the maniacal rush-hour traffic, it took almost two hours to reach Manhattan. My cellphone was on the seat next to me. It didn't ring once. At nine I called the office to say I'd be late, and to check my messages. No word from Ted Peterson. By the time I dropped the car off at Avis and grabbed a taxi downtown, it was close to ten. Just as the cab was pulling up to my office, the phone went off. My hands were trembling as I answered it. It was Phil Sirio.

"How ya doin', boss?" he asked.

"I now know what those kamikaze pilots must have felt like when they were told it was their turn to fly a plane."

"So you made the decision on Peterson?"

"Not yet."

"Just say the word and I'll pick up the phone."

I glanced again at my watch. "Give me two hours," I said.

There was a slew of messages waiting for me on my desk. But none from GBS. I told Lily to interrupt any and all calls for Ted Peterson.

"Is Mr. Zanussi around this morning?" I asked.

"He's at a meeting—and won't be back till after lunch," Lily said.

Thank God for that. It might give me an extra hour or two to play with. Think. Think. Think. I powered up my computer and once again reviewed our client list, in the vain hope that I had overlooked someone—*anyone*—who could cough up a major spread by tomorrow. No possibilities. Though I knew this was a total long shot, I tracked down *CompuWorld*'s regional sales managers in Seattle, Chicago, Houston, and Silicon Valley, wondering if they might have a spare multipage insert going. Coast to coast, they all gave me the answer I was expecting: "Are you nuts?" Bob Brubaker—my counterpart in Palo Alto and probably the most competitive guy in our company—actually turned nasty.

"You pull a stunt like this the day after we're taken over . . . and then you expect me to save your ass?"

"It's not a 'stunt,' Bob. We were badly burned by a client."

"And this 'letdown' is going to impact all of us. To Klang-Sanderling, six blank pages in the April issue will make the entire national sales force look like a bunch of born losers."

"Look, I'm the fall guy here. Okay? It's me they'll be bumping off, not you."

"I promise you, pal, if I go down with you . . ."

"Bob, please, I know this is a difficult time for everyone."

"I've got two alimonies and two kids in college. So don't give me this 'calm down' shit. . . ."

"They're not going to fire you because of my screwup."

"Yeah? Well, if they do, you're dead. Understand me, Allen? *Dead*."

I hung up. Loudly. Just what I needed this morning. A death threat. Psychotic sonofabitch. But I was stupid to have called him. Brubaker was Mr. Hair Trigger—one of those guys who was always two seconds away from detonation. And he was simply articulating what we were all feeling: pure, undistilled fear.

At 11:30, Ivan Dolinsky called. I was feeling so frayed that I told Lily to inform him I was in a meeting. If I spoke to him, I might have lost all control.

At 11:47, Chuck Zanussi called. Again I told Lily to say I was busy, but she came back on the line, informing me that Mr. Zanussi had stepped out of his meeting to make this call and was insistent we speak. I punched line one.

"Well?" said Chuck.

"We're nearly there," I said.

"Horseshit."

"I'm expecting a call from Peterson any moment. . . ."

"You've got thirteen minutes."

"It might be after lunch. . . ."

"Thirteen minutes, Ned."

"For Christ's sake, Chuckie—don't turn this into some death

row scene. Will the governor call with a reprieve before they give him the juice . . ."

"For the next thirteen minutes, I'm still your boss. So I'll do whatever I like."

"Please, Chuckie, I'm begging here, just a little more time . . ."

"Request denied," he said. And the line went dead.

Now I knew what free fall was all about.

"Mr. Sirio on line three . . ."

I looked at my watch. 11:53. I grabbed the receiver.

"So, what gives?" Phil asked.

"Still no word from Peterson."

"Nearly high noon, boss."

"I am very aware of this."

"So what's it gonna be?"

My eyes were closed tight, my pulse sprinting. I replayed the scene in Peterson's driveway. On the verge of blackmail, I'd slammed on the brakes. Could I really go through with it now? Choose, dammit. *Choose*.

"Sorry, Phil. No sale."

He let out a sigh. "Your funeral."

"In about six minutes' time."

"Can I say something here?"

"Shoot."

"You never get anywhere in life being honorable with an asshole."

"Sounds like a good epitaph for me. Thanks anyway, Phil."

"Good luck, boss."

Eleven-fifty-five. So that was that. Game. Set. Match. I leaned back in my office chair. Numb. I had just thrown it all away. Four long years scaling the corporate ladder. All the persuading, the schmoozing, the need to close. You expect it to lead somewhere. You actually get in sight of that place. Ten feet from the summit. And then your footing slips, the ground gives way, and . . . bye-bye.

You play the game. You think you know the rules. But then, one day, you wake up and discover it's the game that plays you.

There was a frantic knock on my door. It flew open and Debbie Suarez came storming in.

"Mr. Allen, I got—"

"Debbie," I said, holding up my hand, "not now, huh?"

"But I've got to show you—"

"No offense, but I've just lost my job and—"

"Will you *puh-leeze* lemme tell you—"

"I'm not your boss anymore. Go bother Chuck Zanussi with—"

She slammed her fist down on my desk—an action so startling that I was momentarily speechless.

"Got your attention now?" she asked. I nodded. "Then read this."

She tossed a piece of paper in front of me. "It just came in by fax. Lily asked me to give it to you."

I stared down at the paper. I saw the letterhead. It contained three letters: GBS. And below this:

Mr. Edward Allen
Regional Manager, Northeast Sales
CompuWorld Inc.
Getz-Braun Publications

via facsimile
Dear Mr. Allen:

I am pleased to inform you that GBS will be proceeding with the multipage insert for their Minerva computer in the April issue of your magazine.

Please have your production department contact our art department to arrange immediate copy transfer.

Sincerely yours,
Ted Peterson

I read it once. It didn't sink in. I read it twice. I still wasn't entirely convinced. I was reading it a third time when Debbie Suarez said, "Whadja do, Mr. Allen? Make him an offer he couldn't refuse?"

As I looked up at her, my eyes were brimming. She noticed, and squeezed my arm.

"You closed, Mr. Allen," she said. "You closed."

The phone suddenly detonated again.

"Mr. Zanussi on line one . . ."

"Lily," I said, "ask him to give you a fax number for wherever he is right now."

"He's adamant that he talk—"

"Tell him I want to talk to him, too. But only after he looks at a document you're going to fax him. Debbie's bringing it to reception right now."

I hung up and turned to Debbie.

"Chuck's going to fire me in two minutes if he doesn't see that fax—so . . ."

"I'm not walking, I'm running."

I dialed Ted Peterson's office. His secretary recognized my voice immediately.

"Mr. Allen," she said, sounding as glacial as ever, "Mr. Peterson is in a meeting."

"Sure he is. And I'm the ghost of Elvis. Look—put me through. I just want to say a fast thanks . . ."

She put me on hold. After a moment, he came on the line.

"Peterson here."

"Ted, I can't thank you enough. And I just wanted to say how grateful I was, and hope there are no hard feelings. . . ."

"Cut to the chase, Allen. Where's this going? Or should I say, what are your terms?"

"*My* terms? You've met my terms. You honored the deal with Ivan. . . ."

"Let's drop the coy crap, okay? You want to play, let's play. I'm sure we can figure out a way to work together on this, and keep everyone happy." I was suddenly lost.

"I don't know what you're talking about, Ted."

"Yeah, right. Well, I guess it was only a matter of time. . . ."

"A matter of time before what? You really have me baffled here, Ted."

There was a long silence. When Peterson spoke again, his voice had lost its acrimony.

"Allen, what exactly is it you know?"

"Only what I heard."

"Which is *what*?"

I chose my words with care. "Just that you got into some rough stuff with Joan Glaston."

There was another long silence.

"That's it?" he asked.

"Uh, yeah."

"Jesus Christ," he suddenly shouted. "You cheap, sneaky little shit. That cock tease was more than happy to make a deal—so don't even think you can milk me for more, you bush league motherfucker."

Then the line went dead.

I frantically redialed Peterson's number. His secretary cut me off before I could finish saying my name.

"I'm glad you called, Mr. Allen. Mr. Peterson asked me to convey a message if you did call back."

"Which is?"

"He wanted to inform you that, though he has authorized the current insert, he will never do business with you again. Nor will he entertain any approaches from your associates. GBS's association with *CompuWorld* is finished."

"Hang on, now . . ."

"There is nothing else to say, Mr. Allen. Except good-bye."

She hung up. And I thought, *Phil was right. You never get anywhere in life being honorable with an asshole. Especially a dangerous asshole—with something to hide.*

SEVEN

"He was probably bluffing," Lizzie said.

"The guy is no bluffer," I said.

"He's into power, right?"

"Thrives on it. Needs it—like a junkie needs crack."

"Well, this is just Ted Peterson's way of letting you know who, in his mind, has the bigger dick."

"If the magazine loses the entire GBS account, and I'm held responsible . . ."

"You're not going to lose GBS. You're an essential outlet for their product. They need you as much as—"

"He's a vindictive sonofabitch, Lizzie."

"I promise you, after Christmas, once he's cooled down a bit, he's going to have no choice but to do business with you again. I mean, if he does boycott *CompuWorld*, his superiors at GBS will eventually begin to notice that they're not advertising in your magazine. And when they bring it up, what's he going to say? 'Oh, I reneged on a contract with *CompuWorld*, so that nasty Ned Allen showed up on my doorstep and embarrassed me into doing the deal. But I got him back by deciding that we should stop advertising in his magazine.' Even Peterson knows that if he gives them a story like that, GBS will ship him back to kindergarten."

She took my hand in hers. "So stop worrying about the schmuck."

Had Lizzie known about the Joan Glaston business—and the truly peculiar way Peterson behaved during our last phone call—she might have been very worried. But I chose not to tell her that part of the story, because I knew she would have been appalled to learn that I had even considered blackmail. But that still didn't lessen my own spiraling anxiety—not just about losing GBS, but about the way Peterson hung up on me. He was definitely hiding something. I mean, the guy actually seemed *relieved* to confirm that I knew about the Joan Glaston incident. So there had to be something else going on here. Something a lot dirtier. And I sensed that the bastard wasn't going to let the whole thing drop. He had regained the advantage, and would now make me pay a ferocious price for tangling with him.

"You forced him to do the right thing," Lizzie said, raising her glass to me. "You won. Be happy. Drink another martini."

"Good idea," I said, raising my hand for the waiter. We were sitting in Circo's, an absurdly extravagant nouveau Italian restaurant on West Fifty-fifth. It was a real expense account place—and we never walked out of there for less than a hundred and fifty bucks. But the food was terrific and the drinks were served in the cocktail-bar equivalent of a fire bucket. Which was fine by me. Especially tonight. Because, after the events of the last sleepless thirty-six hours, all I wanted to do was get drunk. Very drunk.

"At least Chuck Zanussi must have been pleased with the news," Lizzie said.

"Chuck Zanussi showed his true colors today. . . ."

"Always happens when people are under pressure. He was scared, so you became his convenient fall guy."

"He was out for blood."

Not just my blood, but Ivan Dolinsky's. Immediately after he had received the letter from GBS, he called my office.

"This isn't some kind of hoax you dreamed up?" he asked.

"Thanks for the warm words of congratulations, Chuck," I said.

"I'm just asking."

"No, it's totally legit. You don't believe me, get on the horn and call Peterson."

"How the hell did you pull it off?"

"I appealed to his basic Christian morality."

"That guy's got about as much Christian morality as Colonel Gadhafi."

"At least he doesn't tell his subordinates that if a deal isn't closed in thirteen minutes, they're history."

"You know why I had to pressure you like that. . . ."

"To save your own ass." (And, I could have added, *because Kreplin told you to.*)

"Ned—I really wouldn't get into this if I were you. And lose the aggressive tone while you're at it. You cut it fine, but you closed. Congrats. Okay?"

"So I still have a job here?"

"For Christ's sake, of course you do. Forget a day of bad shit between us. You're still my best guy."

And I'm about to plunge a knife in your back.

"Listen," I said, "since we pulled off the GBS deal, am I correct in assuming Ivan Dolinsky can keep his job?"

"What I said yesterday still stands: Hc's out."

"Chuck, that's simply not fair."

"Fair, *shmair.* You pulled this one out of the hat, not Ivan. You've been carrying him for a year. Face facts: He's lost it, Ned. And, given our new circumstances, and the way Klang-Sanderling is going to be monitoring us like we're in the cardiac ward, we just can't afford excess baggage. . . ."

"Give him one more shot."

"He almost cost us our jobs, Ned. The answer is no. And I'm not budging on this one. But look, I'll be pretty generous when it comes to his severance package. Six months' pay, and I'll keep him on medical for twelve months. He can't ask for more than that."

"Tell you what," I said. "I know he's going out to Michigan to see some family over Christmas. The guy's still so fragile that if we sack him before the holidays, he'll totally go under. So let's do it when he gets back, on January fifth."

"You're back from vacation on the second. Do it then."

"Not on my first day back, Chuck. I mean, I don't exactly want to kick off the New Year by telling someone they're toast. Monday, January fifth—Ivan goes. Okay?"

Chuck grumbled a lot about how this three-week reprieve was going to cost the company money. So I tried a different tactic, pointing out that it would be lousy for staff morale if Ivan was terminated before Christmas.

"They see Ivan get the bullet, all they're gonna be thinking is, Who's next? And that's going to distract them from their work. Which is exactly what we don't want—given that we need everyone to exceed their targets for the next couple of issues and impress the shit out of Klang-Sanderling. . . ."

"All right, all right," Chuck said wearily. "He goes on January fifth. And meanwhile, I want you to start scouting around for someone to fill his shoes. On the quiet, natch."

Natch, Chuck—but here's a hot off-the-record tip: You yourself might be interested in applying for the job. . . .

Of course, I didn't mention to Chuck anything about Peterson's war whoop—or my fears that we might have permanently lost GBS. And when I recounted for Lizzie my conversation with Chuck, I also conveniently failed to elaborate on why I really fought to keep Ivan on staff until January 5.

I was on the verge of telling her the news many times, but my mind kept jumping back to a conversation I'd had with Klaus Kreplin earlier that day.

He called just after lunch. No greeting, no small talk, he didn't even say hello. Just:

"Your father-in-law died in 1991."

I worked hard at stifling a laugh. I failed.

"You think this is funny?"

"Yes, Klaus. I actually do."

"Funny, no. Mildly entertaining, yes. And very imaginative."

"I just had to get on home, Klaus. I was dead tired."

"No, you were in a situation you didn't like. And you found a way of removing yourself from that situation which caused no offense to anyone. A clever stratagem. This kind of resourceful lateral thinking I like. Just as I admire your fidelity to your wife—though, during my abbreviated experience of marriage, I personally reached the conclusion that faithfulness is a useless and thankless concept. Still, one must respect such virtue. . . ."

"I'm not that virtuous, Klaus."

"This I know—otherwise you would never have found a solution to the GBS problem."

"I certainly didn't do anything unethical to get the ad back. . . ."

"Of course you didn't. I imagine you were simply . . . *resourceful*. My sincere congratulations."

Sincere? Try smarmy.

"So, now that we do not have to terminate you, you are ready to assume the role of publisher on January second?"

I took a deep breath. "I'm ready."

"May I remind you once again that the appointment is conditional on your secrecy. Not a word to anyone."

Jawohl, mein commandant. As the second round of martinis arrived, I decided I simply had to follow Kreplin's orders. Telling Lizzie now, I convinced myself, wasn't crucial. The situation at work was too delicate. Hell, it wasn't as if I was keeping a life-or-death situation from her (bar the fact that I was betraying Chuck Zanussi). It was good news, after all. And there was nothing intrinsically wrong about putting good news on hold. Especially as it was only for a few weeks.

"Do you really think you'll have to get rid of Ivan as soon as we're back from vacation?" Lizzie asked.

I thought back to the call I made to Ivan sometime after lunch—how he started to sob when I told him that Peterson had capitulated. But as he rattled on, promising to be the company's biggest earner next year, I found myself thinking, *You better start delivering the goods, pal. Because if you pull another stunt like this one, I won't be able to save you again.*

"I'm hoping that the delay might work to Ivan's advantage," I told Lizzie. "If he can score another couple of big deals between now and early January, I might just be able to win him a reprieve. But I really don't want to think about that until January second. . . ."

After the last thirty-six hours, I frankly didn't want to think about anything to do with business, let alone the fact that I was trying to tap-dance my way through a moral minefield. I kept telling myself, *As long as no confidences are blown, life will become considerably less complicated after the second of January. Chuck will go. You will pretend—to both him and Lizzie—that you knew nothing in advance about his demise and your sudden promotion. Ivan will keep his job. After some ass-kissing diplomacy (over a lunch at Le Cirque, perhaps) Peterson will come to his senses and resume adver-*

tising in the magazine. Kreplin will forget about the near loss of our biggest account.

And nobody will ever know the elaborate network of fibs, obfuscations, and near illegal behavior I had woven in order to save my butt.

As it turned out, life at *CompuWorld* did return to its normal semi-manic state rather quickly. And though we now had to put up with a steady stream of corporate visitors from our new head office in Hamburg (anal-retentive manager types who were dispatched across the Atlantic to teach us the Klang-Sanderling way of "organizing efficient interoffice communications"), we all adapted quickly to the demands of our new owners. And they, in turn, never became heavy-handed in their dealings with us. Kreplin kept his word about the staff remaining intact. There was no blood on the floor, no heavy-handed flexing of Teutonic muscles, no sudden terminations. Kreplin and his cronies were perfect models of corporate efficiency and diplomacy. And on the Friday before Christmas—the day that the first installment of the bonus checks was handed out—they even threw an after-work cocktail party for the entire staff.

It was held in a large function room on the twenty-ninth floor of the Regal U.N. Plaza Hotel—and, in true Kreplin style, it was extravagantly catered. An endless supply of Moët et Chandon. Elaborate finger food (raw sirloin on pumpernickel, mini-sushi, quail egg tartlets), and—this was quite a stylish touch—a gift of a Mont Blanc ballpoint pen for each of the eighty guests. Kreplin made a little speech, in which he actually sounded warm and human, welcoming us into the Klang-Sanderling "family" and assuring us of his certainty that the Mont Blancs would be put to good use in the coming year, making the deals that would transform *CompuWorld* into the second biggest periodical in the American computer market.

Extended drunken cheering greeted that last comment, because it reinforced something we all wanted to believe: Klang-Sanderling was behind us all the way.

"I don't need a fancy pen," Debbie Suarez complained when I ran into her at the bar after Kreplin's speech. "I just need all my bonus money."

"So do we all, Debbie," I said, reflecting that my $25,000 bridge loan would now not be paid off until the beginning of February. At least I had been able to solve one of Debbie's money problems a few days earlier, when, as promised, I had a little conversation with the bursar at Faber Academy. After much wheeling and dealing, and playing of the liberal compassion card, I finally got this fine, upstanding Quaker to reluctantly agree to defer half of Raul's tuition until the end of January.

"I am, of course, sympathetic to Ms. Suarez's situation," the bursar said, "and to the fact that she is a single parent who is also looking after her elderly mother. But we still must have some assurance . . ."

I said, "Look, our new owners, Klang-Sanderling, are the fourth-biggest publishing conglomerate on the planet. . . ."

"All I'm asking for, Mr. Allen, is a letter on company stationery, signed by you as Ms. Suarez's superior, guaranteeing that the forty-five-hundred-dollar tuition balance owed to Faber Academy will be paid by the first of February."

"You've got it," I said, though—as I was faxing the letter over to the school—I did momentarily reflect on the fact that, until the second of January, I was in no position to guarantee anything. But hell . . . who was going to know about this letter anyway?

"I spoke to that *maricón* bursar at Faber this morning," Debbie said, handing me another glass of champagne. "He said he got your letter, and that he was really makin' an exception here—'cause it's usually money up front or no school. But he told me that it was your phone call that swung it. 'Your boss, he's some sonofabitch salesman.' "

I laughed. "I'm sure he didn't use 'sonofabitch,' Debbie."

"I owe you big, Mr. Allen."

"All part of the job, Debbie."

She leaned into me and kissed me fully on the lips. I was a little startled by this spontaneous show of affection, but at least had the presence of mind to keep my lips shut. Debbie herself was even more flustered. Taking a giant step back from me, she blushed deeply.

"Oops," she said.

"Yeah," I said, "oops."

"Oh, Mr. Allen, I am such a jerk. . . ."

"Don't worry about it," I said.

"Too much champagne," she said.

"It is a common excuse, no?"

Debbie spun around and there was Klaus Kreplin, beaming broadly at us.

"Nice speech, Klaus," I said, trying to remain composed.

"I am not interrupting anything?" he asked, his eyebrows arching slyly.

"Nothing at all," I said. "Klaus, I'd like you to meet Debbie Suarez."

"Ah, yes," he said, "the brilliant Telesales star you always tell me about."

Now it was my turn to blush. Trust Kreplin to maximize our embarrassment. He took her hand, raised it to his lips, and kissed it.

"Charmed," he said. Judging from her *what-the-fuck-is-this?* reaction, I doubted very much if anyone had ever kissed Debbie's hand before.

"Yeah, uh, likewise," she said, at a loss for words. "Will you guys excuse me?"

And she hurried off across the room.

"A delightful young lady," Kreplin said, "as you obviously agree."

"It was a kiss, Klaus. Nothing more."

"Oh yes, I forgot. You are, of course, the 'prince of virtue.' "

I smiled thinly.

"But we are all tempted by misconduct, aren't we?" Kreplin said.

"Life is nonstop temptation," I said.

"Ah, you are a philosopher as well. But one, I hope, who understands the value of silence."

"I've said nothing to anyone, if that's what you mean. I do follow orders."

"Edward?" he said, slapping me on the shoulder. "We will make excellent colleagues—of this I am certain."

He reached into the breast pocket of his suit, pulled out a business card, and shoved it into my pocket.

"I am off back to Hamburg tomorrow evening," he said. "On

this card you will find my phone numbers at the head office, at my home, and for my cellular phone. You must call me if there is the slightest problem."

"There will be no problem. I'm in the office Monday and Tuesday, then Lizzie and I fly to Nevis on the twenty-sixth. We're at the Four Seasons there if you need me. Otherwise . . ." I proffered my hand. ". . . see you back in New York on January second."

"I shall be there, Herr Publisher," Kreplin said in a whisper. As he turned to leave, I noticed that Chuck was on the far side of the room, watching us. I gave him a quick wave, a facile smile, wondering if I was looking particularly guilty. Then I strolled over and said, "Helluva party."

"What did Kreplin have to say for himself?" he asked abruptly, the words slurring ever so slightly (well, we had all drunk a lot of champagne).

"Usual Kraut horseshit. And he was congratulating me on the GBS biz. You tell him something?"

"Yeah—I mentioned we had a problem and that you solved it."

I gulped. "That was decent of you, Chuck."

"Yeah, well, I always was a sap."

I remained very composed. "A sap? You? Get outta here. I don't know what you're talking about."

"Don't you?" he asked.

I shook my head, shrugging my shoulders.

"You're not bullshitting me?"

"About what, exactly?"

His mood seemed to lighten. "I think I'm getting paranoid in my advanced middle age."

"I think we've all been through a lot in the last two weeks."

"You can say that again." He stuck out his fleshy right paw. "Despite all the crap that went down, we're still buddies, right?"

"You bet," I said, reaching for his hand. But suddenly I found myself in the middle of an M.B.A. (Male Bonding Alert) as Chuck gave me a drunken, fraternal hug. I was glad he couldn't see my face—for what he would have glimpsed was guilt. Okay, I hadn't sold him out. It was Kreplin's call. But, returning his embrace, I still felt like Joe Judas.

"I've got to get on home," he said. "We're off to MaryAnn's folks in Buffalo tomorrow. Back at the office on the twenty-sixth, if you need me. I envy you the Caribbean, guy. Catch some rays for me."

"I'll see what I can do, boss."

As he headed off in search of his coat, I began to dread January 2—and the appalling scene that would unfold when he got the news.

But I tried to put such thoughts on hold. And for the next few days—in an attempt to get into the holiday spirit—"Herr Publisher" went out and spent money. A lot of money. The way I figured it, half my debts were settled, all my credit cards were now back to zero, the remaining bonus check would cancel out my bank loan. Then, as of January 2 . . .

So why not blow a little dough? It was Christmas, after all. And Dr. Barney Gordon was more than happy to install my new front tooth on short notice (especially since he'd made up the bridge months earlier and had been sending me increasingly testy reminder notices).

"About time you showed up, Mr. Allen," Doc Gordon said when I trooped into his office on the morning of the twenty-third. "We were starting to wonder if you'd left the country."

"I was just incredibly busy."

"Well," Doc Gordon said, "I'm glad you found time for this. But, just in case you get so busy in the New Year that you forget about our bill, our practice now accepts Visa or MasterCard—so you can settle up with the receptionist on the way out. Now, open wide. . . ."

Thirty-two hundred bucks for that little stint in the dentist's chair (though, I have to admit, the new bridgework is a considerable improvement on the battered old false tooth that was shoved into my mouth by some navy dentist twenty years ago).

Anyway, $3,200 for a new front tooth seemed cheap when compared with the $3,400 I splurged on a Jaeger-LeCoultre watch for Lizzie. Okay, okay—without question, an over-the-top extravagance. But I knew she'd been admiring that watch for years. As Herr Publisher I could afford it. Just like I could also afford to FedEx my mom a $2,000 set of Callaway titanium golf clubs—because I felt guilty about not staying in closer touch with her.

And, as Herr Publisher, I could also afford to upgrade Lizzie and myself to first class on our December twenty-sixth American Airlines flight to St. Kitts/Nevis.

"Are you deranged?" Lizzie asked as I shepherded her toward the first class check-in at JFK. "I mean, the watch was a big enough shock."

She had been dumbstruck when, on the previous morning, she opened the elegantly wrapped gift box and found herself staring at the Jaeger-LeCoultre she'd always coveted.

"You're insane, you're totally insane," she said, not sounding at all happy.

"It's just a watch," I said.

"Sure—and the Concorde's just an airplane."

"Then you do like it?"

"It's . . . wonderful. Beyond wonderful. But it scares me. Because we can't afford it."

Now, as we waited behind one other passenger at the first class desk, Lizzie turned to me and asked, "Are you keeping something from me?"

"Like what?"

"I don't know. But the way you're spending money . . . either something's going on, or you've become pathologically self-destructive. I just don't understand this recklessness. . . ."

"It's just money."

"I know how much one of these watches costs. We're talking too much money."

"I can handle it."

"I wish I could believe that," she said.

I kissed her. "Relax. I haven't broken the bank."

We drank champagne all the way to San Juan, then switched to a small sixty-seat aircraft for the fast forty-minute puddle jump to St. Kitts. On this last leg of the journey, Lizzie nodded off for around ten minutes. Watching her sleep, I couldn't block out that persistent little voice which inevitably begins to haunt your inner ear after you've made a dumb call. *You're blowing it here. She knows something's up. You're out of the country now—so to hell with Kreplin's obsessive need for secrecy. She's your wife, for Christ's sake. It's time for a complete about-face. Get it over with. Tell her.*

And I resolved to do just that as soon as we checked into our room.

We landed at St. Kitts, where the mercury was punching ninety and the air had that heady, fragrant kick of cheap rum punch. A Four Seasons minibus picked us up at the airport and drove us past whitewashed shacks to a jetty where we were whisked aboard an inter-island motor launch. The engines revved, we gently cruised out of the harbor, then the captain opened up the throttle and we shot across the narrow bay that separated St. Kitts from Nevis. The sun was incandescent, the water was as level as plate glass, and—I couldn't believe this—looming up ahead was this vast mountain plopped down in the middle of the Atlantic. The top of this mountain was covered in a fine, white dust, making it appear to be frosted with snow. As we approached, I could see that its slopes flattened out and were covered by a deep green tangle of tropical foliage. The foliage stretched out, north to south, for around ten miles, and was bisected by one paved road. Below this made-for-Tarzan habitat was a narrow, pristine strip of pure white sand that appeared to encircle the entire island.

"That's Nevis?" I asked one of the crewmen.

"The one and only, mon."

Lizzie gave me a radiant smile. "I approve of paradise."

Our room was at one end of the resort, far from its noisy epicenter. And it fronted the beach, giving us a wide-screen view of the Atlantic.

As we stood on the little verandah that faced the water, Lizzie asked quietly, "Didn't we originally rule out an ocean view because it was an extra thousand bucks for the week?"

"I thought I'd surprise you."

"You're full of surprises, Ned."

"You've got to admit, it's one hell of a view."

"I suppose the bottle of Dom Perignon was another of your surprises?" she said, motioning toward the ice-bucketed champagne that had been waiting for us on our arrival.

"Sweetheart, it's Christmas," I said, picking up the bottle and tugging on the cork.

"And you're acting like Donald Trump. What gives, Ned? I want to know."

I pulled the cork, I poured two glasses, I handed her one. And said, "On January second, I'm becoming the new publisher of *CompuWorld*."

She flinched as if I'd slapped her. It was not the reaction I was hoping for.

"I've been meaning to tell you. . . ."

"For what?" she interrupted. "Days? Weeks?"

"A little while," I said, sounding sheepish. "Nothing was confirmed until—"

"So you have known about this for quite a while."

"I didn't want to say anything until I was absolutely certain. . . ."

"I don't believe this."

"Klaus Kreplin swore me to secrecy."

As soon as I uttered that sentence, I regretted it. Lizzie's reaction was glacial.

"Secrecy—even from *me*?" she said.

"Take it easy. . . ."

"I will not take it easy. You do this all the time."

"Do what?"

"Lie to me."

"This is hardly a lie, Lizzie. All right, I admit it, I was wrong. I should have told you."

"No—what you should have done was trusted me to keep a secret."

"I do trust you, darling. . . ."

"No, you don't. Nor do you take me seriously enough to want to share anything important in your life."

"You know that's not true."

"Don't you dare talk to me about truth."

"I was just being cautious."

"You were shutting me out, as usual."

"I don't shut you out. . . ."

"Go fuck yourself," she said, throwing her champagne glass on the terra-cotta floor and storming off down the beach. My first instinct was to pursue her. But I held back—in part because I knew from experience of previous domestic skirmishes that it was best to stay clear of Lizzie while she was still fuming, and also because, after that verbal brawl, I needed to give myself ten minutes to calm down.

Jerk. Jerk. Jerk. You never learn, do you?

I drained the glass of champagne, wishing it was something more nerve bracing, like vodka. Then, grabbing the bottle and two fresh glasses, I left the verandah and started strolling along the beach. Past my pale, fleshy compatriots courting skin cancer in the merciless West Indies sun. And the waiters carrying trays of piña coladas. And two little kids throwing wet sand at each other. Past the shack where you could rent sailboards. Past the eastern wing of the hotel. Past the line of demarcation that marked the end of the Four Seasons beachfront. Past a place where local dudes with dreadlocks sold lobsters on the beach. And then onto a stretch of beach where there was nothing but water, sand, and a lush thicket of palms.

It was empty—except for my wife. She was sitting by the water's edge, staring out at the deep blue bay. I walked over and sat down beside her. She didn't acknowledge my arrival. She kept her gaze firmly fixed on the horizon.

"Drink?" I said, holding up the bottle. She said nothing. I poured two glasses and placed one in front of her on the sand.

"Merry Christmas," I said, raising my glass.

"Don't humor me, Ned."

"I'm sorry."

"That's not good enough."

"I'm *very* sorry."

"Do you really want this marriage?" she asked.

"Of course I do. You are everything—"

"Oh, please . . ."

"I mean it."

"I don't know if you do mean it, Ned. You never act like this is a partnership. You run up crazy bills but keep telling me not to worry about it. You keep crucial stuff from me—which leads me to believe that you can't trust me with a secret. You seem to be so totally absorbed in making it all the time—in proving to the world you're 'a player'—that you forget there are two of us in this marriage. In it *together*."

"I don't forget that," I said.

"You do. All the time. And then, when I found out I was pregnant . . ."

I avoided her accusatory gaze. And felt shame.

"I was scared," I finally said.

"You were a selfish asshole, thinking only of yourself and your precious job. And you made me feel very alone."

"It wasn't just the job. . . . I was wrong."

"You're going to lose me, Ned."

I reached for her hand. She didn't push me away.

"I don't want to lose you."

"Then make me believe that."

She picked up the champagne glass from the sand and downed it in one gulp.

"Merry Christmas, Publisher," she said cheerlessly.

By the end of the day an uneasy armistice had been established between us. Over dinner that night, I told her everything about the job offer, assuring her that I didn't scheme against Chuck, that it was Kreplin's decision. She didn't seem entirely convinced. She worried about how Chuck would take the news, and whether I would be perceived within the company as a conniving, backstabbing shit. Then I mentioned the salary and she looked both electrified and concerned.

"That's crazy money," she said.

"We'll be rich."

"We'll be comfortable."

"*Very* comfortable. And you know what they say about money—it gives you options. If we want to buy a co-op, rent a weekend place in the Hamptons, have a kid—"

She cut me off. "One thing at a time, Ned."

Careful here. I kissed her, then put my arm around her shoulders, pulling her toward me.

"You're right," I said. "One thing at a time."

The sunstruck indolence of Nevis eventually forced us to kick back, to slide into low gear for the rest of the week, never waking before ten, breakfasting on the verandah, taking extended hikes on the beach, spending the late afternoons in bed, dodging the company of our fellow compatriots at the resort by eating at one of the funky local lobster shacks on the beach. The days effortlessly merged into one another. My nails grew back, my overloaded nervous system began to decompress. Though everyone at the office had my number, the phone never rang once. Domestic calm had been reestablished—but several times I caught Lizzie glancing at me with concern.

And then the week was over. We saluted the arrival of the New Year with a bottle of champagne and a drunken stroll along the beach, collapsing into the sand and letting the warm water of the bay wash over us. It drenched our clothes. We didn't care. Instead, we lay on our backs and stared up at the floorshow in the sky. After a long silence, Lizzie said:

"Say we didn't go back."

"Yeah, sure . . ."

"I'm serious. Say we just said 'fuck it.' To hell with the career, the pressure, the endless ass-kissing, the nights made sleepless with worry, accumulating all this stuff we don't need . . ."

"What would you suggest? Finding an island like this one, and moving into a grass hut?"

"It's a nice dream, isn't it?"

"Sure, but . . ."

"Yeah?"

"We'd be bored to death within a week."

"You really need it, don't you?" she said.

"Need what?"

"The city. The pressure. The deal."

"Yeah, I need it. Don't you?"

"I used to think so," she said. "Now, I'm not so sure. Anyway . . . so much for my tropical fantasy."

"It's nice in theory. But . . ."

"I know. Back we go. . . ."

"Yeah. Back we go."

And early the next morning, back we went—trading the sun-dappled haze of the West Indies for an ashen Manhattan sky. It was sleeting when we landed. We hit traffic on the BQE and crept slowly into the city, as if we were part of a funeral cortege. The frozen rain kept dripping down. The taxi was overheated, the radio blared Estonian pop tunes, and I was suddenly seized by edgy anxiety. Lizzie—sensing my apprehension—squeezed my hand.

"Thinking about tomorrow?" she asked.

I nodded. "It's a big day."

"You'll be just fine. But remember: It's just a job, Ned."

Sleep eluded me for most of that New Year's night. When dawn broke, I was slouched on our sofa, staring out at the brightening skyline. I showered, I shaved, I put on a dark gray double-breasted suit, I retreated to the bedroom, where Lizzie was stirring.

"You look like a man in charge," she said, kissing me lightly on the cheek. "Good luck."

It was just seven when I left the apartment. The streets were empty. I didn't want to get to the office until around ten. Kreplin had mentioned prior to Christmas that he was going to "do the deed" as soon as Chuck walked in at nine, so it was best if I showed up an hour or so after he had been ushered off the premises.

This gave me three hours to kill. It was a radiantly clear morning—the sky cloudless, the chill bracing yet manageable if you kept moving. So I meandered slowly up Fifth Avenue, grabbed a *New York Times*, ate breakfast in a coffee shop near Grand Central, walked all the way east to the river, then finally ambled back to Third and Forty-sixth. I checked my watch. 9:55. Right. It was time.

I entered our building. I took the elevator up to the 11th floor. The door opened and . . .

There was Debbie Suarez. She was distraught. Her eyes were red and swollen, as if she had been crying for hours. Next to her stood Hildy Hyman. Her face was a mask of shock. They were both carrying cardboard boxes. Between them was a large, muscular woman with a face like prison bread. She was dressed in a navy-blue uniform and wore a policeman-style cap with a logo—CORP SECURE—below the visor.

"Debbie? Hildy?" I said. "What's going . . ."

Debbie began to sob. "The assholes. The fucking assholes . . ."

The security guard nudged them both forward into the elevator.

"They did it to us, Mr. Allen," Hildy said. "Just like I said, those German bastards—"

The elevator doors slid shut and they were gone. I turned around. In front of me were two male members of Corp Secure standing guard by the main doors to the *CompuWorld* office. A woman guard was seated behind the reception desk. Through the glass windows separating the reception area I could see several members of my Telesales team being escorted down the corridor by other Corp Secure heavies. I was stunned. Speechless. Rooted to the spot.

Eventually the guard behind the desk said, "May I help you?"

"I work here."

"You are an employee of CompuWorld Inc.?"

"I'm the regional sales director for—"

The guard snapped her fingers impatiently and said, "Employee I.D."

I pulled out my wallet and handed over the laminated plastic card with the metallic stripe that worked as a key to the *CompuWorld* offices. The guard placed the card next to a clipboard and traveled down a list of names until she found mine. Then she nodded to one of the armed guards by the door.

"Right, Mr. Allen—Lorenzo here will escort you up to Human Resources."

Fear hit. Human Resources was death row—the corporate division which specialized in new hires and terminations.

"Can I see my boss, Mr. Zanussi?" I asked.

"Mr. Zanussi no longer works here," the guard said.

"Well, how about Klaus Kreplin?"

"Mr. Allen, if you will just accompany Lorenzo to Human Resources—"

My voice became shrill. "I'm not going anywhere until I see goddamn Klaus—"

Lorenzo came forward and stood in front of me. He was six foot four, very pumped, with a menacing scowl on his face that said one word: *Behave*. When he spoke, his voice was so quiet I had to strain to hear him.

"I advise you to accompany me upstairs, sir." Tapping me on the shoulder, he pointed toward the elevator.

"What about my I.D.?" I asked.

"We'll hold on to that," Lorenzo said.

We rode in silence to the eighteenth floor. Lorenzo escorted me down a long, narrow corridor of small offices with frosted glass doors. He knocked on one, stuck his head inside, then motioned for me to enter. He shut the door behind me. The office was tiny—

just big enough for a metal chair facing a functional metal desk. After a moment the door swung open and in came a nondescript man in his forties. Suit, tie, horn-rims, a row of pens in his shirt pocket, sandy hair streaked with gray.

"Sorry to have kept you, Mr. Allen," he said, seating himself behind the desk. "Bill Freundlich, Human Resources. Please, take a seat."

He didn't offer his hand in greeting; he didn't make contact with my eyes. Instead he opened the large, thick folder that he was carrying. My photo was pinned to one corner of it. My file.

"You're probably wondering what's going on here," he said in a voice that had been trained to betray no emotion.

"I'm being fired, that's what's going on."

"Not exactly. What has happened is this: CompuWorld Inc. has been sold—"

"They sold us?"

I was shouting. The door flew open and Lorenzo stuck his head inside.

"We're fine here," Bill Freundlich said to him, then looked at me coolly. "Aren't we?"

I sank back into the chair and stared at the floor. Bill Freundlich continued speaking.

"I know this is a shock—but, please, it will be easier for both of us if you just let me explain the sequence of events that are about to unfold."

He waited for me to respond—but I remained silent, firmly directing my gaze down toward the grubby linoleum.

"As I said, CompuWorld Inc. has been sold as of the start of business this morning, and all employees of the company are hereby terminated. However, the parent company, Klang-Sanderling, will abide by all the standard New York State provisions for employee termination. You will be paid two weeks' salary for every year's service to the company. You will continue to enjoy company medical insurance for the first quarter of this year. After that, you will be entitled to extended coverage for eighteen months, according to COBRA law, but will be responsible for monthly payments. And, as an executive with CompuWorld Inc., you will be enrolled in an eight-week executive outplacement program—which, put baldly, is there to help you find a position commensurate with your current corporate standing."

His delivery was anemic, devoid of sympathy. The words washed over me like dirty water. Did blood actually flow through this asshole's veins?

"Now, you will be pleased to know that the outplacement agency to which you've been assigned—Gerard Flynn Associates—is, to my mind, one of the truly topflight specialists in executive reinstatement, with a results-oriented approach that, statistically speaking, has yielded first-rate results—"

I stopped looking at the linoleum and interrupted him. "What about our bonuses?"

He paused ever so slightly . . . but a pause nonetheless. "I will be covering that issue after I deal with—"

"Cover it *now*," I said.

"I would rather—"

"We're due fifty percent of our bonus money on January thirty-first. . . ."

"Correction: When your parent company was Klang-Sanderling, you *were* due half of last year's bonus on the thirty-first. But now, as your parent company is Spencer-Rudman . . ."

I couldn't believe what I was hearing. Spencer-Rudman was the multinational that owned our number-one competitor, *PC Globe*.

"I thought we were being closed down. But now you're saying we're *owned* by Spencer-Rudman?"

"It's very simple," Bill Freundlich said. "Klang-Sanderling has sold CompuWorld Inc. to Spencer-Rudman who, in turn, has decided that *CompuWorld* will cease to exist."

"You can't be serious."

"I'm afraid I'm very serious, Mr. Allen. But it's probably best if someone from Spencer-Rudman explained this fully to you."

Freundlich lifted the phone, dialed three numbers, muttered, "He's here," then hung up.

"In fact, the gentleman in question asked me to buzz him when you were in my office."

A knock on the door. And in walked Chuck Zanussi.

"Hi, Ned," he said breezily as Freundlich slipped out of the office, closing the door behind him. "Guess you didn't expect to see me this morning."

I'd lost the ability to speak.

"Cat got your tongue, 'Herr Publisher'?"

I wanted to run out of the room.

"If you're surprised, you can't even begin to imagine how I felt when, the day before Christmas, a friend of mine at Spencer-Rudman tracked me down in Buffalo to tell me that they were about to buy the *CompuWorld* title. Guess we were all doing too good a job of invading *PC Globe*'s market share—because, according to my friend, the guys at Spencer-Rudman were getting worried about the way we were nipping at their heels, and how the 'commercial arena' wasn't really big enough for three computer magazines. So that's when they decided to buy us up, close us down. And you want to know the really funny thing about all this? It seems they approached Klang-Sanderling about the sale in the middle of December. Around the same time you were conspiring with Klaus Kreplin to take my job."

He paused to let that last comment sink in.

I said, "Chuck, believe me, I did not conspire with Kreplin. He wanted you out . . ."

". . . and offered you my job, right?"

"I told him . . ."

"Oh, I can guess what you told him. 'Chuck brought me into the company. Chuck taught me everything I know about sales. Chuck is my friend . . .' " He gave me a dark, sour smile. "Fortunately, my friend at Spencer-Rudman really *is* my friend. Because he offered me a job. Supervising the closure of *CompuWorld*, then assuming the role of group publisher for all software and computer magazines at Spencer-Rudman. He even said I could hire a deputy. Naturally, I thought of you—until he gave me a blow-by-blow account of a conversation he had with Kreplin a couple of days ago, after Klang-Sanderling agreed to the sale. 'Chuck Zanussi, he is a very fortunate man to be hired by you. Because he was to be terminated next week, and Ned Allen had agreed to be his successor.' "

Another uncomfortable pause.

"Well, Ned, as I'm sure you can appreciate, I was just a tad troubled to hear that you were planning to, professionally speaking, have me whacked. . . ."

"Please listen to me. I was not planning—"

"I will not listen to you. Because nothing you say matters anymore." He stood up and leaned over the desk. "But know this: If I have my way, you will never, ever work in this business again."

He walked to the door and shot me a final lethal smile. "Happy New Year, Ned."

The door closed. I sank back into my chair. I was in a hall of mirrors. A labyrinth without an exit. And the implications—both professional and financial—of what had just gone down were only starting to register in my brain. The world was spinning out of control—and I was so stupefied that I hardly noticed the reentrance of Bill Freundlich. He sat down again and continued his bloodless drone—but I was so far away by that point that I only caught the occasional phrase. *Your final paycheck will be mailed . . . Gerald Flynn Associates will be expecting you on . . . We do regret the sudden nature of this . . .*

Then Freundlich stood up and Lorenzo entered the room, announcing that he would accompany me to my office, where I would be given fifteen minutes to clear it out. I was so unsteady on my feet that Lorenzo kept one hand under my left elbow as we walked back down the corridor and entered the elevator.

"Y'okay?" he asked as the doors slid closed.

"No," I managed to say.

We plummeted to the eleventh floor. The doors opened. And there, standing in front of me, was Klaus Kreplin. Initially he recoiled in surprise when he saw me. But then he gave me a *che sarà, sarà* shrug, a thin, weaselly smile spreading across his lips.

"What can I say, Edward? Except, sorry, it's busi—"

He never got to finish that sentence. I caught him in the mouth with my right fist, then punched him hard in the stomach. He doubled over. I slammed my fist into his face again. As he hit the floor, I lost all control, kicking him in his chest, his head, his teeth. The entire assault was a mad, delusional rush, lasting no more than five seconds. The Corp Secure guards came rushing forward, and Lorenzo suddenly had my left arm bent upward in a half nelson.

But I was oddly detached from all that was going on around

me. It was as if I was hovering above this scene, watching it unfold, an innocent bystander. Until I unflexed my right fist and felt an electric jolt of pain race up my arm. Suddenly I was back on earth, howling in agony.

Then I looked down at the floor. Klaus Kreplin was lying in a pool of blood. And he wasn't moving.

TWO

ONE

Nancy Auerbach's office was spare, utilitarian, institutional. She had a firm handshake and a steady, piercing gaze—the sort of gaze that made you feel as if you were being instantly assessed and evaluated. Which, of course, you were—as it was her job to form a professional opinion about you.

She was all business. Five minutes earlier, when I first walked into her office, she greeted me with a crisp staccato monologue that almost sounded rehearsed.

"Mr. Allen, hello there, I can call you Ned, can't I? . . . I'm Nancy Auerbach, your outplacement facilitator. Find us okay this morning? . . . So here we are, and we're going to be working together for—how long is your program?—right, here it is, eight weeks. Well, we're certainly going to be getting to know each other over the next two months. Can I get you anything, Ned? Tea? Coffee?"

"Could I have a glass of water, please? I need to take some pills."

"Water's no problem," she said. "Water we can do." Swirling around in her desk chair, she reached for a bottle of Perrier and a glass, located on a tray. She swung back and set them in front of me.

"Need a hand?" she asked, glancing down at my right arm. The wrist and the top of the hand were mummified in white surgical tape. My fingers protruded from this medical wrap, but the third, fourth, and fifth ones had been bound together with an elastic bandage. "No pun intended."

"I can manage," I said, using my thumb and forefinger to unscew the top of the Perrier bottle, then pouring myself a glass with my left hand.

"God, those fingers of yours are really black and blue."

"More black than blue," I said, reaching into my suit pocket for two bottles of pills, flipping them open, and popping one tab from each into my mouth.

"You on painkillers?" Nancy Auerbach asked as I washed them down with water.

"Yeah, and anti-inflammatories."

"That must have been some accident."

"It wasn't an accident, Ms. Auerbach."

She looked me straight in the eye. "I am aware of that."

"You know what happened?"

"I know *exactly* what happened."

She cleared her throat. "Now what we have to look at, Ned, is the professional complexity of your case and how it may impact your future prospects. But first, I think we should begin by identifying your career objectives and discussing how to maximize program benefits to your advantage."

Career objectives . . . maximizing program benefits . . . professional complexity. Nancy Auerbach spoke a new language: *Outplacement-spiel*. A language I would have to master quickly.

The phone rang. "Mind if I take this, Ned?" She grabbed the receiver and was deep in conversation within seconds.

". . . Now all we've got to do here, Matt, is lose Banker's Trust from your resumé."

As she rattled on, I studied Nancy Auerbach with care. Tall, fifty-something, clean-limbed, long, elegant fingers (no wedding ring, pictures of her two teenage children on her desk—a divorcée), a gray herringbone suit. Definitely East Coast. Probably born and bred in Fairfield County, spent summers at the Greenwich Country Club, went on from Rosemary Hall to Smith or Skidmore, hooked up with some jerk lawyer named Brad, did the raise-the-kids-in-the-suburbs thing until the marriage went down in flames, whereupon she hit the job market again and established a born-again career counseling the downsized victims of corporate America.

". . . Matt, you know their P.O.V. . . . Of course, I hear you, and, yeah, moving to Rochester isn't my idea of a good time either. But that's the deal. It's re-lo or no-go. . . ."

I could see her occasionally stealing a glance in my direction—her gaze constantly returning to my damaged hand, my blotchy fingers. It was almost as if she was keeping an eye on me. Wondering if I was some kind of hair-trigger psycho in a designer suit—the sort of maniac who was destined one day to walk into a McDonald's carrying an AK-47 and announce to the assembled diners, "After I finish this Big Mac, I'm taking you all with me."

You know what happened?

I know exactly what happened.

No doubt, so did everyone in the computer magazine business. The curious saga that led to the demise of *CompuWorld* had made all the papers; the *Wall Street Journal*, the *Times*, even *Newsday*, reporting in their business pages how we were tossed like a hot potato from Getz-Braun to Klang-Sanderling to Spencer-Rudman, only to be bumped off like some upstart street punk who'd dared to take on Mr. Big. Though the *Times* report was only three paragraphs long, the *Journal* devoted half a column to the story. With a real whopper of a final paragraph:

> According to sources within *CompuWorld*, the shocking news of the title's demise provoked considerable consternation among the magazine's employees—especially since, prior to the Christmas holiday, they were assured of *CompuWorld*'s future by Mr. Klaus Kreplin, group publishing director of Klang-Sanderling. The resentment felt toward Mr. Kreplin was vented by one *CompuWorld* manager, Edward Allen, the magazine's regional sales director for the Northeast. On being told of his termination, he physically assaulted Mr. Kreplin. No charges were filed against him.

Yes, that was true. But what the *Journal* (thankfully) failed to mention was that, after I attacked Kreplin, there followed a terrible two-minute period when I thought I had actually killed him. Lying motionless on the floor, blood cascading from his nose and mouth (now missing a front tooth), Kreplin was immediately surrounded by two of the Corp Secure staff. Quickly determining that he was unconscious, they attempted to revive him using crude methods. They slapped his face, they shook him hard by the shoulder, they shouted into his left ear. Then one of the women guards felt for a pulse.

"Oh Jesus, he's arrested!" she screamed, and began administering CPR by slamming her fist into Kreplin's chest. There was a loud groan as Kreplin snapped back into consciousness and reacted with displeasure to having a couple of ribs broken.

The cops were called. While we waited for them to arrive, Lorenzo handcuffed me to a chair (at least he had the decency not to use my freshly fractured right hand). Two ambulance men arrived first. Kreplin kept groaning loudly as they loaded him onto a stretcher and carted him off. After Kreplin was gone, I asked Lorenzo if he could uncuff me.

"Sorry, my man. Just doing my job." Then he leaned forward and whispered, "But lemme give you a little tip. Next time you want to clock a guy, use the heel of your hand. Causes maximum damage to him, minimal to you. You take a swing at someone with a clenched fist, you're both gonna be heading to the ER."

The police finally showed up. They took me uptown in a squad car.

At the station house I was booked for assault. I was also given the opportunity to make one phone call. Thank God, Lizzie was at her desk. When I told her where I was—and what had landed me there—she let out a gasp. But she was at the precinct in less than thirty minutes. Walking into the squad room where I was being held, she hugged me, then said that a lawyer was on his way.

The officer who booked me was on the phone. When he put it down he turned to us and said:

"Cancel the lawyer. I've got good news for you on all fronts. Your victim's okay. He's badly bruised and missing a front tooth, but there are no internal injuries, except for a couple of busted ribs. Anyway, the lawyer told me they won't be pressing charges against you. As far as I'm concerned, you're outta here, guy."

As Lizzie helped me to my feet, the cop said, "Free piece of advice. Next time you thump someone, don't be a jerk and use a clenched fist. . . ."

My hand was now feeling like a bag of flesh stuffed with broken glass. In the cab en route to Lenox Hill Hospital, shock finally descended. Lizzie, sensing just how bad I was, squeezed my operable hand and whispered, "Hang in there, darling."

And then the lights in my brain went off.

When I came to, I was stretched out on a hospital trolley in the emergency room. Standing by me was a doctor in a white coat. He was holding up an X ray.

"Welcome back," he said. "Want to see what you've done to your hand?"

He lifted the X ray above my face and pointed to some delicate bones in three of my fingers. Still adjusting to the hospital glare, I had to squint to see them.

"You fractured the fourth metacarpal on the third, fourth, and fifth fingers. First time I've ever seen a metacarpal hat trick like that. You must have used a clenched fist."

"Is it serious, Dr. . . . ?"

"Harding. Jeff Harding. I'm the resident E.R. orthopedist here at Lenox Hill. If you were a concert pianist, your career might be over. In your case, it's just going to be eight to ten weeks in an elastic bandage . . ."

Eight to ten weeks. Terrific. Just when I'd be interviewing for a new job. That is, if anyone would now dare hire me. And even if they somehow didn't know about the assault before the interview, they'd sure as hell ask about my black-and-blue fingers during it.

". . . so the long-term prognosis is excellent."

Only from where you're sitting, Doc.

The hospital released me an hour later. In the cab downtown I told Lizzie, "No one will ever hire me again . . ."

"That's not true. Everyone in the industry knows how successful you were. And they also know that you were screwed. Trust me:

People will sympathize with you. You went crazy for a moment, that's all. It was sort of understandable, given the circumstances. And it's not like you have a record of violent assaults."

"The money thing's scaring the crap out of me. I mean, without the second half of the bonus . . ."

"Don't even think about that now."

". . . and the bank will be putting the thumb screws on me when they learn . . ."

"Ned, *please*. You're in shock, they've got you doped up with painkillers, so everything's going to seem a little scary right now. But it will work out."

Lizzie was right. The pills had me so doped that the weekend vanished in a blur. There were occasional moments of lucidity, during which I obsessed out loud about my ruined career, and Lizzie had to keep reassuring me that all would be fine. And on Sunday evening I did manage to take two phone calls. The first was from Phil Sirio.

"Boss, I know you're at home recuperating—but word got around about what you did, and I just had to tell you: It was a beaut."

"Thanks, Phil."

" 'Course you shouldn't have used a clenched—"

"I know, I know. How're you taking the news?"

"I'm kind of pissed off, you know. Especially about the bonus biz. Leaves me a bit light."

"How much you out?"

"Fourteen."

"Ouch."

"Everyone got burned. But they owe me."

"So what are you going to do now?"

"This and that. I got friends. I'll be okay. And you, boss?"

"I don't know. After what I pulled, the only job I'm probably suited for is as a bouncer."

"You'll land, boss. Don't sweat it. And remember: When you socked that Kraut fuck, you were doin' it on behalf of all of us. So Phil here owes *you* one. You ever got a problem, I'm here. Understand?"

"You're a class act, Phil."

"Later, boss."

The second call was from Debbie Suarez. As usual, she sounded as if she was on speed.

"I gotta tell ya, I just gotta tell ya, it made my day when I heard you popped him. You're my hero, Mr. Allen. I mean, I know you broke your hand, but it was worth it, right?"

"I'm not too sure about that, Debbie."

"I know what you're thinkin', but they're gonna be linin' up to give you work. I mean, you're the best."

All this talk about how I was a shoe-in for a big new job was making me nervous. It was terminal-ward talk—everyone being far too cheerful to the guy with two months to live.

Trying to change the subject, I asked Debbie how she was going to manage financially. She grew quiet and said, "I already got a job."

"That was fast."

"Yeah, well, it's Chuck Zanussi who offered it to me."

"I see," I said.

"I know, I know—he's an asshole. But he called me at home yesterday, asked me to be part of the Telesales team at *PC Globe*. And I kinda had no choice. . . ."

"It's great news, Debbie."

"Honest—I really wanted to tell him 'No way, Jose.' But I was desperate. . . ."

"You don't have to explain. . . ."

"You know what really makes me want to kick that German in the *cojones*—if they hadn't sold the company until tomorrow, my mom would have just made it on to my insurance. It's totally unfair, y'know?"

"Believe me, Debbie. I know."

"But this is great, you'll love this—I called the money guy at Faber Academy on Friday after I got the news, all upset, telling him I wasn't gonna be able to pay him the additional four-five I owed the school at the end of January. Guess what he told me: Because my boss had written him a letter on company stationery guaranteeing the money, the company would have to cover it."

For the first time in days, I managed a small smile. According to the standard corporate takeover rules, when Spencer-Rudman bought *CompuWorld*, they also agreed to honor all commitments to its creditors (even though they were immediately killing off the title). Thanks to my letter, Raul Suarez's third-semester tuition at Faber was now going to be paid by Debbie's new employers.

"Like I told you at the party," Debbie said, "I owe you a lot."

"Keep in touch, Debbie."

The next morning, Monday, heavy snow returned to Manhattan. Lizzie had to go to the office—and I sat up in bed, watching in silence as she dressed. That's when it hit home. She was in a suit, I was in pajamas. She had a future, I didn't.

Sensing my gloom she said, "Do yourself a favor. Take a couple of days before calling the outplacement people. When you go in there, you want to give a confident impression. . . ."

"You're saying I look like a disaster?"

Lizzie was taken aback by my angry tone—but her voice remained considerate, soothing. "I'm just saying, you're still probably suffering from a bit of trauma. . . ."

"What are you, my goddamn shrink?"

She looked at me, stunned by what I had just said. So was I. Immediately, I was on my feet, burying my head in her shoulder. "I'm sorry, I'm sorry, I'm sorry." She disengaged herself, and took my face in her hands.

"Don't do this, Ned. Please."

"I really didn't mean . . ."

"I *am* on your side. Remember that."

"I do."

She gently kissed my forehead. "I've got to go. I'll call you later, see how you're doing."

As soon as she was gone, I collapsed back into bed, pulled the sheets over my head. How—*why*—could I have turned on her so viciously? Attacking the only real ally I had in life. She was right: I was suffering from aftershock. And I was in no state to put on a happy face in front of an outplacement counselor. I needed to stay indoors until my equilibrium was restored.

I reached for the phone. I called our local florist and arranged for a big bouquet of roses to be sent to Lizzie's office. I asked them to enclose a card with the following message:

I am so sorry.
I love you.

For the next few hours I lay slumped on our sofa, staring out at the snow. My hand was still hurting like hell. I popped more pain-killers. I dozed off, and woke an hour later to the sound of our intercom buzzer. Stumbling over to it, I hit the speaker button and heard a static-laden voice:

"This Edward Allen?"

"Uh-huh."

"Crosstown Messenger Service. Got a letter here for you."

I buzzed him in and waited by the door until he got off the elevator. He wore knee-high black boots.

"They make you do deliveries in a blizzard?" I asked.

"Yeah," came the voice from inside the helmet. "They do."

I signed for the letter, gave him a $5 tip, then ruefully thought, *You really can't be so loose with cash anymore.* With a nod, he turned and clumped down the hallway, as if powered by batteries.

The envelope was embossed with Spencer-Rudman's letter-head. Nervously, I tore it open. And read:

Edward Allen
16 West 20th Street
New York, NY 10011

Dear Mr. Allen:

As you know, *CompuWorld* ceased to exist as a title on January 2, 1998. Having been employed by the magazine since 1994, you are entitled, as part of the standard severance package, to two weeks pay per year of employment, plus any unpaid vacation time.

You are also entitled, under COBRA (Consolidated Omnibus Budget Reconciliation Act), to continue your corporate medical insurance for eighteen months (i.e., July 2, 1999). Your monthly premium was $326.90. Should you wish to enjoy continued coverage, please send us a check for this amount by February 1. Please ensure that all future Blue Cross payments reach us by the first day of each month.

According to our records, you took your allotted two weeks of vacation time during 1997. You are due eight weeks of pay (4 years × 2 weeks).

Your annual salary was $60,000, or $1,153.84 per week. This means that your eight weeks' pay comes to $9,230.76.

We note that on December 20, 1997, you wrote a letter on *CompuWorld* stationery to a Mr. Joseph Myers, the bursar at Faber Academy School, guaranteeing that a $4,500 tuition fee owed by a Miss Deborah Suarez, a former employee of *CompuWorld,* would be paid by the company. Our Legal Department informs us your former position at *CompuWorld* did not give you the authority to write such a letter, let alone guarantee such payment. By doing so, however, you have legally bound the company to honor this financial liability.

Our Legal Department informs us that we could file suit against you for impersonation. Given your recent loss of employment—and to spare you the costs involved in defending such a case—we have deducted the $4,500 sum involved from your final payment of $9,230.76. A check for $4,730.76 is enclosed.

Please be informed that, should you wish to contest this course of action, we will have no option but to file suit against you.

Should you have any further questions about this matter, please address your enquiries to Ms. Heather Nussbaum at Human Resources, Spencer-Rudman.

Sincerely,
Michael Krusiger
Director, Human Resources
Spencer-Rudman

I balled up the letter and tossed it at my window. Then I staggered over, picked it up, unballed it, and carefully removed the check that had been stapled to one corner. I couldn't afford to be throwing money away.

I fell back on the sofa, absently smoothing out the crumpled check on my knee. The bastards. Spencer-Rudman was a massive multinational corporation with an annual turnover well beyond the $3 billion mark. To them, 45 hundred bucks was chump change, the price of a pack of Juicy Fruit gum. To a guy like me—suddenly unemployed, in deep, serious debt—it was a small fortune. And yet, the vindictive shits insisted on sticking me with the bill, even though they knew I was only helping out Debbie. What does doing a good deed get you? *Nada*.

Given your recent loss of employment—and to spare you the costs involved in defending such a case . . . Such humane, charitable people! And then there was the business of my medical insurance. That spineless bastard at Human Resources told me I would "enjoy" company medical coverage for the next eighteen months. What he failed to mention was that I'd have to pay for it. $326.90 a month! First they rob you of your bonus. Then—to really kick you in the teeth when they know you're desperate—they nickel-and-dime you out of a miserable few thousand bucks.

The phone rang. I reached for it.

"Ivan here."

He sounded beyond despondent.

"I was going to call you today," I said.

"I was planning to visit you at the hospital, but when I called on Saturday they said you checked out. You still in pain?"

"Definitely. And how are you doing?"

"Considering bankruptcy court. My ass depended on that second bonus check. Eight-nine they owed me. And all of it was already spent."

"Tell me about it."

"And did you hear what happened over the weekend?"

"Do I want to?"

"I just got off the phone with Phil Sirio. Seems Chuck Zanussi called everyone on the Northeast outside sales team—Maduro, Bluehorn, and Phil—offering them jobs at *PC Globe*. Everyone, that is, except me."

I was on the verge of balling up that check again, but I stopped myself. "I don't believe it. Anyway, when Phil called me last night, he didn't mention he had a job offer."

"That's because Phil only got the call an hour ago. Then he phoned around, found out that Zanussi had called Maduro and Bluehorn yesterday, and wondered if I'd been offered anything."

"So they're all going to be licking Zanussi's ass at *PC Globe*?"

"Maduro and Bluehorn grabbed it, but Phil called Zanussi a scumbag and told him he'd rather work for the Department of Sanitation."

"He is a great man, Phil."

"Anyway, I spent the last hour trying to get through to Zanussi at his new office. Ten minutes ago, his secretary calls back: 'Mr. Zanussi wishes to inform you that there is no position for you with *PC Globe* or any other Spencer-Rudman publication.' "

"I'm really sorry, Ivan."

"I'm fucked, Ned. Finished."

"Ivan, it's just been seventy-two hours since all this went down. They put you in a program, right?"

"Yeah, some outplacement company called Gerard Flynn Associates."

"Same as me. Well, look, the bottom line is, they're there to get you a job. And they will find you something new. You'll land. I don't worry about you, pal."

This was a total lie. Our industry was a small one—and word would leak out that Ivan was the only member of the *CompuWorld* outside sales team not to be offered a job by Chuck Zanussi. Even if he did eventually find something, when his prospective employer called Chuck for the lowdown on Ivan, I doubted the vindictive sonofabitch would give him rave reviews. To Zanussi, Ivan and I were the two guys who nearly cost him his job. And he was going to make us both pay heavily for it.

"Thanks for the encouraging words," Ivan said. "I need them. You doing anything for lunch today?"

"Between the snow and my hand, I'm not really planning to leave the apartment."

"Tell you what," Ivan said. "You know I live right near Zabar's. I could pick up some cold cuts, a bunch of cheeses, a bottle of red, jump the subway, be down at your place within the hour."

I had enough reasons right then to stick my head in an oven.

"The pills they've got me on have really left me kind of zonked, Ivan."

"Understood, understood."

"See you at outplacement," I said. "And stop worrying."

"Man, I wish I had your calm."

But I was anything but calm. As soon as Ivan was off the phone, I reached for a legal pad and began filling it up with numbers. I was doing the math. And it didn't look encouraging:

ASSETS

CompuWorld settlement	**$ 4,730**
Savings	**8,000**
Stocks, bonds	**5,000**
401k	**9,600**
	$27,330

DEBTS

Chase (bridge loan)	**$25,000**
Credit cards:	
American Express (incl. Nevis vacation)	**9,100**
Diners (incl. Xmas gifts, etc.)	**6,255**
MasterCard	**940**
Visa (Dr. Gordon)	**3,200**
New York Health and Racquet Club (annual fee)	**795**
Barneys store card	**1,250**
	$46,540

MINIMUM MONTHLY OUTGOINGS

Rent (my share)		$ 1,750
Medical insurance		326
Con Ed	say	50
Phone	say	75
Food	say	320
Cable		30
Insurance: home, contents, etc (excl. health)		125
Eating out/entertainment (my share)		800
		$ 3,476

If I cut out restaurants, bars, buying new clothes, books, and CDs, going to the movies, or even dropping $3 on this month's *GQ*—if, in short, I never left the apartment—I could probably eke out a very rudimentary living on $2,676 a month. That's $32,112 a year after taxes—which meant (factoring in federal, city, and state) I would still have to earn well over $55,000 per annum. Unbelievable. And that fifty-five grand was based on dividing the costs evenly between Lizzie and myself. One hundred thousand bucks a year for a minimal New York existence. No wonder I had landed myself in such debt. No wonder my stomach was now feeling ulcerated. If I liquidated the modest amounts of stocks, bonds, and savings I had put aside, I would still have to find $19,210 to clear the remaining debt.

If only I had been a little more prudent during my *CompuWorld* years and built up some sort of finanical fuck-up fund, earmarked for a bad time like this. But I was a high roller—Mr. Fast Lane—who considered himself Teflon tough, resistant to all corporate harm or damage, always able to produce the goods when the heat was on.

But then I threw those punches. And . . .

Don't panic, don't panic. Maybe Lizzie was right: Prospective employers would look at my overall record and not judge me solely on one irrational act. In an interview I could convince them that I had been reacting to extraordinary circumstances, extraordinary pressures. And that—given the chance—I'd be the biggest moneymaker their company had ever seen. I mean, did you see how *CompuWorld* came out of nowhere to surpass *Computer America* as the number-two computer magazine in the country? Now I'm not trying to take credit for its market-share resurgence, but—put it this way—in the course of the sixteen months I was running Northeast, our regional advertising revenues tripled. And the relationships I forged with the biggest names in our industry . . .

Once a salesman, always a . . .

But now I was a desperate salesman. $19,210 worth of desperation. I couldn't afford a long convalescence. I needed to get back into the game. Now.

So I reached for the phone and called Gerard Flynn Associates, and made an appointment with my outplacement facilitator for the next morning.

Which is how I came to be sitting opposite Ms. Nancy Auerbach on this still-snowy Tuesday morning, listening to her finish her telephone conversation with some poor sucker who didn't want to "relo" to Rochester, watching her sneak looks at my bandaged hand, and wondering if she had already filed me away under *Hopeless Cases*.

". . . I said it once, Matt, I said it before—it's your call. You don't want the position, you pass on it, and we go back to the drawing board. But I wouldn't write Rochester off completely. . . . Okay, okay, it's not Paris. . . . Look, we'll have to wrap it up here, I'm in with a client. . . . This time tomorrow is just fine."

She hung up and turned back to me with a forced professional smile.

"Sorry about that, Ned. How's the hand?"

"Still broken."

"A sense of humor. I like it. Humor's really important at a time like this. So is perspective. And—just to kick things off, to start broadly identifying areas of mutual concern—I'd like to ask you this: What is the single biggest concern in your mind right now?"

I met her gaze and said, "Will anyone ever hire me again?"

Her eyes glanced down yet again at my ink-colored fingers. Then she nodded several times, absently biting her lower lip. And in her most logical, rational, I'm-going-to-choose-my-words-carefully tone of voice, she said, "That strikes me as a very sensible concern."

TWO

There were ten of us seated around a table. Eight men, two women. We all wore suits. Age distribution: thirty to mid-fifties. Educational level: minimum, bachelor's degree. Previous mean income: around $75,000. Professional level: middle-management to senior executive. Current job status: all unemployed.

It was 8:30 in the morning on day eight of The Program, and I was about to attend my first seminar on interview techniques. On days six and seven, I sat through classes on subjects like "Getting the Resumé Right" and "Reinventing Yourself in the Information Age" and "Maximizing Personal Strengths After Downsizing." I hadn't wanted to attend any of these "workshops." In fact, earlier the previous week—around day two—I thought that my days on The Program were happily numbered. Because, out of the blue, a job dropped right into my lap.

It happened on Wednesday morning—the day after my first meeting with Nancy Auerbach. The meeting where we identified "career destination goals," and "optimum landing places," and discussed "crafting an advantageous exit statement." The meeting where she admitted that my search for a new position was going to be "a challenging quest."

It was also the meeting where I began to decipher some of her language. *To land*—in outplacement-spiel—meant to find a job. *The exit statement* was the explanation you'd give on your resumé (and, eventually, in an interview) as to why you'd been shown the door by your previous employers.

"Now if, off the top of my head, I were to craft an exit statement for you," she said, "I'd probably write something like, 'Having spent four years as the Northeast's regional sales manager—during which time my division increased its market share by 300 percent—I was downsized when Spencer-Rudman bought the title and decided to close it down.' Short and sweet. Pointing out that you were a success at your job, while also highlighting the fact that your termination came as a result of a corporate takeover, rather than anything of a negative performance nature."

"You mean, like assaulting the group publishing director."

A pinched smile from Nancy Auerbach.

"I like that sense of humor," she said.

"But that is going to be a stumbling block, isn't it?"

"It does create certain impediments. . . ."

"Which are going to make it downright impossible for me to get hired anywhere."

She paused and looked carefully at me.

"You obviously don't want me to sugar the pill?"

I nodded.

"You want it straight?"

I nodded again.

"Okay, I'll give it to you straight. You're in big fucking trouble."

I winced—not because of her prognosis, but because I never expected the very patrician Ms. Auerbach to use bad language. She saw that and gave me a small, mischievous grin.

"I do gather, however, that the man you assaulted was a suitable candidate for a fat lip. What we have to do is make a prospective employer understand that. And also understand that, if they hire you, they won't need extra dental insurance."

"Sounds like an uphill task."

"Let me put it this way: If I can get you to land, then I have scored one of the biggest against-the-odds wins of my career."

The next morning—just as I was knotting my tie (no easy thing with three fractured fingers) and preparing myself for day two of The Program—the phone rang. It was Nancy Auerbach.

"Do I have news for you. Ever heard of a guy called Phil Goodwin?"

"Sure. He's the publisher of *Computer America*. I met him a couple of times at trade shows. Pretty nice guy—considering that he was our main competitor in the marketplace."

"Well, he certainly remembers you. More important, he rates you."

This *was* news. "Really?" I said.

"That's what he said when he called me this morning, wondering if you were still in the market for a job."

I felt a sudden surge of adrenaline. "Are you serious?"

"Completely. His exact words were 'Ned Allen is one of the ballsiest sales guys in the industry. If he's free, I want him.' "

I felt a very pleasant second surge of adrenaline. Followed by a wave of worry. "But he doesn't know about the Kreplin business, does he?"

"Ned—everyone in your industry now knows about that incident. You've become the stuff of legend. But when I raised the matter with Goodwin, he actually seemed more amused about it than anything else. Said something like, 'I respect a sales guy who can throw a right.' Anyway, there's an opening at his magazine for a group sales director, overseeing all regional sales departments, coast to coast. Eighty thousand basic pay. Profit participation. Usual medical benefits. Interested?"

Group sales director of *Computer America*? It wasn't just a fantastic upward career move; it was also a kick in the ass to Chuck Zanussi. It would restore my professional credibility overnight.

"When can I see Goodwin?" I asked.

"He was wondering if you were free today at lunchtime."

We met at the Union Square Café, right around the corner from the *Computer America* offices on Park Avenue South. Phil Goodwin wasn't your typical corporate man. On the contrary, he had something of a swashbuckling reputation. Fifty-five, a shoot-from-the-hip mouth, a fondness for booze, a walrus mustache, bold chalk-stripe suits, and about the surest touch of any publisher in the computer marketplace.

As I approached his table, he mockingly put his hands up in front of his face, as if shielding himself from a blow. Then he pointed to the half-empty martini glass in front of him and asked, "You drink these?"

"Definitely."

"Then we might be able to work together. I hate designer-water wimps."

I sat down. He motioned to the waiter for two more martinis.

"So let me ask you something: Did Kreplin even see it coming?"

"No. It was pretty instantaneous. Even surprised me."

"I met the guy once or twice. Oily little Hun. Think you won yourself some friends when you punched out his lights—that is, as long as you don't make a habit of slugging any of your other bosses in the future."

The martinis arrived. "Here's to fisticuffs," Goodwin said. He took a long, deep sip, flipped open the menu, and told the waiter, "We'll order right now." Then, turning to me, he said, "As soon as this guy disappears with our order, you start talking—and tell me exactly why I should give you this job. But as soon as he's back here with the appetizer, your sales pitch is over. Understand?"

After the waiter disappeared, I sprang into action, giving Goodwin my own spin on the state of the computer magazine market, now that *CompuWorld* was dead. Then I explained how, through subtle repositioning, *Computer America* could not only claim the high-end advertisers and readership (once held by *CompuWorld*), but could also start to elbow in on *PC Globe*'s virtual domination of the middle market. It was a variation on the same spiel I had given to Kreplin when he offered me the publisher's job—only carefully tailored to *Computer America*'s requirements, and free of any self-glorifying bullshit. Because I knew full well that Phil Goodwin hated pretension of any variety. Just as I was wrapping things up, our waiter positioned himself in such a way to indicate to me that he was about to arrive with our appetizers. So, knowing how Goodwin also liked to think of business as a contact sport, I decided to end with a flourish:

"I don't want to maintain the status quo—because now we're in a head-to-head situation with *PC Globe*. It's war. And believe me—given what's gone down over the last couple of days—I want to win that war. It's personal."

The appetizers arrived. Goodwin tossed back the dregs of his martini and called for the wine list.

"Okay," he finally said to me. "You're hired."

I was dumbfounded. "Just like that?" I asked.

"It's my company, my magazine, I can do whatever the hell I like. So if I say you're onboard, then you're onboard. You start Monday. Now what are we going to drink with the food?"

I left the Union Square Café at 3:00 P.M., elated. I was also feeling a little otherworldly. This wasn't due to the amount of booze I'd had, but the way the alcohol and my painkillers had begun to interact. Just around the time I said good-bye to Phil Goodwin and began walking west, a fog descended on my brain, making the world seem dark, murky, full of strange shadows. Though my apartment was just five blocks away, I jumped in a cab. I made it home just as my stomach began to palpitate and swell, the damp claw of nausea grabbed me by the throat, and a projectile torrent of vomit baptized our very white sofa.

Staggering into the bedroom, I pitched forward, collapsing in a heap on the bed. The plug was pulled—and the next thing I knew, Lizzie was yelling in my ear, shaking me hard.

"Ned, Ned, *Ned* . . ."

I groaned and rolled over. The sheets were drenched with sweat, and my mouth tasted like a toxic waste dump. I managed a couple of words.

"Sick. I got sick. . . ."

"I'm calling a doctor," she said, reaching for the phone.

"Don't bother. The worst's over."

"What the hell happened?"

"I think the painkillers didn't mix with booze."

"You were sitting here, drinking on your own?" she said, aghast.

"I had a lunch. Phil Goodwin, publisher of *Computer America*. He likes to drink. I wasn't thinking."

"You idiot. You could have died."

"I'm sorry, I'm real . . ."

"I'm calling Dr. Morgan. . . ."

"Don't, please," I said, knowing that I didn't want a barbiturates-and-booze incident on my medical records. "I just need a shower."

I wobbled my way into the bathroom, threw off my soiled clothes, and stood under a very cold downpour of water until some feeling of coherence returned. Then I brushed my teeth, following that with an extended, two-minute gargle with Listerine which finally expunged that delightful aftertaste of vomit from my mouth. Picking up my clothes, I dumped them in the laundry bin, put on a white terry cloth robe, and prepared to face the music.

The sodden sheets were already stripped from the bed. Lizzie was in the living room, her hands covered with kitchen gloves, trying to clean the vomit-covered sofa with paper towels.

"I'll do that," I said.

"Don't bother," she said, not looking up at me. "It's ruined."

"I'll have it re-covered."

"How?"

"I've got a new job. Group sales director at *Computer America*. That's what the lunch was all about."

"Congratulations," she said flatly.

"You don't sound pleased."

She pointed to the stained sofa. "You have one hell of a way of celebrating your success."

"I wasn't thinking."

"You've not been doing a lot of thinking the past few days."

"I'm sorry."

"And you've been using that word far too much recently."

"I'm sor . . ."

I stopped myself and smiled at her. "Point taken."

"You worry me sometimes."

"It's just been a bad couple of days."

"I hope so."

"And things are on the up-and-up. I've landed."

She glanced back at the sofa. "In more ways than one."

The next morning, after Lizzie went to work, I called Nancy Auerbach and told her the great news.

"What can I say?" she said. "Except, you do surprise me, Ned."

"There's one less downsizing victim for your books. Thanks for playing the go-between."

"You pulled it off, Ned. Not me."

I worked the phones and found an upholsterer who could have our sofa re-covered in the same white canvas fabric within a few weeks. Miracle of miracles, he also had a spare van on hand that afternoon and could pick the now rank couch up at 2:00 P.M. The price of the total job: a thousand bucks. It made me wince. That had been a very expensive blown lunch.

I ran down to my local grocery store, picked up the recent editions of *PC Globe* and *Computer America,* then spent the morning comparing and contrasting their editorial and advertising content, while also checking my *CompuWorld* database for solid accounts I could probably seduce over to my new title. I worked steadily all afternoon, breaking only once to help the workmen remove the sofa. By five I had written the first draft of a marketing strategy for *Computer America*—a plan which I hoped to messenger over to Phil Goodwin first thing the next morning, just to let him know that I was hitting the ground running.

Then the phone rang. "Ned Allen?" asked the woman on the line. "Please hold for a call from Mr. Goodwin."

"Phil," I said when he came on, "I was just sitting here, working on a battle plan for the . . ."

"Ned," he said, "sorry to piss on your parade, but we've got a problem here."

My fractured fingers suddenly began to throb. "Problem? What problem?"

"You know a shithead named Ted Peterson?"

Oh, no . . .

"I know him."

"He called me today on some other related matter, and during the course of the conversation, I mentioned that you were going to be taking over here as group sales director. Within five seconds, the guy went ballistic. Telling me how you were a deceitful sonofabitch whom he refused to work with . . ."

"Me, deceitful?" I said. "The only reason that guy has it in for me is because I forced him to honor a deal he made with one of our sales people; a deal on which he tried to renege—"

"Whatever," Phil Goodwin said, cutting me off. "The bottom line, Ned, is this: Peterson made it very clear that if you came aboard here, he'd switch the focus of the GBS account to *PC Globe* and other print media."

"He's talking garbage. GBS just can't walk away from a major outlet like *Computer America*."

"That may be, but what's troubling me is that he also said that he'd been talking to his fellow media sales guys at NMI, AdTel, Icon, et cetera, et cetera . . . and none of them will now have anything to do with you."

This was the abyss.

"Phil, please, *listen*. Peterson wasn't dealing kosher, so I played a moral card and forced him . . ."

"I don't care if he dresses up as his mother for kicks. The fact remains: GBS is our biggest advertiser. Believe me, I think Peterson is a punk. But my magazine's commercial health depends on his ad input. So—while I don't like giving in to threats—I still have to take onboard his concerns. . . ."

"I'm sure that in a very short time I could easily establish some sort of détente with him. . . ."

"How short a time? Two, three, four months? Sorry, Ned—it's a tough marketplace, I'm still an independent, and I can't afford to lose that amount of revenue."

"We can cover that. . . ."

"Not if the guys at NMI, AdTel, et cetera don't want to do business with you. . . ."

"I know these guys. They'll come around."

"Ned, I just can't take the risk."

"At least give me the chance to . . ."

"This gives me no pleasure—because I really think you're a winner. But—I'm promoting a guy from within the organization as group sales director. He's not in your league—but at least he doesn't have your enemies. Sorry, Ned. And good luck to you. I'm sure you'll land."

The line went dead.

I furiously dialed Nancy Auerbach's direct line. She was still at the office.

"Now, first things first," she said after I gave her a distraught account of my conversation with Phil Goodwin. "Try to calm down."

"That fuck Peterson is ruining me, and you're telling me to be calm!" I was screaming.

There was a very long silence on the phone; a silence which I finally broke.

"I apologize . . ."

"No need. I get screamed at by clients all the time. Part of the territory. You calmer now?"

"A little, yeah."

"Then I think you better face up to something right away. Between the Kreplin business and this guy Peterson, you have no future in the computer magazine business. That phase of your career is over."

I swallowed hard. It was like being told you were being deported from the country in which you planned to spend the rest of your life. Nancy Auerbach sensed my despondency.

"I know this is hard, a real blow. And totally unfair. But that's the way it is. It's a crisis. But remember: In Chinese, the character for 'crisis' means two things—danger and opportunity. Try to think of this as a time of opportunity. And come see me tomorrow."

Later that night, as I sat across the dinner table from Lizzie, I said, "You know what gets me most about this whole business? The fact that it was a dumb little chain of events that set it off. And I keep thinking, if only the company hadn't been sold . . . if only Ivan hadn't lost the GBS account . . . if only Kreplin hadn't offered me the job . . . if only I'd been totally straight with Chuck . . ."

"It's the way things work," Lizzie said gently, taking my hand. "Everyone's a victim of circumstance. And hindsight is just a convenient way of beating yourself up. Your outplacement counselor is right: Consider this a moment of opportunity. And please stop drinking. I really don't want a repeat of yesterday's episode."

I reached for the bottle of red wine in the middle of the table and refilled my glass.

"I've stopped taking the painkillers."

"It's your fifth glass tonight."

"It's only my third. And it never used to trouble you before."

She gave me a sad stare. "Well, it's troubling me now."

I went to see Nancy Auerbach the next morning.

"We're back to ground zero," she said. "And we have to rethink your objectives. If I were to ask you, What's your one true talent? what would you reply?"

"I'm a born salesman."

"Then sales it is."

As I quickly discovered, the Gerard Flynn Associates weren't responsible for getting you a job. Like all outplacement agencies, they acted as a resource center, a place which was plugged into the job market and knew which company was looking for what sort of executive at any given time. They tried their best to match up its clients with corporate employers—but, as Nancy Auerbach reminded me from the outset, it was the client who inevitably found himself a new job.

"We can give you tips on positions that are open, you can use our huge employer database to make contacts, we can teach you how to rewrite your resumé and knock 'em dead in an interview, but, in the end, it's you who has to land. And remember: You only have eight weeks with us. That's forty working days. So make each day count."

Having squandered the first week—courtesy of the *Computer America* disaster—I went into high gear. I spent the mornings in seminars, the afternoons and early evenings working my way through the agency's job database and polishing up my resumé. And on day eight, I sat at that conference table with seven other out-of-work managers, listening to an executive retrainer named Mel Tucker take us through the advanced basics of interview techniques.

Mel Tucker was in his early fifties, balding, built like a cue ball, with a hangdog mustache and a deadpan comedian's delivery.

"Okay, folks—let's get things rolling," he said, standing in front of a chalkboard at one end of the conference room. "Now, at the start, I want to make one thing clear: I'm not here to talk about the theory of interviewing, because there is only one theory of interviewing: It's all about *you* getting the information across.

"The good interviewers are lazy. The bad interviewers are worse. 'So, tell me about yourself.' . . . 'So, Ken, if you were a car, what sort of car would you be?' . . . 'If you could be anywhere in the world right now, where would you be?' . . . You're going to be asked all sorts of dumb questions. But remember this: It's not always the most qualified person who wins in an interview situation; it's the best-prepared person. And so here's a simple no-brainer for all of you to keep in mind before going in for that interview: *Do research.*

"Get to know the job—and I do not mean the title. Sell to the need of the buyer. Don't go in there and tell the guy, 'I do ten things,' because he'll turn around and say to you, 'I don't need ten things—I just need three things, none of which you've got.'

"In this marketplace today, it's not what *you* think they need. It's what *they* need."

He looked out at the eight of us, then pointed to me.

"Okay, you're my first victim, Mr. . . ."

I introduced myself.

"Right, Mr. Allen. Here's a question you're bound to be asked in an interview: Why were you fired?"

I shifted nervously in my seat.

"Bad body language," Mel Tucker said. "You scream nervousness."

I immediately sat still, looked him straight in the eye, and said: "I was a victim of downsizing."

"'*A victim of downsizing,*'" Mel Tucker said loudly. "Sounds like a bunch of guys in ski masks broke into your house and downsized you."

Even I found myself laughing.

"The point here is: Be clinical. Be unemotional about an emotional event. 'They went through A . . . then B happened.' Get on and off the subject as fast as possible. It's like that other great stupid interview question: 'What are your weak points?' Believe it or not, people ask it. With one question, we go from an interview to a therapy session. One client I had—and I'm not joking around—said, 'I'm a spitter. I spit a lot when I talk. And because I'm apprehensive about spitting, I get stressed.' Know what the interviewer must have thought? 'Oh, great—a spitter who probably turns violent.'"

On saying the word *violent,* Mel Tucker stared for the briefest of moments at my bandaged hand. And I thought, *He knows. They all know.*

"And say you come up against that dumber-than-dumb question, 'Define yourself in three words.' Remember: 'Armed and dangerous' is not an option."

More raucous laughter from the class. Was he scoring points off me? Or was I just being paranoid?

At noon we took a break for lunch.

"Hey, Mr. Allen," Mel Tucker said as I was leaving the room, "hope you didn't mind me teasing you about the 'victim-of-downsizing' comment."

"I am not violent," I found myself saying. "No matter what you think, I really don't go around punching people."

He looked at me wide-eyed. That's when I knew I was really being paranoid.

"I take your word for it, Mr. Allen. If you say you're not violent, I'm sure you're not. The thing is, the thought never crossed my mind that you *were* violent."

I now felt beyond embarrassed. "Glad to hear it," I mumbled, and left the room quickly.

It's the shock, I told myself as I walked down the corridor toward the elevator. *You're like a man who's just stumbled into an empty elevator shaft. You're dropping down so fast you can't believe what is happening to you. And you're desperately trying to clutch at something,* anything, *that will break your fall.*

I pressed the "down" button and waited for the elevator to arrive. As the door opened, Ivan Dolinsky walked out. He was a changed man. His grief-laden eyes were bright and animated. His shoulders were no longer slumped. He even had a smile on his face.

"Ned, great to see you," he said, throwing an arm around me and giving me a big hug.

"Afternoon, Ivan. You feeling okay?"

"Never better. In fact, today I've decided something: There is a God."

"Glad to hear it," I said. "What gives?"

His smile was now incandescent.

"I've landed," he said.

THREE

Leave it to Ivan. Just when the guy looked like he was about to drive off the cliff, he suddenly slammed on the brakes, reversed gears, and pulled off something of a coup.

"I've landed."

The job wasn't exactly glamorous—but at least it was *a job*. Over lunch at a little Italian place on Thirty-sixth and Madison where Ivan insisted on dragging me ("My treat, Ned"), he told me that he was now the new tristate sales guy for *Home Computer Monthly,* a new mid-market glossy aimed solely at the suburban domestic market.

"Let's face it," Ivan said, "we're not talking about a magazine in the same league as *CompuWorld.* And the job means a re-lo to Hartford."

"Insurance capital of America."

"Yeah—and not exactly the city that never sleeps. Still, I'm going to be on the road most of the time, the cost of living up there is about a third less than in this town, and what's great about the job is that it's helping build something from the ground floor up."

"Who's backing the title?"

"TransContinental Communications. Ever heard of them?"

Yep. A bargain-basement outfit. Publishers of such cutting-edge titles as *Supermarket Today* and *International Dental Technology* and *VCR Choice*. Not exactly Condé Nast—and notoriously cheap when it came to remunerating its employees.

"Who hasn't heard of TransContinental?" I said. "Is the package decent?"

"Like I said, it's not the major leagues."

"Forty?"

"Thirty-five. Plus seven percent commission on all sales. Major medical after six months. And a three-grand re-lo fee which will pay off a couple of bills."

Just as I thought—a substandard deal, only attractive to the truly desperate. Like Ivan. Or me.

"I've heard of worse packages," I said, trying to sound upbeat.

"Believe me, I'm not fooling myself into thinking that this is a Rolls-Royce deal. And to make the math work, I'm going to have to close at least five hundred thousand a year. But, hey, at least it's a job. Some kind of a future."

He raised his glass of house Chianti and clinked it against mine. "Good times ahead for both of us, Ned."

I felt like asking him, *what good times?* Just as I also felt like verbally assaulting him for setting off the chain of events that cost me the *Computer America* job. But, as always with Ivan, I stopped myself from going on the warpath. It was my call to challenge Peterson on his doorstep—to intimate I had something on him—and I paid one heavy price. Anyway, this was the first time since the death of Nancy that I'd seen Ivan looking even remotely pleased with life, and I certainly wasn't going to ruin his day.

"Are you close to landing yet?" he asked me.

"There are a couple of things brewing," I said. "I'm not worried."

Naturally, I was lying like a rug. And over the next four weeks, my alarm intensified. Because not only was I failing to land, I wasn't getting even a single whiff of employment possibilities. Not that I wasn't trying. I was at Gerard Flynn Associates from 8:30 every morning until they finally closed up shop at 7:00 P.M. I had my own little workstation in their database section, and (when I wasn't learning how to sell my ass in the workshop sessions) I spent much of the day surfing the Net in search of job prospects. I must have sent out over a hundred resumés, to everything from the big magazine companies (Hearst, Condé Nast, and Murdoch all wrote back, saying there were no sales positions open at present), to the glossies that specialized in audio/video/cameras/electronics, to around two dozen big marketing agencies. Again, no dice—though the sales director at *Stereo Review* at least had the decency to call me up at my so-called office (my workstation had a direct line) to tell me that he was impressed with my credentials.

"You're exactly the sort of guy we're after," said Mr. Stereo Review. "Perfect sales background for the kind of high-end thing we do here. The problem is, Ned—and it's the reason I decided to phone you—I called the personnel department at Spencer-Rudman, since they were the last owners of *CompuWorld*. Now, the guy there told me that you assaulted a superior, and were subsequently arrested for the attack. Please tell me this isn't true."

"The charges were dropped. And the reason I hit the guy—"

"So you actually did assault someone on the job?"

"There were extenuating circumstances. . . ."

"I don't care what sort of circumstances there were, Ned. I just can't hire anybody with that sort of blot on their record."

"If I could just explain—"

"Sorry, Ned. Impressive resumé, but . . . who's to say you won't strike someone again?"

It was pretty obvious why I wasn't getting beyond a "sorry-no-vacancies" letter from any of the hundred companies to whom I'd written. Whenever a personnel director ran a check on my employment record, Spencer-Rudman told them the same thing: *Don't go near him if you value your teeth.* Of course, I knew that this was going to happen—but I'd been hoping against hope that someone might just forget to run that check.

At the end of week five of The Program, I asked Nancy Auerbach, "Is there any way that I could stop employers from calling Spencer-Rudman?"

"Only if you completely excise *CompuWorld* from your resumé."

"Sounds like a good idea to me."

"Then how are you going to explain away the last four years? A stint in the French foreign legion?"

"I could say I was . . . I don't know . . . studying, traveling . . ."

"That makes you look like some aging flower child—not a savvy thirty-something professional. Anyway, say someone did hire you on the basis of a resumé that didn't include *CompuWorld*, and then subsequently found out that you'd spent four years with them? You'd be out on your fanny before you had a chance to breathe. Sorry, Ned—like I told you on day one, this is going to be a tough call. But can I give you a piece of advice?"

I shrugged.

"Stop chasing everything in the tristate area. Start thinking about re-lo. The way I figure it, a smaller organization in a second- or third-tier city might overlook the Kreplin business in order to snag someone with big-time experience like yourself. Especially if you can convince them you were under extreme pressure at the time."

"My wife's career is totally New York-based," I said. "She wouldn't want to leave."

"How can you know that," Nancy Auerbach said, "until you ask her?"

But I didn't want to ask her—because, to me, the idea of finding employment outside of New York was an admission of defeat. It would be like a demotion to the minor leagues after an extended stint with the Yankees—and I wasn't willing to consider such a regressive step yet. What's more, circumstances between Lizzie and me were definitely not "right enough" to even consider broaching the issue of a potential move away from Manhattan. Within a week of being fired, my severance package was gone—eaten up by minor necessities like my share of January's rent, the recent telephone bill, and the bank deposit I'd made to pay my health insurance premiums over the next twelve months.

That was over a month earlier. Since that time I had become a kept man—financially reliant on Lizzie for everything.

And everything *meant* everything. When Chase Manhattan Bank began to make "we-have-run-out-of-patience" noises in late January and threatened legal action to recover their $25,000 bridge loan (well, I had missed six payments in a row), I made a radical decision. I liquidated all my remaining assets (stocks, savings, the remnants of my 401k) and paid off the debt in one go. But this meant that I was still $19,000 in the hole to a variety of plastic money folk. More troubling, I had no cash of my own.

It was Lizzie who convinced me to kill the Chase Manhattan

debt. She had always been horrified by my reliance on bridge loans to finance my heavy spending habits.

"The important thing right now," she said, "is that you clear up as many financial obligations as possible—and not get yourself further in the red. Don't worry—I can keep us going until you find something."

Public relations has never been one of the most high-paying businesses. And though Lizzie was a high-flyer at her firm, her take-home pay was around $800 a week. Not bad when we were both working—but having been transformed into a single-income family, we didn't get very far on her $3,200 per month. The $2,200 tab on our apartment left us just a thousand bucks a month to feed, clothe, and heat ourselves. Eating out became a thing of the past, cabs a total luxury. I divested myself of such superfluous items as my cellular phone (it went back to the company from which I leased it). A movie a week became our night out (unless, of course, Lizzie was entertaining clients on the corporate account). And every Monday morning she left me $100 spending money for the week.

To her infinite credit, she never once complained about our diminished financial circumstances. Whereas I, on the other hand, felt increasingly guilty about my dependency.

One Saturday, around five weeks into The Program, Lizzie and I were taking a stroll through SoHo and paused to stare at a women's sleek black suit in the window of Agnes B.

"Overpriced Parisian chic," Lizzie said.

"It would look great on you," I said.

"Sure it would," she said with a laugh.

"Let's buy it now," I suddenly said.

"I was just joking. . . ."

"Come on," I said, gently pushing her toward the door. "Let's get it."

"I don't need it. I don't want it. And anyway, we can't afford it."

"I've got some room on my MasterCard."

"Don't be crazy. It's probably a thousand bucks. . . ."

"I can buy you this," I said angrily.

"Why are you doing this?"

"You want the suit, I want—"

"Ned, *please* . . . Let's just keep walking."

"Why won't you let me . . . ?"

"You know why. Now stop." Her tone was testy.

My shoulders slumped. "Okay," I said quietly.

She linked her arm with mine. "Let's get a coffee somewhere."

We ended up at the News Café, two blocks south on West Broadway. Nonstop CNN on the video monitors. The usual gaggle of bridge-and-tunnel folk pretending they're downtown trendies for the weekend. *I bet every one of you bastards has a job. I bet you can buy your squeeze whatever the hell you want.*

"Tell you what," I said to Lizzie, "as soon as I'm back at work, that suit's yours."

She sighed loudly and shook her head. "You can't stop, can you?"

"Stop what?"

"Stop obsessing about the fact that I'm supporting you. . . ."

"I just don't want to be dependent . . ."

"On me?"

"Yes."

"Great. Just great."

"What have I said wrong?"

"Nothing, nothing . . ."

"I'm turning into a burden and it's worrying me. . . ."

"You are definitely *not* a burden."

"We're broke—because of me."

"It's only for a little while. You'll find something. But what you have to do, meanwhile, is just accept things as they are. I now pay the bills. I'm happy to pay the bills. Just like I'm happy to clear some of your debts."

"No way will I let you . . ."

"Well, I already have."

I looked at her with alarm.

"You did *what*?"

"I paid off some of your Diners Club bill yesterday."

"How much, exactly?"

She met my angry gaze.

"Five thousand dollars."

"Five grand? Are you nuts?"

She reached for my hand, but I pulled it away. "Please . . . ," she said.

"How dare you . . . ?"

"I was just trying to help. I mean, I know how much the watch and the vacation cost you. And I had a little extra cash in my money market account, so . . ."

"My debts are *my* problem, not yours."

"If you're in trouble, then it is my problem. And I'm happy to help you. . . ."

"I don't want your fucking help," I blurted out.

There was a long silence. Lizzie looked at me with total despair. In a near whisper, she finally said:

"Did you hear what you just said?"

"I didn't mean . . ."

She stared out the window of the café, biting hard on her lip.

"Forget it, Ned," she finally said. "Just forget it."

That Monday morning a letter arrived from American Express informing me that my "membership entitlements" were suspended until I settled the outstanding debt of $9,100—which, now being two months overdue, was also subject to a 2.5 percent interest fee per month. In the same mail was a kiss-off note from the New York Health and Racquet Club, ending my membership due to my ongoing failure to fork over the $795 annual fee. I tossed this letter immediately in my "circular file." My right hand was still in bad shape. I had trouble gripping a pen, let alone a racquet. Considering my other problems, being expelled from the New York Health and Racquet Club was something I could live with.

I knew that the American Express letter was just the first in a series of threatening dispatches soon to land on my doormat from MasterCard, Visa, and Barneys. I also knew that—thanks to the usurious rates charged by the plastic money companies—my 17 grand worth of credit-card debt would increase by $425 per month. If I wasn't in a position to clear that debt over the next twelve months . . . presto—it would magically swell to nearly $23,000, growing like cancer at nearly $600 a month.

I had to find some way of getting out of this hole. Fast.

So I finally took Nancy Auerbach's advice and spent much of week six of The Program sending resumés to around a dozen sales and marketing companies outside the tristate area. I restricted myself to corporations within an hour's flight time of New York, thinking that maybe I could commute home on the weekends . . . or, better yet, that I could become the New York–based representative of some out-of-town firm. Within days, a dozen letters arrived care of Gerard Flynn Associates, informing me that none of the companies were in the market for sales personnel at the moment, but they would keep my resumé on file, *blah, blah, blah.*

"I'm getting very worried," I told Nancy Auerbach at the beginning of week seven.

"I can appreciate that," she said.

"I'm totally broke. I need something ASAP."

"Like I said at the outset of the program, we're not miracle workers. We simply function in a consulting capacity. And you know the major obstacle that is impeding you. As I've told you over and over again, we can't wave a magic wand and expunge that from your record. It's always going to be there. You'll simply have to work with the problem."

"In other words, accept that I'm unemployable."

"You're saying that, Ned. Not me."

That night, while Lizzie was out with a client and I was about to squander a portion of my week's money on an $11 pepperoni pizza ordered in from Domino's, Nancy called.

"Your luck may be changing," she said. "Late this afternoon, I got a phone call from a guy I know named Dave Judelson. Used to be a big-deal headhunter in Atlanta. Around two years ago, he got lured to Charlotte, North Carolina, to start up a major headhunting firm there. Anyway, one of the companies he represents, InfoSystems USA, is in the market for a senior guy to take charge of media sales for their company. Now I know this would mean going to the other side of the desk—but, hell, wouldn't you rather be a buyer for a while?"

"Not in Charlotte, North Carolina," I said.

"Last week, you were sending resumés out to Boston, Philly, Baltimore, Washington . . ."

"Yeah—but there's a big difference between Boston and Charlotte."

"Hang on: Charlotte's a real boomtown. One of the fastest-growing banking centers in the country, and also a new favorite among midsize software and information technology companies looking for a cost-effective base without crippling overheads. Now, okay, I haven't been there, but from what my spies tell me, the QOL is really first rate. . . ."

"QOL?"

"Quality of Life. They've got their own NFL and NBA teams, a couple of theaters, a symphony orchestra, good restaurants . . ."

"You know what I said about re-lo. I mean, if I had landed something in Boston or Philly . . . but move to some third-tier city like Charlotte? No way."

"Just hear me out. I faxed Judelson your resumé, and gave you this really big buildup, talking about how you're a born operator, a straight shooter, Mr. One-hundred-ten percent . . . and someone who had an out-of-character experience with his former German employer. Well, ten minutes ago he called back, having spoken to the InfoSystem people, and they want to fly you down the day after tomorrow for an interview. So why don't you talk it over with your wife. . . ."

"Like I told you before, my wife's career is here in New York."

She gave me a skeptical laugh.

"That's your excuse and you're sticking to it, right?"

"Leaving New York just isn't in my game plan."

"Ned, as I've told you before, you are in no position to let pride cloud your judgment. And, who knows? Your wife might really like the idea of leaving the Manhattan circus for a while. There are plenty of public relations opportunities in Charlotte.

"Ask her, for Christ's sake. And, while you're at it, tell her that the base salary is fifty-five thousand, with a generous profit participation plan, a company car, major medical, four months free housing until you find a place, and—here's the real icing on the cake—an incentive fee of twenty grand for the lucky guy who lands the job."

Twenty grand. I would be debt free.

"Are there any strings attached to that incentive fee?" I asked.

"So you *are* interested," Nancy Auerbach said with a laugh.

"I'm just asking."

"They want a minimum twenty-four-month commitment. But

should they decide to part company with you before then, you keep it all."

"Sounds pretty reasonable. Too bad it's two years in North Carolina."

"Welcome to Life . . . where you never get what you want. But, given your circumstances, I don't think you can afford to be too contemptuous of Charlotte. Go on, ask Lizzie. *Tonight*. And call me first thing in the morning."

Twenty grand. Twenty grand. Twenty grand. Two months ago—when Kreplin was dangling that three-hundred-grand package in front of me—twenty grand seemed like nothing. Now it was crucial. Nancy was right: I was in no position to be arrogant about a job possibility in Dixie. All right, it was like being temporarily demoted to the second division. But it was *an opportunity*. A chance to clear my financial slate, jump-start my stalled career, and hopefully eradicate that misdemeanor from my record. And Lizzie—who had always hinted that she wasn't tied to New York—would probably jump at the chance of moving to somewhere like Charlotte, where we could set up house in a rural retreat (within easy driving time of the city). And raise a couple of kids. And invite the neighbors over for weekend barbecues. And join the local country club. And learn to play golf. And start to wear cardigans. And switch our political allegiance to the Republican Party. And tell everybody how leaving the big bad city for little ol' Charlotte was the best thing that ever happened to us . . . while, all the time, I would secretly rue the fact that I was now exiled from the professional major leagues, and permanently trapped in a cozy cul-de-sac of my own making.

Fuck Charlotte. It would kill me. Dead. I powered up my computer and punched out a fast e-mail to greet Nancy on her arrival at the office in the morning.

> Nancy:
>
> After much serious consideration, I simply cannot see myself relocating to Charlotte. Please extend my thanks to David Judelson and InfoSystems USA for their interest in me.

Let's talk this morning and see where we go from here.

Best,
Ned

Short and sweet. No doubt Nancy would think I was squandering one of the few career possibilities that were open to me right now. But were Lizzie to find out about this job prospect, she'd insist I go for it. And if I went for it, I'd probably get it. And if I got it, she'd have us packed and moved to Charlotte in a heartbeat. And then . . .

I moved the cursor to the "Send Now" e-mail button and clicked it. The pizza arrived. I washed it down with a few glasses of cheap Australian Shiraz. Then, bottle in hand, I moved on to the bedroom. Sprawling across our bed, I poured myself another large glass of wine, drank it down, then turned on the little Sony television and stared mindlessly at some prime-time junk while upending the rest of the bottle into my empty glass.

The next thing I knew the phone was ringing. I opened one eye. Morning light was flooding the room through a crack in the curtains. My head felt the after-effects of all that low-grade wine. The empty bottle was now on the bedside table, next to our radio alarm clock, which read 9:03 A.M. I could hear Lizzie answering the phone in our kitchen. I made it to my feet, fell into the bathroom, emptied my bladder, and plunged my head into a sink of cold water. Then I wandered into the living room, blinking with surprise when I saw that a duvet and a pillow now adorned our foldout guest cot. Lizzie finished her conversation and joined me in the living room. She was already dressed for work. From the despondent look on her face I could tell that I was in serious trouble.

"Didn't hear you come in last night," I said.

She didn't reply. She just gave me a long, hard stare.

"Did we have a visitor?" I said, nodding toward the cot.

"No, I slept there," she said.

"Why?"

"Because I found you asleep with an empty bottle of wine in your arms. And I don't like sharing my bed with a drunk."

"It was just a little wine."

"You mean, like it was just a little job offer in Charlotte?"

I sat down on the cot. I ran my hand through my hair. I tried to stay calm.

"How did you know . . . ," I finally said.

"That was your outplacement counselor, Nancy Auerbach, on the phone. As soon as I answered, she said: 'Oh, Mrs. Allen, I'm really sorry to hear that you and Ned decided not to explore the Charlotte option.' When I politely asked her to explain, she told me. Everything."

"I was going to discuss this with you last night. . . ."

"But you drank yourself into unconsciousness instead."

"Uh, yeah."

She stared at the floor and shook her head.

"Why are you lying to me?" she whispered.

I stood up. "Darling, I'm not . . ."

"For Christ's sake, Ned, she just told me you sent her an e-mail late yesterday, turning down the job. So what's this 'I-was-going-to-talk-about-it-with-you-last-night' crap?"

"I just knew this was not the right move. . . ."

"You still should have discussed it with me."

"Okay," I said sheepishly, "I was wrong."

"That's not good enough, Ned. Once again, you've shut me out. . . ."

"I'm not shutting you out. . . ."

"Well, that's what it feels like. Because by shutting me out, you've also made it very clear that you really don't want me in your life."

She was crying.

"Lizzie, please . . ."

"Well, do you want to know something? I don't think I want you in *my* life anymore."

She grabbed her coat and stormed out.

I put my head in my hands. I really was in a nosedive. Plummeting toward the ground. Willing myself to crash. And simultaneously wondering, Why was I piloting myself on this self-destructive arc?

I grabbed the phone and called Nancy Auerbach. Kim, her assistant, told me I had just missed her, and that she was out of the office for the rest of the morning. I asked if there was any way she could get a message to her, informing her that I'd had a change of heart and was still interested in the Charlotte job. Kim said she'd do her best.

Then I punched in the number of Lizzie's cell phone. When she heard my voice her tone became cool.

"Listen, darling," I said, "I know I've been acting like an out-of-control idiot—"

"Ned, I really don't feel like talking with you right now."

"Lizzie, please . . . You don't know how bad I feel. . . ."

"I don't care how bad you feel."

"Look, I've just called Nancy Auerbach, and I've decided to go for the Charlotte interview."

"You do whatever you want, Ned. You always do."

"Hang on, don't you want me to do the interview?"

"If you want to move to Charlotte, that's your business. But I won't be coming with you."

"Lizzie, don't say that. . . ."

She hung up. When I tried to phone her back, I received a recorded message informing me that the cellular phone I was trying to reach had been switched off. Lizzie never turned off her phone. This scared the shit out of me—as did her sudden attack of emotional hypothermia.

Wondering what to do next, I drifted into the kitchen and made myself a cup of coffee. I stared out the window. A cold, ashen day. For the first time since quitting I suddenly had a huge, overwhelming need for a cigarette. Without stopping to contemplate the stupidity of what I was about to do, I threw on my black parka, ran over to our local grocery store, bought a pack of Winstons, returned home, found an ashtray hidden behind some espresso cups, tore open the top of the cigarette pack, screwed one between my lips, lit it up, inhaled deeply, and felt that warm, benevolent caress of nicotine wash through my bloodstream.

Within three minutes I had sucked down my first cigarette. It tasted wonderful. I finished the coffee. I reached for the pack, lit another. Then Nancy Auerbach called. From the static on the line, it was obvious she was on her cellphone.

"So Kim gave me your message," she said. "That's great news you've changed your mind about the Charlotte job."

I took a deep, steadying drag on my cigarette—and said, "Nancy, the situation's changed again. I'm going to have to pass on the interview."

"You're joking?"

"I wish I was."

"What happened?"

"You know what happened. You told Lizzie about me turning down the InfoSystems interview."

"But I only told her because I presumed *you* had talked it over with her."

"Well, I hadn't."

Despite the static on the line I could hear Nancy sigh loudly.

"Ned, this is not a game. . . ."

"I know, I know."

"And from talking to Lizzie, I can't believe that she objected so strenuously to the possibility of a Charlotte re-lo."

"It's my decision."

"I really wish you'd at least fly down there and size up the opportunity."

"It won't work for us."

"You know, with your record, an opening like this shouldn't be rejected so lightly. . . ."

"I am aware of that."

"Okay, Ned. It's your call. But remember: There are only six more days left on your program. And your options aren't exactly overwhelming."

After I finished speaking with Nancy I lit another cigarette. And called Lizzie at her office. She was "in a meeting." I called back an hour later. She was still in that meeting. Thirty minutes afterward I called again. "Sorry, Mr. Allen . . . ," her assistant said. So I phoned again half an hour later. And a half hour after that. Just before 1:00 P.M., I finally got through to her.

"Are you trying to embarrass me, Ned?" she said quietly.

"Look, I simply had to talk to you. . . ."

"And I *simply* didn't have time to speak with you this morning. Not that I particularly wanted to . . ."

"Lizzie, sweetheart, I know I've been a jerk—"

"Ned, I've got some news."

My heart skipped four beats.

"I just found out that I have to go to Los Angeles this evening," she said. "Sherry Loebman, who runs our West Coast office, ended up in the hospital last night with a burst appendix. She'll probably be out of commission for at least a couple of weeks and they want me to mind the store while she's recuperating."

"I see," I said. "Maybe I could hop a cheap flight over the weekend. . . ."

"Ned, I really think what we need . . . what *I* certainly need right now . . . is space."

Space. The most dreaded word in the marital lexicon.

"Space?" I said. "Why do you need space?"

"You know why."

"I don't."

"Things aren't right."

"Wouldn't it be better if, at least, we tried to talk through . . ."

"Yes. Of course. But after I'm back from L.A. I really think the time away will do us some good. Clear the air. Give us a little critical distance."

"I don't want to lose you."

She fell silent. All I could hear was the slight hum of the phone line. Finally she said, "I don't know what I want right now, Ned. A lot of stuff has been building up. . . ."

"I know, I know, it's been a fucking awful couple of weeks. . . ."

"Not weeks, Ned. We haven't been connecting for months. Way before you got fired."

"I don't get this."

"That's part of the problem. . . ."

"Define the problem. Please."

There was a difficult silence. Then she said, "I simply don't trust you right now, Ned. Because I'm not exactly certain who I'm dealing with anymore."

Long, stunned silence.

"Oh, Lizzie, Jesus . . ."

"Look, I've got to go back into another meeting. I'm catching the six P.M. American flight."

"Can I at least take you to the airport?"

"I'm really tied up all day—I'm sending one of our interns over with my key to pack a few things for me. Her name's Sally, she'll be dropping by in about an hour. And I'll be leaving straight from the office for Kennedy."

"I'm going to call you in L.A. Every day. Where are you staying?"

"Ned, let me call you."

"Where are you *staying.*" It was no longer a question.

She sighed with resignation. "I'll be at the Mondrian."

"Lizzie . . ."

"Got to go. 'Bye."

I sat there, holding the receiver, feeling lost. I finally put down the phone. After a moment I picked it up again, index finger poised over the numbers. But I didn't know who to call. For the first time in my life, I didn't really know what to do next.

"I'm not exactly certain who I'm dealing with anymore."

Nor was I.

FOUR

"Hi there, Mrs. Ruth Edelstein? It's Ned Allen here, from PC Solutions. I hope this is a convenient time to talk. . . ."

Mrs. Ruth Edelstein sounded around ninety years old. "Whatcha say your name was?"

"Ned Allen. PC Solutions. Now, I note from our records that you bought a GBS Powerplan computer from us in September of nineteen ninety-five. . . ."

"It was my son."

"Sorry?"

"My son Lester, he bought the computer."

I glanced up at the monitor in front of me. "But, according to our information, the computer was registered in your name."

"That's 'cause Lester bought it for me."

"Then it is *your* computer?"

"Never use it. Sits gathering dust on the breakfront. Total waste of money."

"Well, surely, your son bought you the computer so you could use it."

"Nah. Lester bought it 'cause he and that cheap wife of his moved out to Phoenix, and he had this numbskull idea that he could keep in touch with me using this . . . *whatchacallit?*"

"E-mail, perhaps?"

"That's it. I tell him, 'I'm seventy-seven years old, I've got arthritis, you expect me to type you a hello every morning? You feel guilty about not bringing me to Phoenix, drop a dime, pick up the phone.' "

"Well, e-mail is probably the most cost-efficient way of communicating. . . ."

"Lester is a big-deal dermatologist, he doesn't need to worry about a two-buck phone call."

"Well, say you *did* start using the computer. Wouldn't you want the most up-to-date software package available? Because that's what PC Solutions is offering you this month. An incredible software bundle, including Windows 95, Netscape Navigator, Visual Basic, Power C, the new nineteen ninety-eight Grolier Encyclopedia, Al Unser, Jr., Arcade Racing—"

"Al Unser, the racing car guy?"

"The very one. And I have to tell you, Mrs. Edelstein, once you start playing this game, you'll never want to—"

"Me, a racing car driver? That's your idea of a joke?"

I kept plowing ahead with my spiel.

"Now, were you to buy all this software separately, it would cost you over a thousand dollars. But PC Solutions is offering you this fantastic bundle for just three twenty-nine, ninety-five, including next-day FedEx delivery."

"Young man, did you hear me the first time? Never once have I touched that dumb computer. . . ."

"Don't you think it's time to learn?"

"No." And she hung up.

I let out a tired sigh, readjusted my headset, moved the cursor down to the next name and phone number on my screen, clicked on dial, and waited for the ringing phone to be answered.

"Hi there, Mr. Tony Gottschalk? It's Ned Allen here from PC Solutions. Hope this is a convenient time to talk. . . ."

It was the Wednesday after my program had ended, and I was on day three of my new job. Check that: my new *temporary* job. After turning down the potential media-sales gig in Charlotte, I'd spent the last six days of The Program trying to find something, *anything*, that might tide me over while I continued to hunt for a permanent position.

"Now I know you're going to cringe when I mention it," Nancy Auerbach said.

"Try me," I said.

"Have you, maybe, considered something in telesales?"

I cringed.

"I know, I know," Nancy Auerbach said. "After being a sales manager, it's kind of a comedown. But you said you needed the money. So . . ."

"Tell me the name of the company."

And that's how I ended up at PC Solutions: "The At-home Computer Superstore." The guy who hired me, Burt Rubinek, was a class-A geek: bad skin, Coke-bottle glasses, a polyester short-sleeve shirt (even though it was early March), a plastic pen holder in his breast pocket. Our interview was a virtual non-event. I entered his little cubicle of an office, where he was bent over his wastepaper basket, cutting his fingernails. When he polished off his pinky he acknowledged my presence with a brief nod, silently flipped through my resumé, and then said, "If you're willing to do this job, times must be tough."

I gave him my rehearsed reply: "I'm in a transitional phase at the moment. But, believe me, I can sell."

He stared down at my resumé and muttered, "We'll see about that." Then he told me the terms of the job. I was going to be placed in "the software section," initially pitching a $329 software bundle package. The pay would be five bucks an hour, forty hours a week, no overtime, no medical. But I'd get a 10 percent commission for every bundle I sold. The minimum quota was fifteen units a week. If I failed to reach that quota, I would be out, no exceptions to the rule.

"Fifteen sales a week shouldn't be hard," I said.

He chewed on a cuticle. "I like an optimist," he said. "You start Monday."

So, finally, after eight weeks of outplacement counseling, I had landed. In a job that I already despised—even before I had started work there.

"Think of it as a stopgap," Nancy Auerbach had said during our final "formal" conversation together. "And even though, officially, your program is over at the end of today, I'll keep my ear to the ground for anything in senior sales that might suit you."

"So," I said, "I suppose I really blew it, not following up on the Charlotte job."

"It's your marriage, not mine—though, even in my jaundiced

experience, talking things through with your spouse usually avoids a lot of grief. But I hope things work out, Ned. On all fronts."

From my daily conversations with Lizzie, I couldn't really tell how things were working between us. For the first week of her absence she maintained the ill-at-ease-with-me tone that she'd adopted prior to her departure. But when I called her on the day my program finished—and told her about landing the telesales gig—she thawed for a minute or two.

"You really don't have to take a demeaning job like that."

"I need the money. . . ."

"As I've said, over and over again, I'm happy to support us. . . ."

"I need to be doing *something*," I said, lighting up a cigarette. "I'm bored shitless. And I miss you."

She ignored that last comment and said, "I've got some news." My heart now skipped five beats. "Sherry Loebman—the woman I've been sitting in for—has had all sorts of complications since her appendectomy. And I've volunteered to continue filling in for her."

"For how long?"

"I'm going to be here for at least another two weeks."

"I see," I said. "Am I still an embargoed person in L.A., or can I come visit?"

"You've got a new job, remember?"

"I get the hint," I said.

Another awkward silence, during which I puffed heavily.

"Are you smoking?" she asked.

I certainly *was* smoking again. After two weeks back on the habit, I was now inhaling a pack a day, and developing a nice phlegmy cough. Re-embracing cigarettes was like rediscovering—in the midst of bad times—a dangerous but chummy old friend, someone who'd gladly help me through this current crisis . . . at a price. But I wasn't thinking about the long-term risks to my cardiovascular system, or the dangers of lung cancer, or the fact that my dad was a corpse at forty-seven, thanks to the killer weed. I wanted, *craved* the disreputable company of cigarettes. Just like I also wanted and craved all the junk food I could stomach. And sleep was now only possible after downing a six-pack of Busch (chosen for its unapologetic cheapness) every night.

Of course I knew that I was now on a high-trash diet. But I

didn't care. Professionally and personally, I was now a full-fledged fuckup. With the zeal of a convert, I had abandoned all discipline, rejected moderation, embraced the disaster that was me. Three months ago I was a paragon of ambition and high-performance drive, my trajectory level stratospheric. A reckless moment, a couple of bad breaks, a bit of major inattention on the domestic front, and suddenly . . .

"Allen! What time is designated as start of business in this company?"

This was Burt Rubinek talking. Check that: This was Burt Rubinek bellowing. It was my fourth day on the job—and as I was quickly discovering, Rubinek's passive nerd act was total camouflage. Lurking behind that geek exterior was the soul of a sadist: someone who needed to give everyone around him nonstop grief.

"Did you hear me, Allen?" Rubinek boomed again. I looked up from my computer terminal. Rubinek was standing ten feet away from me, smack dab in the middle of a room that was known as the cattle car. It was the size of half a football field, crammed with cubicle-like workstations. Each workstation had a computer terminal, a desk chair, a headset. There were 120 workstations in the cattle car, divided into six subdivisions, each of which was assigned to telemarket specific PC Solutions products. Computers and software was the biggest division (with over eighty telesales operators working the phones), while the remaining forty employees handled direct sales of faxes, printers, modems, and exciting accessories like customized mouse pads ("Send us a photo of any loved one, and we'll have it made up as a laminated computer mouse pad within seven working days!").

Burt Rubinek was constantly prowling the corridors and alleyways of the cattle car. Like a Marine Corps drill sergeant, he saw it as his duty to threaten and castigate his underlings, reminding them that, in the great scheme of things, they were worthless pieces of shit. Watching him at work, I couldn't help but think that he was getting his revenge for some really awful years on the school playground.

"Allen? Are you deaf, or are you simply on a different astral plane this morning?"

I poked my head out of my cubicle. All around me my coworkers were staring straight ahead at their terminals—a habit we all fell into whenever Rubinek decided to berate someone, out of fear that he might catch our eye and turn his poisonous attention to us.

"I didn't hear the question, Burt," I said.

"So you *are* deaf."

"I was just preoccupied with—"

"I WILL REPEAT THE QUESTION ONCE AGAIN: What time is designated as start of business in this company?"

"Eight-thirty," I said quietly.

"Very good. Very good. Eight-three-oh. We are at our desks at eight-thirty, ready to make our first calls at eight-forty-five. And what time did you walk in this morning?"

"Around eight-thirty."

"Wrong! You arrived here at eight-thirty-six. How many minutes late were you?"

"There was a delay in the subway. Someone jumped under a train at Thirty-fourth Street. I think he used to work here."

Nervous titters from a few of my neighboring coworkers. When they saw Rubinek's face go crimson (a sure sign he was about to declare war), they immediately refocused their eyes on their computer screens. He approached my cubicle and lowered his voice to a near whisper.

"A comedian, huh?"

"I was just trying to lighten things up, Burt."

"My name is Mr. Rubinek. You were six minutes late this morning. And you were insubordinate."

"It was a joke, *Mr. Rubinek*."

"I didn't hire you to do stand-up. I hired you to push the product. And to show up not *around* eight-thirty, but *at* eight-thirty. Your quota this week is now eighteen units."

"Oh, for Christ's sake . . ."

"You don't like it, there's the door." He glanced at the big digital clock that hung on the main wall of the cattle car. 8:44:52. Everyone else in the cattle car fell silent, watching the seconds tick down.

"Right, people . . . ," Burt Rubinek shouted. The clock turned 8:45. A loud bell sounded. The selling day had begun. Suddenly the room erupted into babble, as all 120 telesales operators began chasing the first sale of the day, everyone fearfully conscious of the weekly quota they needed to reach in order to report back to work next Monday.

Rubinek turned back to me and said: "Eighteen units by close of business tomorrow, or you're out of here."

"That's not fair, and you know it," I said.

He gave me a wall-to-wall smirk. "You're right. It's not fair. I do know it. And I don't care."

As he sauntered away in search of another target, I felt like ripping off my headset, upending my computer terminal, and marching to the nearest elevator. But I managed to muster the last remnants of my self-control and instead gripped the sides of my desk so tightly I thought I was about to snap my tendons.

Careful, careful. He obviously knows you were once a sales manager. Just as he has also checked into your background and found out about the Kreplin assault. And he's such a twisted bully, he now wants to see if he can inspire you to detonate again.

So I inhaled my pride, turned my attention to my computer screen, lined the cursor up with the first phone number of the day, and . . .

"Hi there, Ms. Susan Silcox? It's Ned Allen here, from PC Solutions. Hope this is a convenient time to talk. . . ."

It *was* a convenient time to speak with Ms. Silcox. As she explained, she was a housewife in Shaker Heights, Ohio, and she had just done that postfeminist thing of giving up work to look after her five-month-old son, Michael. She surfed the Net whenever she had a free moment ("It makes me believe I'm still connected to the outside world and not imprisoned in babyland all the time"), so, sure, she'd be happy to upgrade to our $329 software bundle. "Hang on, I'll just get my credit card. . . ."

Got her. Not that she needed much persuasion. This sort of "tele-home-marketing" was aimed directly at the domestically incarcerated—people like Ms. Silcox, who were stuck at home, felt bored, lonely, sequestered, and looked upon the telesales rep as a temporary friend, someone who was happy to listen to their complaints about a husband who was on the road four days a week. Or a daughter who was a big-deal executive at one of the Hollywood studios, but hadn't bothered to call her widowed mother in St. Louis for the past three months. Or the husband in Sacramento forced into early retirement at fifty-seven, who was now spending nine hours a day in cyberspace because he didn't really know what else to do with his time. Or . . .

As I quickly discovered, the trick to tele-home-marketing was to come across as a sympathetic voice in the telephonic wilderness. Unlike the sort of telesales we used to practice at *CompuWorld*, we weren't dealing with a large, established company client base. At PC Solutions, we hustled individual consumers—99 percent of whom certainly didn't need what we were plugging. So what you had to peddle them was fellowship. Within the space of a few short minutes, you had to become their buddy, their ally, their confidant. You didn't sell them a product; you sold them a sense of personal affiliation, the subtext of which was: *We have a relationship here*. It didn't matter that this relationship would last only for the duration of the phone call. The object of the exercise was to connect. Once you connected, you closed.

The problem was: Only one in twenty customers was willing to let you make that connection. Most of the time your call was greeted with an immediate dismissal—which was still infinitely preferable to the sort of bored schmuck who took up twenty minutes of your time, hemming and hawing, making you repeat your sales pitch two or three times, then finally telling you, "Nah, it's not for me."

Clowns like that were commonplace within the PC Solutions customer base. My average working day involved seventy calls, fifty of which were of the "instant hangup" variety. Of the remaining twenty, at least fifteen of these customers had no intention of buying anything from you . . . but were delighted at the opportunity to talk at your expense. (During my second day on the job, for example, I spent twenty minutes playing grief counselor to a woman in Myrtle Beach, Florida, who had just lost her pet Pekingese. When I finally got her back to the issue of the software bundle, she then informed me, "Oh, I sold my computer to a friend a year ago.")

In the end, there were only five calls a day where you had the chance of closing. And since the weekly quota was fifteen sales, it's no wonder that there was such a desperate atmosphere in the cattle car. Remember those old turn-of-the-century photos, showing hundreds of hollowed-eyed workers hunched over sewing machines in a factory, desperate to fulfill their daily allotment of thirty potato sacks? There were times during the working day when I'd stand up for a moment from my terminal, stretch my hypertense shoulders, look out on the frantic, heads-down landscape of the cattle car, and think, This is the sweatshop of the future. A place where—like some Union Square shirt factory in 1900s New York—the workers survive or perish, depending on whether they meet their quotas. Cyberspace meets the bottom line.

Having closed the sale to Ms. Susan Silcox of Shaker Heights, Ohio, I had now moved thirteen units this week. Considering that it was only 9:05 on Thursday morning, I wouldn't have worried terribly about reaching the quota of fifteen units by 4:45 on Friday afternoon. But thanks to Rubinek's punitive action against me, I was forced to find an additional three sales within the next two days. Not impossible, but . . .

The rest of the morning was a total strikeout. Every number I tried didn't answer or was an instant "no sale." At 11:45 I took a fifteen-minute lunch break: five minutes gobbling a soggy egg salad sandwich bought at the snack bar situated on the ground floor of our office building, the final ten minutes spent standing outside the main entrance in the bracing cold, wolfing down two Winstons in the company of a dozen other nicotine addicts from the cattle car.

"Heard you gave the Jellyfish some lip this morning," said a Latino-looking guy who introduced himself as Jamie Sanchez (and who devoured four Salems in the same time that I smoked my two cancer sticks).

"You call Rubinek the 'Jellyfish'?"

"Yeah—'cause the guy's a blob with nasty tentacles that sting. How many extra units did he give you?"

"Three."

"You gonna make it?"

"I have no choice. Does he pull this shit often?"

"Man, the Jellyfish lives to pull everybody's chain. There was this guy, Charlie Larsson, thirty-something, real educated and respectable, used to be some kind of a trader at Kidder, Peabody before some big layoff. . . . Anyway, the Jellyfish hated his button-down ass, and was on his case day in, day out. Kept finding reasons to up his quota, kept calling him 'Mr. Big Shot Wall Street.' One afternoon,

Charlie couldn't take it no longer, and suddenly, out of nowhere, he put his fist right through his terminal screen. Poor bastard had to be rushed to Roosevelt Hospital with his hand still inside the monitor. Didn't see him ever again."

"Why the hell does PC Solutions allow Rubinek to behave this way?"

"Simple: He makes them money, so they love him. Anytime someone complains to management, they tell the Jellyfish, who immediately doubles their quota for the week, which means they're, like, automatically dead. Life in the cattle car is kind of cut and dry: You don't like how the game is played—tough. Problem is, where are you gonna go after you walk out the door?"

I didn't want to consider such a question, so I hurried back up to my workstation and made call number twenty-two of the day.

"Hi there, Mr. Richard Masur? It's Ned Allen here, from PC Solutions. I hope this is a convenient time to talk. . . ."

"PC Solutions? I've been hoping to hear from you people for a while. Got a problem with my Windows 95 CD-Rom drive. It doesn't run the disk automatically anymore. . . ."

Bingo. "Well, that's officially a problem for Microsoft. And since you bought your computer from us in February 'ninety-six, I'm afraid that your software warranty is long expired. However, the good news is that we're offering brand-new cutting-edge software in a phenomenal bundle for only . . ."

Sold. Ninety minutes later, I closed unit number fifteen. Thank you, Ms. Sherry Stouffer, a self-employed yoga instructor from Cambridge, Mass. Eighty-two minutes after that (the "order dispatch software" on our server logs the exact time of the sale), I sold unit sixteen to a Mr. A. D. Hart, a freelance writer in San Jose, California. And then, at 4:31—a mere fourteen minutes before quitting time—I scored the final coup of the day, as units seventeen and eighteen were bought by the reverend Scott Davis, a Unitarian minister in Indianapolis, who was planning to install the bundle in his church computer and make a gift of the second bundle to an inner-city poverty project in which he was involved.

I was on a winning streak—one of those gold-dust moments in sales where everything suddenly changes gears, and the music of chance is on your side. Five sales in five hours! It was a windfall beyond my dreams. My increased quota for the week already reached—a full day before the Friday deadline. As I stood up from my terminal at 4:45 P.M., I couldn't help but feel that luck might just be returning to my corner.

As I headed toward the elevator, Rubinek blocked my path. He already had the printout of today's sales figures in his hand. Staring down at the accordion-like pages, he said, "Get desperate and call a couple of friends, Allen?"

I maintained a mildly befuddled tone. "What was that, Mr. Rubinek?"

"Five sales in one afternoon, that's what. Which makes me wonder if you might have resorted to friends or family to save your bacon."

"I just had a good day, that's all."

As I tried to walk away he blocked my path again.

"If you're such a goddamn sales whiz, maybe I should increase your quota to eighteen units every week."

I suddenly felt that surge of intrepidness which always hit whenever someone underestimated my ability. "Mr. Rubinek, I will achieve whatever quota you set."

"Six more units by close of business tomorrow, or you're history."

He walked away, then turned back and said, "I don't like you, Allen. I don't like you at all."

He liked me even less when, by 1:14 on Friday afternoon, those six new units were closed. I was the Golden Boy, I could do no wrong. Or, at least, that's how I felt as I headed off for the weekend. As I walked by the Jellyfish's office, he gave me the petulant scowl of a bully who had been shown up. For today, anyway.

I didn't do anything stupid with my paycheck—because the recovered sofa showed up just after I arrived home from work that afternoon and the delivery guy had a COD invoice, which (as the acronym indicates) had to be paid on the spot, forcing me to write a check for funds I didn't have in my account (but which would be on deposit Monday morning when the first week's money from PC Solutions hit my account). The sofa looked whiter than white. Lizzie would be happy.

As he was leaving, the delivery guy asked me, "Your wife away?"

"How'd you know that?" I asked.

"You kidding me?" he said as he scanned the apartment. Stacks of empty fast-food cartons, brimming ashtrays, crushed beer cans, a half dozen dishes with congealed food stacked high in the sink, an overflowing garbage can.

"Piece of advice, bud," the delivery guy said. "If you don't want to make the acquaintance of a divorce lawyer, I'd get a maid in here before your wife comes home."

He was right: The apartment currently looked like a stretch of industrial wasteland. I resolved to spend the rest of the evening thoroughly cleaning it. Just as I also resolved to disassociate myself from cigarettes and eat nothing but sushi for the next two weeks, as (according to our bathroom scales this morning) my weight had ballooned—by twelve pounds—to 187, and I was having major difficulty squeezing into my pants.

But before I commenced this weekend of clean-living virtue, I decided to have one final cigarette, chased with my last can of Busch, while listening to my phone messages. There was only one. It was from Lizzie. She sounded pleasant in a distant sort of way.

"Hi there, it's just me. It's around nine A.M. L.A. time, so you won't be hearing this until you get home from work tonight. I've got to fly to San Francisco this morning to see a client, then I'm rendezvousing with a bunch of people from the office at this hotel near Carmel. Kind of a last-minute thing, but I've never been along that section of the Pacific Coast Highway, so . . ."

I sank down on the couch. *"Rendezvousing with a bunch of people from the office at this hotel near Carmel."* What bunch of people? And why didn't you leave me the name of the goddamn hotel?

". . . since I probably won't be back at the Mondrian till after midnight on Sunday, it's probably best if you reach me at the office on Monday. And I do want to talk to you on Monday because . . ."

Please don't say *I've got some news*.

". . . well, you should know, there's some talk around the office about me possibly extending my stay out here for, maybe, four to six months. . . ."

The cigarette shook in my hand. Ash fell onto the whiter-than-white sofa. I stared at it.

"Anyway, nothing's definite or decided. But call me Monday and we'll talk it all through. 'Bye."

Click.

I sat on the sofa for a long time, unable to move, the cigarette burning down to the filter, forcing me to douse it in the can of Busch. One thought blanketed my mind: *I've lost her.* Even if this weekend in Carmel was just an innocent outing with a bunch of workmates, she still didn't want me to have the name and number of the hotel. And if it wasn't innocent . . .

Jealousy was a word that never entered my domestic vocabulary. Nor was infidelity. I played the monogamous game—and, to the best of my knowledge, so did Lizzie (I would have been astonished to discover otherwise). But now . . .

Stop it, stop it. You have no evidence that she's suddenly up to no good. She just doesn't want to hear the sound of your voice right now. On the scale of marital disasters, not wanting to talk to your spouse ranks pretty high—but at least she's not screwing some other guy.

Still, the realization hit: If her company was planning to extend her stay at the L.A. office by at least four months, and if she remained unenthusiastic about the idea of my joining her on the Coast, then our future prospects together were nothing short of dismal.

I grabbed the phone, punched in the 310 area code followed by the number for Lizzie's West Coast office. I asked to be put through to her secretary.

"Ms. Howard is away until Monday. May I ask who's calling?"

"Her husband."

"Oh."

"She didn't leave a number where she can be reached over the weekend?"

"I'm not allowed to give out that information."

"Like I said, I *am* her husband."

"I'm sure you are, but I still can't give out that number. . . ."

"Can you at least get a message to her?"

"I can try. Is it urgent?"

I wanted to say it was an emergency to ensure that Lizzie did call me back. But I figured that she'd be unamused to discover that the "emergency" was simply a ruse to make her phone me. And I didn't need any further black marks against my name in Lizzie's book. So all I said was, "Just tell her, if she wants to talk, I'll be home all weekend."

"I'll make sure she gets the message."

By Sunday afternoon, I was wondering if Lizzie *did* get the message. Because she hadn't called me yet. As my anxiety grew, so, too, did my obsessive need to tidy up my life. So I became relentlessly preoccupied with neatness. I purged the refrigerator of all high-calorie crap. I rid the apartment of junk-food boxes, brimming garbage bags, and all other trash. I emptied ashtrays, and cleaned the bathtub, and scrubbed sinks, and vacuumed carpets, and dusted with Pledge. I laundered sheets and washed windows, and even rearranged my sock drawer. I made a visit to my local D'Agostino's and came back with six bottles of mineral water and two bags brimming with fresh fruit. I stuck to a fruit-and-water diet all weekend, and shed three pounds by Sunday. Though I didn't manage to go cold turkey on the cigarette habit, I still restricted myself to three a day. And on Sunday afternoon, in an attempt to work off some excess flab (and major stress), I grabbed my tennis racket and a couple of balls, and headed over to a playground off Twentieth Street and Ninth Avenue, where there was a handball court that worked just fine as a backboard.

It was a cold, gray afternoon, and I had the playground to myself. As I slammed the ball against the wall—practicing my ground strokes, sharpening my backhand, and musing on the fact that this was not exactly the New York Health and Racquet Club—I suddenly heard a voice behind me.

"Preparing for the Open, Allen?"

I turned around and found myself looking at Jerry Schubert. He was standing with a very tall, very thin blonde woman in her early twenties. Without question, a model.

"Is this your local club?" Jerry asked as I shook his hand.

"Yeah, and I'm its only member. Do you live around here?"

"No, I'm down in SoHo. But Cindy here is the Chelsea-ite."

He introduced us. Cindy Mason had a deep southern drawl.

"Where are you from, Cindy?"

"Little ol' town called Charlotte, North Carolina."

"I've heard of it," I said.

"You're awful good with a racket," she said. "D'you play professionally?"

"If I did, I wouldn't be on this playground."

"I saw the piece in the *Journal* about the *CompuWorld* business," Jerry said, then added with a smile, "and about the way you improved German-American relations."

"Yeah—that was my fifteen minutes of fame."

"Do you know what Mr. Ballantine said after reading the story? 'That guy has done something that ninety percent of the American workforce dream about.' "

"Oh, everyone was really impressed—except any and all future employers."

"Are things tough now?"

"You could say that—computer software telesales isn't exactly my idea of a good time."

"I did telesales for a week when I first came to New York," Cindy said. "It was the pits."

"Believe me, it still is. But I'm sure I'll find something better by the time I'm forty. How are things with the Great Motivator?"

"Booming. He's got a new book out in midsummer, followed by a thirty-five-city promotional tour. And we've also been diversifying a bit. Setting up a couple of interesting investment projects. Give me a call sometime. I'll buy you lunch and tell you all about them. You still have my number?"

I nodded. And accepted Jerry's outstretched hand.

"Don't be a stranger," he said.

"Real nice meeting you," Cindy said. "Hope you find a better tennis partner than that ol' wall."

As they headed off down the street, Jerry put his arm around Cindy's narrow waist and she leaned her head against his shoulder. And I felt a desperate stab of envy. He had a career, a woman, a future. Everything I once had. Until the mistakes were made, and that life was suddenly gone.

I kept pounding tennis balls against the wall until the onset of evening forced me to return to the empty apartment. I maintained my fruit-and-water diet, I smoked my designated evening cigarette, I squandered a few more hours in front of the television, I went to bed and couldn't sleep. At midnight, I tried Lizzie's hotel room in

L.A. No answer. I popped some melatonin tablets and drank a mug of chamomile tea. At one, I called L.A. again. "Sorry, Ms. Howard is still out." I channel-surfed, and ended up gazing mindlessly at an infomercial for a revolutionary teeth-whitening system. At two, I gave the Mondrian Hotel one last call. Lizzie was still out. So I left a message asking her to call me anytime. Then, resisting the temptation to drink a sleep-inducing beer, I fell back into bed, taking with me the latest Tom Clancy novel. It had the desired effect. After fifteen minutes my brain finally closed down.

And then it was morning. And the phone was ringing. I squinted at the clock radio, remembering that I had forgotten to set it. 8:03. Shit. Shit. Shit. I'd never make the eight-thirty punch-in time at PC Solutions. The Jellyfish would be delighted; it would allow him to double my quota for the week. I'd blown it. Yet again.

I sat up in bed, my head still fogged in with sleep. The phone kept ringing. I managed to pick it up and mumble a "Yeah?"

"Am I speaking to a Mr. Ned Allen?" asked a brisk-sounding woman. A telemarketer, no doubt.

"Are you selling something?" I asked.

The woman was annoyed. "I am not selling anything. I am simply trying to find a Mr. Ned Allen. Is this Mr. Allen?"

"Yeah, that's me."

"My name is Detective Debra Kaster. . . ."

Now I was totally confused. "I'm talking to a cop?"

"You are talking to a detective from the Hartford, Connecticut, P.D."

Hartford? Why the hell would a cop be calling me from Hartford?

"I'm sorry," I said, "I'm kind of half awake. And late for work. Could you maybe call me back?"

She ignored that request and said, "Do you know a Mr. Ivan Dolinsky?"

I was suddenly very awake.

"Ivan? Sure I know him."

"What's your relationship to him?"

"Has something happened?"

"Please answer the question, Mr. Allen."

"I was his boss for two years. Is he okay?"

"He left your name and number in his note. . . ."

"Note? What note?"

There was a long silence. And I was suddenly shuddering. Because I knew what she was going to tell me.

"I regret to inform you that Mr. Dolinsky took his life last night."

FIVE

She was waiting for me at the station. Late forties. Five foot two. Silver hair. A navy-blue pantsuit that accentuated her slight chunkiness. A bulge on her hip where her service revolver was not-so-discreetly hidden beneath her blazer. A handshake that temporarily blocked all circulation to my fingers.

"Ned Allen?" she asked as she approached me on the station platform. "Detective Kaster."

"Nice of you to pick me up," I said.

"All part of the service. Thanks for getting up here this morning. We like to settle these matters as quickly as possible. Was your boss okay about you taking the day off?"

"No."

"Oh, he's one of those, is he?"

"Understatement of the year."

"You want, I can call him myself, explain why we needed you here."

"Thanks, but it wouldn't do much good. The guy scores zero on the sympathy front."

In fact, when I had called the Jellyfish right after getting the call from Detective Kaster—and explained that I was needed at the Hartford morgue to identify a body—he asked, "Was the deceased a family member?"

"No, a guy I used to work with, but—"

"If it was a family member, you'd be entitled to three days off on full pay. But if he was just a guy you used to work with—"

"Look, he's got no real next of kin, so . . ."

"That's his problem. You gotta go up to Hartford, you lose your pay for today. If you're not here tomorrow, you lose Tuesday's *and* your quota jumps by three. Got me?"

"I'll be there tomorrow," I said, and then hung up before I said something that might get me fired.

We got into Kaster's unmarked Ford Escort. She fastened her seat belt, turned the key in the ignition, reached into the glove compartment, and pulled out a pack of Merit cigarettes. "Hope you also don't object to these?"

I dug around in one of my overcoat pockets until I found my Winstons. "Fellow addict," I said, inserting a cigarette between my lips.

"We're going to get along just fine," Detective Kaster said, pushing in the car's cigarette lighter.

We pulled out into traffic and followed the signs for downtown.

"This is going to be a three-stop trip. First the morgue, which is in a suburb called Farmington, around ten minutes from here. After you make the identification, then we'll move on to Mr. Dolinsky's apartment before heading over to his office at *Home Computer Monthly*. His boss . . . ," she flipped open a little black notebook, ". . . a Mr. Duane Hellman, asked if he could see you. I think he's kind of upset about what happened."

"What exactly *did* happen?"

"Mr. Dolinsky went up the pipe."

"He *what?*"

"Gassed himself. In his car." She reached for the notebook again, flipped it open, read from her notes as she drove. "A nineteen eighty-seven Toyota Corolla, found in Elizabeth Park at two-thirty-three A.M. last night by a patrol car on a routine nighttime beat. The deceased had parked in a wooded area near a little lake. The two officers found a garden hose taped to the exhaust pipe, the other end of the hose inserted into the right front passenger window, all car windows taped shut, the engine running, the car filled with fumes . . . In other words, your classic 'up-the-pipe' suicide. Must get one of these a month."

I sucked hard on my cigarette and stared out the window.

"Judging by the preparations Mr. Dolinsky made, this was no cry for help. The officers found a receipt from a Wal-Mart on the front seat. From the time on the receipt"—another glance at the notebook—"five-thirty-eight P.M. yesterday, it seems Mr. Dolinsky bought the the tape and the garden hose at the Wal-Mart in nearby New Britain, then drove straight to Elizabeth Park."

5:38. On a dark, bleak, winter night. If, on the way to that Wal-Mart, Ivan had been delayed by just twenty-two minutes, then the store would have been closed by the time he arrived. Forcing him, perhaps, to put off his death for another day. And maybe, come morning, the all-encompassing sense of hopelessness would have passed.

"Bet I know what you're thinking," Detective Kaster said. " 'If only he'd called me. If only I'd known just how bad he was. If only . . .' Am I right?"

I shrugged.

"Worst thing about suicides is the way it punishes those who were left behind. But . . . can I be blunt here? He obviously wanted to go. Because we found a bottle of whiskey and an empty bottle of Valium on the seat next to him. It was his own prescription, which makes me wonder, Did he have a history of depression?"

I explained about the death of his daughter, the collapse of his marriage, the problems at work, the way *CompuWorld* was suddenly killed off.

"Sounds like Mr. Dolinsky was juggling some pretty big problems," Detective Kaster said.

"What gets me is that six, seven weeks ago, Ivan was in the best shape I'd seen him for years. He'd just landed this new job, he was really upbeat about the future . . ."

"You speak to him since that time?"

"Nah, I've been kind of preoccupied. Did he leave any note, any explanation?"

Back to the notebook. "There was a letter on the dashboard. Short and sweet: your name and phone number, and a personal message for you: 'Tell Ned I'm sorry for making him tidy up after me again.' That was it."

I exhaled loudly, and felt my throat contract as it stifled a sob.

"Was he erratic on the job?" Detective Kaster asked quietly.

"After the death of his daughter, yes."

"And you had to cover for him a lot?"

"I suppose so."

"Then he considered you his friend."

My eyes began to well up.

"Yes. I was his friend."

We entered the town of Farmington, then drove on to the campus of the University of Connecticut School of Medicine and Dentistry. The office of the Hartford medical examiner was located in an off-white concrete building. We parked the car. As we approached the front entrance an ambulance swung by us, heading toward the rear of the building.

"The back is where they make the deliveries," Kaster said quietly. Then she added, "We're going to make this as fast and simple as possible. The Hartford M.E. prides itself on its streamlined service."

Inside the building a uniformed cop was talking with the morgue's receptionist. Detective Kaster approached the front desk, flipped open her badge, pointed in my direction. Then she nodded for me to follow her into the "family room." Simple, functional furniture. A coffee machine. A notice on one of the walls giving the extension numbers for assorted hospital chaplains.

Without thinking, I had pulled out a cigarette and had it at the ready between my fingers. So had Kaster.

"No smoking in the hospital, please," said the white-coated official who entered the family room. He glanced at a clipboard. "Mr. Allen, we're ready for you now."

I expected the usual cop-show morgue scene. The meat-locker room with a wall full of shiny metal doors. Some Peter Lorre–type attendant pulling open one of the refrigerated compartments. A blast of cold air hitting me in the face as the attendant grabs a handle and pulls out a slab on which a body lies covered in a white sheet. Then, after asking me if I'm ready, he slowly uncovers the face. . . .

But the Hartford M.E. had sanitized the experience of identifying a body. We were brought into what appeared to be a lounge—with a blue couch and two chairs, and a video monitor (its screen draped with a white cloth) positioned on a small table. The official introduced himself as Dr. Levon and said that he had conducted the postmortem examination on Ivan. He asked if I had any questions before the identification began. I shook my head. He approached the set. I couldn't help thinking, *This is like a sales conference, and the guy in the white coat is going to use some audio-visual materials to make his pitch.* He asked me to sit down. I found a chair, stared straight ahead at the monitor.

"Ready?" Dr. Levon asked. I nodded. He lifted off the cloth. The set was already on—and I found myself staring at the ashen face of Ivan Dolinsky.

The shot was a closeup. The harsh lights gave Ivan's blue-gray skin a spectral glow. Unlike the face of my cancer-victim dad—who looked like some Amazonian shrunken head by the time he died—Ivan's features hadn't been ravaged by the carbon monoxide and Valium cocktail that killed him. He looked at rest, his haunted, burdened face finally free of the multiple torments that had stalked him in the last few years. I found myself stifling another sob. We all try to plan our lives so carefully, don't we? We're like kids with a set of building blocks—methodically putting one brick atop another. The job, the home, the family, the crap we buy—brick upon brick, we pile it high, praying that this is a stable, lasting construction. But if adult life teaches you anything, it's this: Nothing is fixed, solid, durable. And it doesn't even take a cataclysm for the entire edifice to come crashing down on you. Just one small jolt will do.

Dr. Levon asked, "Is that Mr. Ivan Dolinsky?"

I nodded. And felt like adding, You want to know the real cause of death? *Failure to close*. That's what killed him. Closing was the yardstick by which he measured his personal worth. After the death of Nancy, after his divorce, his ability to sell was the one thing that kept him afloat. It was his trade, his craft, the thing he was good at. Until that skill abandoned him as well. And then . . . maybe, it was just a matter of time.

Catastrophe is such a random business, isn't it? Ivan was a hostage to happenstance. Like the rest of us.

Referring back to his clipboard, the doctor asked a few general questions. He then informed me that the body would be ready for release to a funeral home at nine the next morning, and did I know to whom Mr. Dolinsky's remains should be sent? I said that, to the best of my knowledge, there was no family—only an ex-wife, now living (if my memory served me well) somewhere near Naples, Florida.

"Would you mind getting in touch with her and finding out what sort of arrangements she wants to make?" the doctor asked.

"We'll give her a call from my office," Detective Kaster said, then sharply asked, "Does that wrap it up, Doc?"

"Uh, yeah," he said, handing me the clipboard to sign the official identification. Then he hit the off button on the remote control, and Ivan Dolinsky faded to black.

On the drive over to Ivan's office Detective Kaster said, "You hanging in there?"

"It's kind of a strange experience, isn't it? Seeing it on TV."

"Yeah," she said, lighting up a cigarette, "you almost expect them to cut away for commercials. *We'll be right back with the body after this message from . . .*"

Ivan's final home was a tiny one-bedroom unit in a 1960s motel-like building off a gasoline alley in a grubby corner of West Hartford. Having earlier retrieved the key from the landlord, Detective Kaster let us in. The apartment was just two cramped rooms—a living room with a galley kitchen, a metal table and chairs and a cane sofa with smudged floral cushions; the bedroom with nothing but a queen-size bed with a floral headboard, a cheap white veneered chest of drawers, a pocket size bathroom, badly tiled, with an avocado-colored sink and toilet. There was Woolworth's art on the apartment walls. A stack of cheap paperback thrillers by the bed. Aside from a couple of suits and shirts hanging up in the closet, the only personal touch that Ivan had brought to this dump was a half dozen framed photos of Nancy, positioned throughout the apartment so she'd always be in his sight.

The detective turned to me. "Any idea where he'd like his personal possessions to go?"

Personal possessions. When he moved to Hartford, he sold what little furniture he had in his West Eighty-third Street studio. So now, the sum worth of Ivan Dolinsky was two suitcases full of clothes, a pile of Tom Clancy and Ken Follett novels, the ten-year-old Toyota in which he took his life, and a half dozen pictures of his dead child.

"Give everything to charity," I said, gathering up the framed photos. "I'll get these to his wife."

We made a lengthy pit stop at the Hartford precinct where Detective Kaster had a desk. It was a two-step cinch to find the phone number of Ivan's ex-wife, Kirsty, in Florida. She was listed under her married name in Naples. I let Detective Kaster break the news to her. About three minutes into the conversation, Kaster put the call on hold and said, "She wants to speak with you."

I'd only met Kirsty Dolinsky twice before: once at some *CompuWorld* family outing by a lake in the Poconos around four years ago; the second time at her daughter's funeral. I tried to conjure up my initial impression of Kirsty—a small, angular woman, around ten years younger than Ivan (making her now close to forty), highly strung, and super-anxious about keeping an eye on Nancy, especially whenever she wandered near the lakefront.

When Detective Kaster handed me the phone, Kirsty was sobbing.

"Oh, Jesus, Ned. Lie to me. Say he didn't . . ."

"I'm sorry, Kirsty. I'm so sorry."

Her sobbing escalated. When she got a grip on herself, she said, "How'd he do it?"

I told her about the car. This prompted another long torrent of tears. As quietly as possible, I said, "There are a couple of, uh, practical matters we need to discuss." And then, through gentle interrogation, I found out that Ivan wanted to be cremated, that he'd probably like his ashes sprinkled on the Gulf of Mexico (where they often vacationed during the early years of their marriage), and could I get them sent on to her (I scribbled down her address), because, no, she wouldn't be coming north for the funeral.

"I have this new job here—receptionist at the Ritz-Carlton in Naples. Not exactly glamorous, but it pays the rent. I'm on nights the next three days, so it would be kind of hard to take the time off. . . ."

She broke off again, crying. "You know what I keep thinking?" she said. "If Nancy had lived, if that fucking meningitis hadn't shown up . . ."

She couldn't finish that sentence. Her sobbing was now out of control.

"Kirsty," I said, "is there anyone there to look after you right now? Your husband, maybe . . ." I'd heard from Ivan that she'd married a local tennis pro shortly after moving to Naples.

"That ended ten months ago," she said, her voice now steely, semicontrolled. "I've got no one."

I didn't know what to say. She knew that.

"I've gotta go, Ned. Thanks for dealing with everything."

Click. She was gone.

As I turned to explain the gist of that conversation to Detective Kaster, it struck me that I'd probably never speak to Kirsty Dolinsky again. She would now vanish from my existence. A blip. Like so much in life.

Detective Kaster sprang into action. Within fifteen minutes she found a funeral home that would take the body and prepare it for incineration the next day. The first available slot was 3:30 P.M. at a crematorium on the outskirts of Hartford. They'd also provide a reverend to say a few words.

"Ask them to get a rabbi," I said, remembering that Nancy was buried at a Jewish cemetery in Queens.

"Are you going to be the only mourner?" she asked.

I picked up the phone, found the number for *PC Globe* in Manhattan, and asked to be put through to Debbie Suarez.

"Mr. Allen! This is incredible! I was gonna call you today. See if you was free for lunch or somethin'. Howyadoin'?"

"Could be better. They treating you right at *PC Globe*?"

"It's not like old times with you, but hey, a girl's gotta make a living, right? You okay, Mr. A.? You don't sound okay."

I told her exactly why I wasn't okay. For perhaps the first time in her life, Debbie Suarez was at a loss for words. After around thirty seconds of silence, I asked, "You still there, Debbie?"

"Just about," she said, her voice barely audible. "Why?"

"I don't know. Maybe he never really got over the Nancy business. Maybe he just gave up. I just don't know."

I could hear her swallowing hard. "When's the funeral?"

"Tomorrow. Three-thirty. In Hartford." I gave her the address of the crematorium. "You think you could maybe take half a day off, grab the train up here? Otherwise it's just going to be me in attendance."

"I'm gonna do my best to get there, Mr. A. Promise. And I'll also call the old gang—Dave, Doug, Phil, Hildy. See if they can make it, too. We all liked him. . . ."

She started to sob.

"One last favor," I said.

"Anything."

"As soon as you get off the phone, I want you to march into Chuck Zanussi's office, and tell him exactly what happened. And make sure he understands it was a suicide."

"I'm on my way now."

It was just a ten-minute drive from the precinct to the offices of *Home Computer Monthly*. They were located in a small industrial park bordering I-93—and judging from the prefab building in which they occupied the first floor, the magazine looked like the nickel-and-dime operation I had suspected.

There were a lot of nervous glances at the detective and me as we were escorted through a corridor of desks to the office of the publisher, Duane Hellman. He was around thirty-two—a big mop of greasy black hair, a shiny blue suit, a wet, weak handshake. He was visibly anxious in our presence.

"You asked to see Mr. Allen?" Detective Kaster said as we sat down.

Duane Hellman picked up a pencil and began to absently tap it against his desk. "Can I get you folks anything? Tea? Coffee? Diet Coke?"

"You can get to the point, Mr. Hellman," Detective Kaster said. "We don't have all day."

He kept tapping that damn pencil against the desk. "Ivan told me all about you. Said you were just about the best damn boss a salesman could have. Really built you up as some kind of amazing—"

I didn't want to hear this, so I cut him off.

"Do you have any idea why he killed himself?" I said.

The pencil-tapping now escalated to double time. "I've got to tell you, I was just shocked as heck. I mean, Ivan was only with us six or so weeks, but everyone liked him. And he seemed to be in pretty good spirits—"

"Please answer the man's question," Detective Kaster said, sounding peeved. "Why do you think he killed himself?"

Hellman swallowed hard, averted his gaze, tossed the pencil aside. When he finally spoke, his voice was nothing more than a croak.

"I let him go on Friday."

It took a moment to register. "You *what*?"

"Friday was his last day here," he said.

"Because you fired him?"

"I didn't want to . . ."

"Answer the goddamn question."

"Easy, Mr. Allen," Detective Kaster said.

Duane Hellman was now the color of talcum powder. And he looked genuinely frightened of me.

"I liked him, he'd already closed a couple of small things, I really didn't want to let him go. But . . ."

"What do you mean, *you* didn't want to let him go?" I said. "You were his boss—so it was your decision whether he stayed or went."

Hellman picked up the pencil again. Tap-tap-tap.

"He'd become a liability," he said.

"What do you mean by that?" I challenged.

"I mean . . . he was going to cost us if he continued working here."

"If he'd already closed a few things, if you actually *did* like him, then how the hell could you call him a liability?"

Tap-tap-tap. Tap-tap-tap.

"What happened was this," Hellman said, trying to sound composed. "One of our main advertisers informed me that they would cancel all future spreads with us if Ivan continued on in his job."

"What advertiser said that?" I demanded.

Hellman leaned his forehead against the palm of his hand and stared down at his much-doodled-upon desk blotter.

"GBS."

I went numb, rigid.

"Ted Peterson?"

Hellman, still focusing on his blotter, nodded slowly.

"And you bought his threat?"

"I tried to argue his case, but Peterson was adamant."

"And so you kicked Ivan's ass out, no questions asked."

"They're GBS, for God's sake. We depend on them. . . ."

"And Ivan Dolinsky depended on you."

Hellman had begun to sweat, two large watery globules cascading down his beefy face.

"Look, if I knew . . ."

"Did he plead . . . ?"

"I can't tell you how upset—"

"Did Ivan plead with you . . ."

"It wasn't my call . . ."

"DID IVAN FUCKING PLEAD WITH YOU FOR HIS JOB?"

I was hovering over Hellman's desk, yelling. With gentle firmness, Detective Kaster took my right arm and led me back to the chair. Hellman had both hands over his head, as if he'd expected me to punch him. I could hear him whimpering.

"Yeah," he said. "He pleaded."

A long silence. Finally broken by me.

"Murderer."

SIX

It was pointless to return to Manhattan that night. Anyway, after that scene in Duane Hellman's office, I needed several stiff drinks—and Kaster, now officially off duty, was only too happy to keep me company.

Which is how we ended up at an old-style steak joint called Kappy's in a residential corner of West Hartford—where, over the next four hours, Kaster and I bought each other rounds of bourbon and beer, devoured a London broil apiece, and eventually started trading secrets. Hers was a biggie: Just last month, after over twenty-five years in the closet, she had come out as a lesbian.

"It kind of surprised me how everyone in the department took it in their stride. Especially when I showed up at a departmental party with my squeeze, BethAnne."

"What's she do?"

"A plumber."

Having shared this revelation with me, it was my turn (according to the unwritten rules of "strangers drinking together") to divulge a confidence or two. So I told Kaster about the business with Kreplin, and my assorted professional and marital troubles since then.

"You're lucky you didn't slug that nerd Hellman," she said, tossing back her bourbon, " 'cause this time you would've been booked for assault. Have you always been a hair-trigger kind of guy?"

"Only since all this shit started."

"Well, I'd stop it. Like now. And since I'm handing out loads of free advice tonight"—she gave me a tipsy smile—"here's another pearl of wisdom from the dyke detective. I'd give your wife as much space as she needs right now. Know what women hate more than anything in guys? Neediness. You come across desperate to her, you can forget about winning her back."

I kept that advice in mind when I checked into a nearby Marriott motel, which the detective recommended. It was 10:00 P.M. I slumped on the bed and checked my messages at home. No word from Lizzie. So I called her office in L.A. Her secretary, Juliet, was working late.

"I passed on your message from Friday, Mr. Allen. But Lizzie never returned to L.A. yesterday—she had to go straight from Carmel to San Francisco today for a last-minute business thing. Now she's caught up there in a dinner, so we don't expect her back in L.A. until tomorrow. Another message?"

"That's okay."

Instead, I called the Mondrian and asked to be put through to Lizzie's voice mail. I left a simple, straightforward message, in which I explained about Ivan's suicide, how I had ended up identifying the body and arranging the funeral, and wouldn't be back in the city until late Tuesday night. I didn't get emotional. I didn't leave a number in Hartford where she could reach me. I didn't come across as beseeching. As Kaster recommended, I played it cool and sounded very much *in control*. Whereas I was feeling anything but controlled. And I wanted to scream into the phone, *I'm going crazy. . . . I miss you. . . . Please, please, let me jump a plane to the Coast and try to sort things out*.

Why is it that, if we say what we actually feel to the most important person in our lives, we often risk losing that person altogether?

I pondered that question again at three-thirty the next afternoon as I stood outside the crematorium with Detective Kaster, puffing away on a cigarette. A taxi drew up outside the crematorium. The door opened and Debbie stepped out, accompanied by Phil Sirio. I went running over and threw my arms around both of them. I could tell they both looked a little startled by my newly accumulated weight, and by the cigarette clutched between my fingers.

"Thank you," I said. "Thank you so much. I thought I would have to do this alone."

"No problem, boss," Phil said. "Workin' for my brother in the restaurant supply game these days, so I can come and go as I please."

"Yeah, and Mr. Zanussi had no problem giving me the afternoon off," Debbie said.

"How'd he take the news?"

"He went all quiet. I hope the man felt shame. You doin' okay?"

"Could be better."

"What's with the cigarette?" Debbie asked.

"Just a temporary lapse."

"You crazy, Mr. A.? That shit'll kill you. . . ."

"Only if he really works at it," Detective Kaster said, wandering over to join us. I introduced her. But we were interrupted by the oily, black-suited funeral director, clipboard in hand, glancing at his watch like a time and motion analyst.

"I think we should start," he said. Under her breath, Detective Kaster added:

"Because the next customer shows up in half an hour."

The chapel was a plain, simple room. White brick walls, a sandstone floor, varnished pine benches, an imitation marble bier upon which sat the simple wooden coffin I had chosen for Ivan. As they entered, Debbie and Phil did a double take at the sight of the coffin. Not that they didn't expect to see it—but there's always something deeply disquieting about the sight of that box. Because you know that, inside it is someone who, up until a day or so ago, was as alive as you are now. And because you also know that box is your destiny, too.

We all sat together in the front row. The rabbi entered. Early sixties. Black suit, black tie, black yarmulke. We'd spoken on the phone earlier that morning, after I'd had a chat with the funeral home about final arrangements. The rabbi asked what I wanted for the service. Keep it simple, I said. Prayers—but no eulogy. The idea of a stranger extolling Ivan's essential decency and goodness to an empty funeral chapel was just too much to bear.

The rabbi stood to the right of the coffin and began to intone some prayers in Hebrew, his eyes clenched shut, his body gently swaying back and forth like a tree branch in the wind. Then, in

English, he said that he would now say the Kaddish—the prayer for the dead—for our departed brother, Ivan.

At first, his voice was almost imperceptible. But very quickly it swelled into a deep, haunting baritone—fervent, potent, profoundly tragic. And though none of us understood a word of what he was incanting, the emphatic force of those prayers said it all. A man had died. A life had ended. Attention must be paid.

Debbie had covered her face with one hand and was weeping quietly. Phil stared stonily at the coffin, doing his best to control his emotions amid the full-frontal assault of the Kaddish. Even Detective Kaster seemed curiously moved by the terrible loneliness of this service. And me? I just felt . . . adrift. My bearings lost. Wondering why an ethical man like Ivan went under, while an unscrupulous shit like Ted Peterson flourished. And thinking just how easy it was for everything to come unhinged.

Abruptly the Kaddish ended, the final baritone chords reverberating against the chapel walls. Then, after a moment's silence, there was the hum of machinery as the coffin slowly descended from view. The rabbi approached and shook hands with each of us. The unctuous crematorium supervisor ushered us out into the light. I glanced at my watch. The entire service had taken ten minutes.

Detective Kaster had to head back to the precinct. She gave me her card, a peck on the cheek, and told me if I ever needed a plumber I should call BethAnne. I thanked her for everything.

"Go easy," she said. "Especially on yourself."

The funeral director called us a cab. He also discreetly asked me for a credit card ("We accept everything except American Express and Diners"). We declined his offer to wait in "the family lounge." The sun was still bright, the March cold tolerable. I lit up a cigarette and received reproachful looks from Debbie and Phil. But they said nothing. Because the service had rendered us all mute. And because we were all staring at the now smoking chimney.

The funeral director returned with an invoice and a credit card slip for me to sign. I looked down at the price: $3,100, including basic embalming, coffin, transportation, the service, the incineration. Death was not cheap. I also noticed that the charge slip had been made by one of those old-style, by-hand imprint machines.

Thank God for that. Had it been a new, instant-verification machine, my MasterCard would have been instantly declined . . . though I don't know exactly what the oily undertaker could have done about it. Except, maybe, pulling the plug on the furnace before the job was fully done.

"You haven't told me where I should dispatch the ashes," the supervisor said. I handed him the piece of paper on which I had written Kirsty Dolinsky's name and address.

"Included in the charge," he said, "is second-class postage anywhere in the U.S. We can, however, FedEx the ashes for an additional charge of twenty dollars. Guaranteed next-day delivery, of course."

Phil Sirio said, "I don't want Ivan goin' second class." Then, whipping out a large roll of money, he peeled off a twenty, scrunched it up into a ball, and dropped it right at the director's feet.

"There's your extra twenty," he said with unconcealed contempt. "And if I hear that Ivan ain't in Florida tomorrow, *you* are gonna hear from me."

We caught the 4:20 Amtrak express back to Penn Station. We sat in the bar car. Phil nursed a beer, I threw back a bourbon on the rocks, Debbie quickly killed a rum and Coke, then started to cry. Loudly.

We drank all the way back to New York. Phil kept plying me with bourbon, and I found myself unable to stop talking—the whole god-awful story of the past ten weeks spilling out in a torrent of words. It really was like an extended stint in the confessional box. And though Phil and Debbie couldn't offer me absolution, they were, at least, two pairs of sympathetic ears.

"Man, what's your wife doin', running away from you at a time like this?" Debbie said.

"What's been happening is not exactly her fault," I said. "I mean, it takes two to blow a marriage, doesn't it? And I haven't exactly been the easiest guy to be around recently."

Thankfully, we didn't dwell too long on the state of my marriage, as Phil really wanted to vent a lot of rage about Mr. Ted Peterson.

"That white-bread, preppy piece of shit," he said. "The guy

comes across all Mr. Brooks Brothers, Mr. Fairfield-fucking-County—but at heart he's just some vengeful *goombah*. I know hit men who've got more morals than this clown. I don't like saying it, boss, but you should've—"

"I know, I know. I was trying to do the right thing."

"What did I tell you at the time? You can't play nice and noble with an unethical fuckhead. You should've let me make that call."

Debbie asked, "What are you talking about?"

"*Fugedaboudit*," Phil said and dropped the subject. When we reached Grand Central, Phil insisted on dragging us to the bar of the adjoining Grand Hyatt Hotel for a final drink. Four hours later—when, underneath the table, Debbie began to stroke my thigh with her hand—I decided it was time to call it a night. So I stood up and said, "Listen, folks, I got to go. Again, I can't thank you enough for making it up to Hartford. . . ."

Debbie staggered to her feet. "If you're goin', I'm goin'. I gotta get home to Raul."

I reached into my pocket for my wallet. "Phil, lemme help out with the damage. . . ."

"Your money's no good here," he said. Then, scribbling a couple of numbers on a paper cocktail napkin, he said, "Here's my number at my brother's office. You need me, you know where to find me."

Standing up, he gave me a hug and shoved the napkin into the breast pocket of my jacket. Outside the hotel I hailed a cab. As I was opening the door for Debbie she grabbed me by the arm, giving me a tipsy smile.

"Ride downtown with me," she said.

"I'm wasted, Debbie. Beyond wasted."

"Drop me home, it's not out of your way, then you can take the cab 'cross town. I've got some stuff I wanna say."

Reluctantly I climbed in after her, determined to remove her hand from my thigh if she began to stroke it again. I had enough problems right now.

Debbie gave the driver her address and we headed south. Then, reaching into her purse, she pulled out a folded piece of paper and handed it to me.

"This is for you," she said.

I opened up the paper. It was a check. Made out to me. For forty-five hundred dollars.

"What the hell is this, Debbie?" I asked.

"You know what it is."

The check swam in front of me. I was drunk. "Really, I don't."

"The money you gave Faber Academy for Raul's tuition. . . ."

"I didn't give the school money. It was *CompuWorld*. . . ."

"Mr. Allen . . ."

"You really can call me—"

"Okay, okay, *Ned*. A couple of nights ago I was at the school. Some parent-teacher thing. And I got talkin' to the bursar, who's actually an all-right guy. Anyway, he told me that Spencer-Rudman called him up a couple months ago, making this big stink about the letter you signed saying *CompuWorld* would guarantee the money I owed the school. And when he told them a guarantee's a guarantee, they said, yeah, yeah, yeah, they were gonna honor it, but you had no authority to write that letter. And you were gonna get stuck with the bill. The shits did stick you with the forty-five hundred, didn' they?"

"Debbie . . ."

"I *know* they did . . . 'cause I got this new friend, Paula, up in accounts. Yesterday morning, before you called, I got her to pull your file, look up your payout. I got to tell ya, Mr. Allen . . . *Ned* . . . I cried when she snuck me the letter they wrote you."

I stared down at the check. "It wasn't exactly me playing fairy godfather, Debbie. *They* decided I was going to be Mr. Charitable."

"Yeah . . . but the thing is, you didn't fight it. And you didn't make me feel bad by letting me know. . . ."

"Not my style."

She put her hand over mine. "I like your style."

I gently removed my hand and tore the check in two.

"I knew you were gonna do that," she said, then added with a laugh, "But that's not why I wrote it."

We fell silent. Then Debbie said, "Thank you."

As directed, the cab stopped at Nineteenth and First, right near one of the dark entrances to that 1950s Lego-labyrinth of middle-income housing called Stuyvesant Town. There were a couple of seedy-looking characters loitering on the street.

"How far's your building?" I asked Debbie.

"Halfway to the river," she said.

That settled the matter. I pushed some money through the cabbie's window. "I'll walk you to your door."

We said nothing as we headed into Stuyvesant Town. When we reached the door, she said, "Come inside, see Raul. . . ."

"I'm really fried. . . ."

She dug out the key from her purse and opened the front door. "It'll just take a minute. Anyway, don't you want to see where your money's going?"

"Just a minute, then," I said—but I was really talking to myself.

The apartment was on the ground floor. It was very cramped, very thrown together. Old sagging charity shop furniture. Foldout drying racks filled with freshly washed clothes. An elderly television and VCR. Raul's school paintings Scotch-taped to the walls.

There was a tiny alcove off the living room, furnished with a bunk bed. On the top bunk lay the snoring figure of Debbie's mother. Raul was asleep in the lower bunk. Long, curly black hair, perfect unblemished skin, a slight hint of a smile as he slept. An angelic innocent.

"He's beautiful," I whispered. Debbie nodded in agreement.

"Time to go," I said. We stepped away from the alcove. I moved to kiss her good night on the cheek. But suddenly we were all over each other, my hands in her hair, on her breasts, up her skirt, the two of us stumbling backward toward a doorway, collapsing on her bed, my brain sending out danger signals, the signals being drowned out, her hands grabbing my shirt, a final faint admonishing voice inside my head: *This is insane* . . .

Fade to black.

Daylight. A shaft of daylight, to be exact, sneaking through a tiny gap in the blinds. I opened one eye. A serious mistake. The light hit the optic nerve, sending an electrical charge of pain into the deep recesses of my skull. I opened the second eye. *Bang. Crack. Wallop*. Now my head felt as if it had been cleaved by an ice pick. My mouth was Sahara-dry. My eyes felt puffy, my face bloated and greasy. And, for a moment or two, I found myself wondering, Where the hell have I crash-landed?

And then I noticed that I was naked, lying next to an equally naked Debbie Suarez. She was comatose, snoring deeply. I felt that free-floating horror, known to every man or woman who has woken up, on the morning after, to discover themselves in a place they shouldn't be, lying next to someone they shouldn't be lying next to. And though I could try to blame the booze, the lateness of the hour, the emotional burden of Ivan's death, the heat of the moment, and any other excuse you care to mention, the fact remained: This was a fuckup of my own making.

I glanced at my watch: 7:12 A.M. I had to get out. Fast. I sat up in bed and, as quietly as possible, lowered my feet to the floor. As my toe touched the frayed carpet, I noticed (with immense relief) a spent condom on the floor—and, with a bit of mental effort, vaguely remembered Debbie interrupting the impassioned proceedings to dig around in the drawer of her bedside table for a Trojan.

The used condom was the good news. The bad news was revealed to me by the mirror on the wall next to her bed. There was a small but unmistakable hickey on the right side of my neck, and a few discernible scratches near my throat. Thank God Lizzie was still in L.A., and would be there for at least another week. Because it was pretty clear what activity had led to these scars.

My clothes were in a crumpled pile by the bed. I scooped them up and slinked into the bathroom. My suit looked as if it had been balled up and used for an impromptu basketball game. I dressed quickly, spread an inch of toothpaste on my forefinger and rubbed it around my gums in an attempt to rid my mouth of its rank morning-after taste. Then I snuck back into the bedroom. Debbie was still down for the count, and I was deeply relieved. Quite frankly, I didn't know what to say to her. Except *oops*.

I slowly crept to the bedroom door, gently opened it, then shut it behind me. Only ten steps separated me from the front door of the apartment. I heard Grandma's thunderous snoring coming from the top bunk. Like a thief terrified of setting off a hidden burglar alarm, I tiptoed my way across the living room. Then I heard a voice:

"Can you spell *discovery,* please?"

I spun around and there, sitting in the apartment's little breakfast nook, was Raul. He was dressed in Power Rangers pajamas, digging into a bowl of Sugar Pops. He had a schoolbook opened, and was doing some homework with a small stub of a pencil. He was a big kid for a six-year-old. I put my finger to my lips and approached him.

"What was the word?" I asked.

"Discovery," he said loudly.

"Let's not wake your grandma."

"Discovery," he whispered. "I've got to fill in the sentence, *Thomas made an interesting . . .*"

"D—I—S—C—O—V—E—R—Y."

He mouthed each letter as he wrote them into his workbook.

"What discovery did Thomas make?" I asked.

Raul stared down intently at the workbook again, and read, "'*Thomas was going on a. . . .* How do you spell *journey*?"

"How do you think you spell *journey*?"

"J—O—R . . ."

"J—O—*U*—R . . ."

"J—O—*U*—R—N—E—Y."

"Good spelling," I said, squeezing his shoulder. "I've got to go. . . ."

"Are you Mommy's friend?"

"Yeah, I'm a friend of your mom's."

"Are you going on a J—O—U—R—N—E—Y?"

"I'm going to work. Please tell your mom I'll be in touch."

"My name is Raul. That's R—A—U—L. How do you spell your name?"

"N—E—D."

He gave me a shy smile. "Later, Ned."

"Later, Raul."

I hopped a cab across town. It was 7:48 by the time I reached my building. A fast shower and shave, a change of clothes, a cup of coffee, a handful of Raw Energy vitamins, and then a sprint uptown in time for the eight-thirty punch-in at PC Solutions. I dreaded to think about the greeting I would get from the Jellyfish. Eighteen units was the punishment for missing work on Tuesday (not to mention being docked a second day's pay). I'd have to do a lot of closing between now and Friday afternoon if I wanted to have a job next week.

I turned the key in our door and was surprised to discover that it wasn't double-locked. When I swung the door open, I heard the sound of running water from the kitchen. Then, with a growing sense of alarm, I saw a small overnight bag to the immediate right of the door.

Lizzie was back.

My first instinct was to run—to quietly back out the door, hit the fire stairs, and vanish from view until my war wounds healed. But in my panic, I stepped away from the door and it slammed behind me.

The kitchen tap suddenly went silent.

"Ned?" Lizzie yelled from the other room. I reached for the door, but before I could open it, she was standing in front of me. She was wearing a business suit, having obviously just arrived off the red-eye from L.A. She seemed bewildered as to why, having just arrived, I was now clutching at the door handle. Then I turned fully around and her face suddenly tightened—initially with shock, then anger, then desperate hurt.

I watched as she caught sight of the scratches and the dime-sized hickey on my neck. But most of all, I saw her register my terrible guilt.

She closed her eyes and shuddered. Then she opened them again—and the look on her face was now one of pure despair.

"You asshole," she whispered.

"Lizzie, please . . ."

"Fuck you," she said and marched into the bedroom. I raced after her, but the door slammed shut in my face. She locked it. I rattled the handle, banged the door with my fist, begging her to open it, telling her I could explain everything . . . even though I knew there was no explanation for what I did. Except complete and total stupidity.

After about three minutes of banging and pleading, I slumped to the floor, feeling spent and genuinely scared. The bedroom door suddenly opened. Instantly I was back on my feet.

"Lizzie, you've got to let me try and . . ."

Then I saw that she had a suitcase in each hand.

"Sweetheart," I said, "please don't leave."

She dropped the suitcases at my feet.

"I'm not leaving," she said. "You are."

"Hang on a minute. . . ."

"I pay the rent now; I pick up all the bills, so if this marriage is ending, I don't see why *I* should leave. . . ."

"This marriage is *not* ending."

"You're right. I was using the wrong tense. It's over."

"Darling . . . ," I said, trying to touch her shoulder. She swatted me away as if I were a wasp.

"Don't you goddamn touch me. . . ."

"Okay, okay," I said, trying to lower the emotional temperature. "Could we just sit down and talk—"

"Talk? TALK?" she screamed. "You screw someone else and then you want to *talk* about it?"

She went storming into the living room. I followed.

"It wasn't like that. Nothing happened."

"Nothing happened? You can actually stand there—covered in evidence—and tell me *nothing happened*? Get out of my life."

I began to sob. "I was drunk, I was stupid, I was all over the place after the business with Ivan, I didn't mean—"

"I don't want to hear your bullshit excuses, Ned. . . ."

"At least give me the chance—"

"Give *you* the chance? After I got your message about Ivan, I dropped everything and flew cross-country all night—because I thought, 'Okay, he deserves the chance . . . *we* deserve the chance.' And what do I discover?—that my piece-of-shit husband doesn't even have the aptitude to tell his floozie not to bite his neck."

"She's not 'my floozie'. . . ."

"I don't give a shit who she is, *what* she is. We are finished."

"You can't just end it—"

"I can't? Who are you to say I can't?"

"I made a mistake. A terrible mistake."

I sank down onto the sofa and put my head in my hands. Lizzie stood and watched me cry. As my weeping intensified, she didn't move, didn't soften, didn't stop staring at me with dispassionate contempt. When I quieted down, she spoke.

"I made a mistake, too," she said, "thinking there was a chance of putting this all back together again."

Her voice broke, her eyes began to fog with tears. "How could you? How fucking could you . . . ?"

"I didn't mean—"

"Who cares what you 'meant,' Ned. You did it. Knowing full well our marriage was on shaky ground, you still went ahead and did it. And there's no excusing that."

She wiped her eyes with the back of her hand. Then, picking up the two suitcases, she walked to the front door, opened it, and deposited the bags in the hallway.

"You're going now," she said.

I didn't move.

"Did you hear me? I want you out of here," she said.

"Please, Lizzie . . ."

"There is nothing more to say."

"There is *everything* to say. . . ."

"I'll be talking to a lawyer today."

"Say I refuse to go."

"Then I'll get the lawyer to make you go. With an injunction. You want an ugly scene, Ned? I'll give you an ugly scene."

I was in a no-win situation. I'd blown it—and no amount of arguing or begging would bring her around. So I stood up and walked to the door. My hand on the knob, I turned and was about to launch into one final plea. But before I could say a word, she cut me off.

"I don't want to know," she said.

She walked into the bedroom, slamming the door shut behind her. Silence. Then I heard her crying.

I approached the closed door.

"Lizzie . . . ," I said softly.

Her crying abruptly stopped.

"Fuck off and die," she said.

I remained paralyzed to the spot. I scanned the apartment frantically, as if there were something there—a wedding photo, a vacation memento, a dumb little trinket we bought together on a whim—that would make everything better, end the crisis, bring us back together again. But all I saw was sleek interior design and polished wood floors and big bright windows that framed the midtown skyline with all its vertical promise. And I thought, *There's nothing of us here. Nothing at all.*

Then, as instructed, I walked to the front door. I opened it. Is this how a marriage ends? An opening and a shutting of a door? Is that what it all comes down to?

The door closed behind me. With a thud.

SEVEN

I had $7.65 in my pocket. And it was raining. Not a mild little drizzle, but a near monsoon. I lugged my bags through this downpour to Sixth Avenue and spent ten minutes trying to find a cab. No luck. I checked my watch. 8:18 A.M. Even if I hauled my suitcases over to the subway, there was no way I was going to make the 8:30 A.M. punch-in time at P.C. Solutions. So I found a phone booth and called the Jellyfish. Before I had a chance to say I'd be late, he interrupted me.

"Why weren't you at work yesterday?" he asked.

"When I called on Monday, I warned you that I might have to stay in Hartford for another day."

"No, you just said you'd be out Monday. Then *I* told you that if you did miss Tuesday, you'd be docked a day's pay, and your week's quota would rise to eighteen units. But I didn't give you *permission* to be absent for the day."

"I must have misunderstood you, Mr. Rubinek," I said, trying to sound calm. "But, as I told you, a good friend of mine died."

"That's not my problem. Your quota is now twenty-two units. And an additional three units on top of that if you're not here at eight-thirty. You've got nine minutes."

I suddenly heard myself saying, "Fuck you, you sadistic geek." Then I slammed down the phone—after which I thought, *I have just resigned.*

Having finally told that pathetic monster what I thought of him, I felt a buzz of triumphant satisfaction. That lasted about a nanosecond—at which point I remembered that I was homeless and jobless, and that my worldly assets now totaled $7.40.

I considered my limited options. I could try to check into a hotel, but none of my credits cards would permit such an extravagance (and if I wrote a personal check for the room it would bounce like a basketball, allowing the bank to prosecute me under federal law). So I needed to throw myself on the mercy of a friend. But who? After last night's insanity I really didn't want to make contact with Debbie Suarez because I was terrified that she might interpret my call as an expression of ongoing romantic interest. She was a widow with a kid, after all. If she found out that Lizzie had left me, she'd probably zoom in on me like a heat-seeking missile. Right now I was about the worst catch imaginable. I was trouble—and she, of all people, didn't deserve trouble.

There was, of course, Ian and Geena—but I could already hear Lizzie's rage when Geena called her in L.A. to say that I'd scrounged a bed for a couple of nights. And I was certain Ian and Geena would feel rather used when Lizzie informed them of the real reason why I was locked out of my apartment. Who else? Phil Sirio. Bingo.

I dug out my wallet in search of the cocktail napkin on which he'd scribbled his phone numbers. But as I shuffled through assorted wallet debris (credit card slips, taxi receipts, old business cards) I found myself staring at Jerry Schubert's card. He'd asked me to call him ("*Don't be a stranger*")—and, unlike Phil, he did live in Manhattan. Surely he'd help out an old Brunswick High pal for a few days. I fed a quarter into the phone and nervously punched in his office number. After keeping me on hold for a moment, his secretary put me through.

"Ned!" he said, sounding pleased to hear from me. "I was hoping you'd call. Sounds like you're on the street. . . ."

"You could say that."

"Where you calling from right now? Your West Twentieth Street tennis club?"

"I'm in a phone booth at Nineteenth and Sixth. . . ."

I must have sounded a little shaky, as Jerry asked, "Everything okay, Ned?"

"Not really. I'm in a bit of trouble, Jerry."

"What kind of trouble?"

"Big trouble—as in, I don't know where I'm going to sleep tonight."

"That sounds serious." With a laugh, he added, "Don't tell me your wife threw you out?"

"I'm afraid she actually did."

"Hey, I'm sorry."

"Shit happens," I said weakly.

"Yeah—especially in marriage. Listen, I've got to run into a meeting with Mr. B. Get up to my office—it's 502 Madison Avenue, between Fifty-third and Fifty-fourth—and we'll take it from there, okay?"

The rain was still torrential. There were no cabs on Sixth Avenue. And when I tried to get cash on every credit and ATM card in my wallet, the machine kept flashing the same message: INSUFFICIENT FUNDS. So I dragged my bags down into the depths of the subway, bought a token, and squeezed onto a packed uptown car. My bulky suitcases did not win me friends among my fellow passengers. Especially after I accidentally dropped one bag on the toes of the woman executive standing next to me.

"Watch it!" she said sharply as the bag hit her feet.

"I'm really sorry," I said.

She shook her head with disdain. Under her breath, she muttered the ultimate New York insult:

"Tourist."

I closed my eyes and wished this day were over.

I got off at Fifty-third and Fifth. After dragging the bags upstairs to the street, my shoulders felt as if they were on the verge of dislocation. The downpour had been transformed into a steady drizzle. I struggled east for two blocks, and all but fell into 502 Madison Avenue.

The offices of Ballantine Industries were located in a sleek 1950s skyscraper—one of those proud, vertical testaments to postwar optimism and corporate confidence. There was a security man posted near the elevators. He took one look at my drenched, disheveled state (and my two large suitcases) and immediately filed me away under *Trouble*. He blocked my path.

"Who are you visiting, sir?"

"Jerry Schubert at Ballantine Industries."

He motioned me toward a cluster of chairs. "You can wait there while I call him."

"But he's expecting me."

"I'm sure he is," the guard said, returning to his desk. "Please sit down."

I planted myself on a chair. My overcoat was sodden, my shoes waterlogged, and I felt an internal chill coming on. The guard hung up the phone and said, "Mr. Schubert is on his way down to see you."

Jerry showed up two minutes later, dressed in his overcoat, briefcase in hand.

"You look like a drowned rat," he said with a smile. "Having a bad day?"

"The worst."

"Come on," he said, picking up one of my bags. "There's a car waiting outside."

A Lincoln Town Car was parked at the curb. The uniformed driver relieved us of the two bags and put them in the trunk. We climbed into the backseat. Jerry told the driver, "First stop is 115 Wooster Street, then I'm heading to 111 Broadway, at the intersection of Broadway and Wall Street."

Turning toward me, Jerry said, "I'm off to a meeting with some financial guys, but I'll drop you off at my place on the way."

"Listen, if this is an inconvenience, just loan me a hundred bucks and I can find some cheap hotel for a night or two."

Jerry rubbed his right thumb and forefinger together.

"Know what this is?" he said. "The world's smallest violin. Cut the self-pitying shit, Allen. It doesn't wash with me."

"Sorry."

"If you want a bed, I've got a spare room in my loft."

"Sold," I said. "And I really can't thank you . . ."

He held up his hand.

"Gratitude accepted. What the hell is that on your neck?"

"A hickey."

"Courtesy of your wife?"

"I wish."

He laughed.

"So that's the problem?"

"It's a long story. Everything's a long story."

In the cab going downtown, I told him the entire god-awful tale—from the moment Getz-Braun was sold, to being evicted by Lizzie. When I finished talking, Jerry let out a long whistle.

"That's some epic," he said.

"And it's not over yet—considering that I'm now homeless. . . ."

"Rule Number One of the Jack Ballantine philosophy of life: If you want to bounce back, you *will* bounce back."

"I want to believe that," I said.

Jerry's apartment was between Prince and Spring. It was stark and empty. Bleached floors, plain white walls, a large black leather couch, a television, a stereo, a long steel table and chairs. The guest bedroom was tiny. It accommodated nothing more a double futon and a clothes rack. To call it austere was an understatement—it seemed devoid of any signs of actual life.

"Quite a place," I said.

"I'm hardly ever here," he said, "except for the six hours a night I'm asleep. As long as you're tidy, you can stay here indefinitely."

"I'm very tidy," I said. "And very grateful."

"Do you have any idea what your next move might be?" he asked.

"I'm in the market for anything," I said. "Especially since I'm about to be named Debtor of the Month."

"How deep you in for?"

"Around seventeen thousand."

"Impressive."

"That's one way of looking at it."

"Anyway, first things first. Make yourself at home. Hang your stuff up in the spare room, order in any food you want, 'cause there's nothing but beer in the fridge. You okay for cash?"

"Fine," I said.

"Bullshit." He pulled out his money clip, peeled off two $50 bills, and handed them to me.

"Jerry, I can't accept your charity. . . ."

He stuffed the bills into the breast pocket of my suit.

"Yeah, well, that dumb-ass Maine pride doesn't wash with me. I'm going to be out late tonight. . . ."

"Business?"

"Pleasure," he said.

"The beautiful Cindy?"

"Nah—she's history."

"Jesus, that was fast."

"It usually is with me. Listen, I've got to get to this meeting. We'll talk in the morning. But here's a small piece of advice, Ned. Try to kick back today, and not worry about tomorrow. Because life's going to look a lot better after you've gotten twelve hours' sleep."

"You're a good guy."

"Shut the fuck up," he said with a smile. "Catch you later."

I unpacked my bags, stripped out of my wet clothes, took a long hot shower, changed into a pair of jeans and a T-shirt, and made a pot of coffee. I began to feel vaguely human again—until I thought about Lizzie, and how badly I'd blown it. I checked my watch. It was just before noon. I knew what I was going to have to do. Call her at work, beg her to meet me, apologize profusely, and (if necessary) get down on my hands and knees and plead with her for another chance.

I picked up the phone and punched in Lizzie's office number. Her assistant, Polly, answered. She obviously knew what was going on, because her tone with me was nervously cool.

"You just missed Lizzie," she said. "She had a couple of meetings this morning, and then caught the noon American flight back to L.A. You know, she's still in charge of our office out there."

So she really had dropped everything and flown cross-country to try to reconcile with me. Oh you dumb, stupid asshole, Allen. You walked right into the oncoming headlights.

Polly continued talking. She sounded extremely jittery. "Uh, Ned, I don't know how to say this . . . but Lizzie also asked me to inform you that she . . . uh . . . asked the landlord to sublet the apartment. She also told him that you were not living there anymore, and asked him to arrange for everything to go into storage. So if you need to get any of your stuff, you should call—"

"I have the landlord's name and number," I said.

"Of course you do," she said quietly.

"Please tell Lizzie I'm staying with a friend in SoHo, and that I can be reached at 555-7894."

"Anything else, Ned?"

"Just tell her how sorry I am."

I hung up quickly so she wouldn't hear me burst into tears. It took about ten minutes for me to calm down. Had my father seen me now, he would have been appalled. "When you make a mistake, *acknowledge* the mistake," my father once told me, "then take your lumps in silence. Allen men don't cry."

Nor do they fuck up as badly as I had fucked up.

I resisted the temptation to steady my nerves with several shots of Jerry's malt whiskey. And when I felt myself in need of a cigarette, I walked over to the kitchen, turned on the sink tap, and doused my pack of Winstons. No more booze, no more tobacco, and I was going to start jogging tomorrow morning. I thought about Jerry's quotation from the collected sayings of Chairman Ballantine: *"If you want to bounce back, you will bounce back."* True. The problem was: Would Lizzie ever give me the chance to bounce back again?

I spent the afternoon on Jerry's sofa, browsing through the complete works of Jack Ballantine (which were displayed prominently on Jerry's thinly populated bookshelves). You needed a serious sense of irony to wade through these self-empowerment gospels. Knee-deep in football metaphors, they appeared tailor-made for the guy I used to be—the slick, on-the-make salesman who wanted to believe that there was an actual recipe for success, a strategic formula you could use in order to *maximize your goals* and *achieve optimum results*.

But though I laughed at Ballantine's endless gridiron references, I did find myself wincing when I read the following passage in the Great Motivator's current best-seller, *The Success Zone*:

> In business, we define ourselves by our ethical posture. The profit motive is a *great* motive—but it becomes an even greater motive when commingled with scrupulousness. The business arena is a tough one—so when you're making a forward charge, always be sure to back it up with a strong zone defense. But believe me: If that forward charge is not played according to the rules—if you, as the quarterback, attempt

> to gain ground through illegal maneuvers—then any touchdowns you make will always seem like false triumphs. Because secretly you'll know that one day, someone will figure out just how you scored those points.

At *CompuWorld,* I'd always tried to abide by the rules, to maintain an ethical posture. Until that bastard Kreplin offered me Chuck's job, and Peterson pulled the rug out from under Ivan, after which I began to play things fast and loose. Legally speaking, I hadn't been "unethical." I'd never overtly blackmailed Peterson, and I was sworn to secrecy by Kreplin about my "promotion" to publisher. But *I* knew I had let my scruples slide. Once you dabble in the amoral, you lose your bearings. And drift. Right out to sea.

I only left the loft once that afternoon, to hike down to the local grocery store and stock up on fruit, vegetables, and fizzy water. By nine that night, after a hearty rabbit-food dinner, exhaustion set in. I climbed into the futon and conked right out.

I was out cold for eleven hours. When I finally awoke and made it to the kitchen, I caught sight of a note left for me on the steel dining table. Next to it was a crisp $100 bill.

> Hombre:
> Hope you slept. Here's some extra cash, in case you need to buy yourself a new toothbrush. But try to hang by the phone this morning, just in case we need to speak with you.
>
> Later,
> Jerry.

I read the note several times over, wondering what the hell Jerry meant by that just-in-case-we-need-to-speak-to-you line. Unless, of course, working for the Great Motivator had turned Jerry hoitytoity, and he was now using the royal "we."

I pocketed the cash, feeling faintly embarrassed about accepting Jerry's charity. Then I drank a glass of orange juice and went out for a run.

My plan was to jog straight up West Broadway and then do a fast circuit around Washington Square Park before heading south again. I got as far as the intersection of West Broadway and Houston (in other words, around five blocks) before I doubled over with a sudden sharp stitch in my chest.

No, it wasn't a coronary. Just a stern reminder from my cardiovascular system that I was seriously out of shape . . . and that cigarettes are wonderful for your health.

I killed the rest of the morning cleaning the loft. It was something to do—and it also helped ease the guilt I felt at accepting my host's charity. Around noon the phone rang. It was Jerry's secretary.

"Mr. Schubert is tied up in meetings all day. But he'd like you to meet him for dinner at Bouley Bakery at nine. The address is—"

"I know where it is," I said, remembering that Lizzie and I had eaten there once, and that it was absurdly overpriced. "He was also wondering if you wouldn't mind picking up a couple of his suits at G & G Dry Cleaners, behind the SoHo Grand Hotel."

"No problem. Any other errands he needs run for him?" I wondered if she heard the eager-to-please nervousness in my voice. Because, at this juncture, Jerry was the only thing standing between me and the street—and I was willing to do just about any reasonable task he requested to stay in his good books.

"That's all he mentioned," she said. "He'll see you at nine."

Bouley Bakery was located in Tribeca—a mere ten-minute walk from Jerry's loft. I arrived at nine. There were only ten tables in the restaurant. I was shown to the one booked under the name of Schubert. At 9:15 there was still no sign of Jerry, and I kept dodging the persistently pleasant waiter's question, "A pre-dinner drink, sir?" because, after dropping $30 on groceries and paying $22 to the dry cleaners for Jerry's suits, my entire worldly net worth was $148, and ten bucks for a martini would have reduced said worth by 6 percent. Since I didn't know where the next $200 might be coming from, I had to be prudent.

So I politely informed the waiter that I'd hold on for my friend's arrival. I kept my head buried in the menu to avoid eye contact with the maître d'—because if Jerry didn't arrive, I'd be forced into the embarassing position of telling him that we wouldn't be needing one of his ultra-precious, five-week-waiting-list (unless you're Ballantine Industries) tables for the night.

Or I could save face and order dinner.

With appetizers starting at $14, entrées at $29, and four bucks minimum for a bottle of water, I might just make it out of there for $65, including tip and tax. God, $65 a head for dinner was nothing to me a couple of months ago. I'd toss down a credit card as if it were a negligible $2 poker chip—and not think about the financial consequences. When it came to money, I wasn't simply reckless, I was totally inattentive. I raced through cash; I never bothered to think about the implications. I never really saw beyond the next deal, the next designer suit, the next designer meal in an over-hyped restaurant. Here's the true definition of a fool: somebody who is so busy struggling to get somewhere that he loses the very thing that gives his struggle some meaning.

"Looking sad, Ned."

I glanced up from the menu and saw that Jerry had arrived.

"Just pensive, that's all," I said.

He sat down, called for some drinks, then asked, "This pensiveness—might it be due to your wife?"

"It might."

"Are you missing her badly?"

"Beyond badly. It's killing me."

"Then do something about it."

"Like what?"

"Like get back on your feet. I promise you: Once you haul yourself together, she'll return."

"Not after what I pulled."

"Was that the first time you got caught?"

"It was the first time I ever did *anything* like that."

"Jesus—are you a Boy Scout?"

"I love my wife."

"Congratulations. But hey, such fidelity is pretty impressive, I guess. And believe me, she definitely knows just how much you love her. . . ."

"After what I did, I don't think that matters."

"Look, all women know that men can be jerks. Especially in

that department. And, hell, it was a one night stand after a friend's funeral, and while the two of you were separated. I promise you—once you get yourself together again, you'll win her back."

The drinks arrived. I lifted my glass of Perrier.

"Jerry, I really can't thank you—"

"Allen, *please*—ease up on the indebtedness. You're making me feel like Saint Jude."

"Okay, okay—but I will say this: You are saving my ass."

"You're going to save your own ass, Allen. Know why? Because you're a natural born salesman. And guys like you always come out on top."

"Even with someone trying to kill your career?"

"I wouldn't worry too much about this Ted Peterson guy."

"Jerry—he's like the Terminator. He won't quit until I'm history."

"Did you say he works for GBS?"

"Yeah—he's head of their media sales department."

"Want me to get him off your case?"

"I want him dead."

Jerry laughed darkly. "That service we can't provide. But I'm sure Mr. Ballantine knows somebody in the GBS management structure. Mr. B. knows somebody *everywhere*. Anyway, after a call from us to the right person, I'm certain Peterson would be ordered to back down. In fact, I bet GBS doesn't even know what he's really up to."

"Thanks for the offer, but I think the damage he's caused is irreversible. I mean, Ivan's dead, and so am I, vis-à-vis the computer business."

Jerry stared down at the glossy surface of his martini and asked, "What do you like most about selling?"

"Talking somebody into a yes."

"Does what you're selling matter much to you?"

"Not at all. The selling game isn't about the commodity—it's about convincing. So, yeah, as long as the product in question isn't illegal, I can sell it."

"That's good to know."

"Why?"

"Because what I want you to sell for us is hardly illegal. In fact—as anyone on Wall Street will tell you—it's pretty cutting-edge stuff. . . ."

"Sorry," I said, interrupting him, "but I think you've lost me somewhere."

He looked up from his drink—and gave me a sardonic grin. "You're not following me?"

"Not exactly."

"Okay, I'll cut to the chase. Would you be interested in a job?"

EIGHT

Jerry Schubert was a master of suspense. After dropping that little bombshell about offering me a job, he then informed me that he never discussed business until after dessert. It was a cruel but shrewd stratagem, a way for Jerry to gauge whether I was someone who, when desperate, overplayed his hand—and would instantly make a grab for the dangled carrot.

I certainly *was* desperate—but I also realized that this was a test. Having spent much of the previous afternoon immersed in Ballantine's self-empowerment gospels, I remembered several paragraphs from *The Success Zone,* in which the Great Motivator let it be known that he considered desperation to be a weakness, a cardinal business sin.

> Never show the other guy that you think you're fighting a lost cause. Consider this no-hope situation: There's only twenty seconds remaining in the fourth quarter, it's the third down, and you're behind 14–10 on your own 30-yard line. Do you panic, do you give in to fear? Only if you want to lose. The true winner is the guy who eyeballs fear and doesn't blink. Instead, he comes out of that huddle knowing that the next pass he throws is going to be a touchdown.

No doubt, Jerry also subscribed to this philosophy. So I didn't commit the blunder of appearing overanxious. Instead, I let Jerry dictate the conversational agenda. When he mentioned that we'd talk turkey when the coffee arrived, I casually nodded in agreement. So, over three courses and a bottle of Cloudy Bay chardonnay, we spent the next hour catching up on each other's lives. After I supplied him with the fast-forward edition of my last fifteen years, Jerry finally got around to giving me a few telling details about his time after Brunswick High (though not mentioning anything about the "thrown game" scandal for which he was eventually cleared). Following graduation, he'd won a full ice hockey scholarship to St. Lawrence University—but couldn't hack it scholastically, and jumped at the opportunity to join a minor-league Canadian pro team in Alberta.

"I was just twenty at the time, and figured I had the world by the scrotum because I was a big swinging-dick pro hockey player. And even though I was only making three-fifty a week, I felt like Wayne Gretzky. Next stop: a million-dollar contract with the NHL."

Of course, the million-dollar contract (and the move upward to the world of major-league hockey) never materialized. Instead, Jerry remained stuck on this nowhere Alberta team, playing against bumpkins, in front of crowds of bumpkins, in bumpkin towns like Sault Sainte Marie, Yellowknife, and Medicine Hat. Six years evaporated in a flash. So, too, did a marriage to a journalist in Alberta—which, according to Jerry, lasted all of about five minutes. Suddenly he was twenty-six. He was now being paid a whopping $600 a week to be head-butted by bozos on skates. His knees were starting to get wobbly, and the team doctor was predicting major orthopedic problems ahead if Jerry didn't retire. Fast.

So he drifted down back across the American border, landing in Detroit, where an ex-player he knew from the Canadian minor leagues was now running a small corporate security agency.

"I was seriously bust, I didn't have a college degree, and *nada* in the way of prospects. Though I didn't exactly relish the idea of working as a freelance security goon in Motown, the money wasn't bad. And I was desperate."

For around a year Jerry played bodyguard to a variety of semi–high-level automobile executives—guys who lived in fear of getting whacked by some dubious union boss, or who had the usual kidnapping paranoias. Occasionally he would also be hired out to watch over a visiting bigwig, like Jack Ballantine, who spent ten days in Detroit during 1990. He was investigating a potential shopping complex project near Grosse Point, and wanted to be guarded by a local guy who knew the territory. Jerry hit it off with Capitalism's Great Quarterback ("I think he liked my hockey credentials"), and about a week after Mr. High-rise returned to New York he received a call from somebody in the Ballantine organization, informing him that Mr. B. was in the market for a new bodyguard. Would he like the job?

"I was on the plane to New York within seconds of putting down the phone. That was seven years ago, and I've never looked back. Because Mr. B. runs his business on a very simple premise: If you look after him, he looks after you. I mean, even after his whole real estate empire went to the wall, he still kept me on the payroll. Know why? Because, as he said to me at the time, 'When a quarterback gets tackled, he needs his best defensive guard by his side to make sure he doesn't get sacked again.' "

Ballantine also knew that Jerry had professional aspirations beyond the role of security goon. So when he decided to reinvent himself as a self-empowerment guru, he promoted Jerry to the role of middleman—letting him liaise with his publishers, his literary agent, and the lecture tour company that initially booked Ballantine's speaking engagements.

"After Mr. B.'s first book, *The 'You' Conquest*, became a major national best-seller, he allowed me to do a lot of the running on the deal side. I mean, the first book sold for three hundred thousand, the second for one point eight million, the third for two point six million, and he can now command around fifty grand per lecture. Last year alone, he did something like two hundred motivational talks—which adds up to some pretty impressive math, wouldn't you agree?"

I nodded. Many times.

"Now, of course, the Great Motivator is such a one-man industry that I've hired a team of three coordinators to handle all his touring logistics. Which is fine by me—because, to be frank with you, I was starting to get a little bored with the entire self-empowerment biz. Having helped make it such a success, there was kind of a 'been there, done that' feeling to it. Since Mr. B. is also somebody who doesn't like to stand still—and is always thinking about the potential for business expansion—he agreed that it was time we consider other entrepreneurial prospects. And after studying assorted investment possibilities, we decided to embark on something rather adventurous, yet potentially very lucrative. Ever heard of private equity funds, Ned?"

The coffee had just arrived at the table. So, too, had the pitch. I sat up straight and made certain I was looking focused.

"Are they like mutual funds?" I asked.

"Not exactly. Mutual funds are a very restrictive, conservative form of investment. They're what Mr. B. calls the Missionary Position School of High Finance—because, though effective, they're not exactly the sexiest way of making financial whoopee. You see, mutual funds are heavily regulated. You can only invest in listed companies, you're very restricted in terms of the investments you're allowed to make, and you're also operating in an incredibly crowded marketplace. Do you know that the American public invests fourteen billion a month in mutual funds? And the pool of money tied up in these funds is so large, the return on the investment is only what the market sector has to offer—at the absolute most, twenty percent in a truly fantastic year. Which—if you're a play-it-safe kind of guy—probably works for you.

"But, when it comes to money and everything else in life, Jack Ballantine is definitely not a 'safety first' type of guy. Neither am I. Which is why we decided to avoid the entire mutual fund business. But then we discovered this thing called private equity funds—which turned out to be a whole different speculative ball game. And perfect for anyone with a gambler's streak."

The way Jerry described it, running a private equity fund was a bit like betting on some very untried horses. It was a collective investment scheme in which a group of speculators bought stakes in companies that were not yet established (or listed on the stock exchange), and that needed capital in order to expand.

"Essentially, the game works like this," Jerry said. "We, as the operators of the fund, approach financial institutions and wealthy private individuals, encouraging them to invest in our equity partnership. Then we seek out new businesses that are developing potentially hot new products. If we think the business in question is an exciting investment, we use some of the fund's money to buy an equity stake in the company. When it goes public, we already possess a very lucrative chunk of its stock. If we choose the right company, the investment returns can be fantastic.

"Say, for example, we've backed a tiny software company that has developed a new cutting-edge Internet browser. In exchange for one million dollars' worth of capitalization, we now own half of its shares. Then a couple of midsize Net providers decide to incorporate this new browser into their software. Suddenly our little Internet browser company is a hot investment prospect. After an initial public offering, it's floated on the stock exchange for thirty million. We've earned fifteen million on our one-million-dollar investment. And that's just the start of our profitability. Because if its stock price climbs higher, we could be on our way to making a small fortune."

I came in here.

"In other words, the object of the exercise is to spot the next Microsoft when it's still just a burgeoning little company."

"I knew you'd pick up on this quickly," Jerry said. "Microsoft is exactly the sort of dream investment that every private equity fund would like to make. Say, back in the late 1970s, you met these two computer geeks named Bill Gates and Paul Allen, who were just developing this weird thing called DOS, and were looking for some urgent capitalization to move their business forward. And say you threw them two million in exchange for a five percent equity stake in their little company. Do you know what that stake would be worth today, had you held on to the stock?"

"Several hundred million?"

"Try billions. Of course, stumbling across the new Microsoft is our ultimate fantasy. By and large, however, we're looking for intriguing small companies that could yield us a minimum initial return of fifteen to twenty percent when they go public, and that could, of course, be worth far more, should their stock prices continue to rise.

"It is a gambler's kind of investment. But if you talk to any fund manager on Wall Street, he'll tell you that private equity funds are the hottest investment possibility going. And there are plenty of institutions and well-heeled individuals out there who are willing to put around ten percent of their investment funds into the hands of private equity managers. Because everyone knows that, if you bet on the right company, the payoff can be huge."

My excitement was growing by the minute. This was exactly the sort of professional arena I'd always dreamed of entering—the arena of high finance, a realm which made selling space in a computer magazine seem negligible, déclassé. It would be a huge career jump. I'd finally be playing in the major leagues.

Jerry motioned for the waiter to replenish our coffee, then said, "Now you're probably wondering about our own private equity fund, and how you might fit into its general structure."

"I'm listening," I said.

The fund was called Excalibur. It specialized entirely in new technology. It had been operating for six months. It currently consisted of private investors, most of whom had past business dealings with Jack Ballantine. However, given his newfound fame as the Great Motivator, Ballantine's name was not directly attached to the fund. Ever since his real estate business went to the wall, Mr. B. had become deeply sensitive about having himself identified with any form of overt financial speculation, given the press's penchant for mocking him whenever possible. So—for sound public relations reasons (and to avoid any conflict of interest with Ballantine's self-empowerment empire)—the fund was "an autonomous entity," registered offshore to a holding company that was owned by a subsidiary of Ballantine Industries. But, of course, the IRS was aware of the fund's existence.

"Officially speaking, offshore funds aren't subject to American tax. However, the Internal Revenue Service expects any American with offshore interests to come forward on a 'good citizen' basis and report his involvement in such a fund. Which, of course, we have done. Because the IRS can turn nasty if they discover you're duping them." He arched his eyebrows. "And because we're *such* good citizens."

To date, the fund had invested in just one single info-technology operation in eastern Europe. What it now needed was new investment possibilities. And Jerry wanted me to use my extensive network of info-tech and software contacts to "talent-spot" emerging companies that might make exciting investments.

"You have to find us that group of geeks operating out of a garage in Palo Alto who have just worked out a way of tripling the speed of the Pentium chip. Or that three-man operation in Spokane that has developed a new, improved, emergency recovery utility for software programs. And if you succeed in both selling the fund and scouting out lucrative new companies, you could end up a very well-off guy."

He then explained the package. Because the fund was still very new and not yet profitable, he could "only" pay me a basic salary of $60,000. However, I'd receive a 3 percent equity stake in any companies I talent-spotted, and in which the fund ultimately decided to invest.

"Think about it. Say you convince us to buy a two-million-dollar, fifty percent equity stake in that Spokane software company. It floats on the exchange for forty million. That's an instant twenty-million gain for us, and you own three percent of that stock. In other words, an immediate six hundred thousand. Pick us just two winners like that every year, and you're going to be, financially speaking, nicely set up."

I couldn't believe what I was hearing. This wasn't just a job—it was a pursuit that could potentially transform my entire professional life. I would be able to eradicate all my debt, build up some capital, regain a little self-respect. And, in the process, hopefully win Lizzie back.

"So what do you think, Ned?"

"I think this is exactly what I've been looking for."

"Well, life is all about timing. Because I've been scouting around for someone like you, with your sales and computer business background. And when you called me yesterday, I couldn't help but think, so that's what they mean by synchronicity."

"There's only one small logistical problem," I said. "I'm going to need to take advantage of your spare bed for a few more days while I look for a new apartment."

"Why go to the expense of finding a new place? You stay as long as you like at the loft. Like I said to you yesterday, I'm hardly ever there."

I couldn't believe my luck. Not having to worry about rent for the immediate future meant I could pay off my debts *pronto*.

"By the way," Jerry said, "though I appreciate the gesture,

there's really no need to clean the place yourself—I've got a woman who comes in twice a week to do that for me."

"Hey, I've got to do something to ease my guilt. . . ."

"As far as I'm concerned, you're not a freeloader—you're an *investment*. Somebody who is going to make us a lot of money."

"That's what I'd like to do," I said.

"That's what you *will* do."

"So when do I start?" I asked.

"After you play tennis with Jack Ballantine."

Initially I thought this was Jerry's idea of a joke. But he was absolutely serious.

"I told Mr. B. that, besides being a first-rate salesman, you were also a *monster* tennis jock. Know what he said? 'Well, before we hire the guy, let's see if he can kick my butt on the court.' "

I was suddenly nervous. "Do you mean that the job is contingent on whether or not I beat him?"

"No," Jerry said. "The job is dependent on whether or not he likes the way you play the game."

I tried to protest that I was really out of shape, and not the behind-the-baseline gunslinger of high school. But Jerry just shrugged and said that Ballantine was expecting me at nine the next morning at the Health and Racquet Club, and if I wanted the job I'd better be there.

"Does it have to be the Health and Racquet Club?" I asked.

"It's where Mr. B. always plays. In fact, he was one of its founding members."

"I was a member there, too," I said.

"But not anymore?"

"I kind of let my membership lapse."

Jerry smiled knowingly. "How much do you owe them?"

"It really doesn't matter. . . ."

"How much, Ned?"

"Eight hundred," I said with an embarrassed gulp.

"That's nothing," Jerry said, reaching into his pocket and pulling out a substantial wad of cash.

"Jerry, you really don't have to do this. . . ."

"All I'm doing," he said, counting off eight $100 bills, "is making certain your game with Mr. Ballantine tomorrow goes off without a hitch. So get there early and make certain the club management have this money in their hot little hands before Mr. B. shows up. We don't want an embarrassing scene."

"How will I pay you back?"

"From your first equity stake."

"But say I don't get the job?"

"You *will* get the job. Just remember one thing. When you're out there on the court with Ballantine, *play to win*. It's the only game he understands."

I tried to remember that advice the next morning when I found myself waiting nervously in the lobby of the New York Health and Racquet Club, anxiously awaiting the arrival of Jack Ballantine. As Jerry suggested, I had shown up twenty minutes beforehand to deal with the little matter of my overdue annual fee. The club manager, a petite, pumped woman in her forties named Zelda, wasn't exactly effusive when I walked in the door.

"Ah, Mr. Allen," she said dryly, "we'd thought you'd left the country."

"I have been out of town a bit," I lied, "but you've been on my conscience."

With that I handed her an envelope, filled with eight $100 bills. "This should bring us up to date."

"Better late than never, I suppose—even if we did have to send you six letters. . . ."

"Like I said, I've been away a lot. But I do apologize. . . ."

"You do realize, of course, that this simply cancels out last year's overdue fees. Your membership, however, still remains lapsed. So if you want to play here again, you'll have to reapply."

"Well, I'm a guest today."

"And I suppose whomever you're playing with is a fully paid-up club member?" she asked with blatant sarcasm.

"He is," said a nearby voice.

Zelda looked up and was stunned to find herself staring at Jack Ballantine. He was standing right behind me, dressed in a gray Ralph Lauren tracksuit and carrying a tan leather tennis bag.

"Morning, Zelda," Ballantine said, flashing her a big white smile. She became instantly obsequious.

"Oh, Mr. Ballantine, how nice to—"

"You giving my guest a hard time, Zelda?"

"Of course not, Mr. Ballantine."

"Sounded that way to me."

"There was just a little confusion about an old membership matter."

"But that's settled now, right? And my friend won't have to reapply again for membership, will he?"

"Absolutely not, Mr. Ballantine. We'll reinstate him right away. And I do apologize to you, Mr. Allen. . . ."

"Apology accepted," Ballantine said on my behalf. Then, tapping me on the shoulder, he said, "Come on, kid," and I followed him toward the locker room.

As soon as we were out of earshot, Ballantine turned to me and said, "Isn't power a joke?" Then he proffered his hand. "Nice to meet you, Ned."

"Mr. Ballantine, I'm really sorry you had to get involved back there. . . ."

"Why the hell should you be sorry? How much did you owe the club?"

"Eight hundred. But I did pay it off. . . ."

"Just so you could play tennis with me?"

"Well, uh, yes."

"Kid, that's both smart and dumb. Smart because you *have* impressed me. But dumb because you must never, *never* get all cowed and kiss-assy about a debt as trivial as eight hundred bucks. Remember, you're talking to a guy who was two hundred million in the hole five years ago—so, to me, eight hundred is not even chump change. Now get your ass into that locker room and then out to Court Four. Our hour starts in three minutes."

I was changed and on the court within two minutes. Ballantine had taken off his tracksuit and was wearing a pristine white Ralph Lauren polo shirt and matching white tennis shorts. Standing in the middle of the court, he was doing some rather conspicuous stretching exercises and enjoying the fact that everyone on the adjoining courts was noticing him.

"Over here, kid," Ballantine said, motioning me to where he was standing. "Jerry tells me you're quite a killer on the court."

"Maybe once upon a time. Now, I'm just average."

"*Never* call yourself average. Especially when you have the ability to kick ass. You can still kick ass, can't you, Ned?"

"Uh, sure, I guess."

He tossed me a tennis ball.

"Well, let's see you try to kick mine."

Within five minutes, it was pretty damn clear to me that Jack Ballantine really *did* play to win. As I hadn't been on a tennis court for several months—and also felt somewhat tentative about coming out fighting (despite his "let's-see-if-you-can-kick-my-ass" exhortation)—he won both his service games to love and broke me during a cliffhanger game that went to deuce five times.

Suddenly he was up 3–0 and shooting me quizzical, *why-aren't-you-trying-here?* looks from across the court. That's when I suddenly stepped up my game and began making him run for every point. Ballantine was a classic serve-and-volley player. He tried to ace you off the court. If that failed, he'd hit deep, then race to the net. To him, a point was to be won with a few quick punishing shots. Like a heavyweight boxer, he wanted to finish you off fast. But like most heavyweights, he began to falter when forced into a lengthy brawl. And I gave him a very lengthy brawl, turning as many points as possible into extended rallies that had him dashing all over the court. I also began to crack his high-velocity first serve, which, though brimming with brute force, didn't have the necessary topspin or sneaky angle to make it unplayable. That was the thing about Ballantine's tennis—it was forceful and dynamic, but it lacked finesse. By keeping him on the move, I was able to exploit the twenty-year age gap between us.

Before he knew it, I'd broken back twice and held service twice, and was now up 4–3. There was a tense eighth game that Ballantine just managed to take on a lucky netcord at forty-thirty. But I powered ahead, winning the next service game to love. And then Ballantine lost the plot, hitting two double faults and a wild lob, which suddenly handed me three set points. Facing loss, Ballantine never once radiated fear or concern. He simply hit back hard, reeling off a trio of aces that brought us to deuce. Then I made an unforced backhand error into net, and blew the game with a bad volley that ricocheted way out of court.

Now it was 5–5, and I knew that I was going to let him win. It wasn't that the fight had gone out of me. Rather, having come back from a 3–0 deficit to holding three set points, I'd shown him I was a battler. But I also knew that, having let Ballantine back into the set, it would be a strategic error to suddenly decimate him. This man was the only thing standing between me and unemployment. I needed to hand him the win—and, in doing so, show him I knew who was boss.

And thanks to a few unforced errors, and a couple of less-than-blatant double faults, Jack Ballantine beat me 7–5. The club buzzer sounded, ending our hour on court. I approached the net, hand outstretched. But before he took it, Ballantine gave me a stern stare.

"Why'd you throw the set?" he asked.

From his sharp tone I realized this was not the moment to trade in you-won-fair-and-square bullshit. So I returned his stare and said, "Because I really want the job you're offering me. And because, as you yourself said in *The Success Zone*, there are times in life when it is strategically advantageous to lose a game or two."

Ballantine allowed himself a small smile. Then, finally shaking my hand, he said, "Welcome to the team."

NINE

My office was tiny. It was an eight-by-eight closet, furnished with nothing more than a steel desk, a steel straight-backed chair, and a phone. This cubicle was situated in the backwater of the skyscraper that housed Ballantine Industries. Whereas the hub of Ballantine's empire was located in a large, stylish suite of offices on the eighteenth floor of the building, I found myself at the extreme rear of the third floor. This was the low-rent district of the office building—a long, dingy corridor lit by fluorescent tubes, with twenty or so frosted doors behind which worked JOHN MACE: PRIVATE INVESTIGATOR, THE BENTHEIM COLLECTION AGENCY ("No Debt Is Too Small"), and MANSOUR & SONS: INT'L RUG MERCHANTS. My cubbyhole was at the end of this corridor. Its minuscule window afforded me a panoramic view of a neighboring airshaft. Besides being deficient in natural light, the office also lacked all basic business amenities. It depressed the hell out of me.

"I know, I know," Jerry said when he saw my stunned reaction, "it's not exactly a lavish setup. . . ."

"That's the understatement of the year," I said. "Couldn't you find me something up there with all of you on the eighteenth floor?"

"As I told you before, we really are a lean operation. So our space is at a premium—to the point where two secretaries share the same office. Anyway, as you know, the fund has to be kept separate from Ballantine Industries. I tell you, they love to hate Mr. B. in this town—and they really can't stand the fact that he's bounced back as a best-selling author. So the moment some goddamn financial journalist or gossip columnist finds out about Mr. B.'s connection to Excalibur, we're going to start seeing all sorts of bad press disparaging the fund. And once a private equity fund's image is tainted, it's dead. And you can kiss your job good-bye."

I certainly didn't want to do anything that might jeopardize the fund—because, after all, it was my lifeline, the means by which I would pick myself up again. But I still felt deeply let down by this office—and said so.

"Okay, I agree with you," Jerry said. "It is definitely not ideal. But, hey—as Mr. B. probably told you yesterday—yours is a real pioneering kind of job. You're helping build something from the ground up. And if it works as well as we think it should, then we'll be able to rent you a penthouse here."

Indeed, Mr. Ballantine did hit me with the same sales pitch. After our tennis game, we headed to the club's lounge, where the Great Motivator gave me a demonstration of his formidable self-empowerment skills. Like any canny guru, he had the ability of making me feel as if I were the most important person he had ever met—and that he saw in me the potential for . . . well, *greatness*.

"You know what I like about your tennis game, Ned?" he said, sipping a glass of orange juice. "The fact that it's tough but tactical. I saw what you were doing out there. You were trying to wear this old guy down. But you didn't attempt to slam-dunk me off the court. You played a very consistent game, and you didn't mind waiting a while before winning a point.

"Now, to me, that sort of strategy is the key to true salesmanship. You displayed steadiness and diligence, you never overplayed your hand, but knew exactly when to move in for the *coup de grace*. And that's why I'm certain you will not only succeed brilliantly with Excalibur . . . but you also might get rich in the process. Because, my friend, what I see in you is exactly what I also see in this brave new world of private equity funds: *unlimited potential*."

Okay, maybe Ballantine was laying it on a little thick. But, having been on a downward curve for the past few months, I was more than receptive to such ego stroking. He obviously knew what I had been through—because everything he said was designed to rehabilitate my battered self-confidence.

"You're not just a fighter, Ned. You're also a survivor. Takes one to know one, kid. I've gone to the wall, too—and, believe me, I understand just how bad it hurts. Especially when it's not just your professional dreams that are destroyed, but your personal ones as well. And I'll let you in on a little secret, Ned. On the pain meter, the collapse of my second marriage made the collapse of my real estate business seem like nothing more than a sprained ankle. I'd never felt agony like that in my life."

My eyes fogged over. I turned away from Ballantine, not wanting him to see my distress.

"Sorry," I said, rubbing my eyes. "I really don't know why I'm . . ."

"Don't ever fucking apologize for *feeling*, Ned," Ballantine said. "Feeling is good. Feeling is *right*. Feeling means you understand loss and regret. And unless you understand loss, you will never experience *growth*. Growth leads to positive change. And positive change always results in success. That's the upward trajectory you're now on, Ned. So every time you feel that overpowering sense of loss about the collapse of your marriage, tell yourself this: 'By acknowledging the pain, I am beginning the journey back to success.'"

It's funny how, when you are at your most vulnerable and needy, you lose all sense of irony—and take comfort in sentiments that you would normally find laughable. Of course I knew that Jack Ballantine was talking psychobabble. But in my emotionally raw state, it was exactly what I wanted to hear. Because he innately understood that I now felt like a very abandoned, very scared little boy—suddenly all alone in the big bad world and desperate for a daddy. And he was going to fill that role. He was going to be the father of my dreams—the guy who totally believed in me and would nurture me back to self-respect.

And if, in exchange for such nurturing, I had to put up with a shoe box office, so be it. It was a small price to pay for the faith that Jack Ballantine had in me.

"All right, I'll live with the office," I told Jerry, "but can I at least buy a few crucial things to make it functional?"

"No problem," Jerry said—and later than afternoon handed me an envelope with $5,000 in cash.

"Will that be enough to get you started?" he asked.

"More than," I said. "I'll make certain you have receipts for everything I buy."

"Sure, sure," Jerry said absently. "Just remember: If you're getting anything delivered, don't have it sent care of Ballantine Industries. It should go to you directly at the Excalibur Fund."

"You mean, just in case the sales guy at CompUSA turns out to be a reporter from the *New York Times*?"

"Very funny," Jerry said with a grimace.

CompUSA, on Thirty-eighth and Fifth, was the first stop on my shopping expedition. I bought a desktop IBM Aptiva, a fax/modem, a laser printer, an answering machine, and an Office Software Suite. The salesman worked hard at appearing New York blasé when he saw me whip out a fat roll of $100 bills—but his eyes betrayed him.

"Where do you want it delivered?" he asked.

I printed the Excalibur Fund's office address. Glancing down he asked, "What kind of fund do you work for?"

"The kind of fund that makes people money," I said.

He glanced again at the wad of cash in my hand.

"I can see that," he said.

Leaving CompUSA, I walked one block east to an office furniture shop on Madison and Thirty-seventh, where I found a stylish secondhand beechwood veneer desk, a black-and-chrome desk chair, and a high-tech Tizio desk lamp—all for just under $1,200. The manager of the shop let me use his phone. I called the phone company and arranged for a separate fax/modem line to be installed in my office on Monday, and also asked that they deliver a modern Touch-Tone phone. Then I walked up to Forty-second Street and Lexington and shelled out $199 for a cellular phone at one of those cheapo electronic goods emporiums that crowd the eastern side of Grand Central station.

I had one final errand on my shopping run. I dropped by Kinko's on Fifty-fourth between Madison and Fifth and placed an order for Excalibur Fund stationery and a thousand business cards with my name and title—FUND EXECUTIVE—situated in the lower right-hand corner.

After helping me choose an elegant light gray paper for the stationery, the Kinko's printing clerk asked, "Do you have a company logo or typeface you'd like us to copy?"

I handed over a very glossy, well-produced brochure. THE EXCALIBUR FUND was embossed in silver letters on the cover.

"Could you use the same typeface for the stationery and the cards?" I asked.

"No problem," he said, flicking through the pages of the prospectus. "Is this your baby?"

"Sort of."

"Pretty impressive. Will it make you rich?"

"That's the idea."

Or, at least, that's what I wanted to believe. The fact was, I really didn't know how (or if) the fund would work. All I knew was what Jerry told me over dinner. To date, the fund was made up of a half dozen private investors (FOB's—Friends of Ballantine), each of whom had entrusted $1 million to the fund. So far the fund had backed one small company, Micromagna, which had just gone public.

"We did pretty well out of the initial public offering on Micromagna," Jerry said. "Anyway, it's now up to you to use *your* contacts to find us the hot new companies of the future."

The Excalibur Fund sales brochure was the key document in the search for new investors. Jerry had shown it to me when we returned to the loft after the Bouley Bakery dinner.

"We recently had this printed," he said, opening his briefcase and handing me the sales brochure. "I wrote it myself. I'll disappear for a half hour, grab a shower. Read it through, see what you think."

During the next half hour I read this document several times (I wanted to be well up on the workings of the fund before I played tennis with Ballantine the next morning). It was an exceedingly smooth piece of salesmanship, opening with a "mission statement":

> In today's dynamically charged financial world, where the serious investor has a myriad of potential investment opportunities, a well-balanced portfolio is a crucial commodity. Opt for maximum safety and you will never achieve any substantial return on your capital. Opt for maximum risk, and you can end up playing a dangerous game of financial roulette.

> This is why most fund managers today suggest a sensibly diversified portfolio, in which secure low-yield investments are offset against more speculative ventures. But even those investors with a venturesome spirit do not want to engage in reckless gambles. They want a financial investment that is designed to maximize profitability, yet provide potential long-term stability.
>
> In short, they are looking for the exciting, yet discerning, investment opportunities that THE EXCALIBUR FUND can provide.

The sales brochure then went on to explain the "dynamic potential" of private equity funds—how, if properly skippered and managed, they could provide the serious investor with an equity stake in some of today's hottest new companies on the brink of "going public."

> Of course, your investment counselor may point you in the direction of many private equity funds that promise high return, but whose investment strategy is uncertain. After all, the key to all high-yield investments is *choosing* the right venture to back—which is why you need the expertise of the Excalibur Fund.

Excalibur, according to the brochure, had its finger on the pulse of the most vibrant, lucrative industry today: information technology. Through its in-depth knowledge of the software and computer businesses, the fund was able to target emerging new companies with cutting-edge credentials. The brochure then detailed the sole enterprise it had backed to date: Micromagna, an American-owned, Budapest-based software manufacturing company that had "achieved phenomenal success" selling low-cost, high-grade word processing programs within the emerging eastern European market.

There were graphs and charts explaining how the fund operated. There was a detailed explanation of the fund's structure—how it was registered offshore, and divided into three active divisions: the North American (incorporated in Bermuda), the European (registered in Luxembourg), and the South American fund (incorporated in Nassau, the Bahamas). Each division had a talent spotter (based in New York, Luxembourg, and São Paolo), an "international investment specialist" who was actively engaged in discovering the best in new information technology enterprises.

"You didn't tell me you already had people working for the fund in Europe and South America," I said to Jerry when he walked back into the living room after his shower.

"They're strictly freelance talent spotters. But if they start finding us solid investment possibilities, I'll probably hire them both full time. And, I'm telling you, if the returns we've seen on Micromagna are a barometer of the future, by this time next year you won't just be in a bigger office—you'll also be employing a couple of assistants."

Naturally I bombarded Jerry with questions. I was a little concerned about the complex structure of the fund—the way it was registered in three different offshore locales. "Believe me, it's a standard setup when you're dealing with a geographically diversified fund," Jerry said reassuringly. Wouldn't an emerging American info-tech business worry about having unknown Latin American or European investors buying up equity in their company? "Only if they allow those investors to take a fifty-one percent controlling stake in their business. The fact is, Ned, a bunch of struggling computer nerds in a basement aren't going to give a damn who's giving them the money. As long as the cash is helping them develop their product, they're going to be happy. Especially since they know that Excalibur is going to make them rich once we take them public."

I then articulated my most pressing worry: How in the hell was I going to find exciting new companies in the first place?

"Well, you've got a lot of contacts in the computer business, right?"

"Yeah, but most of them are on the media sales side of the business."

"Well, what you're going to have to do, I'm afraid, is start from scratch and research potential investment possibilities. Track down the names of the people running the product search divisions at every computer company worth dealing with. Hit them with a sales brochure and an introductory letter, then talk your way into a meeting with them, pump them for information, and find out what emerging companies are worth betting on. I know it's not the easiest sort of talent spotting . . ."

"Not easy?" I said. "Jerry, what you're asking me to do is the toughest thing imaginable. Especially as the Excalibur Fund has no track record, and no identifiable names attached to it. At least if I could mention that Mr. Ballantine has given the fund his imprimatur—"

"You know that's impossible. And I'm going to need your assurance that you will never mention his name in connection with—"

"Jerry, I get the message. Jack Ballantine has *nothing* to do with Excalibur. All I'm saying here is this: I want to do a good job for you. I want . . . *need* to make this a success. But, quite frankly, I'm scared shitless about the prospect of cold-calling even minor computer companies, trying to sniff out hot new investment prospects."

"I hear—and *appreciate*—what you're saying. You want to do well. *We* want you to do well, too. And we also don't expect you to be an overnight miracle worker who's going to discover us the next Netscape by the end of next week. We know that this sort of intelligence gathering is a gradual operation. Just like we also know that once you've found your investment for us, the force will be with you—and you'll find yourself on a roll.

"But, trust me here, we really are taking a long-term view on Excalibur. As far as Mr. Ballantine and I are concerned, you've got six months to feel your way into this business and score your first significant investment contract. In the meantime, you're assured of your base salary—that's eleven-fifty a week—and free rent *chez moi*. Not a bad deal, if I say so myself."

No, it wasn't a bad deal at all, considering that my other employment prospects amounted to zilch. And I was reassured by the fact that Jerry and Ballantine both understood that this really was a start-from-scratch operation.

Of course, I still had major apprehensions and misgivings about this nebulous, embryonic product. But when you're desperate, you will grab at any reasonable proposition, no matter how amorphous it might seem. Especially if the man dangling the carrot is the legendary Jack Ballantine. So every time I questioned my ability to sell Excalibur, I remembered that Ballantine himself created a real estate empire out of nothing.

So I decided to put all my reservations regarding Excalibur on hold and go to work, telling myself—in true Ballantinian style—that the only thing standing between me and success was my own sense of doubt.

And nothing—not even that god-awful *toilet* of an office—was now going to dent my belief in the fund. Because it was my potential salvation.

So I hit the ground running. After leaving Kinko's I returned to my office, called Janovic Paint on West Seventy-second Street, and asked them to deliver three gallons of off-white emulsion, a half gallon of white gloss, a roller and tray, two brushes, a can of turpentine, and some drop cloths. When they demanded a credit card, I convinced them to accept payment COD.

The paint arrived at four that afternoon. It was Friday, and since I wanted to have the office painted by first thing Monday, I picked up the phone and called Jerry, explaining about the paint job and asking him if I might be able to get a building key from him for the weekend.

"No problem," he said. "I'll call the super and ask him to drop one by you. But it's one hell of a way to spend your weekend, Allen."

"It's cheaper than hiring someone to do it. And you know what they say about a fresh coat of paint. . . ."

"Let me guess. It makes everything seem brighter?"

"And it allegedly covers all the cracks."

"Believe me, there's only one thing that really covers *all* the cracks, and that's money. Something you should be making a pile of soon enough."

"Speaking of money . . . if I have any business expenses . . ."

"Just put them on your own credit card and then we'll reimburse you."

"Well, there's a small problem with my credit cards," I said.

Jerry needed no further explanation. "How much do you need?" he asked.

"A thousand would liberate my MasterCard."

"Done," he said. "I'll leave the cash at reception on my way out."

"Are you going to be around for a beer later tonight?"

"No can do. Mr. B. just told me he wants me to fly to L.A. tonight and sort out some problems we have with the West Coast segment of his upcoming book tour."

"I wish I was en route to Los Angeles," I said absently.

"Don't think about her, Ned."

"Easier said than done. Have a good weekend."

"You, too. Try not to paint too hard."

But, of course, I did paint hard, because I was hoping that work would somehow keep my mind off Lizzie. So I threw myself into redecorating the office. I arrived at eight o'clock Saturday morning and left at ten that night. On Sunday I put in a thirteen-hour day—and by the time I headed out into the night, my little room appeared twice its size, thanks to a fresh coat of white paint. The following morning my new desk and chair arrived, along with all the CompUSA equipment—and my office suddenly looked like a stylishly small business operation. I got down to business. Working my way through my address book, I made around three dozen calls to assorted contacts in a wide range of computer companies around the country. Every call was a strikeout. Either my contact was "in a meeting," "out of town," or simply "unavailable right now."

Trying not to be dismayed, I got my IBM computer up and running and went on-line, using Yahoo to find the names of every computer company in the country. Amazingly, there were over 12,500 listings. Over the next three days, I systematically worked my way through this list, narrowing down the field to around six hundred companies that might be worth pursuing. Another three days were spent phoning each of these companies to find out the name of the individual in charge of research and development. Once this task was completed, I spent the next two days sending out over six hundred sales brochures, each with a cover letter (on the new Excalibur Fund stationery) in which I introduced myself and Excalibur, informed the recipient that we were on the lookout for exciting new info-tech investment prospects, and said that I'd be calling to set up a one-to-one meeting shortly.

It was slow, tedious work—but at least it did make me feel productive. However, keeping myself preoccupied did not do what I wanted it to do: block out all thoughts of Lizzie. I was still missing her terribly. It had been nearly two weeks since she had flown back to the coast, and I had been phoning Los Angeles daily, calling both her office and her hotel room. But she wouldn't take my calls. At first her secretary, Juliet, kept telling me the same thing: She was in a permanent meeting. After a few days of this "otherwise engaged" crap, Juliet finally came clean: Lizzie didn't want to speak with me, and was also screening all her calls at the Mondrian to make certain she didn't inadvertently get connected to me.

This freeze-out treatment didn't stop me from faxing her a long, pleading letter—in which I essentially called myself a jerk, told her she was the best thing that had ever happened to me, said I couldn't live without her, and comprehensively begged for forgiveness.

The letter had been sent over a week ago. To date, Lizzie's answer had been a devastating one: total silence. A silence which let me know that she wasn't in the market for a reconciliation.

With typical salesman's persistence, I kept up the barrage of phone calls—hoping against hope that, in time, the Berlin Wall she had constructed between us would finally crumble. Now it was late Friday afternoon, I had just returned to the office after sending out the last one hundred Excalibur sales brochures to assorted companies, and decided it was time to steel myself for the daily call to L.A.

"Hello, Lizzie Howard's office."

"Hi, Juliet, it's—"

"Oh . . . Mr. Allen." Her tone said it all: *Leave me alone, you loser.*

"Is she in?" I asked.

"No—she's gone out of town for a few days. But she did—"

"She's away on business?"

"Of course."

"Where, exactly?"

"Mr. Allen, I am not in a position to say . . ."

"Okay, okay. Could you just give her a message that—"

"You're at 212-555-7894, and during office hours your number is 212-555-9001."

That stopped me short. "Yeah. Those are the numbers. And please, *please* tell her that all I want is five minutes on the phone."

"I do have a message from Lizzie for you."

"You do?"

"Yes, that's what I was trying to tell you. . . ."

"So tell me now."

I could hear her reaching for a notepad. Her voice assumed that official intonation, much beloved of court stenographers.

"Lizzie asked me to inform you that she's been appointed acting head of the L.A. office for the next six months, and that you will be hearing from the law firm of Platt and McHenry regarding your legal separation. . . ."

"*What* legal separation?"

Juliet suddenly sounded sheepish. "Mr. Allen, I'm just reading what she dictated to me. Platt and McHenry will be contacting you about drawing up a legal separation agreement between you, so your lawyer should contact—"

"I don't have a lawyer," I said, and slammed down the phone.

I fought the urge for a cigarette. I fought the need for a drink. I simply put my head in my hands. Then the phone rang. I picked it up, said hello, and heard a blast of Spanish-inflected English in my ear.

"The fuck you been, Ned?"

Oh, God. Debbie Suarez. Since that night I hadn't plucked up the courage to call her again . . . even though I knew she had been trying to contact me, as she'd left about five messages on my old home phone number. The subletters hadn't moved in yet, so I was still able to access the voice mail at my former apartment. Just yesterday I'd finally gotten around to changing the message, leaving the number at Jerry's loft and my new office for anyone trying to reach me. Yeah, it was slimeball form to dodge Debbie's calls. But not only was I still deeply embarrassed about ending up in her bed, I was also a little preoccupied by the fact that our one-night fling had triggered the end of my marriage.

"Hi, Debbie," I said, sounding anxious.

"The fuck is wrong with you?" she said. "You share my bed, then you disappear?"

"It's a long story. . . ."

"And then you never call me, even though I phone you over and over. . . ."

"It's a *really* long story."

"I want to hear it."

"Debbie, please . . . This has not been an easy time for me."

"You don't want to see me."

"I do, but . . . life has been really complicated lately."

"You sayin' I'm gonna complicate your life?" She sounded hurt.

"Of course not. It's just . . . I'm all over the place."

"A cup of coffee, that's all I'm asking."

"Okay, okay."

And we arranged to meet at a Starbucks on Fifty-third and Park at 6:00 P.M.

But when I walked into Starbucks sixty minutes later, it became quickly apparent that Debbie was interested in more than a quick latte. She kissed me fully on the lips, holding me close. She ran her fingers through my hair and gave me a big love-struck smile. As we sat down at a small table, she took my hand and squeezed it tightly. She scared the shit out of me.

"I gotta tell ya, I figured you'd left town or somethin'," she said.

I gently withdrew my hand from hers. "Things got a little complicated after Ivan's funeral." And I explained about my eviction from the apartment and from the telesales job. She suddenly had my hand in hers again.

"Oh, Mr. A. . . . *Ned* . . . I feel terrible. How'd your wife find out?"

"I was, uh, kind of marked by the experience."

She let out a nervous giggle. "I know, I know . . . all my fault. But that's the problem with you being so irresistible. . . ."

"Debbie . . ."

"Now I know why you've been so hard to find. Where you stayin'?"

"A place belonging to a guy I went to school with."

"You know, you need a place, you can always stay with me. Raul asks about you every day. Says you helped him with his homework. I tell ya, he really, really likes you. Keeps asking me when he's gonna see you. . . ."

I said nothing. I simply avoided her gaze and stared at the table, feeling truly awful. Suddenly, Debbie put the brakes on her manic monologue, her eyes moist.

"I'm embarrassing you," she said. "I'm embarrassing *me*."

"You're not embarrassing anyone. . . ."

"If I was you, I'd be thinking, this woman sounds desperate. . . ."

"I don't think that."

"Well *I* think that. 'Cause ever since that piece-of-shit husband of mine got his ass shot off three years ago, there's been nobody in my life, nobody in my bed. Not even for one night. Until you. And you know . . ."

Her voice grew quiet, little.

". . . I've always carried this big fucking torch for you. That night at the Christmas party . . . it wasn't because I was drunk. It's how I felt. I'd wanted to kiss you for—"

"Debbie . . . Don't."

". . . and so when you came back to my place, I thought, hoped, *prayed* that maybe this would be the start of . . . especially after Raul told me how much he liked you."

"I'm sorry. I'm really sorry."

"Don't apologize, man. I don't need your sympathy. I just need . . . *you*. Or, at least, that was my bullshit dream. You. Me. Raul. Some fairy tale . . ."

"Debbie . . . I love my wife."

"Your wife's left you."

"I know. I blew it. Sleeping with you was—"

"Don't say it."

I nodded. We lapsed into silence. Debbie covered my hand again with hers.

"She's gone, Ned. I'm *here*."

As gently as possible, I said, "You know that's not how it works. I wish it were. But . . ."

"Shut up," she whispered.

"Okay," I said.

She withdrew her hand, reached into her bag for a little packet of Kleenex, extracted a tissue, and quickly dabbed at her wet eyes.

"You know what I was thinkin' today?" she said. "Just how damn tired I am. How everything is one big, long struggle. Never enough money. Never enough time with your kid. Nonstop worry—about the rent, the tuition, the medical bills, and paying Con Ed, and whether you'll have a fuckin' job next week. You keep hoping it's gonna all get easier. But secretly you know it'll never happen.

So, when you get down to it, all this struggle only makes sense if there's one basic thing in your life: someone waiting for you when you get home at night."

"At least you've got Raul," I said.

"Tell me about it. Sometimes I think he's the only reason I get up in the mornin', spend the day screaming down a phone, selling bullshit."

She took a deep, steadying breath. And stood up.

"I gotta go, Mr. Allen."

"I'm *Ned*."

She shook her head.

"See you around, Debbie."

"No, you won't," she said, and headed for the door.

I walked over to the Lexington Avenue subway and caught the downtown local. When it stopped at Fourteenth Street, I had to fight the urge to jump off, dash three blocks east to Stuyvesant Town, knock on Debbie's door, fall into her arms, embrace Raul as my newfound son, make a teary speech about family values being the *only* values, and then lead the three of us, arm in arm, off into the sunset.

If only life could be scripted by Hollywood.

Instead, I stayed on the train to Canal Street, walked north to Jerry's place, and checked the phone for messages. There was just one—from, of all people, Ian Deane.

"Well, hello there, stranger. Geena and I were wondering where the hell you were. Then, when I was talking to Lizzie yesterday . . ."

I didn't wait to hear the rest of the message. I rapidly punched in Ian's number and hoped to God he was home. He was.

"So what did Lizzie say?" I asked as soon as he picked up the phone.

"And a good evening to you, Mr. Allen," Ian said with a laugh.

"Sorry, sorry. It's just . . ."

"Understood. How are things?"

"I've been better."

"Then why the hell haven't you called?"

"You know why, Ian. And I'm sure Lizzie told you *why*."

"Yeah, she did say something to Geena about . . ."

"How I fucked up."

"It happens."

"I was so stupid. . . ."

"Okay, okay, it was a dumb call. But we all make dumb calls from time to time."

"Not *that* dumb."

"You still should have gotten in touch with us, Ned."

"I really thought you wouldn't want to talk to me. . . ."

"For fuck's sake, Ned. We're your friends. And we're not going to take sides here."

"Not even Geena?"

"All right, I have to admit that she has been leaning a bit toward Lizzie. Especially because of the . . . uh . . ."

"Yeah, I hear you. . . ."

"But hey, don't expect me to get all righteous with you. I mean, stuff like that . . . It was kind of a drunken accident, right?"

"Yeah, I drank too much, then tripped and ended up naked in another woman's bed. . . ."

"You got unlucky, that's all."

"You mean, I got caught."

After a pause, Ian said, "Yeah, I guess that's what I mean. But hey, it's not a war crime."

"No—but my marriage is dead because of it. She's not coming back, is she, Ian?"

"Well, from what I could gather, Lizzie's still pretty upset about things. And, yeah, I think you've got an uphill battle ahead of you. . . ."

"Right."

"And I also sense that she needs some space right now. . . ."

Space. That fucking word again.

"But, who knows?" Ian said. "Given time, she might not . . ."

"What? Hate me so much?"

In the background I could hear Geena calling Ian.

"Listen, we're about to eat. And tomorrow we're off to Bermuda for a week. But we're back next Sunday. So I'm going to expect a call, understand? Take care. And remember: You've got an ally here."

As I put down the phone, I couldn't help but think what a jerk I had been to file Ian away under *Arrogant Manhattan Prick*. Yet again, my Maine-boy envy—my need to compete at all costs—had made me overlook a glaringly obvious truth: Ian Deane considered himself my friend.

And though I wanted to take his friendly advice—and temporarily desist in my campaign to win Lizzie back—I left five messages for her over the weekend.

Then, on Tuesday morning, a letter arrived (via Federal Express) at the loft.

Ned:

I'm not trying to play hard to get, or be a bitch. But after what happened, I just think it's best if we cut each other a bit of slack right now, and keep some distance until we both cool down.

Juliet told me about your reaction to my message. In retrospect I do think it was wrong of me to call in lawyers so soon—and I apologize for that. But I would appreciate it if you would please stop phoning. It's not helping the situation.

I'll be in touch when I'm ready to be in in touch—i.e., when I know what my next move will be.

Lizzie

Searching around Jerry's apartment, I found a yellow legal pad and a pen. Sitting down at the dining room table, I wrote:

Dear Lizzie:

Hindsight is always 20/20, isn't it? I cannot change what happened—though, Christ, I'd pay just about any price to do so.

I blew it. I blew it. I blew it. And I miss you more than I can say.

But . . . okay, if you don't want me to call anymore, I will honor your request.

Know this, though: Every time the phone rings, I will be hoping it is you.

I love you.

Ned

On the way to work I dropped the letter into a mailbox, and thought, *It's her move now. And if she chooses not to respond to this, then I'd better start accepting that it is truly dead between us*.

Two weeks later I still hadn't had a response from Lizzie, and was lurching into total despair. Not just because it was clear that my wife really didn't want anything more to do with me—but also because I'd yet to have one positive response to my mailing of Excalibur sales brochures. Check that: After making over two hundred calls, not one product manager had deigned to even speak with me. "Sorry, we're just not interested" was the message I kept receiving over and over again from secretaries, personal assistants, and other species of underling. Jerry was out of town on business for most of this time, so I didn't have to supply him with an ongoing progress report, or feed him some spiel about how everything was coming up roses.

But I knew that, if I kept striking out on the sales front, I would eventually have to come clean with Jerry and admit this simply wasn't working. And why wasn't it working? If you're a good salesman, there is only one real reason why you can't peddle something: because people don't like the product.

Still, I kept on phoning, contacting around fifty companies a day on my list. *"Sorry, we're not looking for private investment right now."* . . . *"Sorry, we already have other equity funds interested in us."* . . .

But then I had a lucky break. A guy named Dwight Capel called me one afternoon. He told me he was an MIT grad, running a small company in Medford, Massachusetts, that was currently developing a new state-of-the-art graphics board (the hardware component that allows computers to run full-motion video programs).

"We've got a real cutting-edge product, but we've got no budget to get the damn thing marketed properly. So when your brochure and letter arrived I thought maybe this is the sort of investment we've been looking for."

When I asked if I could come up and see him in Medford, however, he informed me that he'd like me to meet his financial advisor, who also just happened to be his brother. His name was Elliot Capel. He was a senior fund manager at Federal & State, a Boston-based pension fund company, and Dwight had given him the Excalibur material the night before.

"So give Elliot a call—and if he's enthusiastic about what you're offering, then I guess we might just do some business together."

Getting through to Elliot Capel was no easy task. For two straight days he was busy. Finally, in desperation, I called him at 6:30 P.M. on the third day—and he picked up the phone himself.

"Well, this is some fluky coincidence," he said after I introduced myself, "because I finally got around to reading the Excalibur sales brochure this afternoon."

I was suddenly animated.

"Fluky coincidences are the way some of the best business deals get started," I said. "And I'd really love to build on this coincidence, and come see you to discuss how your brother's company could benefit from Excalibur investment."

"Have you been with the fund long, Mr. Allen?"

"Ned—please. But the answer to your question is no. Just a few weeks, to be exact. But, of course, I am incredibly excited by Excalibur's overall potential and—"

"So you had nothing to do with structuring the fund or writing the sales brochure?"

"Like I said, I've just been hired by the fund."

"And have you ever worked in the private equity fund business before?"

"Uh, no. This is a career change for me. But look, Mr. Capel, if you could find a window in your schedule during the next few days, I'd be delighted to fly up to Boston and meet you."

"How about tomorrow, say around eleven A.M."

Got 'em! Finally, the first breakthrough meeting.

"Eleven works fine for me, Mr. Capel. And if you have time to do lunch, I'd love to take you. . . ."

"Lunch is out. And I can only give you, at most, twenty minutes of my time. But if you still want to come up here and see me, that twenty-minute window is yours."

"I'll be there, sir."

"Only I have to tell you, Mr. Allen—the only reason why I'm willing to see you is because you come across as a sound guy who doesn't seem to realize that he's selling a very unsound proposition."

My hands were suddenly sweaty.

"I don't exactly follow you, Mr. Capel."

"Okay—I'll give it to you straight, Mr. Allen. There is absolutely no way that I would let my brother take even a dime from your fund. And the reason is a simple one. To my professional eye, the Excalibur Fund is complete and total bullshit."

TEN

Elliot Capel was a man of his word. He gave me exactly twenty minutes of his time, then politely showed me the door. The meeting was over before I knew it. I left Capel's office on Copley Square and walked down to Boston Common. Though it was a stunning day—a cloudless sky, a soft breeze—I wasn't exactly taking it in. Nor was I paying much attention to the manicured pleasures of the Common, or the hint of brine in the moist air, or the amazing abundance of leggy women in short skirts. I was too preoccupied, too lost in troubled thought, to notice anything.

"So tell me," Elliot Capel had said as soon as I sat down opposite him, "who exactly is behind the Excalibur Fund?"

I chose my words with care.

"It's made up of a consortium of businessmen—"

"Obfuscation," he said, cutting me off.

"Sorry?" I said.

"You're obfuscating, Mr. Allen. Better known as trading in bullshit."

His voice was temperate, cool, vaguely academic. With his gray worsted suit, his button-down Oxford shirt, his striped bow tie, and his horn-rimmed glasses, Elliot Capel did look the professorial type. He tapped his fingertips together as he spoke, and kept his pale blue eyes focused on me with such intensity that I felt as if I was under interrogation. Which, essentially, I was.

"I'm really not *obfuscating* here, Mr. Capel," I said. "Like I said, Excalibur is an umbrella organization, made up of three companies—"

"Three *shell* companies, Mr. Allen."

"*Shell* companies?"

"That's what I said, Mr. Allen. You sound surprised."

"I was just under the impression . . ."

"What?"

". . . that the three companies that made up the fund were . . ."

"Legitimate, perhaps?"

"Well, yes."

"They might be. Because there are plenty of offshore companies that are thoroughly legitimate. Then again, why would a legitimate company have a board of directors made up of a Bahamian lawyer and his secretary?"

"I'm not exactly following you. . . ."

"I had one of my assistants run a company check on the so-called South American division of your fund, Excalibur S.A., incorporated in the Bahamas. Its chairman is a Nassau lawyer named Winston Parkhill, and there's only one other member of its board: a woman named Ceila Markey . . . who, we discovered after a few phone calls, happens to be Mr. Parkhill's secretary.

"Now this bit of news intrigued me, so I asked my assistant to check up on the European and North American divisions of the fund—registered, if I'm not mistaken, in Luxembourg and Bermuda respectively. Guess what he found out? In both instances, the company's structures were exactly the same: a local attorney, his secretary, and no other board members. Of course, this is not an unusual setup for certain offshore companies. But what it does indicate—to me, anyway—is that the individual or set of individuals behind your fund do not want to have their names directly attached to Excalibur. Once again, there may be a perfectly valid, tenable reason for their secrecy. . . ."

I had to stop myself from saying, *Yes, there is. Jack Ballantine is worried about all the potential negative press that might hit Excalibur were he revealed to be the man behind the fund*. Elliot Capel continued.

"Then again, there may be a perfectly valid, yet *unlawful* reason as to why no names are attached to the fund. That's the thing about offshore shell companies. You can never tell exactly who or what is behind them. I mean, do you *personally* know the people behind the fund?"

Trying to keep my nervousness in check, I gave him the answer that Jerry told me to give if this question arose during pitch meetings.

"As you know, Mr. Capel, the names of the principals behind many private equity funds often remain confidential. But as you undoubtedly saw in our prospectus, Excalibur has the backing of such leading financial institutions as the Luxembourg Trust Company, the Bahamian Bank of Commerce—"

"*Leading financial institutions?* Who are you trying to kid here? The Luxembourg Trust Company is an insignificant private bank . . . though compared to the Bahamian Bank of Commerce, it looks like Chase Manhattan."

Avoiding his gaze, I said, "I really wasn't aware that those banks were so small—"

"You don't seem to be aware of a great many things about the fund you're selling."

"Like I said yesterday, I'm kind of new to this business."

"Clearly. So what did you do before you landed yourself in this game?"

I gave him an abbreviated version of my resumé. He listened with interest, especially when I explained how I stumbled into the Excalibur Fund after hitting the skids.

"So this was, in truth, an 'I'll-take-anything' kind of job?" he asked.

"Well, I was pretty desperate—but I also thought it might be a stepping stone—"

"To what? A career as a white-collar criminal?"

"You're not serious, are you?"

"Put it this way, Mr. Allen—if I were in your shoes I'd be very wary of my employers, and would probably check out their background with care."

"Believe me, they're extremely legitimate people," I said.

"Well, if they *are* legitimate, then why is Micromagna such a dubious operation?"

I tried not to appear stunned. Micromagna was the centerpiece of the fund. I chose my words carefully. "What do you mean by 'dubious operation,' Mr. Capel?"

"I mean, quite simply, that Micromagna doesn't exist."

My cellular phone rang. I was jolted out of my reverie. Elliot Capel's voice abruptly stopped replaying in my head, and I found myself back on a park bench at Boston Common, staring blankly at a well-pruned bed of roses. I reached into my briefcase and answered the phone. It was Jerry's secretary.

"Mr. Allen, I have a message for you from Mr. Schubert. . . ."

"May I speak with him myself?"

"I'm afraid he's out at meetings all day, but he did ask me—"

"It's kind of important," I said.

"He's with Mr. Ballantine, and he left strict instructions not to be disturbed, but he does want to see you tonight."

"That makes two of us."

"He's planning to attend a SOFTUS reception at the Parker Meridien Hotel on West Fifty-seventh Street this evening, and was hoping you might meet him there at six."

"Tell him I'll be there."

And—I felt like adding—tell him that I've also just met a mutual fund manager named Elliot Capel who has been scrutinizing our fund. And he discovered that Excalibur is nothing but three very empty shell companies, all of which have the alleged endorsement of three tiny, questionable financial institutions. Not only that—Mr. Capel then told me that he had his assistant call International Directory Assistance and ask for the number for Micromagna in Budapest. Want to hear something hilarious, Jerry? Micromagna has an unlisted number. Who the hell has ever heard of a business having an unlisted phone number? In short, Mr. Capel reached the conclusion that Micromagna might not be an authentic, functioning enterprise. Which, in turn, has led me to wonder, What the fuck is going on here?

All the way back to New York I rehearsed the speech with which I was going to confront Jerry this evening—a speech in which I would demand to know why the structure of the fund was so damn suspect. And if he didn't give me the answers I wanted, I'd . . .

What? Quit? And then find myself a nice cardboard box in which to bed down for the night on West Broadway? Resigning now would mean instant destitution, total disaster. I needed this job. I needed to make it work. Surely there must be some very plausible reason why the company was structured in such a cryptic way, and why Micromagna didn't have a listed phone number. I mean, this fund was ultimately Jack Ballantine's baby. Though he might not want his name attached to it, it could ultimately be traced back to him. So—given that the press were still circling him like famished vultures—there's no way he'd be up to anything shady. No way at all.

I was back in Manhattan by five and hopped a cab straight to the Parker Meridien. I wasn't thrilled about rendezvousing with Jerry at the SOFTUS reception. After all, this annual convention of American software manufacturers had always been a key business event during my years at *CompuWorld*. It was also the place where I had first met Lizzie. So attending this reception would be yet another reminder of how badly I had screwed up my life. I wanted to dodge it—but I needed to see Jerry urgently and get some answers to some difficult questions.

"Holy shit, it's Ned Allen."

As soon as I walked through the doors of the Parker Meridien ballroom I felt as if I was on a trip down memory lane, in which my entire former history in the computer magazine business passed before me. The "holy shit" comment came from Don Dowling—the circumferentially challenged media sales honcho of AdTel. Offering me his outstreched paw he took a melodramatic step backward before I could shake it.

"Not planning to punch me, are you, Ned?"

I managed a smile. "Very funny, Don," I said, grabbing a glass of water from a passing waiter's tray.

"What the hell brings you here?" he asked. "I'd heard you left the business."

"Yeah—but I'm now in a related business. High finance, to be exact. A private equity fund dealing exclusively in new technology. And, you know, Don, I'd love to do lunch sometime. Especially as we're on the lookout for young new companies that might need some capitalization. . . ."

Don Dowling was already looking past my shoulder, hoping to catch someone else's eye.

"I don't believe it . . . Bill Janes!" he shouted to someone in the near distance. Then, turning back to me, he said, "Great seeing you, Ned. Hope whatever you're doing works out. . . ."

"About that lunch idea I was mentioning . . . ?"

"Call my secretary," he said, then swiftly headed toward the other side of the ballroom.

A minute later I bumped into Dave Maduro, my former outside sales guy for Massachusetts.

"Dave!" I shouted. "How the hell are you?"

He seemed startled to see me—as if I were someone who, having been presumed dead, was suddenly back stalking the living.

"Oh, Ned," he said. "This is quite a surprise."

"You're looking good, Dave. How's *PC Globe* treating you?"

"Fine, fine . . . ," he said distractedly.

"Any of the old gang here tonight?" I asked.

"Saw Doug Bluehorn around somewhere. But Chuck's out of town, schmoozing some potential new advertisers in San Jose."

Well, that was a relief. I'd been dreading the prospect of encountering Chuck.

"Family good, Dave?"

"Yeah, great . . . ," he said, and (like Don Dowling) his eyes started looking for someone who could rescue him from me.

"Listen," I said, trying to keep the conversation going, "I get up to Boston from time to time and would love to pick your brain about new software outfits. . . ."

"Sure thing, Ned," he said. "You know my number. . . ."

Everywhere I turned inside the Parker Meridien ballroom I was greeted with uneasy diffidence by former business associates. Or I noticed someone whispering something into the ear of a colleague—who, in turn, would steal a quick glance in my direction. I could just imagine what was being muttered.

See that guy over there? Ned Allen. Used to be a player when he worked for CompuWorld. *Then he punched out his German boss. . . . Yeah, he was the guy . . . and from what I hear now, the poor sucker can't even get arrested. . . .*

It was obvious that I terrified my former colleagues. Because I was the sum of all their fears: the fuckup they all dreaded becoming. I felt like a freak show exhibit: *The loser. The has-been*. And unable to find Jerry among this packed throng, I decided it was time to head for the door.

But then I heard his voice.

"Ned, Ned . . . over here," Jerry shouted.

I spun around and saw him standing in a distant corner of the room. He waved hello and motioned me to approach him.

But then I saw who was standing next to Jerry. And I suddenly froze.

It was Ted Peterson.

Peterson himself appeared shocked to see me as well. But when he tried to walk off, Jerry grabbed him by one shoulder. Then, pointing a finger in his face, he appeared to harshly reprimand him. Peterson turned ashen. I couldn't believe what I was seeing.

"Ned!" Jerry shouted at me again. I had no choice but to approach him. He was now all smiles.

"I just wanted you to meet an old friend, Ned," Jerry said. "You do know each other, don't you?"

"Yeah," Peterson said, "we know each other." He proffered his hand. "How're you doing, Ned?"

I kept my hands behind my back.

"*How am I doing*?" I asked. "Go fuck yourself—that's how I'm doing."

"Easy now, Ned," Jerry said.

"*Easy? Easy?*" I said, my voice becoming loud. "This piece of shit doesn't deserve *easy*."

"That's all in the past now," Peterson said quietly.

"*The past! The past!* You destroy my career and kill Ivan Dolinsky, and now you want bygones to be bygones?"

I was yelling. The room had grown quiet. Everyone was staring at us. Jerry put a steadying hand on my arm.

"Ned, knock it off now."

I angrily shrugged him off.

"This fucker should be prosecuted. Not just for driving Ivan to his death, but for attempted rape."

"You are way out of line, mister," Peterson yelled.

"Why? Because I'm telling the truth about how you did a little unwanted crotch-grabbing last year at Grand Cayman—"

"All right, all right," Jerry said, trying to intervene.

"You have no proof," Ted yelled.

"Her name was Joan Glaston . . ."

"You know shit."

". . . and the only reason she didn't bring charges was because you bribed her . . ."

"You watch it."

". . . but only after she kicked you in the balls."

That's when he went for me, lashing out with both fists. But before he could connect, Jerry jumped between us, grabbing Peterson's arms in the sort of ferocious grip that he used to employ on the ice.

"I want you out of here," Jerry barked at me.

"With pleasure," I said, then turned and threw my drink in Peterson's face. "That's for Ivan."

"YOU'RE A DEAD MAN," Peterson screamed, struggling to break free of Jerry's grip.

"Out, NOW," Jerry yelled—and the crowd of onlookers parted as I made a dash for the door.

Outside the hotel, I had to lean against a lamppost until I calmed down. Then, once I regained my equilibrium, I began to walk. Heading south on Sixth Avenue, I was so distracted by what had just gone down that I didn't realize how much ground I was rapidly covering until I looked up and realized I was at Twenty-third Street. I wanted to collapse into a bar and soothe my jangled nerves with half a bottle of Jack Daniel's. But I was still adhering to my clean-and-sober regimen—so I just kept going farther south. Through the Village, past SoHo, into Tribeca, across Wall Street, then finally hitting the end of the line: Battery Park. I wasn't aware of time, or of the distance involved—because my brain was trying to make sense of everything that had happened today. I could find no logic to what I'd seen and heard.

All I could come up with were questions. Such as: *What the hell was Jerry doing, talking to Ted Peterson? . . . Why did he reprimand him so fiercely? . . . Knowing my checkered history with the asshole, why did Jerry never mention the fact that he knew Peterson? . . . What, in short, was going on between them?*

And when I finished pondering these questions, then I had to consider all the doubts that Elliot Capel raised about the fund.

I headed north from Battery Park, walked back through the empty canyons of the financial district, cut east through Chinatown and Little Italy, then finally wended my way back to Wooster Street. Heading down the east side of the block, I could see that the lights were on in the loft. For the first time in around a month, Jerry was home before midnight. I wasn't surprised. After what I'd pulled in the Parker Meridien, he was obviously lying in wait for me—and planning, no doubt, to fire my ass.

I wanted to dodge this confrontation—to keep on walking through the night in the hope that, come morning, the gravity of my situation might have possibly improved. But I knew that, according to the Ballantinian Principles of Business Management, eluding responsibility (especially after committing an error of judgment) was considered a major mortal sin (almost up there with scoring a touchdown for the other side). "Always face the music, own up to the mistake, take your lumps," Jack Ballantine advised in *The Success Zone*, "because when we acknowledge fumbles with manful dignity, we learn."

There was no getting around it. I would have to "acknowledge the fumble" and then embrace homelessness with manful dignity.

Jerry was seated on the sofa when I entered the loft. He was deep in conversation on the phone, so I headed into my room and began to pack my clothes. After five minutes Jerry walked in. Noticing the open bag on the futon, he asked, "What the hell are you doing?"

"Leaving."

"Why, for Christ's sake?"

"I figured, after what happened at the Meridien . . ."

"What you did was dumb. *Totally* dumb. But . . . part of the blame lies with me. Because I should have told you that Peterson was working with us."

"What?" I managed to say.

"You sound shocked," Jerry said.

"I *am* shocked."

"It's a recent development. And anyway, he's just helping us in an advisory capacity. Keeping his ear to the ground for new companies that the fund might want to consider for investment."

"Why didn't you tell me?"

"Because, knowing your past with the guy, I figured you might have taken the news badly."

"You figured right. I mean . . . I can't believe this, Jerry. The guy is my nemesis. Arch Enemy Number One. Not to mention a completely evil fuck. And now you want to work with him?"

"He's an important player at GBS. He could be very useful to us. And when I met him three weeks ago—"

"This has been going on for *three weeks*?"

"Ned, cut the betrayed-spouse routine. We're talking business here. I was introduced to Peterson through a couple of business contacts, he seemed like a smart operator with his finger on the pulse of the industry, so I offered him a consultancy deal with us—which, strictly speaking, is not in line with GBS rules, but all we're talking about is me taking him out once a month for lunch and picking his brain about new companies. Anyway, knowing how much you loathe Peterson . . ."

"With good reason."

"Right, okay, he acted appallingly toward you. . . . So, knowing that, I really didn't want to get you upset about what was, *is*, nothing more than a consultancy situation which doesn't really concern you. Having said that, what happened tonight changes things a bit."

"In what way?"

"That was Mr. Ballantine on the phone when you came in. Word's already gotten back to him about the scene in the ballroom. Know what he told me? 'You've got to admire Ned for tearing a strip or two off the bastard. But it was still an asinine call.' "

I shrugged and said, "Guilty as charged. I'm sorry."

"Apology accepted. And unpack your clothes while you're at it. Nobody's firing you."

"Thanks, Jerry."

"But we still have a situation on our hands here. GBS is the biggest global player in the computer industry. Ted Peterson is our conduit to them. He may be a sonofabitch, but he's *our* sonofabitch. We don't want to lose him. So here's what Mr. Ballantine suggests: You take him out to dinner and smooth things over with him. . . ."

"No fucking way."

"Ned, when Mr. B. 'suggests' something, it is tantamount to an order."

"Does he understand my history with Peterson?"

"Completely. And, of course, he is on your side. But, like I said earlier, this is business—and, as Mr. B. is fond of remarking, in business you often have to sleep with assholes. Anyway, he thinks it would be character building for you to confront Peterson *mano a mano* over dinner, and reach some sort of détente with the guy."

"I still don't like it."

"*C'est la* fucking *vie*, Ned."

"Say I refuse."

"Then, I'm afraid, you *will* be packing your bags."

It was the response I was expecting. And dreading. I threw my hands up in the air—the universally recognized gesture of capitulation.

"Okay, okay, I'll meet the guy."

"Attaboy."

"But say he refuses to meet me? Especially after the shit I said about him in public?"

"He won't refuse to meet you."

"How can you be so certain?"

"Because I know he wants this consultancy. Badly. In fact, he really *needs* it."

"But why? He's a big swinging dick at GBS."

"A big, swinging, *overextended* dick. With the usual upper-middle-class money problems. Trying to make ends meet on three hundred grand a year. It seems Ted just can't do it for less than three-seventy-five. Which means he's got a mounting debt dilemma. A dilemma that could easily be solved by playing swami to our fund."

The phone rang. Jerry reached for it. He had a fast, hushed conversation with the person on the other end of the line, then hung up.

"That was my date for tonight. My seriously pissed-off date, who I was supposed to have met at the Odeon thirty minutes ago."

"You can blame me."

"Believe me, I will. You free tomorrow night?"

"Yeah, I suppose so."

"I'm going to try to set up this dinner with Peterson for then.

Probably near his office in Stamford. It's best to get this all behind us as quickly as possible. How was Boston, by the way?"

"I wanted to talk to you about that. The guy I was seeing at Federal and State—"

"It's great you got to see someone there. They're real comers in the mutual fund game. . . ."

"Yeah, but the guy I saw . . . Well, he had, uh, a few questions about Excalibur. . . ."

"Look, I really don't have time to deal with this now."

"How about tomorrow over breakfast?"

"I'm doing breakfast in Philly. And then I'm off to Wilmington and Baltimore for back-to-back meetings. Won't hit the city until around ten. But hey, I'll meet you here at ten-thirty, we'll catch a drink somewhere, and you can tell me all about what happened in Boston and how you sorted things out with Peterson. I'll get Peggy to set the dinner up with his secretary—and she'll call you as soon as she has details of when and where."

Sure enough, at eleven the next morning the phone rang in my office. Jerry's secretary, Peggy, came on the line to say that dinner with Mr. Peterson had been arranged for seven that evening in Connecticut in the atrium of the Hyatt Regency Hotel, located on the Post Road in Old Greenwich.

"Mr. Peterson will be driving to the Hyatt directly from his office," Peggy said. "But if you catch the six-oh-four Metro-North train from Grand Central, you'll be in Old Greenwich by six-forty-eight. And then it's just a ten-minute cab ride to the restaurant. So the two of you should meet right on time."

That is exactly what should have happened, had the 6:04 from Grand Central not ground to a halt outside of Port Chester for nearly a half hour, thanks to a major signal failure. Using my cell phone I called the restaurant and said I would be late. Already dreading this face-to-face with Peterson, I now felt my apprehension level skyrocket.

At Old Greenwich station I called a cab. It took ten minutes to arrive—which meant that I didn't reach the Hyatt Regency until nearly 7:45 P.M. The atrium had a themed decor: a suburban Garden of Eden, with a stream, gravel paths, and semitropical trees. Peterson was seated at a corner table. He looked terrible. His skin was pasty, there were deep black circles of fatigue under his eyes, his fingernails were ravaged. He had the aura of someone who hadn't slept for days and was in a state of ongoing trepidation. And he was drinking. Heavily. As I sat down at the table, a waitress was placing a fresh Scotch on the rocks in front of him. He already reeked of Johnnie Walker.

"Thanks for being prompt," he said.

"Didn't they give you my message? The train . . ."

"Yeah, I got it. Drink? I'm about three ahead of you."

"A Perrier, please," I said to the waitress.

"What are you, a Mormon?"

"I'm just not drinking, Ted."

"Well, that makes one of us," he said, taking a deep swig of his Scotch.

"Believe me," I said, "I don't want to be here, either."

"That was some fucking show you put on at the Parker Meridien last night. I really want to thank you for that."

"You deserved nothing less."

"You're really out to get me, aren't you?"

"Oh, *please*. Who made the phone calls to that dweeb at Home Computer Monthly, threatening to pull the GBS account if they didn't fire Ivan? Who pulled the same shit with Phil Goodwin to keep me out of a job?"

"And who forced my hand on that advertising spread for *CompuWorld*?"

"You reneged on the deal, remember?"

"And you tried to play hardball with me . . . which kind of got my back up."

"Oh, I get it. You're one of those *business is war* jerks. If somebody gets your back up, that entitles you to destroy their career. . . ."

"I operate according to a very basic principle: *You fuck me, I fuck you*. I think it's called the 'law of the jungle.' "

"No—it's the law of immoral assholes like you. . . ."

The drinks arrived, forcing me to bite off that sentence in midstream. As the waitress placed the fresh Scotch in front of Ted, he drained his previous glass.

"Are you going to be ordering dinner?" she asked.

"I'm not hungry," Ted said.

"Me, neither," I added.

As soon as she was out of earshot, Ted hissed, "Want to know a little secret? I really don't give two shits what you think about me. And I really wouldn't start playing the moral card with me. Especially since I know what you're up to."

"I'm up to nothing."

"Of course you'd say that. But I know . . ."

"What?"

". . . the game you're playing."

"What goddamn game?"

"Don't go all naive on me, pal. You don't think I catch the drift, the *subtext* of this meeting? Believe me, you can tell your boss, Jerry, I get the point. Loud and clear."

I stared at him, mystified.

"You've lost me here."

"Have I now?" he said, emitting an acrimonious little laugh. "Man, you're better than I thought at the bullshit-spinning game. Then again, I'd expect no less from a true disciple of Jack Ballantine's."

I felt a jolt of fear. Ted saw it and smiled. He also snapped his fingers at the waitress and pointed to his now empty glass.

"I don't know what you're talking about," I said.

"Did Jerry program you to say that?"

"Nobody programs me . . ."

"Sorry, sorry. I forgot you're not a Moonie—just a convert to the Church of the Great Motivator."

"I don't work for Jack Ballantine."

"Yes, you do. Because I work for Jack Ballantine, too."

"Now I'm really lost," I said.

"Sure you are. You 'know nothing.' Nothing at all."

"Really I don't . . ."

"Then what are you doing here tonight?"

"Jerry wanted me to see you . . ."

"There you go."

". . . in the hope that we could, maybe, sort things out."

"Well, you can tell him that I do not automatically bend over when threatened."

"I am *not* threatening you."

"This whole fucking thing is a threat," he said loudly. Then, noticing that he had attracted the stares of a few nearby diners, he leaned forward and whispered, "Tell Jerry my position hasn't changed. Two hundred grand up front, an eight percent taste on all future deals. Otherwise . . ."

His Scotch arrived. He drained it in one gulp.

"Otherwise *what*?" I asked.

"Otherwise . . . well, put it this way: Knowledge is power."

"I still don't get what you're talking about," I said.

He looked at me with drunken admiration.

"You're good. You're *real* good. I now see why they hired you. You're perfect. . . ."

"Perfect for *what*?"

He stood up. "I really have nothing more to say on the subject. Except this: You're going to get found out. You, Jerry, Mr.-Fucking-High-rise. It's one of the only rules of life. We *all* get found it. It's just a matter of time."

With that, he turned and staggered away. He didn't get very far, as the six whiskeys he'd thrown back suddenly kicked in and he stumbled right into a waiter carrying a tray of food. The tray smashed to the floor, the waiter skidded into a table, and Peterson ended up collapsed against a banquet table. Within seconds the maître d' was on the scene. Helping Peterson up, he caught a whiff of his breath and began to frog-march him toward the door. I threw some money down on the table and caught up with them in the lobby. The maître d' was holding Peterson by the arm in an attempt to keep him vertical.

"Can I give you a hand there?" I asked the maître d'.

"Is he with you?" the maître d' asked me.

"I'm afraid so."

"Well, he's drunk and I want him out of here, now. You okay to drive?"

"I was only drinking Perrier—you can check with your waiter."

"Then I'm making it your responsibility to get him home. And when he sobers up tomorrow, tell him he's barred from here. Permanently."

He handed Peterson over to me. Grasping him by the arm, I led him out the door and into the parking lot.

"Where are your car keys?"

"Fuck you," he said, the words slurring.

I tightened my grip on his arm and, with my free hand, quickly frisked him. Then I reached into the left pocket of his suit jacket and removed his keys. They were attached to a ring with a BMW logo.

"What color is your car?" I asked.

"Black."

"Where'd you park it?"

He pointed to a distant corner of the parking lot.

"There," he said.

"Great," I said and led him off in search of the BMW.

The sun had just set, the lot was surprisingly large, and there wasn't much in the way of street lighting—so the hunt for the black BMW was a tiresome business, especially as I was having to maneuver a drunk at the same time. Peterson had now veered into incoherence, and kept bumping into fenders and hoods. Scraping his shin against a parked Volvo, he muttered a threat: "You do that again, I'll hit you back."

"Come on, come on," I said, taking hold of him by the back of his belt. "The sooner we get to the car, the sooner you get home."

After five minutes of lurching through this obstacle course of parked cars, we finally reached the BMW. But as I leaned Peterson up against the passenger door and bent down to unlock it, I heard a voice behind me.

"Tell you what, pardner—say we all give him a lift back."

Keeping a grip on Peterson, I spun around. There, standing behind me, were two dark, heavyset guys. They were both wearing baseball caps and sunglasses. They were both carrying guns. Within seconds they had converged on us. When I tried to scream, I felt something cold and metallic nuzzle the side of my head. It was a small nine-millimeter pistol placed directly against my left temple.

"I'd shut the fuck up if I was you," Thug Number One said, a hint of Dixie in his voice. Grabbing the car keys from me, he tossed them to Thug Number Two. He had his gun held against Peterson's heart—but the whiskey had muddled Ted's brain so badly that he wasn't really cognizant of what was happening. Thug Number Two unlocked the rear door, shoved Peterson inside, then joined him in the backseat and threw the keys back to Thug Number One. He led me to the driver's door, opened it, and told me to get inside. As Thug Number Two covered me with his gun, Thug Number One ran around to the front passenger door and climbed in. Then, dropping the keys into my lap, he said:

"Drive."

"You want my money, take my money," I said. "Just let us—"

I didn't get to finish that sentence. Thug Number One rammed the barrel of the gun against the side of my head again—only this time he made certain I felt some pain.

"You want instant brain surgery, you keep talking."

"Okay, okay," I muttered, terrified.

"Now drive the fucking car."

I put the key in the ignition and turned it. The engine fired on the first try. I slapped the gear stick into first and headed toward the lot's exit. As soon as we were moving, Thug Number One removed his gun from my head, but kept it ready in his lap. Glancing into the rearview mirror, I could see that Thug Number Two had also lowered his pistol. Not that he really needed it—Peterson was now sprawled across the backseat, deep in an alcoholic stupor.

"Okay," Thug Number One said. "Here's how this is gonna work. You're gonna do exactly what I tell you to do, drive exactly where I tell you to drive. You open your mouth, you get shot. You try to get help, you get shot. You run a red light, you get shot. You reading me here?"

"I'll do whatever you—"

He jabbed me in the leg with the gun.

"I said, *no fucking talking*. Now turn right."

We headed north along the Post Road, then took a right under the interstate and headed downhill toward Old Greenwich. My hands were sweating so badly they kept slipping down the wheel. And my eyes were watering with pure, undistilled fear, because I was certain that they were going to kill us.

Pulling onto the main drag of Old Greenwich, Thug Number One ordered me to make a sharp right underneath the railway bridge, followed by a fast left down a road that ran parallel with the tracks. After fifty yards, we reached a railway crossing with safety gates on either side of the tracks. Thug Number One turned back to his colleague and asked, "This the place?"

Thug Number Two nodded. He told me to pull the car off the road and cut the headlights.

We sat there for a minute or two, the silence punctuated by Peterson's snores. Then, in the distance, we heard the faint rumbling of an approaching train, followed by the bells and flashing lights of the descending safety gates.

"Now," said Thug Number One. Immediately, Thug Number Two was pulling Peterson out of the car, getting him on his feet and walking him, double time, toward the crossing. The gates started to descend. Thug Number Two squeezed Peterson and himself under the descending gate just before it fell into place. They were now inches away from the railway tracks. And I suddenly knew what was about to happen.

"Oh, Jesus Christ," I said. "You can't, you—"

"Just sit tight," Thug Number One said softly, his gun back up against my forehead.

I stared numbly ahead, watching as Thug Number Two led Peterson between the two rails. Peterson was swaying back and forth, oblivious to where he was or what was about to happen. Suddenly they were both caught in the full spectral glow of the train's headlights. The engine driver frantically began to blow the whistle, brakes shrieking. Thug Number Two let go of Peterson and made a dash off the tracks. The driver's whistle was now screeching nonstop. Peterson appeared almost bemused by this sound, and turned toward the train, blinking in the light. Then, suddenly, he realized where he was. His mouth opened wide. The whistle drowned out any scream. Thug Number Two had climbed over the gates and was running toward the car. Peterson attempted to jump to safety, but he tripped, his head landing on a rail, just as the train . . .

I covered my face with my hands. For an instant, the world fell silent. Then Thug Number One turned to me and smiled.

"Looks like you just committed a murder," he said.

THREE

ONE

They ordered me to drive back toward Old Greenwich station. Halfway there, Thug Number One directed me to stop on a narrow, darkened road near a large park, and to cut the headlights. The road was empty of traffic—though I did notice a car parked in the near distance.

"We're getting out," Thug Number One said. "Now this is how we're gonna end our little collaboration. You're gonna sit here for five minutes while we drive away. Then you're gonna drive to Old Greenwich station, park the car, and take the next train into the city. Jerry's expecting you back at his place."

"Jerry?" I said hoarsely.

"Yeah, Jerry. Now before we say good-bye, I just want you to be aware of one little thing. If you think you're gonna get out of this by going to the police, you are very wrong. Because all you'll be doing is indicting yourself for first-degree murder. Of course you might be considering another alternative—like maybe pulling a disappearing act. Well, if you do vanish, then we will make certain that the police get a tip-off about you being the number-one prime suspect in this case. And the Feds will be chasing your ass by tomorrow morning.

"So do the smart thing—and do nothing, except, of course, get yourself back to Jerry's place. And I'd be prompt if I was you—because he wanted you to know that, if you're not there by midnight, he'll make that call to the cops. You've got just under three hours to make it to Manhattan, so I wouldn't stop anywhere for a drink if I was you. Understand?"

I nodded.

"You got any questions?"

I shook my head.

"Glad to hear it. Now we've got one last piece of housekeeping to deal with. My friend and I are gonna give the car a nice little rubdown of anywhere we might have touched. Of course, should you try to drive away before this domestic chore is completed . . ."

"I won't try to drive away."

"You know something? I'm beginning to like you more and more."

"I'm pleased," I muttered.

"Now sit tight, 'cause this'll just take a sec."

With that, they both got out of the car, pulled out handkerchiefs, and comprehensively polished every surface. It took about five minutes. I sat there, a cold sweat streaking down my back, my fingers gripping the steering wheel tightly. It was the only thing keeping me steady right then. When they finished, Thug Number One motioned for me to roll down my window.

"Well, here's where we say *adios*. And remember—once we drive away, you wait five minutes before heading back to the station. And believe me, we'll know if you duck away earlier. Real nice working with you, pardner."

I watched as they walked the hundred yards to their car. It was parked far enough away from the BMW—and on a pitch-black stretch of road—to make it impossible for me to recognize its make and model. Driving away, they kept their lights off until they turned a corner and vanished from my view, ensuring that I wouldn't be able to note its license plate number. Their meticulousness was frightening—because it meant that Peterson's murder (and my role in it) had been planned with painstaking care.

Sitting behind the wheel, staring at the clock on the dash, waiting for the five minutes to expire, I was suddenly sick. I stumbled out of the front seat and collapsed to my knees just as a cascade of vomit poured out of my throat. I kept retching until I nearly convulsed.

I'd been set up, primed to take the fall. And Jerry had been the author of this plot.

"This whole fucking thing is a threat," Peterson had shouted at me in the restaurant.

But I'd said nothing threatening. In fact, the dinner was supposed to be a stab at reconciliation. So why the hell did Peterson act as if I was there to put the thumbscrews on him? Unless, of course, Jerry told him in advance that I was going to play the heavy, and demand . . .

Demand what?

"Tell Jerry my position hasn't changed. Two hundred grand up front, an eight percent taste on all future deals. Otherwise . . . well, put it this way: Knowledge is power."

What did Peterson know that gave him such alleged "power"? A power that evidently so threatened Jerry that he'd had him thrown under a train? Granted, Peterson had figured out that Ballantine was behind the fund—but was that a reason for whacking the guy? Did it have something to do with the two hundred grand he was demanding?

"You're going to get found out. You, Jerry, Mr.-fucking-High-rise. It's one of the only rules of life. We all get found out. It's just a matter of time."

Those final comments—his *last words*—kept reverberating in my head. A murder had been committed. The police would be looking for a suspect. And I was, without question, the man they'd come searching for, because everything, *everything* pointed to me.

I *was* going to get found out.

I would have to run. But if I ran, Jerry would hand me to the cops on a platter. Anyway, running away took work, planning, cash, time—and time was definitely not on my side. In fact, if I wasn't back at Jerry's loft in . . .

I glanced at my watch. The five-minute detention had passed. It was now 9:15. And given the way he so carefully plotted Peterson's death, I was certain that, unless I was at his loft by midnight, Jerry would act on his threat to turn me in.

So I got myself up off my knees, slid back into the car, and shakily drove the five minutes to Old Greenwich station.

I left the car in a distant corner of the parking lot. Using the tail of my shirt I wiped down the steering wheel, the door handle, and anything else I might have touched. Then I tossed the keys into a drain and boarded the 9:27 back to the city.

The train was almost empty. There were only two other passengers in my car, and they glanced over at me with interest—noticing, no doubt, the shirttail hanging out of my trousers, the rumpled state of my suit, the residue of vomit on my lips, the fear etched into my face. After I took a seat at the rear of the car, the conductor came onboard and announced, "Looks like there's been some sort of accident up ahead, so we're not going anywhere for a little while."

I stiffened—and wondered if anybody noticed.

"D'you know what's going on?" asked one of the passengers.

"Seems there's a body on the tracks around a mile south of here. I believe it's on the northbound side, but the cops have temporarily closed the line in both directions."

The next few minutes were the longest of my life. I had to resist the immediate temptation to dash off the train, grab a cab, and order the driver to take me to Manhattan. That would have meant calling attention to myself. The people on the train and the driver would remember me as someone who seemed both jumpy and desperate to get out of town. But I was also worried about being stuck for so long that I might just miss Jerry's midnight deadline. So I resolved to bail out and find a taxi if the train wasn't moving within forty-five minutes.

Happily, the train jerked into motion after only ten minutes had passed. Initially, we crept along the tracks. It only took a minute to reach the scene of the "accident." There were four cop cars, an ambulance, and a slew of official-looking folk crowding alongside the tracks. The rear of the ambulance door was open, and I could see the shape of a corpse through a white plastic body bag. A uniformed cop stared up at the train. Instinctually, I lowered my head, then thought, *Did he see that? . . . Is he reaching for his walkie-talkie right now and radioing the cops at the next station to pick up a potential suspect on the southbound Metro-North train*?

"Real pretty scene, huh?"

I jumped and found myself staring at the conductor. He observed my overreaction with amusement.

"Scare ya? Sorry."

"Didn't see you coming," I said. "I was just . . ."

I pointed to the window.

"Yeah, it's a real mess. And when we were sitting at Old Greenwich, waiting for 'em to clear the line, word came through that the driver of the train saw two men on the line. But they only found one body."

"No kidding?" I said.

"Yep—it's all kind of suspicious, if you ask me. You going straight through to Grand Central?"

I nodded and handed him a $20 bill. He punched a ticket and returned it to me with the change.

"Have a good one, sir."

No chance of that.

Thankfully, after the train inched by the accident scene it picked up speed. I spent the journey staring out the window at the dark void of night, my brain swamped by images of Peterson's final moments on the railway tracks. And then I saw myself seated on that park bench in Boston Common the day before, mulling over Elliot Capel's suspicions about the fund. My instincts had told me to abandon ship, to quit the job on the spot. But I stayed put. Just as I stayed put after I first read the Excalibur prospectus and felt uneasy about the legitimacy of the fund. Just as I pleaded for this job without ever considering what I might be actually called upon to do.

And now each of those decisions suddenly seemed huge, monumental, life-defining, whereas earlier I must have spent no more than a few seconds formulating them. Is that all it takes to make a wrong choice? A few anxious milliseconds—when you're so desperate, you'll grab at almost anything offered?

We reached Grand Central just after eleven. I hailed a cab and was at the loft forty minutes before the midnight deadline. Jerry was seated at the kitchen table, talking, as usual, on the phone. He hung up as soon as I entered.

"So how was the dinner with Peterson?" he asked pleasantly.

"You know exactly how it went, you sonofabitch."

"Sorry—I don't."

"Oh, really?" I said. "Well then I'll tell you. After dinner, two guys with guns hustled us into Peterson's car, made me drive to a quiet little spot near the Old Greenwich train station, and watch while they threw Peterson under an oncoming New Haven express. So that's how my goddamn evening went, Jerry. . . ."

"I'd lose that unpleasant tone of voice if I were you," he said, standing up and opening a kitchen cabinet.

"I'll give you any 'tone' I want. Especially since the two guys who killed Peterson let it be known that you were the brains behind this operation."

"Did they really say that?" he asked mildly. Then, holding up a bottle of Scotch and two glasses, he asked: "Feel like a whiskey? I think you can use one after what you've been through."

"Fuck your whiskey."

He shrugged. "Suit yourself," he said, pouring himself a shot.

"Why did you order Peterson to be killed?"

"What are you talking about? I didn't kill Peterson. *You* did. There's nothing connecting me to the crime whatsoever. I mean, all I told you to do was take him out for dinner. Next thing I hear, he's fallen under a train. Nasty way of ending someone's life, Allen."

I sank down into the sofa and put my head in my hands. He came over and crouched down beside me, and continued to speak in an easy, matter-of-fact tone.

"Think about it. Everyone knows you despised Ted Peterson because he destroyed your career. And everyone who attended the SOFTUS reception last night would be able to testify to the level of your hatred, thanks to that shouting match. I bet you were also the last person to be seen with him—as, no doubt, the maître d' at the Hyatt Regency would also tell the cops. You left together, too, didn't you? And, from what my associates just told me, he was totally smashed at the time, and you appeared to be entrusted with the job of getting him home.

"Now let's face it, Ned, the scenario I'm describing will be music to the ears of the local district attorney for Fairfield County. Not only does he have you at the scene of the crime, he also has a motive, to boot. What's more, only a few minutes after killing him, you boarded a train. Surely, there must have been a conductor on duty who saw you. Just as I bet there were a couple of passengers in the same car who could easily pick you out of a lineup."

I felt another wave of nausea—but there was nothing left to bring up.

"Now I know that, under police interrogation, you'd probably weave some story about working for Ballantine, and how the Excalibur Fund was owned by us. Well, there's absolutely no record of your ever being employed by us—and the fund, as I already told you, is divvied up between three offshore-registered companies. Yes, we do pay taxes on the fund's revenue—we are good citizens, after all—but the holding is constructed in such a way that, on paper, it can never be traced back to Ballantine Industries. In fact, there's no way that the actual company owner's identity can be divulged. Under U.S. law this information is also confidential.

"So, you see, Ned—we are clean, and you are . . . well, a murderer."

I hit Jerry. With the open heel of my right hand. Catching him right on the nose. He fell to one side, his hands covering his face. I grabbed a heavy glass ashtray off the table, and was about to bring it down on his head.

"Go on," Jerry taunted, "do it. And get indicted for two murders while you're at it."

I froze, the ashtray raised above my head. Then I let it drop on the sofa. I followed, slumping back down into the cushions. Jerry picked himself up off the floor, walked over to the kitchen, opened the fridge, filled a dish towel with ice cubes, and held it against his bloodied nose.

"That was dumb, Allen," he said. "Very dumb."

I forced myself up from the sofa.

"I'm out of here," I said.

"I'm afraid you're not going anywhere. If you do, then the police will be tipped off that you are the man they are looking for."

I said nothing.

Jerry removed the ice pack from his nose, studied the dish towel for blood, shrugged, and tossed it into the sink.

"You don't even throw a good punch," he said.

"What do you want?"

"Want? Me? I want nothing, Allen. Nothing except your loyalty. Because the scenario I've been describing will only be played out if you do something rash. Like blab to the newspapers. Or go on the run. Or try to leave the job."

"The police will be on to me very fast."

"No way. Sure, there will be talk in the papers about some guy having been seen with Peterson—but, unless the cops are tipped off, who will know it's you? I mean, before meeting him at SOFTUS, when was the last time you made contact with Peterson?"

"Before Christmas."

"There you go. Anyway, if, for some accidental reason, you were fingered, I'd help you with an alibi. Sure you were seen arguing with Peterson at the Parker Meridien. But on the night he died, you were out of town on business."

"How will I ever prove that?"

"Give me one of your credit cards." When I hesitated, he barked, "NOW."

I dug out my wallet and handed over my MasterCard (the only one that was usable).

"You had to fly to Miami for the day on fund business. You stayed at the house of a Victor Romano. . . ."

"Who's he?"

"One of the original investors in the fund. An FOB. Anyway, he'll vouch for you. And by this time tomorrow, using your MasterCard, I'll have a New York–Miami airline ticket dated for today in your name. I'll also arrange for a rental car receipt, just to make things look really convincing."

"Isn't that illegal?"

"Only if you get caught. And believe me, you won't get caught. Because it will all be authentic documentation."

"How the hell will you arrange that?"

"I know people. . . ."

"I'm sure you do."

He objected to the tone of that last comment. "You want an alibi or not?"

"What I *want* is to be out of this situation."

"Well, that's not going to happen. So a solid alibi is your only shot at beating the rap."

"You know, even with the manufactured alibi, it's not going to be that clear cut. The cops are obviously going to question Peterson's secretary. And they'll find out that I had dinner with him."

"No, they won't."

"But you had Peggy call his secretary to set up the dinner."

"Well, actually, I called him directly, myself."

"But surely, he *told* his secretary about the dinner. Or wrote it down in his business diary."

"Believe me, he didn't."

"You can't know that. . . ."

"I *do* know that. Because the dinner with you was not something he would've wanted anyone to know about."

"Stop talking in fucking riddles, Jerry. *Why* would he have been so secretive about meeting me?"

"It doesn't concern you."

"Of course it concerns me, Jerry. It's my ass on the line."

"Ned, as long as you don't eat at the Hyatt Regency again, you are not going to have any problems. No one will ever place you at the scene—and, in the wholly unlikely event that they do, well, you'll have the Miami alibi to fall back on. So, you see, you're in the clear. In fact, if I were you, I'd go out and celebrate. Buy yourself a new suit. I hear there's a sale on at Armani. . . ."

"How can you fucking stand there, joking with me about buying a suit, after authorizing a whack. . . ."

"Tsk, tsk, tsk. As the great Ronald Reagan once said, 'There you go again.' But, okay, I will attempt an explanation. There was a problem in that Mr. Ted Peterson was trying to harm our fund—and, in the process, the reputation of Mr. Ballantine. It seems his personal financial problems were so acute that he had no choice but to resort to blackmail—he had begun to threaten us, saying he'd spread misinformation about Excalibur unless a substantial payoff was forthcoming."

I was about to say, *You mean, the information that the fund is bogus?* But I stopped myself. Knowledge might be power . . . but it also can be dangerous to your health.

"But though the alleged intelligence he had on the fund was completely spurious, the fact remains: Mud sticks—something Mr. Ballantine knows all too well. Had Peterson played the blackmail card, that little shit could have undermined the credibility of everything connected to Ballantine Industries—including your job. Would he have played that card? It's doubtful. But, if you've read *The Success Zone*, you'll know that one of the great Ballantinian business strategies is this: *Doubt breeds apprehension. So go on the offensive and shut down all avenues of doubt.* That's all I did. I shut down Peterson. And then I closed off any avenue of doubt I might have about you by ensuring your ongoing allegiance to me."

"You trapped me."

"That's one interpretation. If I were you, however, I'd look upon this situation as an opportunity. As long as you maintain your silence and do your job, you will flourish. We really do reward loyalty—and, as I know you're an ambitious guy, I'm sure you'll rise quickly up the organizational ladder. Especially when I report back to Mr. Ballantine that *(a)* you carried out a very unpleasant task with tremendous efficiency, and *(b)* you can be trusted."

He looked at me with a grin that was verging on the triumphant.

"Can you be trusted, Allen?"

I swallowed hard.

"I can be trusted." *Because you've got me. And because there's no way out.*

TWO

I spent a long night staring at the ceiling, sinking deeper into despair, not wanting to close my eyes for fear of seeing Ted Peterson's head being pulverized on that railway track yet again. My mind kept running through the entire scenario, looking for an angle, a slant, a loophole, an escape clause . . . *anything* that might spring me from this entrapment. I found nothing. Jerry had me cornered, boxed in. He now controlled my life. If I displeased him—or refused to do as ordered—he could snatch that freedom away from me with one anonymous phone call to the police. Besides eliminating the Peterson problem, this entire frame-up had been designed to ambush me; to make me entirely reliant on Jerry for my life. And he, in turn, now had a dependent pawn who would do his bidding.

Lizzie. Lizzie. Lizzie. I wanted to race to the phone, call L.A., tell her everything. But if I did I would lose her forever. Once she heard how I had been ensnared (*correction*: how, through bad judgment, lack of acumen, and desperation, I had allowed myself to be trapped), she would write me off permanently.

Sleep eventually hit me around five. Two hours later, there was a loud pounding on my bedroom door.

"Get out here," Jerry shouted. "Ted Peterson's the talk of the town."

I threw on a bathrobe and headed into the living room. Jerry was already showered and dressed for work. He was standing near the television, coffee cup in hand, watching the news on a local cable station called New York One. He turned up the volume as I entered, just in time for the 7:15 news summary. The Peterson story was the top item. The square-jawed anchorman, Fred Fletcher, looked gravely into the camera.

"Connecticut police are today investigating the suspicious death of an Old Greenwich computer executive who was struck by a Metro-North train around nine last night. New York One's Mary Shipley is live at the scene at Old Greenwich. Mary?"

As the camera jump-cut to that train crossing in Old Greenwich, I sucked in my breath. Mary Shipley, an angular woman in her thirties, was standing in front of several police cars, with about a dozen plainclothes and uniformed cops looking busy in the background.

"Fred, the Connecticut State Police are baffled as to how Edward Peterson, a thirty-three-year-old executive with Global Business Systems in Stamford, met his death when he fell under a New Haven–bound express train at 8:41 last night. From what the police can ascertain so far, Mr. Peterson, a resident of Old Greenwich, told his wife that he would be returning home late from work. His car was later found parked at the Old Greenwich Metro North station, but the police cannot figure out how his body ended up at this crossing, which is located almost a half mile away from the station, and is in the opposite direction of his house. And there are unconfirmed reports that the train's engineer informed the police that he saw two men on the tracks.

"It's quite a mystery, Fred—and one in which the police are definitely *not* ruling out foul play. Reporting from Old Greenwich, this is Mary Shipley for New York One."

Jerry hit the "off" button and the picture dissolved.

"*'It's quite a mystery, Fred,'*" Jerry said, mimicking Mary Shipley's voice. "Don't you love this country? Human tragedy reduced to a snappy sound bite. Next thing you know, Peterson's death will be a Movie of the Week. Or an episode of Miss Marple."

"They're going to figure out it was me. . . ."

"Will you please relax? They will not find out because *I* will not let them find out. You're on the team. And I protect my players."

He jumped up from the couch. "Better get my ass in gear," he said, heading toward his bedroom. Then he turned back to me and said, "Oh, one small thing I meant to ask you. I need you to fly down to Miami tomorrow."

"Fund business?" I asked tentatively.

"Absolutely. You're going to meet with a representative of Victor Romano. I mentioned him to you last night. . . ."

"The man who's supplying me with the Miami alibi?"

"You have an excellent memory. Anyway, Mr. Romano is making a new contribution to the fund—so it's been arranged that you'll collect it at noon tomorrow, from his representative at the bar of the Delano Hotel, then catch the two P.M. flight to Nassau and deposit his contribution in the fund's account at the Bahamian Bank of Commerce."

I suddenly felt very nervous.

"Mr. Romano makes *cash* contributions to the fund?" I asked.

"He has highly diversified interests, especially in his construction and hauling businesses—and much of it is done in cash."

"Isn't it illegal to transport cash from American soil to an offshore bank?"

A sly smile from Jerry.

"Only if you get caught. According to federal law, if you take over ten thousand dollars out of the country you're supposed fill out a customs form declaring the amount. But, quite frankly, that defeats the idea of moving money to an offshore bank—because once you fill out that customs form, you've set up a paper trail. And before you can say *audit*, the IRS is knocking on your front door."

"But say some customs guy does stop me. How am I going to explain a briefcase filled with cash?"

"Ned, since you don't look like a member of the Cali drug cartel, the odds are about ten thousand to one against some customs guy stopping you before you board the plane. Because they have bigger fish to fry. And because it's *only* money."

"But won't the airport X-ray machine pick up the money bricks?"

"Not if the cash is spread out across the top and bottom linings of a computer bag. We're talking about an inch and a half of padding on each side—which means a hell of a lot of money can be stuffed into one case . . . especially if it's in large denominations. And as long as it's packed flat and loose, it won't be detected when it goes through the X-ray machine."

"You don't mind if I check the bag to make certain there's nothing illicit or contraband—"

He cut me off. "Ned, if I say that it's only money, then it's *only* money. Do you read me?"

"Yeah, I read you."

He glared at me. "You are going to carry out this assignment, aren't you?"

His tone said it all. *This is an order. And you follow orders, or face the consequences.* I sucked in my breath.

"I'll do whatever you ask," I said quietly.

"That's what I like to hear," he said. "I'll get someone to drop the tickets off at your office later today."

As he headed out the door, he turned back to me and said, "Allen, you're being smart. And I like smart."

Thirty minutes later I took the same route uptown. It was an unseasonably warm morning—but I was indifferent to the humidity, the sun, the din of jackhammers digging up the street near the Canal Street subway station. I was in a room of my own, shut off from everything around me. Then again, why should I even be cognizant of life when I didn't have one anymore?

When I reached my office I fell into my chair and threw my feet onto the desk, kicking away a pile of Excalibur sales brochures. They scattered to the floor. I saw no reason why I should pick them up. Instead I found myself staring at their glossy covers. They looked so official. So professional. So greedily promising. Instead they were the reason a man was dead, and I had been transformed into an indentured servant. They were the cornerstone of the shiny trap that had been laid for me. And now I knew why Jerry had stuck me in such a tiny office. He was giving me a taste of my future as his prisoner.

Around noon there was a knock at the door. Still slouched in my chair, I craned my head and shouted, "Yeah?"

The door opened. And then I heard a voice I knew.

"Howdy, pardner."

I stiffened—and found myself staring at a dark, heavyset guy dressed in an oversized black suit.

"You wouldn't happen to be Ned Allen, would you?"

His voice had a distinctive southern twang. And though I'd last seen him wearing a baseball cap and sunglasses, I knew immediately that our previous encounter had been in the parking lot of the Hyatt Regency last night, when he held a gun to my head.

This was Thug Number One.

"Cat got your tongue?" he asked me.

"Yeah, uh, I'm Ned Allen. And who are you?"

"I'm From Upstairs, that's who I am. Got something here for you."

He handed me a large, padded manila envelope.

"Here's your plane ticket for tomorrow. You're booked on the seven-ten A.M. American flight from La Guardia, you land in Miami at ten-fifteen, and then grab a cab to the Delano Hotel. You're meeting a Mr. Burt Chasen in the bar of the hotel—try one of their piña coladas, by the way . . . they're killers—and then it's a cab straight back to Miami International for the one-fifty American Eagle flight to Nassau. You're in Nassau at two-fifty-five, you take a cab directly to the Bahamian Bank of Commerce. The manager, Oliver MacGuire, is expecting you. You're booked back on the five-forty-five P.M. flight to Miami, you change planes, and you jump the seven-twenty-five P.M. American flight back to New York. You got all that?"

"I think so."

"*Know* so."

I wasn't exactly surprised to hear this. Jerry was ultracautious about leaving any sort of paper trail that could link me to Ballantine Industries. I was paid in cash; I was reimbursed for my expenses in cash. No doubt my office and my plane tickets were paid for out of an Excalibur Fund account that had no link whatsoever to Ballantine. And from the first day I began work there, I had essentially been barred from showing my face at Ballantine Enterprises on the eighteenth floor. Jerry was right: Even if I went to the cops or the newspapers and spun a tale about dubious offshore equity funds that were run by my employer, Jack Ballantine, they wouldn't find a damn shred of evidence to associate me with him.

"You'll also find four hundred bucks in cash, which should cover all the cabs you'll be taking to and from the airports. If there's anything left over, buy yourself a good dinner."

"You're very efficient," I said.

"That's my middle name."

"Ah, so that's what I'm supposed to call you—'Mr. Blank—Efficient—Blank.' "

He narrowed his eyes. "Is that your idea of a joke?"

I met his stare, and did my best to check my nervousness.

"Haven't we met somewhere before?" I asked.

He didn't blink. "I've never seen you before in my life."

"You sure?"

"I'm real sure. And I'm sure you're *real* sure, too."

It was time to end this line of questioning. Fast.

"I must have mixed you up with someone else," I said.

"Yes, you must have." He opened the door. "Have a nice time in Miami. You obviously like going there a lot."

"I've never been to Miami."

"Yes, you have. You were there yesterday, remember?"

His eyes were still rigidly focused on me. I finally blinked.

"Of course," I said. "Yesterday, indeed, I was in Miami."

"That's right. You were there. And in that envelope you're holding, you'll find a couple of things to refresh your memory. Pleasure meeting you."

The door closed behind him. I immediately ripped open the envelope. Inside was the ticket for my upcoming trip—and another ticket to Miami in my name, dated the day before, with the outbound/inbound coupons torn out to give the appearance that it had actually been used. There was also a receipt, with an attached credit card slip, from Alamo, showing that I had rented a Mustang convertible the day before at Miami International Airport. My MasterCard fell out of the envelope—as did three photographs—evidently taken with special high-speed night film, clearly showing me guiding a visibly drunken Ted Peterson out of the Hyatt Regency.

I stared at those pictures for a very long time. Then I reached into the envelope and removed the last item. It was a tiny dictaphone. Through the little plastic window, I could see there was a tape already in the machine. I pressed the "play" button. The recording quality was poor—especially as the clatter of silverware dominated the tape. But despite the background noise, you could still hear what was being said:

"I wouldn't worry too much about this Ted Peterson guy."

"Jerry—he's like the Terminator. He won't quit until I'm history."

"Did you say he works for GBS?"

"Yeah—he's head of their media sales department."

"Want me to get him off your case?"

"I want him dead."

"That service we can't provide."

I hit the "stop" button and put my head in my hands. The evil sonofabitch had taped us during that dinner at Bouley Bakery—the dinner where he had pitched me the job. Jerry probably couldn't believe his luck when he heard me mention Ted Peterson the previous day, when Lizzie kicked me out and I threw myself at his mercy. And, supreme strategist that he was, he suddenly saw a way of dealing with his Peterson problem, while simultaneously checkmating me.

But what exactly *was* the Peterson problem? What did Peterson have on Jerry, on Ballantine, on the fund? And what wrong card did he play that made Jerry "shut him down"?

I tore the photographs into little pieces. I removed the tape from the dictaphone and crushed it under the heel of my shoe. I scooped the debris into the empty manila envelope. Then I picked up the phone and called Jerry.

"Thank you for crudely reminding me how blackmail works."

"I'm not blackmailing you," he said, sounding amused.

"Okay . . . semantically speaking, you're right. It's not blackmail, it's *coercion.* A show of brute force. A reminder of who's boss."

"Sorry, sorry—I really was being crude. Point taken, and my humble apologies. I guess I do overplay my hand from time to time."

An example of which being the way you arranged for Peterson to be decapitated by a New Haven–bound express.

I chose my words carefully. "I do know what my position is, Jerry."

"I was just checking, that's all. Just making certain you were onboard with us."

"I am onboard, Jerry."

"Then the matter won't be raised again."

"And you'll stop taping all our conversations?"

"I haven't taped *all* our conversations, Ned. Just selected ones." And he hung up.

I grabbed the manila envelope and left the office. As I headed down Madison, I saw a garbage truck parked two blocks south, on the corner of Fifty-first Street, and tossed the envelope into its swirl of trash. Then I stopped by a newsstand and bought an actual piece of garbage—the *New York Post.* The story I was looking for covered the top half of page three.

COMPUTER EXEC MEETS MYSTERIOUS DEATH IN FALL UNDER TRAIN

The *Post* devoted over twelve paragraphs to the story (which, by tabloid standards, made it *War and Peace* length). It essentially covered the same ground as the report on New York One, with two exceptions. The *Post* managed to get a quote from the engineer, Howard Bubriski, in which he confirmed that there were two men on the line right before the impact, ". . . and one of them appeared to get out of the way just in time." The second new item came from an "undisclosed source," which stated, "According to business colleagues at GBS, Peterson had seemed troubled and depressed recently, and was evidently preoccupied by some private problem. . . ."

Better known as rubbing Jack Ballantine the wrong way.

I drifed further downtown, stopping at a New World Coffee on Forty-third Street for a sandwich and an iced latte. Sitting there, I read the *Post* story several times over, relieved to note that, so far, no one had placed Peterson at the Hyatt Regency prior to his "little accident." As I was perusing it for the fourth time, my cell phone rang.

"Boss, did you see the fuckin' *Post*?"

"Phil?"

"The one and only. Howyadoin'? You must be doin' pretty good after Mr. Ted 'Asshole' Peterson took a little dive under that train."

"Phil, can I call you straight back on a land line?"

"No problem," he said, and gave me a 718 number in Queens. I gulped down my coffee and dashed out to a pay phone. Dropping a few coins in the slot, I quickly punched in Phil's number. He answered after one ring.

"Something wrong, boss?" he asked immediately.

"Yeah, there is. First things first: Is this a secure line?"

"Absolutely."

"Good."

"You in trouble?"

"Big trouble."

"How big?"

"As big as it gets."

He paused for a moment. "Don't tell me, boss . . . It's the Peterson thing?"

"You sure this is a secure line?"

"On my mother's life . . ."

"Okay, okay," I said.

"You have something to do with him getting whacked?"

"Not exactly, but . . . I'd better not say."

"Understood. How can I help, boss?"

"You know 'people,' don't you?"

"Sure. I know people who know people who know people . . . if you catch my drift."

"Well, I need some information."

"You got it."

"Ever heard of a guy called Victor Romano?"

"Nope. Is he a made guy?"

"Haven't a clue. All I know is, he's got a construction and hauling business in Miami. But I have a feeling that's not his only line of work. . . ."

"I'll make a couple of calls, get back to you."

"No—let *me* get back to *you*."

"You've got me worried, boss."

"I've got me worried, too."

But as worried as I was, there was no way I could dodge my trip to Miami. And so, at 7:10 the next morning, I found myself at the rear of an American Airlines Boeing 757, heading south. Flying me economy class wasn't just Jerry's way of reinforcing my indentured status, it was also to ensure that I remained nice and anonymous. After all, unless you're obstreperous, air hostesses rarely remember the faces of people in the back of the plane.

The temperature in Miami was a cool hundred. But I didn't have much direct contact with the heat. Hopping an air-conditioned cab to the Hotel Delano in South Beach, I walked straight into the air-conditioned lobby. The bar was empty. I climbed on a stool, ordered a Perrier, and waited. After five minutes a stringbean-thin man with a pencil mustache, thinning hair, and a cheap, ill-fitting light blue suit came in. He looked like an accountant. He was carrying a black computer case. He sat on the stool next to mine and put the case down between us. He raised his finger toward the barman and asked for a Coke. Then, keeping his eyes focused straight ahead, he said, "Ned Allen?"

When I turned to face him, he said, "No need to look at me. Just answer one simple question: What's my name?"

"Burt Chasen."

"You pass the test. The case is at your feet. There's three hundred and fifty grand inside, along with the little document the bank needs. Don't pick it up until after I've left the bar. And tell Mr. Schubert we might want to make another deposit next week."

He downed his Coke and put five bucks on the bar.

"I'll take care of the drink," I said.

"We're not together, remember?"

With that, he turned and left. Still nursing my mineral water, I moved my foot to the right and hooked it under the handle of the case. I kept it there until I finished my drink. Then, tossing down a couple of dollars on the bar, I picked up the case, retreated to the nearest bathroom, locked myself in a toilet stall, and opened it.

Inside was a Toshiba laptop computer. I lifted its cover, hit the power switch, watched as the screen flickered into life, then turned it off. On top of the computer was an envelope. Inside was an official-looking invoice—from Exeter Industrial Equipment Inc. (with an address in Tampa, Florida) to a company called the Veritas Demolition Corp. The invoice contained an extensive list of machinery bought by Veritas for the sum of $350,000. It was stamped *PAID.*

The computer rested on a layer of thick shockproof padding, designed to cushion the machine against any accidental jolts. I removed the laptop, ran my fingers along the interior edges of the case, and discovered that the padding was held in place by Velcro. I carefully pulled down a small corner of the padding. Sticking two fingers up underneath, I managed to pry out two $500 bills. Turning to the padding at the top of the case, I disengaged the Velcro and discovered that the shockproof stuffing here was made up of $1,000 bills. Pushing the padding back into place, I ran my fingers down every inch of the case, making certain that there was nothing else secreted inside it. When I was satisfied that it was clean, I repacked the computer. Zipping the case closed, I headed for the front door of the hotel and grabbed a cab straight back to the airport.

It was eleven-forty-five by the time I was back at Miami International—a mere ninety minutes after I had landed from New York. Noticing that I was just carrying hand luggage, the check-in clerk at American Eagle asked if I wanted to rush for the earlier twelve-fifteen flight to Nassau. "Absolutely," I said, and, boarding pass in hand, went charging for the gate. There was one rather nerve-wracking moment, when I had to hand over the case to a security officer who then tossed it on the conveyor belt for the X-ray machine. As I passed through the metal detector, I tracked the case's progress, hoping that Jerry was right about flattened money not registering a suspicious outline on an X-ray screen.

The case passed inspection and slid down to the end of the ramp. A well-dressed elderly gentleman accidentally made a grab for it. Within seconds, my hand was gripping his arm.

"I think you've picked up the wrong case, sir," I said.

He looked down at the black computer case in his hand.

"Oh, hey, you're absolutely right, son. Real sorry about that."

He passed me the bag and then reached for a vaguely similar black case at the bottom of the conveyor belt. I decided that he had made a legitimate mistake.

"No problem," I said.

The sixty-seat puddle-jumper took just forty minutes to leapfrog over to the Bahamas. I still had another uneasy few minutes while waiting to clear Bahamian customs. But the uniformed officer waved me through, and I flagged a broken-down taxi outside the terminal. We passed through the outskirts of Nassau. Once downtown, we cruised down Bay Street (Naussau's Fifth Avenue, according to the driver), then turned right and parked outside a small, squat concrete building, painted pink. A brass plate to the right of the door announced that I had arrived at the Bahamian Bank of Commerce. I stepped inside, and entered a large open-plan room with bad florescent lighting, peeling blue walls, and scuffed linoleum. An elderly air-conditioning system wheezed like a consumptive. Scattered around this room were a half-dozen steel desks at which a half-dozen rather matronly Bahamian women were sitting. If there hadn't been IBM computers on every desk, I could have sworn I had just walked into a 1960s Caribbean time warp. At the rear of this room were two glassed-in offices, both painted in what could only be described as electric green, furnished with the sort of cheap cane furniture you expect to see in a down-at-the-heels Hawaiian resort. Elliot Capel was right: the Bahamian Bank of Commerce didn't exactly inspire confidence.

"Hello there, Mr. Allen," said the woman at the desk nearest the front door.

"Uh, hello," I said, taken aback that she knew my name.

"Mr. MacGuire told us you were coming, and to keep an eye out for you. Go straight on back—he's expecting you."

Oliver MacGuire was a Bahamian gentleman around forty. He was nearly six foot four and had that seriously pumped look of someone who worked hard at fending off a middle-age spread. There was a framed portrait of Queen Elizabeth on his wall, next to one showing a younger version of himself in cricket whites. He was wearing white today, too: white cotton trousers, a white linen shirt open at the neck, and white canvas shoes. Not exactly the Wall Street banker look.

"It's so nice to meet a foreign depositor for a change," he said, shaking my hand.

"You've never met anyone from our fund before?" I asked.

He gestured for me to sit in the cane chair facing his desk.

"I don't get to meet most of my offshore clients. They are, by and large, invisible."

"So who opened the Excalibur account here?"

"That sort of information is confidential, but your Bahamian lawyer, Winston Parkhill, handled all the paperwork. Have you met him yet?"

"I only joined the fund around a month or so ago. But don't you need an individual name attached to the account?"

"Under Bahamian law, if a company is incorporated here, there is no need for an individual's name to be affixed to the account. All we need is the name of a local agent, like your lawyer, Mr. Parkhill. If, however, you yourself wanted to open an account with us, we would be legally obliged to open it in your name—though, of course, if your Internal Revenue Service ever came knocking on our door, we would not feel under even the slightest obligation to let them know whether or not you had an account with us." He smiled. "Welcome to the world of offshore banking—where you can actually tell the U.S. government to go to hell."

"I should open an account with you," I said. "Just for the pleasure of thumbing my nose at the IRS."

"By all means," Mr. MacGuire said, reaching into a side drawer and pulling out two printed forms. "We'd love to have you as a customer. All we require is some proof of identification—a passport would do—and your signature on these forms. We usually demand some reference from another financial institution, but seeing how you're already 'associated' with an existing account, we could waive that requirement."

I took the forms, folded them, and slid them into the inside pocket of my jacket.

"I'll think about it," I said. The $1,150 a week I was being paid by Ballantine Industries didn't exactly give me the wherewithal to explore offshore banking options.

Mr. MacGuire focused his attention on the case beside my chair.

"I gather you are making a deposit today," he said.

I placed the case on his desk, opened it, and removed the laptop. Then I yanked off the top padding. Money came cascading down into the center of the case: a waterfall of $500 and $1,000 bills. I turned the case over and released the other padding, sparking off another downpour of cash. Mr. MacGuire didn't bat an eye.

"There's three hundred and fifty thousand dollars in there," I said.

"And you also have the 'source of funds' documentation?"

"There's an invoice in the case, if that's what you're talking about."

"That's what I'm talking about," he said. "Under our new anti-money-laundering legislation, Bahamian banks cannot accept deposits over $10,000 without written proof of its origins."

He paused for a moment, and absently tapped his left index finger against my bag. "Of course, that doesn't mean that we must carefully investigate whether such documentation is legitimate . . . or, for that matter, ask questions about the intriguing means by which the money arrives on our shores. It's a lovely case, Mr. Allen. Beautiful leather. Where'd you buy it, if you don't mind me asking?"

"It was a gift."

"Of course it was," he said, standing up. "I'll just have someone count this."

He headed out into the front office with the case. He returned a minute later.

"Shouldn't take too long," he said. "We're used to dealing with cash around here."

"How did the earlier deposits for the fund arrive?" I asked.

"Through a third party. But, to date, your deposits are only . . . what . . ." He tapped a few numbers into his computer, then squinted at the screen. ". . . six million, two hundred eighty-four thousand, five hundred and thirty-two dollars." He looked at me carefully. "If you don't mind my saying so, that is not a substantial amount for a private equity fund. I mean, two hundred million is, in my experience, a more typical amount, though usually that's based on fifty million in cash, with the rest leveraged up. And, of course, when you're talking about a fund of that dimension, there are usually just three to four major institutional investors involved."

"You seem to know a great deal about this sort of thing."

"You mean, for a Bahamian banker?" he said dryly.

"No offense intended."

"None taken. The reason I know so much about equity funds is that I spent twelve years working in London for a little company called Lehmann Brothers."

If his aim had been to embarrass me he'd succeeded.

"Lehmann Brothers . . . Wow. What made you give it all up?"

"And exchange it for this ramshackle little bank? Have you ever been through a January in London, Mr. Allen?"

"I've never been to London."

"After twelve Januarys in London, you'd happily take a cut in pay and conditions in exchange for a glimpse of the sky. Anyway, I'm a Bahamian. This is my country. I wanted to come home. And the offshore banking business here is constantly amusing—especially as it affords me the opportunity to meet colorful businessmen like yourself."

"I'm not 'colorful,' Mr. MacGuire."

"Mr. Allen, anyone who shows up at my office carrying a computer case containing three hundred and fifty thousand dollars is, in my book, a colorful character."

The phone on his desk rang. He answered it, spoke a dozen or so words, hung up, and looked back up at me.

"Your three hundred and fifty thousand dollars are all present and accounted for."

He pulled a large buff-colored receipt book toward him, picked up a pen, filled in the receipt and the stub, grabbed a stamp, inked it, slammed it down twice in his book, then tore off the receipt and handed it to me.

"Now it's official," he said. "You can pick your case up at reception. And, of course, don't forget your laptop."

I stood up, tucked the Toshiba under one arm, then thanked him for his assistance.

"I'm sure I'll be seeing you again soon," he said.

"That depends."

"On what?"

"On how fast our fund investment grows."

He gave me a conspiratorial smile.

"Or on how many cash-filled computer cases you can carry at one time," he said.

I said, "I'm not a courier, Mr. MacGuire." But, of course, I knew that I was now whatever Jerry Schubert wanted me to be.

A puddle-jumper to Miami, a fast connection to New York, and I was back at La Guardia by 10:20 that night. On my way out of the terminal I picked up a copy of the *Post*. The Ted Peterson story may have been relegated to page five, but the headline still made me shudder.

COMPUTER EXEC IN RESTAURANT CLASH
HOURS BEFORE DEATH

As I had feared, the maître d' at the Hyatt Regency restaurant, Martin Algar, had (according to the *Post*) come forward and informed the police that Peterson had been in his establishment on the evening that he met his death under that Metro-North train. Algar told the cops that Peterson was not alone in the restaurant, but was seen having a heated discussion with a fellow suit at a corner table—a discussion that eventually erupted into a frequently loud argument.

The final paragraph of the story really made my day:

> Connecticut State Police are now eager to question the white male seen leaving the hotel with Peterson. He has been described as being in his early thirties, around six feet tall, of medium build, with sandy hair, and wearing a light gray suit.

No doubt a police artist was currently sitting across a table from Mr. Algar, creating a composite sketch of the alleged perp. No doubt as well, several of Peterson's GBS colleagues were being interviewed by the police. "Did he have any known enemies?" they'd be asked. And they'd all say the same thing. "Well, this guy called Ned Allen had a real ugly shouting match with Ted the night before he died."

As I slid into a Manhattan-bound cab, my phone rang. As soon as I answered, Jerry asked, "How did it go?"

"No hitches," I said.

"Glad to hear it."

"Did you see tonight's *Post*?"

"I always read the *Post*," he said in a tone that indicated I shouldn't bring up such matters during an easily traceable call. "It's a wonderful newspaper. Full of interesting tales. Are you in a cab right now?"

"Yeah."

"Then meet me at Fanelli's. I'll buy us a late dinner."

Fanelli's was the neighborhood watering hole—possibly the only old-style bar and grill still left in SoHo. There was no traffic on the BQE, so I arrived there just before eleven. Jerry was already seated at a table in the little dining area beyond the bar. It was a slow night. We were the only customers in the back room.

"Rule Number One of modern life," Jerry said after I sat down. "Never, *never* discuss anything of a sensitive nature on a cellular phone."

"I'm scared shitless, Jerry."

"Why? Because some fucking hotel maître d' says he saw Peterson with a suit?"

He pulled my copy of the *Post* off the table, turned to page five, and read out loud: *"Early thirties, around six feet tall, of medium build, with sandy hair, and wearing a light gray suit.* The guy could be talking about half the male population of Fairfield County."

I spoke in a near whisper.

"But say somebody tells the police about my confrontation with Peterson at the SOFTUS reception? And say they ask me to take part in a lineup for the restaurant manager?"

"You are being totally paranoid here. To begin with, so what if you were seen arguing with Peterson? If the cops ask around GBS, they'll probably find half a dozen other people who had screaming matches with the guy. Because he was the sort of asshole who went through life picking fights with everybody. Second, if the cops do come to question you, you've got the Miami alibi. And once they see you have legitimate proof that you were elsewhere when the murder was committed, they're not going to be hauling you up to Connecticut."

I said, "I really wish you'd give me some sort of clue as to why Peterson was so dangerous to you."

"Ever heard of the old American expression, What you don't know won't hurt you? I'd follow that advice if I were you. But know this: If, for some extraordinary reason, the heat starts taking a real interest in you, we'll take action to pull you out of jeopardy. I said it yesterday, I'll say it again: As long as you're on our team, you have nothing to worry about."

I almost found myself thanking him. Then I thought, *This is what they call the Stockholm syndrome—when the hostage suddenly begins to look upon his captor as his protector.* So I said nothing, and simply acknowledged his last comment with a nod.

"Now we have a little business to discuss," he said. "I need you to fly to Atlanta on Monday, and see another new fund client. Bill Simeone. He's also making a cash investment in Excalibur. . . ."

"And, let me guess, you want me to collect it, then jump a flight to Nassau, and deposit it in our account."

"You are a very clever guy."

Jerry reached into his jacket pocket and pulled out an envelope.

"Here are your tickets. I'm afraid it's a six A.M. start. And, after your meeting at the airport with one of Mr. Simeone's representatives, you'll then have to fly on to Miami before changing planes for Nassau—"

"I need to know something."

"No, you won't be carrying anything contraband. And yes, Mr. Simeone is a completely legitimate businessman, who runs one of the biggest food processing plants in the South."

"That only answers part of my question."

"What's the other part?" he asked equitably.

"Has my job description changed?"

He had to struggle to control a smile. "Let's say it has *evolved.* Because, over the past few days, we have made a corporate decision to transform Excalibur into a fund that is wholly made up of private investors. Which, I'm afraid, means that—"

"I'm now the fund's courier—its bag man."

He ignored my harsh tone.

"Given the large volume of cash investments I have recently managed to acquire for the fund, I'm afraid that we do need you to perform this courier function. I know it's not what we hired you for. And I also know that it's not utilizing your formidable talents as a salesman. However, once we have achieved the fund's twenty-two-million-dollar investment objective—"

"Twenty-two million! I'm going to be on that plane to Nassau day in, day out."

Jerry's voice remained as smooth as ever.

"I'm afraid that, for the next few months, you will be racking up the miles. However, once we've reached our objective—"

"What? You'll start having me run coke out of Colombia? Or are you going to start exploring the possibilities of weapons sales to Iraq?"

A long pause. Jerry drummed his fingers on the table, then looked back up at me.

"I will say this just once: If you do not like the work I am offering you, you are free to leave. But do understand what the consequences of that action will be."

"You'd planned this all along, hadn't you? From the moment I showed up at your office, you thought, Here's the perfect stooge."

"You credit me with far too much advance planning and guile. I'm no different from most reasonably successful businessmen: When I see an opportunity I simply take it."

He extended the airplane tickets toward me. "So, tell me: Are you flying to Atlanta or not?"

Now it was my turn to drum my fingers on the table. But after a moment, I reached up and snatched the envelope from his hand.

He gave me an approving nod.

"I promise you, this entire courier operation will only take a few weeks. And, believe me, it usually takes them several months before the customs guys decide to target a frequent flyer. So there's absolutely nothing to worry about."

I said nothing.

"Okay, then—let's order," Jerry said.

"I've lost my appetite."

Jerry used my lack of hunger as an excuse to rendezvous with his new woman of the week. As soon as he left, I went to the restaurant's pay phone and dialed Queens.

"Yo, boss," Phil said. "How's it going?"

"Worse and worse. Ever heard of a character named Bill Simeone?"

"Nah—but I do have some info on that Victor Romano guy you were asking about."

"Is he a Boy Scout?"

"An *Eagle* Scout. Yeah, he does have a legitimate construction and hauling business—but he's also been investigated by the Feds for everything from gun-running to drug stuff and two murders of so-called former associates. But the Feds couldn't make anything stick."

"Jesus," I said.

"You working with this Eagle Scout?"

"Sort of."

"Is that wise?"

"Let me put it this way: I don't have much choice in the matter."

THREE

Bill Simeone's representative turned out to be a chauffeur. He was dressed in a dark blue blazer and wore a classic black peaked driver's hat with a shiny black visor. As arranged, I met him in the arrivals area. He held a sign with my name on it. When I approached him he asked me to follow him to his vehicle. Once inside I found a computer case on the backseat. I opened it up. It was empty. I squeezed the top and bottom padding. It felt well-upholstered.

"Two hundred and eighty thousand, sir," he said. "You'll also find an envelope with the necessary paperwork."

"Fine," I said.

"Are you staying with Delta for your next flight?"

"No, American."

As he drove me over to the American Airlines terminal, I opened the nylon duffel I had brought with me. I pulled out the laptop and a few file folders and packed them into the computer case. Folded, the duffel fit easily into an inside pocket of the case. I scanned the enclosed paperwork. It was an invoice from Fay & Sons (a Dallas-based management consultancy firm) to a San Antonio company called Cooper-Mullin for $285,000 in fees. The document looked legitimate. I doubted whether Cooper-Mullin was.

The driver pulled up in front of the American terminal. "Have a good flight, sir."

One hundred minutes to Miami. A sixty-minute stopover. An hour to Nassau. And a knowing smile from Oliver MacGuire as I entered the bank.

"And you said you wouldn't be back so soon," he said, shaking my hand.

"I was wrong."

"How much do you have today?"

"Two hundred and eighty thousand," I said, handing him the case.

He arched his eyebrows slightly.

"Your fund is evidently taking off."

"Evidently."

The bag was handed over to a cashier named Muriel. We waited for her to count the money in MacGuire's office, sipping Cokes. I handed him the invoice that accompanied the cash. He gave it a cursory glance, then tossed it into a basket full of papers on his desk.

"So tell me, Mr. Allen . . . exactly what sort of business ventures is your fund investing in?"

"By and large, new information technology companies."

"And your investors—they are, *by and large*, individuals with cash-based businesses?"

"I'm just the courier—so I don't know any of them personally."

"Of course you don't," he said pleasantly. "And why should you? Ignorance is bliss, after all." He beamed at me, enjoying my discomfort.

"Like I said, Mr. MacGuire. I'm just the errand boy. I pick the money up, I bring it to you, I return to New York with the receipt. I ask no questions, I keep my head down, I do as I am told."

"Do you want to be doing this job?"

"What do you think?"

He looked at me with concern. "If I were in your position I would be very careful, that's what I think."

I met his gaze. "And why do you say that?"

"Well . . . look what happened to poor Ted Peterson."

I nearly fell off my chair.

"You knew Ted Peterson?" I asked.

"Yes, I knew Mr. Peterson."

"As a client?"

"Yes, he did have an account with us. Terribly unfortunate thing that happened to him, wasn't it?"

"His death made the papers here?"

"No, but we do get the *New York Times* in Nassau. As you can imagine, I was shocked when I read of his accident . . . if, of course, it *was* an accident. The police haven't ruled out foul play as yet, have they?"

"No, they haven't," I said quietly.

"Evidently you were also acquainted with Mr. Peterson."

"I used to be in the computer business—so, yeah, we'd met a few times."

"And that was the extent of your association?"

"Yes," I said carefully, "just the occasional professional encounter over the years."

He gave me another amused look. "Then you didn't know . . ."

"What?"

". . . that Ted Peterson was the gentleman who actually opened the Excalibur Fund account with us?"

Now I was completely lost. Before I could do anything except register shock, the phone on MacGuire's desk began to ring. He answered it, mumbled a few words, then hung up and pulled the receipt book toward him.

"Two hundred and eighty thousand dollars exactly," he said, writing out a receipt.

"Why didn't you mention the Peterson connection yesterday?" I asked.

"Because I wanted to get to know you first," he said casually.

"Hang on—didn't you say that the fund's local lawyer opened the account?"

"No—you misunderstood me. The lawyer simply handled the paperwork. But it was Peterson who showed up here with the opening Excalibur deposit last year."

His stamp came crashing down on the receipt. "Of course, he opened his own personal account with us at the same time."

"Did he have much in it?"

"That's confidential. But, let me put it this way: It wasn't insubstantial. And though I know he's only been dead a few days, the lawyers for his estate haven't been in touch with us about it."

"Do you think nobody knows that the account exists?"

"It's still too early to say."

"I don't understand something: If he opened his own personal account by mail, then why didn't he make his deposits by mail?"

"Because they were all in cash—and because, like many of our customers, he probably didn't want a paper trail linking him to this account."

If, as Jerry alleged, Ted Peterson had been in serious financial trouble, then how had he been able to make cash deposits to an offshore account in his name? After all, a major multinational like GBS didn't exactly pay its executives in cash. And according to Jerry, Ballantine Industries only started paying him a consultancy fee three to four weeks ago. So where was he getting the money?

"Did Mr. Peterson ever tell you who was behind the Excalibur Fund?" I asked.

"What an absurd idea," MacGuire said, handing me the receipt. "Of course he didn't say a word about the names of his associates. And even if he had informed me, I wouldn't tell you. A Bahamian banker is like a priest: He cannot reveal anything that has been confessed to him." With a laugh, he added, "But he can't offer absolution. All he can do is bank someone's money—and tender investment advice, if requested. So I asked Mr. Peterson no questions about anything to do with his accounts here. Nor about the individuals behind the fund. Nor about the origin of the six million dollars with which he opened the Excalibur account."

I blinked.

"Peterson showed up here with six million in cash?" I said. "How the hell did he carry it?"

"He hopped a cruise boat from Miami, if I remember correctly. And came ashore with five duffel bags, stuffed with money. It took four of my staff an entire day to count it all. Six million is a lot of cash."

"Did he make any further deposits to the account afterward?"

"No. The account received no additional funds until yesterday, when you showed up—which, I suppose, makes you Mr. Peterson's successor." He glanced at his watch. "You must now excuse me. I'm due to play tennis with our finance minister in less than half an hour."

"One final question . . ."

Mr. MacGuire stood up. "You must be brief. If I'm late, the minister may raise our base rate of interest."

"Why did you tell me to be careful?"

He shrugged his shoulders, then said, "Because couriers are always expendable, that's why."

All the way back to New York, I kept thinking, *So Peterson was my predecessor as the fund's bag man—which meant that he had been in cahoots with Jerry and Ballantine for longer than three weeks. Which, in turn, also meant . . .*

My brain switched into rewind mode. I suddenly remembered the telephone conversation I had had with Peterson right after he capitulated on the *CompuWorld* advertising spread. When I said that I knew all about the Joan Glaston incident, he actually sounded relieved—as if that was a penny-ante misdemeanor compared to . . .

What? My mind reeled backward to that morning I drove north to Old Greenwich and confronted Peterson in his driveway. He had frozen when I mentioned Grand Cayman, then turned back toward me, his eyes filled with apprehension.

Grand Cayman. Something had gone down during that visit to Grand Cayman, which had set in motion . . .

Hang on. Maybe it was in Grand Cayman that he found out . . . *what*?

Found out something that made his encounter with that Metro-North express an inevitability?

Peterson had looked so jittery and high-strung when talking to Jerry at the SOFTUS reception. Had Jerry been threatening him the way he subsequently threatened me? Maybe he'd been trying to turn Peterson into his stooge—and having failed, decided I was the perfect candidate. Jerry had cleverly stage-managed my "accidental" encounter with Peterson at the SOFTUS reception. And then he pulled off a master stroke when he insisted that I meet Peterson at the Hyatt Regency. . . .

Talk about a perfectly executed double play. Peterson silenced, me trapped—and all it took was a little devious planning. And I would now remain permanently trapped. Unless . . .

Here's where I drew a blank. Because I still couldn't figure a way out of this situation. All I could think was, *Couriers are always expendable*.

And I was the new courier.

I was back in New York by five that afternoon. I headed home to the loft, checked my messages (none), threw on a pair of jeans and a T-shirt, and decided to take myself out for an early dinner in the Village. But as I approached Bleecker Street, my cellular phone rang.

"Ned?"

It took a moment for the voice to register.

"Lizzie?"

"Hi, there." Her tone was pleasant, polite.

"This is a surprise," I said, then quickly added, "a *nice* surprise."

"I called your office, but your voice mail told me to try your cellphone."

"Yeah—I was out of town on business this morning. Just got back. Where're you calling from?"

"My office."

"In L.A.?"

"No—here in New York."

"You're in town?" I asked, trying not to sound excited.

"I've been here since Thursday on business. Staying with Ian and Geena—the apartment's still sublet."

Maintain a casual tone.

"And when are you heading back to the Coast?"

"First thing tomorrow morning," she said.

"I see," I said quietly.

"Listen . . . uh . . . my schedule's been really jammed . . . and I've got this dinner thing tonight. . . ."

Her nervousness was palpable. She hadn't wanted to make this phone call.

"I understand, Lizzie," I said. "It's just really nice to—"

"Look," she said, "could you meet me somewhere in midtown in about a half hour? I won't have much time, but . . ."

"Name the place. I'll be there."

"The Oak Bar at the Plaza."

"I'm not really dressed . . ."

"Don't worry about that. Listen, I've got to take another call. A half hour, okay?"

I ran to the subway—and actually managed to arrive at the Plaza on time.

Lizzie had already found us a corner table in the Oak Bar.

"Hope you haven't been waiting long," I said, leaning across the table to kiss her. She pivoted her face and let my lips land on her cheek. Not a good start.

"I just arrived a minute before you." She gave her watch the fastest of glances. "I'm afraid I've only got twenty minutes."

"You look great," I said.

Actually, she looked wonderful. Her face was tanned. She was sleek. She looked like she slept eight hours a night and ate her greens. She had evidently adapted well to southern California.

"You look good, too, Ned."

I tugged on the T-shirt. "If there'd been more time, I would have dressed for the occasion."

She shrugged. "My fault. I shouldn't have sprung this on you at the last minute."

"I'm glad you did."

We fell silent for a moment. She gave me a tight, nervous smile, then drummed her fingers on the table and said, "Shall we order?"

"Sure." I raised my hand. A waiter was on the scene immediately. I pointed to Lizzie.

"A martini," she said. "Straight up, with a twist. And you?"

"A mineral water," I said.

The waiter nodded and left.

"*Just* mineral water?" she said.

"It's become my staple drink these days. Haven't touched anything alcoholic in . . . well, since just after you left."

"I'm surprised. You loved your booze."

"I loved a lot of things." I looked her straight in the eyes. "I still do."

She stared down at the table. I quickly changed the subject. "What brings you back to the city?"

"A couple of big meetings. The company offered me two choices: either become the full-time head of the L.A. office or return to New York as a junior vice president."

"Nice options. What's it going to be?"

"I'm coming back. L.A. was fun for a couple of months, but there's too much sun."

"Yeah, that would get on my nerves, too. When do you move back?"

"Monday morning. I'd rather not head back to L.A. right now, but I've got a few last-minute pieces of business to finish up."

"Why do they need you here so fast?"

"Because we've just landed a big new account. Ballantine Industries."

I gulped.

"That is a big account," I said.

"Yeah—and a handful, I imagine. According to his much flaunted reputation, Jack Ballantine is a total piece of work. Still, it's an incredibly lucrative account, and quite a challenge—especially since the first piece of business I've got to handle is his new self-empowerment book."

"You mean, *The Best Defense Is Offense*?" I blurted out.

"Very impressive."

"Well, uh, you know my connection with Jerry Schubert. . . ."

"Yeah, I was actually speaking with Jerry on the phone today. We're going to be doing a lot of liaising together on the book project. I didn't realize you'd been living with him."

"Yeah, he offered me his guest room after we . . . ," I said, trying to sound cool.

"Right," she said. "Anyway, I finally get to meet the great man tonight. We have a dinner date. At Le Cirque, his choice of venue—which is why I've only got a few minutes to spare."

"Is Jerry going to be there?"

"No, he's been called out of town."

Well, that was a small mercy.

"Anyway," she continued, "I think Ballantine wanted to make it dinner *a deux*. I gather he's a major ladies' man."

"I'm sure you can handle yourself."

"Believe me, I can."

"Anyway, congratulations on landing the account," I said. "It's great news."

"I'm not so sure about that. From what I've heard, Ballantine doesn't have nervous breakdowns—he gives them. Still, it'll keep me busy—which is the main thing these days."

I didn't meet her cheerless gaze.

"You working?" she asked.

"Sort of."

"For whom?"

I had to be cautious here. I had to lie.

"Well, after I lost the telesales job . . ."

"I didn't know. I'm sorry."

"Don't be. Every day there was taking a year off my life. Anyway, once that ended, I got desperate, walked into an employment agency, and asked them to find me anything going. And they placed me in a job with a financial services company. They're Seattle-based, and I'm essentially running their New York office. It's sort of a 'communications' job. Tracking the movement of funds, arranging courier services for clients, that kind of thing. Funny thing is, my office is in the same building as Ballantine Industries."

"Do you like the work?"

"It isn't really my kind of thing."

"Then quit."

"I need the job. I owe money."

"To whom?"

"AMEX, Visa, Barneys—the usual suspects. I think I'm still on their 'Ten Most Wanted' list."

"If you need money, I can help."

"That's really sweet, but . . ."

"You're still paying off our week in Nevis, aren't you? And my watch. And . . ."

"It's my problem. Anyway, you gave me that loan, remember?"

"It wasn't a loan. It was a gift."

"Whatever it was, I'm slowly beginning to sort things out on the money front."

"You're still making me feel guilty."

"Why? My debt is not your fault, Lizzie."

"I was seeing someone else."

The sentence landed in front of me like a lobbed hand grenade. I tried not to wince. I looked down. Her index finger was etching circles inside the empty ashtray on our table. I said nothing.

"Did you hear what I said?" she asked softly.

"Yes. I heard. And?"

"He was serious. I decided I wasn't."

"It's over?"

She nodded. "Yeah. Just. He was nice. Solid. Dependable. Dull."

"A lawyer?"

"How did you guess?"

"I didn't. It was just a shot in the dark."

"You met him once, a few years ago. Peter Buckley."

"Isn't he Mosman's in-house counsel?"

She nodded.

"He's based here, right?" I asked.

"He does a lot of business on the Coast. So he was back and forth a lot. . . ."

"And you? Were you back and forth a lot?"

Inadvertently, she covered her mouth with her hand.

"A bit," she said. "I'm sorry."

The drinks arrived. We did not raise glasses. She took a large gulp of her martini, her eyes blinking rapidly as the alcohol hit. I envied her that jolt.

"I want you to know something," she said, "and you must believe me: This didn't start until after we separated."

"Okay," I said.

"I was so fucking angry with you."

"And now?"

"I don't know."

"I miss you. I cannot tell you how much I miss—"

"I'd rather not hear this."

"It was a dumb, drunken mistake."

"It doesn't excuse it. . . ."

"I'm not trying to make excuses."

"It wasn't just the fact that you cheated on me. You pushed me away. I wanted to help you. You hated me for trying."

"I have never hated you."

"You didn't want a child with me."

This stopped me short. "I was scared, that's all."

"Why didn't you say that?"

"Because . . . I was scared about admitting I was scared."

"You could never really talk to me, could you? Especially when it came to 'the big stuff.' Never show any weakness, any fear."

"No, I couldn't. And I now know I should have said a lot of things."

"Me, too. We dodged . . ."

"Everything," I said. "And I really regret . . ."

"I regret how things turned out, too."

She took a long sip of her martini, draining half the glass. "Anyway . . . ," she said.

I covered her hand with mine.

"Come back," I said.

She withdrew her hand. "I saw a lawyer yesterday," she said.

"I see."

"It'll all be pretty straightforward, if you don't contest the divorce."

I stared into my glass.

"Do you really want to end it?"

"I think so."

"*Think*?"

"Yeah, *think*."

"If you're not sure . . ."

She glanced at her watch.

"Ned, not now."

"It's just . . . I find this really hard, Lizzie. I just wish . . ."

"I've got to go," she said.

"Can I see you when you're back?"

She stood up. "I don't know. I find this hard, too."

She quickly squeezed my hand and dashed off before anything else could be said. I wanted to go after her, but knew better. So I forced myself to remain seated, staring at Lizzie's half-finished martini. I reached for it, pulled it close to my lips, but then set it back down. I didn't feel virtuous. Just depressed. I asked for the check. Eighteen bucks for a martini and a mineral water. Jesus. Reluctantly, I dropped a twenty on the table. I headed off.

Suddenly a waiter came out of the bar holding my $20 bill.

"Sir," he said, thrusting the money back into my hand, "your guest took care of the bill on her way out."

My throat tightened. I blinked and felt tears.

"Thanks," I said.

I headed back to the loft. I didn't know what to do, so I watched television. But I couldn't concentrate on the screen. Lizzie and Ballantine. Lizzie and Peter Buckley. Lizzie and fucking Jerry Schubert. Without question, it was his brainstorm to get Mosman & Keating to take over Ballantine's public relations. And I'm certain he requested that Lizzie Howard handle the account personally. Having snared me, now he was going to pull her into his ever-spreading web—to really make sure that I wasn't going anywhere.

I tried to sleep. I failed. Around 4:00 A.M., after hours of ceiling-gazing, I decided what I was going to do. It was a "bet-the-farm" gamble—but one that had to be made. I got out of bed. I showered, I left the loft and walked uptown to Twentieth Street, then headed west to Eighth Avenue. It was now 4:45 A.M. With just over a half hour to kill, I sat in an all-night coffee shop, drinking around three pints of fully caffeinated black java. I kept thinking that now was, without question, the moment to re-embrace cigarettes—yet I somehow managed to resist that temptation.

Then, shortly after 5:15, I walked half a block west on Twentieth, parked myself opposite a well-maintained brownstone, and waited.

At 5:20 A.M. a long, black, Lincoln Town Car pulled up in front of 234 West Twentieth Street. Five minutes later Lizzie emerged from Ian and Geena's apartment. As she walked toward the car, she looked up and saw me crossing the street, approaching her. Her face registered incredulity, then dismay.

"Oh, Christ, Ned. *Why . . .* ?"

But then she stopped and saw what only your most intimate ally can see: real fear.

"What has happened?"

"Please," I said. "Let me ride with you to the airport."

She hesitated for a split second, but then gave me a fast nod.

As the car pulled away I noticed that the glass partition between the driver and the rear seat was down. As if reading my mind, she asked the driver if we could have a little privacy.

A motor hummed as the glass partition slid up into place. When it was closed, she looked at me.

"So . . . ," she said.

"So . . . ," I said. And began to talk. Taking her step by step through everything that had happened since Jerry bailed me out of jail. I spared her no details. I made no apologies for my bad judgment. It all came spilling out. Though she said nothing, her eyes grew wide—especially when I detailed the events in Old Greenwich earlier that week, and explained how Jerry was now my jailer.

She didn't interrupt me once, though I knew what she was thinking: *I'm about to work for these people?*

When I finally finished, there was a long silence. I reached for her hand. I expected her to pull back or push me away. But she took it. And held it for a moment. Tightly.

FOUR

She offered me money. She offered me a plane ticket to the destination of my choice. She said I should disappear, escape into the great American nowhere, assume a new identity, and hope that my vanishing act would convince Jerry that I planned to remain silent. I could even drop him a note, outlining my position: You leave me alone, I'll leave you alone.

"He doesn't work that way," I said. "You're either on his team or you're the enemy. And all enemies are to be annihilated. I promise you, if I leave town, he'll have me on the FBI's Most Wanted List in a heartbeat."

"Then you've got to go to the police."

"And do what? Come on like some deranged conspiracy theorist? The story I'd tell them would sound so unhinged, they'd shove me into a rubber room at Bellevue—and then book me for murder one after Jerry tipped them off. All the cops would have to do is get the restaurant manager to I.D. me. And once they took statements from any of the two hundred witnesses who saw my screaming match with Peterson, everything else would fall right into place, and I'd be doing a life stretch at Bridgeport—or wherever the hell Connecticut has their maximum security prison."

"I can't believe it's that desperate."

"Believe me, it's completely desperate."

She squeezed the palms of her hands against her eyes. "You idiot. You stupid idiot. How, *why* did you take the job? Especially when it smelled so bad?"

"I had no money. I had no home. I had no prospects. And it was Jack Ballantine. Do the math."

She pulled her hands away from her face.

"Do you blame me?" she asked quietly.

"No way."

"I blame me."

"Don't."

"I was unforgiving."

"You were hurt."

"Yeah, and I wanted to punish you for that. And, oh, Christ, did I ever."

"I made the bad calls, not you."

"I gave you no choice."

"I panicked myself into believing this was my only option. And once you panic, you lose all judgment."

We pulled into Kennedy Airport, and drove up the ramp to the American Airlines terminal. The driver opened the trunk and placed Lizzie's bag by the curb.

"I don't know how to help you," she said.

"Can I at least call you?"

"I guess so," she said flatly. Then she got out of the car, grabbed her bag, and hurried into the terminal. She did not look back.

The car drove me back into the city. As we approached SoHo, I asked the driver to let me out on Broadway and Spring. It was just after 7:00 A.M. I found a telephone. I dialed Queens.

"Sorry to get you so early, Phil."

"No problem, boss. You still sound like a gun's at your head."

"Believe me, it is. You find anything about this Simeone guy?"

"Yeah. Runs a couple of big food processing plants in Georgia, South Carolina, and Alabama. But he also has a couple of businesses south of the border."

"What kind of businesses?"

"A ketchup factory in Mexico City, a couple of sweatshops in Bogotá and Medellín . . ."

"Medellín?" I said. "Isn't that the coke capital of the world?"

"You read your *National Geographic,* boss. Anyway, nobody I spoke with said that he's in any way connected to the white powder biz. But there's no doubt that he knows people down there who are in that game. You doing any business with this joker?"

"Just transporting some of his cash to an offshore bank."

"Nice work," he said sardonically.

"I have no choice."

"You are in some serious shit."

"I need a straightforward yes or no, Phil. In your considered opinion, do you think the money I'm carrying could be from south of the border?"

"In my considered opinion, abso—fucking—lutely. I mean, the white powder business is about as cash based as you can get. And the money has got to be lodged somewhere, *capeesh*?"

I sucked in my breath. "Thanks for the opinion."

"Boss, get out of this."

"I would if I could."

Back at the loft, I sat down on my bed. Within seconds I was asleep—and when I woke again, it was late afternoon and the phone was ringing.

"Where the hell have you been?" Jerry asked when I finally got around to picking up the phone. "I'm still in L.A.—but I must have tried your office and cellphone half a dozen times."

"I had a bad night. Couldn't sleep. So I was making up for it now."

"You're supposed to be working for us, remember? Which means keeping regular office hours."

"Oh, for Christ's sake, Jerry—bag men don't keep office hours."

"If I say I want you here . . ."

"Aye, aye, sir."

"You're going to Dallas tomorrow."

"Great."

"It's another airport rendezvous. You'll be meeting a representative of a fund client named Chuck Battersby. And then you'll be heading straight on to Nassau via Miami. I'll have the tickets messengered down to you at the loft."

"Fine," I said tonelessly.

"Mr. Ballantine said that he had a delightful dinner with your wife last night. Sorry: your *estranged* wife. 'An absolute charmer' is what he called her. 'Bright, beautiful, funny as hell—Allen must have screwed up royally to lose her.' His exact words, Ned."

Between clenched teeth I said, "Is there a point to this, Jerry?"

"None whatsoever. Though I guess you should know that we've engaged Mosman & Keating to handle Mr. Ballantine's PR—and I personally requested that Lizzie take charge of the account."

I didn't want to intimate that I had seen Lizzie yesterday—or had previous knowledge of this development. So all I said was, "You're a very clever guy, Jerry. First me, now Lizzie."

"It's called 'keeping it in the family,' Ned. And you know what a family-oriented business we are—and how we look after each other. Speaking of which, I understand your picture's in the papers, and on television."

"What?" I managed to say.

"Not a picture, actually. More of an artist's sketch. Anyway, got to fly. Have fun in Dallas."

As soon as he hung up I grabbed the television remote and turned on New York One. I had to wait ten minutes for the headlines. The Peterson story was the third item. The anchorman spoke of "intriguing new developments in the death of Ted Peterson, the GBS computer executive killed Wednesday night after being hit by a northbound Metro-North train at a railway crossing in Old Greenwich, Connecticut. On the scene at Old Greenwich is New York One's Mary Shipley. Mary . . ."

Jump-cut to Mary Shipley. Still looking angular and serious. Still standing in front of that train crossing in Old Greenwich—the sight of which had my heart thumping at double time.

"Fred," Mary Shipley said, "the mystery surrounding the death of computer executive Ted Peterson is growing daily, with Connecticut state police now saying that coroner reports show that Mr. Peterson was severely intoxicated when he fell under a New Haven–bound Metro-North train on Wednesday. According to the Stamford coroner's office, the level of alcohol in Mr. Peterson's blood was nearly ten times over the legal limit. It still isn't clear whether Mr. Peterson had been driving that evening. He was seen earlier that night leaving the Hyatt Regency Hotel with *this* man . . ."

The camera cut away and showed a police sketch of a thirty-something guy with tired eyes, terse lips, and the usual sullen, "wanted murderer" expression. A tie and jacket were sketched in below his neck. I'd seen better likenesses of myself—and was relieved that it wasn't so identifiably me.

". . . whom police are seeking for questioning. He's a white male in his early to mid-thirties with sandy hair, around six feet tall, and of medium build. He was dressed in a suit the night of Ted Peterson's death. This same man was allegedly spotted by a Metro-North conductor boarding a Grand Central–bound train at Old Greenwich within an hour of Peterson's death. Connecticut state police are speculating that this was the same individual who was seen by the engineer on the tracks right before the accident."

The camera cut back to Mary Shipley.

"Reporting for New York One . . ."

I hit the "off" button, and thought, *As soon as I leave the loft, I run the risk of being nabbed. That police sketch will have made this afternoon's edition of the* Post. *And it will also be shown on* Live at Five, Eyewitness News, *and every other local television news program. And even if the police portrait left a lot to be desired, someone somewhere is bound to spot the resemblance.*

I checked my office voice mail. I received the following message:

"Hi, it's Lizzie, and I'm calling you from thirty-three thousand feet. I'm sorry I haven't returned your phone calls recently, but I really did need the space. Anyway, I do think it's time we began to speak about finalizing things—so if you want to call me, I can be reached at my L.A. office today anytime after one o'clock Pacific time."

At first the message baffled me. Then I instantly understood. She was covering for me—making it seem as if we hadn't met yesterday, just in case Jerry was hacking into my voice mail or had my phone tapped (two likely possibilities, given his need to control everything and everyone). And fearing that he also might be recording conversations on the loft phone (and not wanting to risk saying anything confidential on my cellular), I had no choice but to use a pay phone. I threw on a pair of dark glasses and a baseball cap before venturing out—just in case somebody happened to be glancing at the *Post* as I passed by.

I walked west, stopping at a Korean grocer to get five dollars in change. Then, finding a phone booth on a quiet end of King Street, I punched in Lizzie's number in L.A., and deposited $3.75 in quarters when prompted. After putting me on hold for around sixty seconds, her secretary put me through.

"Can you call me back?" I asked. "I've only got two minutes."

"This will only take a few seconds. When are you next in Nassau?"

"Tomorrow."

"Making another deposit?"

"Of course."

"Well, while you're at the bank, I really think you should open an account in Jerry Schubert's name."

"Are you serious?"

"Very. And we're now down to ninety seconds. So, for once in your life, please shut up and listen to me."

I listened. Then, after ninety seconds, Lizzie hung up—and I went back to the loft in search of Jerry's passport.

It was easy to find—he kept it in his unlocked desk drawer. I flipped through it. There were recent entry stamps for Colombia, Ecuador, Brazil, the Cayman Islands, and Luxembourg . . . but not the Bahamas. I studied his signature on the inside flap. I expected Jerry to have an extravagant, bold autograph—but it turned out to be a tight, spindly scrawl. After around twenty attempts on a blank sheet of paper (which I then shredded and flushed down the toilet), I was able to produce a reasonable facsimile of his John Hancock on the two forms required for opening an account at the Bahamian Bank of Commerce. Then I filled in the remainder of the application, using his passport to provide details like his date and place of birth. I also circled *No* on the corner of the form that asked if the applicant wanted bank statements sent to his home address.

I presented these forms to Oliver MacGuire the following afternoon.

"So your friend Mr. Schubert wants to open an account with us?" MacGuire asked.

"Well, just between ourselves," I said, tossing Jerry's passport onto MacGuire's desk, "he's actually my boss. The fund is his baby—and he wants a secure offshore home for his twenty percent commission from all deposits."

"Twenty percent?" MacGuire said, studying me carefully. "That *is* a sizable commission."

I reached down beside me, hoisting up the computer case stuffed with the cash I had collected that morning at Dallas Airport. I placed it on MacGuire's desk.

"Yeah, it's a hefty cut—but look at the money he's bringing into the fund."

"How much today?"

"Four hundred and ten thousand."

"Of which"—he scribbled a few figures on his desk blotter—"exactly eighty-two thousand should be deposited in Mr. Schubert's account?"

"Absolutely."

He studied the forms at length. Finally he shrugged.

"Well, it's not as if you're opening the account in your own name. And you do have his passport. And his signature on the form matches that in his passport, which leads me to conclude that either this is perfectly legitimate, or you are dangerously clever."

Before I had a chance to protest my innocence, he raised a finger.

"Do me a favor, Mr. Allen, and refrain from answering that question. Because it's not my business to know such things. And—I really do *not* want to know. One small thing, however—Mr. Schubert should have supplied you with a reference from a financial institution with which he has an account. But given that he is your boss—and therefore involved with the fund—I think we can waive that requirement."

"He'll be very grateful."

He disappeared with the computer case. When he returned fifteen minutes later he was carrying a small deposit book. He handed it to me. It was made out in the name of Jerome D. Schubert.

"The account is officially opened."

I handed him back the book. "You can keep this on file here," I said.

"You mean, Mr. Schubert won't want to see a record of his deposits?"

"He trusts me."

"Of course he does," Mr. MacGuire said, beginning to write out the receipts.

"I mean, I'll be turning over the deposit receipts to him."

"Of course you will."

"I've been meaning to ask you something. Doesn't Jerry Schubert get Excalibur Fund statements sent to him?"

He gave me a withering glance.

"Excalibur is not his account, Mr. Allen."

"Of course," I said, covering my gaffe. "It's traceable to no single individual. And therefore, no one receives its statements."

"Precisely. But . . ." He motioned me toward him. ". . . I'll let you in on a little secret. The fund's lawyer, Mr. Parkhill, rings me here every time you visit us with a deposit, just to make certain that the money has arrived. And he always inquires as to the amount you have deposited."

"And what will you tell him, now that the money is being spread between two accounts?"

"I will continue to do what I have always done: inform him of the total sum you deposited . . . and say nothing more. Unless, of course, he demands to know the balance of the fund's account—which I will be obliged to tell him."

"May I ask a favor?"

"Try me."

I chose my words carefully.

"If he does ask you for the overall balance, would you please call me?"

He thought about this for a moment.

"Well . . . I don't suppose a phone call would contravene bank regulations. So . . ."

He pushed a pad toward me. I scribbled down the number of my cellular phone. Then I stood up to leave.

"I really appreciate your help," I said.

He shook my hand. "You are playing a very curious game, Mr. Allen. I hope there is some strategy behind it."

No, I just make it all up as I go along.

Before leaving the bank I managed to execute a maneuver I had planned while en route to Nassau. I stopped by the front counter to say hello to Muriel, who always called me a cab after I concluded my business with Mr. MacGuire. She was a thickset woman around fifty, with a bouffant hairdo and heavily rouged lips. She was also a skillful flirt. As I approached the counter, she said, "Hey there, rich man—how much money did you give us today?"

"Not enough to win you over, Muriel," I replied.

"Damn right. I'm sure it's not enough—because I don't come cheap."

"I bet you don't."

"Cab to the airport, hon?"

"Please."

There was no phone behind the counter, so Muriel headed into a back office. As soon as she was out of sight (and I had glanced around to make certain no one was watching), I made a fast grab for two items on the counter: an unused receipt book and an official bank stamp. The entire theft couldn't have taken more than three seconds, and the booty went straight into my case. When Muriel returned there was one nervous moment when I thought she noticed the missing items—but it passed, and she gave me a big smile.

"The taxi'll be here in a second, hon."

"Are you going to run away with me this time?" I asked.

"You propositioning me?"

"Absolutely."

"Man, you are one fast worker."

"The fastest."

"Think I better talk things over with my husband first. He might not like the idea—and I think you've got enough problems already, hon."

All the way back to Miami, Muriel's comment kept pestering me. Making me wonder if I radiated worry—or if Mr. MacGuire and his colleagues knew more about my little predicament than they let on. Surely they were more than a little curious about the origins of the one million dollars I had banked with them this week. I was rather curious as well.

In the departure lounge at Miami Airport I broke a $5 bill, deposited $3.75 when requested, and called Lizzie.

"Did you open the account?" she asked.

"I did."

"No problems?"

"There were a few raised eyebrows—but then the manager, Mr. MacGuire, saw the four hundred and ten grand I was depositing and decided he could live with any doubts he might have about the account's legitimacy."

"Anyway, it *is* a legitimate account—in Jerry Schubert's name. Did you get both receipts?"

"Yes."

"Then you'd better find a safe place to hide the ones pertaining to Jerry's account."

"I even scored a Bahamian Bank of Commerce receipt book and official deposit stamp."

"Was that difficult?"

"It turns out I'm a natural as a shoplifter."

"Listen, I'll be flying to New York on Sunday. I just found out that the company's found me a three-month sublet on Seventy-fourth and Third."

"Can I meet you at the airport?"

"Ned, we're separated. We're staying separated."

"I just thought . . ."

"What?"

"You've been great, that's all."

"I'm just trying to help—because, God knows, you need help. But it's nothing more than that. Understood?"

"Yeah—understood."

"Call me tomorrow with an update. Oh—and see if you can somehow break into Jerry's computer. The only way you're going to get out of this is if you find out exactly how the fund works, and what landed Peterson under that train."

At a newspaper shop near the departure gate, I asked the clerk if they stocked ink pads.

"The only one I've got comes with a complete set of Disney characters."

"Sold."

The flight to New York was half full. I had two seats to myself. After takeoff I opened my computer case, pulled out the receipt book, and filled in a deposit slip in the name of the Excalibur Fund for the amount of 410 thousand U.S. dollars. Then I retrieved the bank stamp, opened the Disney ink pad, inked the bank stamp, and slammed it down on the receipt—giving Jerry alleged proof that the entire Dallas deposit was safe and sound in the fund's account.

I didn't reach New York until after ten that night. The lights were off in the loft—but I was taking no chances. Before taking the elevator upstairs, I left my case in a broom cupboard at the rear of the little downstairs lobby. But Jerry wasn't lying in wait for me, wondering why his passport was missing. The loft was empty. So I returned his passport to his desk drawer, then powered up his computer. Immediately, a prompt appeared:

ENTER PASSWORD.

Damn. Damn. Damn. But not unexpected, as Jerry was ultra-cautious on the security front. I rummaged through his desk drawers, hoping that he might have written down the password in an address book or on the inside cover of his computer's instruction manual. But the very fact that he left his desk unlocked told me what I already knew: Nothing of a confidential nature was kept there. So I tried a variety of password variations:

JERRY
JSCHUBERT
JERRYSCHUBERT
JS
J.S.
JERRYS
BALLANTINE
JB
BALLANTINE IND
BALIND
EXCALIBUR
EXCALFUND
FUND
SUCCESS
SUCCESS ZONE
BRUNSWICK
HOCKEY GUY
HEAVY
BUSINESS IS WAR

When my inventiveness began to peter out I tried his date of birth. No dice. So I reversed that number. Still no luck. But just as I dug out his passport and was about to type in its number, I heard a telltale *clunk* in the outside hallway. The elevator had stopped on our floor. Frantically I shut the computer down, just managing to turn off the monitor and dive onto the sofa as Jerry walked through the door.

"You're up late," he said, tossing his bag by the door. "Everything go okay in Dallas?"

"Not a hitch," I said, trying to appear relaxed.

"And you made your connection to Nassau?"

"With a half hour to spare."

"You've got the receipt?"

"Yeah," I said, reaching into my shirt pocket and handing it over. He glanced at it briefly, then slipped it into his wallet.

"How was L.A.?" I asked.

"Great trip. Plenty of interest in Mr. B.'s new book on the Coast—and I found a new client for the fund."

"I see."

"So it looks like you're off on Monday afternoon to the City of Angels. I phoned our travel agent. She's got you on the three P.M. American flight, you'll be at LAX by six, you'll have a couple of hours at the airport to deal with all your 'business,' then you're booked on the ten P.M. red-eye to Miami, changing there for the seven A.M. flight to Nassau."

"Whatever," I said, thinking that two transcontinental flights in a day would give new meaning to the expression *jet lag*.

Jerry opened the fridge, pulled out a beer, screwed off the top, and took a long swig.

"I need to ask you something, Ned. And understand: I'm doing it as a courtesy."

"Yeah?"

He took another swig of beer. "What would you think if I started going out with Lizzie?"

I tried to show no emotion.

"We're separated, remember? So it's not really my call who she sees."

"We had lunch yesterday."

"What?" I said, sounding thrown.

"We had lunch yesterday in West Hollywood. Strictly business, of course—there's a lot to talk about, vis-à-vis the launch of Mr. B.'s book. But, I've got to tell you—she is one exceptional woman."

"Yes, I'm aware of that."

"So, naturally I got to thinking about . . . well, how I'd like to start seeing her. Especially since she's moving back here. And especially since I definitely sensed that she's interested, too. Of course I could be wrong, but . . ."

I stood up and headed toward the door.

"You could be right, too," I said. "I'm going to get some air."

"I've upset you."

"Yes," I said. "You have."

I didn't bother to wait for the elevator. I charged down the stairs, grabbed the computer case out of the broom cupboard, marched out the door and straight to the nearest pay phone. It was now midnight. As it was her last day in the L.A. office, I gambled on Lizzie working late. Before she could say hello, I yelled, "What the hell were you doing having lunch with Jerry Schubert?"

"Talking business. And lower your voice, *now*."

"He said sparks were flying between you like a forest fire . . ."

"Oh, for Christ's sake . . ."

". . . and that he really felt you were giving off this big romantic *vibe*."

"In his dreams. Now will you please grow up. . . ."

"I miss you, goddammit. I miss you. I miss you. I miss you."

Silence. She waited until I stopped sobbing.

"Are you okay?" she finally asked.

"No."

"Ned, trust me here. I think Schubert is a total asshole."

"Okay."

"But I've got to work with him. And I do think it's worth flirting with the guy. Because, like most men, he shoots his mouth off when he thinks he might just have a chance. And yesterday afternoon . . ."

"Yeah?"

"He asked me if we were ever friendly with Ted Peterson and his wife."

"He really *asked* you that?"

"Yeah, he did."

"But why?"

"Well, trying to be really casual, he mentioned how he'd read about Peterson's death in the paper, and how he knew you had a history with the guy . . . and he was just also *casually* wondering if we'd ever met Mrs. P. And was she somebody who was close to her husband, or knew much about his work. I told him the truth: I'd never met either her or her late jerk of a husband. But it got me thinking . . ."

A long pause. Finally I said, "He's worried that Mrs. Peterson might have stumbled upon some sort of evidence that Ted left at home?"

"Bull's-eye, Sherlock."

FIVE

Two things stopped me from rushing up the next morning to meet Meg Peterson in Old Greenwich. The first was a headline I saw in the *New York Times*. It was on page three of the Metro section:

HOME OF DEAD COMPUTER EXECUTIVE
RANSACKED DURING FUNERAL

Just over a week after Ted Peterson's death on the Metro-North line in Old Greenwich, a new twist has been added to the case, which Connecticut police have been calling "highly suspicious." Upon returning home from his funeral service yesterday, Mr. Peterson's family discovered that their house in Old Greenwich had been robbed.

According to Capt. James Hickey of the Greenwich police department, "The perpetrators took very little of value from the house, yet still ransacked it thoroughly."

The major thefts took place in Mr. Peterson's study and bedroom. "Either these thieves were looking for something specific," Capt. Hickey said in a prepared statement, "or they mistimed the break-in and had to flee when they heard the mourners returning to the house. Whatever the scenario, their actions are beneath contempt."

Fucking Jerry. The guy was beyond ruthless. He had no scruples whatsoever. Lizzie's instincts had been right on the money. Worried that Peterson might have kept some incriminating papers at home, he decided to stage a break-in at *chez* Peterson, disguised to look like a robbery. Only, of course, instead of grabbing jewelry and the family silver, they nabbed Ted's desktop computer, his floppy disks, his papers. And with impeccable, humane timing, Jerry organized the robbery to take place while his family and so-called friends were saying prayers over the guy's body.

So much for me getting to Mrs. Peterson first. Jerry had closed down that possibility.

The second thing that stopped me from visiting Mrs. Peterson was the police. Around 9:00 A.M. Monday morning—only a few hours before I was due to fly to Los Angeles—I received a call at the office from a Detective Tom Flynn of the Connecticut state police. He "just happened to be in Manhattan today on business," and would greatly appreciate the opportunity to stop by my office and ask me a few questions about Ted Peterson. When I explained I was going to L.A. that afternoon, he said, "No problem. I've just wrapped up an interview with someone on East Forty-eighth Street. I could be at your office in half an hour."

"Well, it's kind of a busy morning," I lied.

"I just need fifteen minutes of your time, no more," he said, then hung up before I could say no.

Detective Tom Flynn was in his late forties. Short and wiry, he had the build of a bantamweight boxer and a street kid's face—an aging Jimmy Cagney, now marooned in the Connecticut suburbs.

"Appreciate the time," he said, sitting down in the chair opposite my desk.

"No problem," I said, doing my best to avoid sounding nervous.

"Let me explain something from the outset, Mr. Allen. This isn't a formal interrogation. Nor are you officially under suspicion. And you're under no obligation to answer any of my questions. All this is, is a chat."

"Thank you for the clarification."

"You work for yourself?" he asked, looking around my tiny office.

"Sort of. I'm the North American representative of an international private equity fund."

"Private equity *what*?" he said, already taking notes in a little black book.

I gave him a thumbnail sketch of how private equity funds worked, and how I traveled the country, trying to interest clients in investment prospects. He seemed to buy this lie.

"You used to be in the computer business, didn't you?"

"Computer magazines. I was the Northeast regional sales director for *CompuWorld*."

"And that job ended when . . . ?"

"In early January. Our title was closed down."

He consulted his notebook.

"Which is when you assaulted your boss, a Mr. Klaus Kreplin?"

I felt a stab of fear. Detective Flynn had been investigating my background carefully.

"Yes, there was an . . . uh . . . *altercation* with Mr. Kreplin after the company was sold."

His eyes shifted back to the notebook.

"And he was hospitalized, and you were arrested?"

"The charges were dropped."

"I am aware of that, Mr. Allen. I am also aware of the fact that you did not get along with the late Mr. Ted Peterson."

"He was not my favorite person on the face of the earth."

"Isn't that something of an understatement? According to his secretary . . ."

Oh, God, that charmer.

". . . you had a major business dispute with him just before Christmas. And a Detective Debra Kaster of thc Hartford P.D. informed us that you blamed Peterson for the suicide of a business colleague. Is that right?"

Stop avoiding his eyes.

I stared straight at Detective Flynn and said, "Yes, that's right."

"And then, of course, there was your very public confrontation with Mr. Peterson at a trade reception here in Manhattan on the night before he died."

"Yes—that was the first time I had made contact with him since . . . well, since before Christmas."

"And despite the fact that quite a few months had passed, you still had this major blowup."

"He had done a tremendous amount of professional damage—both to me and to a deceased colleague of mine named Ivan Dolinsky."

Eyes back to the notebook. "The gentleman who committed suicide in Hartford in March of this year?"

I nodded.

"So you hated Peterson?"

Tread carefully here.

"Like I said, I didn't exactly love the guy . . ."

"Then you were happy to see him dead?"

The question was asked in such a casual, throwaway style. But I still cringed.

"No one deserved to go the way he did," I finally said.

"And I suppose you can vouch for your whereabouts on the night of the murder?"

"Yes. I was in Miami. On business."

"Like I said at the outset, this is not a formal police conversation. And there is no onus on you to supply me with evidence of your whereabouts. But if you did have proof of your Miami trip, it would be useful in eliminating you from—"

"Happy to help," I said, interrupting him. Pulling open a desk drawer, I rooted through a couple of files, then pulled out the one marked *Miami* and handed over the plane ticket and rental car receipt. Detective Flynn studied the documents, copied down the necessary details in his notebook, then gave them back to me.

"So you're on the road a lot?" he asked.

"A couple of times a week, but I'm never away for more than a night."

"So if I needed to contact you again . . ."

"I'm here."

He stood up.

"Thanks for your time."

"My pleasure."

He turned to leave, then spun back toward me.

"One final thing," he said, reaching into his briefcase. "Any idea who this guy might be?"

He held up the police artist's sketch of Peterson's last supper companion.

"Never seen him before," I said.

"You're sure you can't place his face?"

"I must know a couple of dozen guys like that. They're a type."

He studied me closely.

"Yeah—they are," he said, and left.

That afternoon, before boarding the 3:00 P.M. flight to L.A., I called Lizzie. It was her first day back at work in the Manhattan office, and she sounded hassled.

"I really don't have much time to talk, Ned," she said. "You know, I only arrived back in town last night."

"How's the apartment?"

"Sterile."

"When can I come up and see it?"

"You never really hear what I say, do you?"

"I heard exactly what you said. But don't expect me to let you go without a fight."

"Ned, you don't have to let me go. I've *gone*. Face it."

I changed the subject. Quickly.

"Did you see the *New York Times* yesterday?" I asked.

"I couldn't believe it. Breaking into Peterson's house during his funeral."

"Just as you predicted. Jerry was worried that Peterson was hoarding something damaging. And now whatever evidence was there is gone."

"I'd still go see his wife."

"On what pretext?"

"She might be able to tell you something . . ."

"Like what?"

"I don't know. I've temporarily run out of brainstorms."

"That makes two of us. And, just to really complicate matters, the cops were around to see me this morning."

She sounded concerned again. "How did that go?"

"I got through it. And I did show him the false evidence of my alleged trip to Miami on the night in question."

"Did he buy it?"

"Seemed to."

A loudspeaker near me announced that American Airlines flight eleven to Los Angeles was now closing.

"Listen, that's my boarding call."

"You on courier duty today?"

"I'm afraid so."

"How the hell did you get yourself into this?"

"The way you always stumble into something—by not looking."

"Be careful," she said quietly.

I got off the plane at Los Angeles International. In the arrivals hall, I handed my computer case to the representative of a Mr. Tariq Issac. He disappeared for several minutes, then came back and sat down on the bench next to me. He placed the case between us on the floor. "Six hundred and twelve thousand," he whispered in my ear.

After he left, I killed almost four hours in the departure lounge before boarding the red-eye for Miami. I fell asleep with my arms wrapped around the case. We reached Miami by six the next morning. I got on the 7:00 A.M. puddle-jumper to Nassau. The money was deposited in the bank by nine-thirty ($122,400 deposited to the account of Jerome D. Schubert, the remaining $489,600 to the Excalibur Fund), and I was back in New York by four that afternoon. I grabbed a taxi to Wooster Street and retrieved the case I was storing in the broom closet in the downstairs lobby. Upstairs in the loft, I pulled out the assorted bank paraphernalia, wrote out a deposit receipt for $612,000, labeled it EXCALIBUR FUND, dated it, inked up the bank stamp, and slammed it down on the receipt. Then I tore it out of the book and left it on the kitchen table for Jerry.

Reaching back into the case, I added the two actual bank deposit receipts to the envelope in which I was accumulating all the previous slips. Then I repacked all the bank stuff, and decided against storing the computer case back in the downstairs broom cupboard. It wasn't a secure hiding place—and if the janitor ever found it and started knocking on doors in search of its owner, my days on this earth might be numbered.

So I took a cab uptown to a stationery shop on Forty-fifth and Lexington where you could also rent a mailbox. I paid a $20 deposit and $20 for the first month's rent on the box—and after being given a key to box number 242, I locked away the contents of the computer case, then dumped the now empty case in a trash can on the street.

As I entered my office building, Jack Ballantine came walking out, with two heavies in attendance. I recognized one of them immediately. It was "I'm From Upstairs."

"Hey, it's my tennis partner," Ballantine said, proffering his hand.

"Nice to see you, Mr. Ballantine," I said quietly.

"We should set up a game again soon."

"Whenever you like."

Inclining his head toward me, he said, "Jerry's been telling me about all the great work you've been doing for the fund."

I glanced briefly at I'm From Upstairs. He looked away. "I'm pleased he's pleased."

"I know it's not exactly what you had in mind. . . ."

Another glance at I'm From Upstairs. "Certain aspects of the work have . . . uh . . . taken me by surprise."

"Well, believe me, I know the effort you're putting into the job—and once this book tour of mine is finished, you and I are going to go out for a long lunch and talk about your future with us. How's that sound?"

"I look forward to it, Mr. Ballantine."

"Oh, a little piece of advice: If I were you, I'd move heaven and earth to get that wife of yours back. She is quite impressive. And . . ." He leaned forward, whispering into my ear.

". . . I know for certain there is someone actively on the chase, if you take my meaning."

I nodded.

"By the way, Ned—you never mentioned anything to Lizzie about your, uh, connection with us?"

"Of course not."

"Glad to hear it. Keep up the good work."

He gave me a coach's punch on the shoulder and headed out to his waiting car. I'm From Upstairs looked through me as he went by.

"I know for certain there's someone actively on the chase." And since that someone happened to be my all-controlling boss, he could also conveniently send me out of town for nearly two weeks

as he actively pursued my wife. Which is exactly what he did. The morning after I bumped into Ballantine, Jerry handed me a stack of plane tickets and an extensive verbal itinerary, which he asked me to copy down (so, of course, no paper trail led back to him). It was an exhausting schedule. Memphis, Dallas, L.A., Miami, Detroit, Miami, Denver, L.A., Houston, New Orleans, Miami—with a stop-off at Nassau after each city.

"Wouldn't it be cheaper to get FedEx to handle all this?" I asked facetiously.

"Do you really expect our investors to entrust so much cash to a courier company? Anyway, having you collect it personally is good customer relations. What's more, you ensure that it reaches the Bahamian Bank of Commerce without a hitch. So our investors know they're in good hands with us."

Our investors. You had to hand it to Jerry—the guy acted as if he believed his own bullshit. I really felt like telling him, *Just between ourselves, why don't we come clean about all this and admit that you're playing banker for a bunch of deeply unsavory characters.* Because, courtesy of Phil and his friends, I was beginning to assemble quite a dossier on our "investors."

"Okay, here's the lowdown on Tariq Issac," Phil said when I called him from Miami Airport between flights. "Lebanese-born, L.A. based, and a big noise in the clandestine weapons game. . . ."

A week later, when I phoned him from Denver, he had a report on our Houston investor:

"Manny Rugoff—independent oil trader, with extensive business interests in Guatemala, Ecuador, and Venezuela. And rumored to be on very tight terms with assorted wise guys south of the border."

"Terrific," I said.

While on the road, I also stayed in regular contact with Lizzie. Jerry really *had* been "pursuing her actively."

"My office is starting to look like a Mafia funeral," she said one afternoon when I phoned from Miami Airport.

"How do you mean?"

"The daily bouquet of flowers from Mr. Schubert."

"Jesus . . ."

"Well, you've got to admire his persistence."

"Has he asked you out yet?"

"Only about two dozen times."

"And?"

"I finally gave in and agreed to have dinner with him tomorrow night."

"Wonderful."

"Ingrate."

The next evening, when I was overnighting at the Dallas Airport hotel, I called Lizzie at her new apartment.

"What are you, my father?" she said angrily.

"I was just concerned. . . ."

"It's one in the morning, Ned."

"And you're alone?"

"I really should hang up on you."

"I simply wanted to make certain . . ."

"What? That I didn't sleep with the guy?"

"Well . . ."

"You are a total jerk."

"A total *concerned* jerk."

I heard her stifle a laugh.

"Sleeping with Jerry Schubert would be a total taste crime."

"But he's a hunk."

"And a murderer—which, believe it or not, doesn't really make him my type."

"Really? I'm surprised. Did he make a move?"

"He took me to a very nice restaurant. . . ."

"Which one?"

"Jo-Jo's on East Sixty-fourth Street."

"We ate there once, didn't we?"

"Yes, we did. For our second anniversary."

"That was a very romantic night."

"I'm not getting into this."

"You know, there are two basic types of seduction technique. The first is where the guy makes the woman laugh all night, and essentially jokes his way right into her bed. The second is where the guy comes across all sincere and touchy-feely, then moves in for the kill. Now I'd bet anything that Jerry's an exponent of the second technique. . . ."

She stifled another laugh.

"Good night, Ned," she said.

Three days later, while changing planes (per usual) in Miami, I managed to catch her at work.

"I was hoping you'd call," she said.

"That sounds promising. . . ."

"How fast can you get back here?"

"I've got two more days' worth of courier duties. Then—"

"Have you seen this morning's *New York Times*?"

"Not yet."

"Ted Peterson's house was broken into again."

"Jesus fucking Christ. Was anything taken?"

"Nothing major—though, according to the story, it was really torn apart."

My mind began to race. Finally I said, "Jerry's people didn't find what they wanted, right?"

"That's how it looks to me. Which means either Mrs. Peterson has stashed whatever evidence they're after somewhere else. Or maybe . . ."

Bingo.

"Peterson himself stashed it somewhere safe," I said, finishing her sentence.

"Safe and *offshore*, perhaps?" she asked.

"Perhaps, indeed," I said.

At the nearest newspaper stand I bought a *New York Times*. Then I ran for my plane. Two hours later I walked into the Bahamian Bank of Commerce.

"You know, you really have become our best customer," Mr. MacGuire said, peering into the briefcase I placed on his desk.

"What can I say? Business is very satisfactory."

"Four point two million dollars' worth of deposits in just under two weeks is more than satisfactory. Especially if, like Mr. Schubert, you're getting a twenty percent commission."

"Yeah—he must have close to a cool million in his account by now."

"Are you envious?"

"He deserves it," I said frostily.

"I'm sure he does," Mr. MacGuire added, arching his eyebrows. "So how much do you have for me today?"

"One hundred and forty-one thousand."

"Modest, by your standards."

Yeah, well—the "investor" in question (Bill Pearle, a big-time scrap merchant in Denver) *is probably just a minor-league racketeer.*

The money was whisked off by Muriel for counting. I tossed the *New York Times* on MacGuire's desk.

"Turn to section two, page five," I said.

"You mean, the story about the second break-in at Mr. Peterson's house?"

"You're way ahead of me."

"Shocking business, isn't it? What on earth do you think they're looking for?"

"Don't you know?"

"Why should I know?"

"Because you were his offshore banker. And because not only did he maintain an account with you, but a safety deposit box as well."

"You don't know that."

"No, but I'd stake a large sum of money on its existence. If I had any money in the first place . . ."

"Mr. Allen, you know that, if such a box existed, I couldn't reveal its existence to you."

"But you could reveal its existence to Mr. Peterson's widow, couldn't you?"

"Provided she supplied me with certain documentation, yes, I could."

"So the box *does* exist."

He let out a sigh, then peered at me with amused annoyance.

"Remind me never to play poker with you, Mr. Allen."

"What documents would she need?"

"Their marriage certificate, his death certificate, and his probated last will and testament, showing that he has left all his financial assets to her."

"Is that it?"

"Yes . . . but we would appreciate it if, at *your* convenience, you would return the stamp and the deposit book that you 'borrowed' from us."

"Give me a few more days," I said.

"You're lucky you're such a good customer."

I missed my connection in Miami that night, so I had to overnight in the airport hotel. I called my office number and checked my messages. There was only one.

"Detective Flynn here from the Greenwich P.D. Could you please call me as soon as possible—either at my office or at home. My numbers are . . ."

I glanced at my watch. It was just 9:15. I punched in the detective's home number.

"Hey, thanks for calling, Mr. Allen. You in New York?"

"Miami."

"When are you back in town, sir?"

"Not for another week," I lied.

"You can't get back here before then?"

"Not unless I want to lose my job."

"Well, I'm going to be blunt with you—we need to see you."

"Why?"

"We want you to take part in a lineup."

"A *lineup*?" I said, the word catching in my throat. "But I thought you had eliminated me from—"

"We had. Then we managed to get hold of some photographs taken at the SOFTUS reception. It seems there was a photographer, hired by SOFTUS, who was roaming the room to take public relations shots of all the guests—photos which, I gather, they were going to use in their trade magazine. As it turns out, there were several shots of you in 'discussion' with Mr. Peterson. They are, it must be said, slightly blurred. Still, earlier today, we showed the entire set of reception photographs to Mr. Martin Algar, the maître d' at the Hyatt Regency, in the long-shot hope that he might spot the individual who left the restaurant with Peterson. Now I must inform you, Mr. Allen, that he pointed to your picture and said that he thought you might be the man."

I wanted to run out of the room. Instead I took a very deep breath and tried to sound calm.

"But that's absurd. I was in Miami. I showed you proof that I was there."

"I am aware of that. Just as I am also aware that the photo was slightly blurred, and that Mr. Algar said he simply 'thought' you were the man he saw with Peterson. And, of course, the fact that you called me at home tonight also shows your willingness to cooperate with our investigation."

"I am definitely not the man you're looking for."

"I am glad to hear that, sir. But given that Mr. Algar has, in effect, given us some reason to question your assertion of innocence, we're going to have to ask you to come in and take part in a lineup. It'll get the whole business over with once and for all. And if he doesn't identify you as the guy with Peterson, then you'll never hear from us again. So when can you get back here?"

Stall for time, stall for time.

"Tuesday," I said.

"No way, Mr. Allen—that's almost a week from now."

"Like I said, I've got meetings set up all around the country this week. . . ."

"And I've got a murder investigation to run—an investigation in which you are now a figure of considerable interest to us. I mean, if Algar had given us a positive I.D., I'd have a warrant out for your arrest right now. But, under the circumstances, I can give you forty-eight hours from tomorrow morning to present yourself at my office. And if you're not there at nine A.M. Friday morning, then a warrant *will* be issued for your arrest. Is that clear?"

"Yes. It's very clear."

"One last thing—you might want legal counsel present at the lineup. Just in case."

He hung up. I fell backward on the hotel bed, terrified. Then I jumped up again and grabbed the phone, ready to call directory assistance for Old Greenwich, Connecticut, and ask for the home number of an Edward Peterson on Shore Road. But then I thought, If Jerry has had his stooges break into his house on two occasions, desperately searching for evidence, then there's every good chance he's also tapped the phone. And, with just forty-eight hours to go, I was only going to have one shot at getting this right, so . . .

I called Lizzie instead. As soon as she answered I said, "Lizzie, I am in the biggest trouble. . . ."

"Oh, I see. . . ." She sounded very distracted.

"You okay?"

"Uh, sure. But . . . I can't really talk right now."

"What do you mean, you 'can't talk'? This is a crisis."

"I mean," she whispered. "I *can't* talk."

My stomach did a somersault.

"Oh, Jesus. . . . ," I muttered.

"I've got to go. . . ."

"He's there, isn't he?"

"Call me tomorrow."

"Jerry is there, isn't he?"

"Yeah."

"Great."

"Trust me," she whispered. And hung up.

SIX

I was on the dawn flight out of Miami. Before boarding I turned off my phone. For the next twenty-four hours I needed to be unreachable, untraceable.

At La Guardia I made two return reservations to Nassau (via Miami) for that afternoon, then rented a car. I hit Old Greenwich by ten. Driving down its central drag, Sound Beach Avenue, I kept my head down, just in case Detective Flynn might be in town . . . or if Martin Algar of Hyatt Regency renown happened to be crossing the main street.

Ten o'clock. If the insane plan I had concocted was going to work, Meg Peterson would have to be home now. And if she wouldn't buy my story, then I would have no choice but to go on the run. Because if I did show up at the lineup, I was heading nowhere but jail.

I turned right at Shore Road. Halfway to the Peterson house a Ford Explorer passed me, heading toward town. It took a moment to register, then the realization hit: Meg Peterson had been behind the wheel of that car. Slamming on the brakes, I did an instant U-turn.

For one brief terrible moment, I thought I had lost the Explorer. But then I saw it turn right down a side street. I ran a stop sign and managed to catch up with it as it cruised down a residential road called Park Avenue. Then it crossed a narrow street and entered a parking lot behind a bank. I pulled in just as Meg Peterson got out of her vehicle. She looked world-weary, deprived of sleep. I screeched to a halt and jumped out of my car.

"Mrs. Peterson?" I shouted.

She turned around and regarded me with contempt.

"If you're from the press, I don't want to talk to you," she said angrily.

I approached her, both hands held up, trying to appear conciliatory.

"Trust me, Mrs. Peterson—I am *not* from the press."

"Yeah, well that's what that bastard from the *Post* told me."

"We've met before."

"I've never laid eyes on you in my life."

"Last December in the driveway of your house, remember? I'm Ned Allen. I used to work for a magazine called *CompuWorld*, and you found me camped out behind the wheel of my car. . . ."

"Yeah, yeah, I remember. Ted said you were chasing him for some advertising spread . . . and that he decided to help you out when it turned out your job depended on this deal."

"That's right. Your husband really did a great thing by—"

"Bullshit. Ted never did a decent thing for anybody. It was against his religion. Now if you will excuse me . . ."

"I really need to talk to you."

"Well, I really don't need to talk to you. I've spent the last couple of weeks talking to the cops, the press, the lawyers, and most especially to my very confused and distressed children. So I am truly sick and tired of talking. . . ."

She leaned against a parked car and tried to stifle a sob.

"Mrs. Peterson, please."

I made the mistake of putting a steadying hand on her arm.

"Don't you touch me. . . ."

"I'm sorry. I didn't mean—"

"Get out of here, or I'll call the cops."

"Mrs. Peterson, just *listen*."

"Get out!"

A few passersby in the parking lot stopped and stared. I had one final shot at this meeting. I had to gamble.

"I know who killed your husband," I said in a near whisper.

At first, she didn't take it in.

"You . . . what?"

I kept my voice low. "I know who killed your husband."

She studied me carefully, and with total distrust.

"And how do you know that?" she asked.

"Because I was there."

She stared at the ground.

"Listen," I said, "can I buy you a cup of coffee?"

"Go away," she said softly. "I don't want to know. . . ."

"I'll just take ten minutes of your time, no more."

"How do I know . . . "

"What?"

". . . you're not *them*."

"Who's 'them'?"

"The men who ransacked my house. Twice."

"Because . . . I work for *them*. And because they're trying to pin your husband's murder on me."

She shuddered.

I said, "Ten minutes—that's all I'm asking. You name the place."

She looked away—and I could see she was desperately trying to make up her mind.

"I'm going into the bank now," she said and started walking away from me. After taking five steps, however, she turned back and said, "There's a coffee shop on Sound Beach. Be there in five minutes."

Thank God, the coffee shop was empty. I settled into a booth right in the back. Ten minutes came and went. I thought, *She'll be showing up here with a cop in tow.*

But five minutes later, she walked in. Alone.

"There were long lines at the bank. . . . ," she said, sitting down.

"I really appreciate—"

"Mister, I don't know who the fuck you are—and after what I've been through, I certainly don't trust you or anyone else on this planet, with the exception of my kids. So you get to the point. *Now.*"

I started to talk. Step by step, I took her through the entire story. I spared her no details. The crisis over the *CompuWorld* advertising spread. The way Ted panicked when I played the Cayman Islands card—but how he turned vindictive when he realized all I had on him was a hushed-up case of attempted rape (her face visibly tightened when I detailed the Joan Glaston incident). I explained how he cost me the *Computer America* job. How he helped spark Ivan's suicide. How I hit bottom and was rescued by my old pal Jerry Schubert, who just happened to work for Jack Ballantine, and for whom her husband also happened to working.

She interrupted me.

"Jack Ballantine?" she said in a whisper. "*The* Jack Ballantine?"

I took her through the Excalibur Fund scam. How I discovered it was bogus. How it was being used as a front for some sort of elaborate, illegal scheme involving hefty amounts of dubious cash. How Ted was somehow involved—and how Jerry set up our confrontation at the SOFTUS reception, followed by an alleged reconciliatory dinner at the Hyatt Regency, after which . . .

She kept her head bowed during my description of the murder. She said nothing when I explained how Jerry set me up as the fall guy, and threatened to turn me in if I didn't transform myself into the bag man. And how, in the course of carting all that highly suspect money to an offshore Bahamian bank, I discovered that a certain Ted Peterson had opened an account there. And how he also had a safe deposit box in the same bank. And how I was certain that this box contained whatever the thugs who ransacked her house were looking for. And how I was due to take part in a lineup at the Greenwich Police Station in just under forty-eight hours, and was certain to be put away unless . . .

"Unless what?" she said.

"Unless whatever's in that safety deposit box can clear me."

"And you need me to gain access to the box?"

"Absolutely. All they'd need at the bank is your marriage certificate, Ted's probated will, his death certificate, your passport, of course . . . You do have a passport . . . ?"

She cut me off. "Are you out of your fucking mind?"

"I know it all sounds—"

"You expect me to drop everything and get on a plane with you? *You*—who may really be the guy who pushed that asshole husband of mine under a train. *You*—who might just be one of the charmers who tore up my house during my husband's funeral, and then came back and did it again. *You*—who'll probably hit me over the head the moment I get into your fucking car . . ."

She was getting dangerously loud.

"Mrs. Peterson, *please* . . ."

"I'm out of here."

"Just hear me . . ."

"I've heard enough."

"You're in debt, aren't you?"

"What?"

"He left you in debt. Serious debt, didn't he?"

"That is none of your—"

"Okay, true, point taken. But know this: There is an account in your husband's name at the Bahamian Bank of Commerce. I don't know how much is in it—but I think it's substantial. And if you will just hear me out for two more minutes, I will explain how I think you might also be entitled to a million dollars."

There was a very long pause.

"Two minutes," she said.

My explanation took about five minutes, but she didn't cut me off. When I finished she said, "Do you have a phone number for this bank?"

I pulled out a notebook and wrote it down.

She reached into her bag and pulled out a cellular phone. I saw her press zero, then ask for AT & T international directory assistance. "Nassau, the Bahamas," she said into the phone. "I need the number for the Bahamian Bank of Commerce. . . . You've got it? Hang on. . . ."

She pulled the notebook toward her, stared at the number I had written down, and then touched each digit with her finger as the operator verified its authenticity.

After she hung up, she looked back at me.

"Okay, there really is a Bahamian Bank of Commerce. Now what's the manager's name?"

"Oliver MacGuire. But if you want to call him, I wouldn't use your cellphone. Someone might be listening. . . ."

"You'll just have to take that risk, won't you?" And she started punching in the number.

"I'd like to speak to Mr. MacGuire, please. . . . Tell him it's Ted Peterson's widow . . . and that a Mr. Ned Allen suggested I call him."

I put my head in my hands and wondered if Jerry really was monitoring her calls.

"Mr. MacGuire?" she said, then suddenly stood up and walked

to the extreme rear of the coffee shop, out of my hearing range. She returned five minutes later, sat down opposite, and tossed her phone back into her bag.

"Mr. MacGuire said that, according to bank regulations, he could not confirm or deny the existence of an account and a safety deposit box in my husband's name . . . but that if I did show up at the bank with all the documentation you mentioned, he would be able to 'help me.' He also said you were legitimate."

"I've got tickets for the one-thirty flight to Miami—which we could just about make if—"

"How do I know that MacGuire isn't being paid by you to feed me some crap about an offshore account in order to lure me out there?"

"You don't. It's your call."

She said nothing for almost a minute. Then she stood up.

"Wait here. I might be a while."

She left the coffee shop. It was 10:47. I was exhausted and emotionally wasted and terrified. I was also starving, so I ordered a large breakfast. Two scrambled eggs, sausages, home fries, toast. But I could only manage to chew a little toast.

11:10. 11:18. 11:31. I kept glancing at the clock, and began to fear the worst—that, on panicked reflection, she didn't buy my story, and had placed a call to Detective Flynn.

11:38. And the door flew open and Meg Peterson rushed inside—carrying a small overnight bag.

"We'd better move if we want to make that plane," she said.

We left the restaurant and walked quickly back to the parking lot, where I'd left my rented car. Heading south on I-95, I kept thinking I was being tailed by a guy in a silver Cutlass, but then saw him drop back into the traffic and decided my paranoia was in overdrive.

"I have to be back by noon tomorrow, no later," she said.

"You'll be back."

"What time do we get to Nassau tonight?"

"Just before six, if we make the connection."

"Won't the bank be closed?"

"If MacGuire knows we're coming, I think he'll be there."

She pulled the phone out of her bag, and hit the redial button.

"Mrs. Peterson, let's wait until we get to a pay phone. . . ."

"I'm not getting on that plane unless I know he'll see us tonight."

"They're probably listening. . . ."

"They're not the CIA. . . . Hello? Yeah, Mr. MacGuire, please. Mrs. Peterson here again. . . . Hello, Mr. MacGuire? Meg Peterson . . . Listen, Mr. Allen and I will be arriving from Miami tonight at six. Now I've got to be back in the States by noon tomorrow, so . . . You sure that won't be a problem? . . . Terrific. Okay, really appreciate that. . . . See you then."

She turned off the phone. "He said he'll be waiting for us at the bank around six. Sounds like a very accommodating guy."

"I'm a good customer."

"I bet you are."

"Who'd you get to look after your kids?" I asked.

"My sister. She lives in Riverside. She'll pick them up at school, and they'll stay at her place tonight."

"What did you tell her?"

"Just that the prime suspect in Ted's death was whisking me off to the Bahamas for the night."

"I see."

"You have no sense of humor."

"I lost it on January second of this year."

"What went wrong on January second?"

"*I* went wrong."

"I know that feeling. My 'I-went-wrong' date was July twenty-seventh, nineteen eighty-seven."

"What happened then?"

"I married Ted Peterson."

She told me a little about herself—how she was raised just outside of Philadelphia, attended Wheaton, went to New York after graduating, and was doing rather nicely in advertising when she met wonderful Ted.

"He was Mr. Ivy-League charm. Mr. Corporate Big Shot. The shit I was destined to marry."

"Why did you, then?"

"He reminded me exactly of my dad."

Within two years, she knew the marriage was bad news. But

Ted had been transferred to GBS's head office in Stamford, and Meg was pregnant with Child Number One.

"So it was suburban nightmare, here we come," she said. "And, at Ted's urging, I made the dumb mistake of giving up work."

"You could have resisted," I said.

"I guess I have a talent for unhappiness."

Child Number Two followed eighteen months after Child Number One. And Meg found out about Ted's first affair.

"A barmaid at this dump in Stamford he used to drink at after work."

"Classy."

"His middle name."

"How'd you find out?"

"She called up the house, pissed, crying, boozed up, saying how Ted had promised her the moon, the stars, and her very own trailer. Of course he denied everything. Just like he denied investing two hundred grand in some Bordeaux vineyard that went down the toilet. Or losing a hundred and fifty thousand in some crazy hedge fund. Or taking a second mortgage out on our house. Or landing us in such fucked-up shape that I actually had to beg my dad for ten grand last month. And now you tell me the bastard had money socked away the whole time. It was probably going to be his running-away money—the disappearing act he always hinted he might pull someday. Leaving me and the kids with all his debts."

"Exactly how bad were his debts?"

"Try six hundred thousand dollars' worth of bad."

"Jesus."

"Yeah—at work Ted was considered Mr. Achiever, Mr. One Hundred and Ten Percent. But, at heart, the guy had this totally reckless, self-destructive streak. It was as if he kept trying to see just how far out on a limb he could go. At least when he went under that train I came into around three hundred thousands' worth of life insurance. But there's still another three hundred grand to clear—and the house is definitely destined for the auction block if this offshore account of his doesn't save our ass."

"Trust me, it will."

"Never say those two words to me again."

"Sorry . . ."

" '*Trust me.*' That was Ted's endless mantra. 'Trust me, I'm not sleeping with anybody else.' . . . I'm just screwing them. 'Trust me, we're in terrific financial shape.' . . . but do the kids really need new shoes? Trust me, trust me, trust me . . ."

"Why did you stay?"

"Cowardice. Stupidity. Low self-esteem. The usual classic 'wifely' reasons. But I did tell him around a month ago that I wanted out. Some of my girlfriends knew that I'd mentioned the 'D' word to him, and wondered if he threw himself under the train because he was so depressed about the prospect of me divorcing him. You know what I told them? 'Ted would never kill himself over something so trivial as losing his family.' "

"But he was still pretty desperate about the debt he'd landed you in."

"So desperate he got into bed with some pretty nasty characters—like this Jerry Schubert guy."

"Take it from me, Mrs. Peterson: Desperation is a dangerous thing."

Just before we pulled into La Guardia Airport, I glanced in the rearview mirror and thought I saw that silver Cutlass again. But then it was gone.

We made the 1:30 Miami flight. We dashed for the 5:00 P.M. puddle-jumper to Nassau. And Mr. MacGuire was waiting for us at the bank. I could see Meg Peterson's amazement at the shabby funkiness of this venerable offshore financial institution—but MacGuire's innate graciousness instantly won her over. She presented him with the requisite documents. He studied each carefully—especially Peterson's probated will. Finally he asked to see Meg's passport. Then he passed judgment.

"Mrs. Peterson, from the documentation you've shown me, I can confirm that your late husband did have an account with this bank. And though it is also clear that you are the beneficiary of this account, I cannot allow you access to the funds in his account until we receive the standard court order to allow their disbursement."

"I'll get in touch with my lawyer tomorrow."

"Once I receive their green light, the money is yours."

"And how much money might that be?"

Mr. MacGuire tapped a few keys on his desktop computer.

Then, squinting at the screen, he said, "One million, one hundred and twenty-eight thousand, seven hundred and fifty dollars."

For a moment Meg Peterson froze. Finally she said, "Are you serious?"

"I am very serious."

A small smile formed on her lips. "Well, if you are very serious, then I am very, *very* pleased. Would you mind repeating that figure again, Mr. MacGuire?"

He did.

"Thank you," she said.

"Now, in the matter of his safety deposit box," Mr. MacGuire continued, "I do not think that we need worry about getting approval from his estate for you to inspect its contents, as he did leave written instructions that it should be opened by his beneficiary in the event of his death. He also recently made the unusual provision of posting a key to the box back to me for safekeeping."

He opened his top desk drawer and pulled out a large key ring as well as a single tiny key with a tag marked B21. We left his office and walked down a narrow back corridor to a steel-reinforced door. It had five locks, all of which MacGuire systematically opened. Inside the small, dark room was a table and chairs and two walls of safety deposit boxes. MacGuire put the tiny key into the box labeled B21, then asked Meg to turn the lock. The little door swung outward. Mr. MacGuire pulled out the long steel box and placed it on the table.

"Now, if you would like privacy while you inspect it . . . ," he said to Meg.

"I'd like you both to stay," Meg said.

"Are you sure?" MacGuire asked.

"Safety in numbers," she said, and lifted the lid on the box. Inside was a small microcassette recorder, twenty microcassette tapes, a handful of documents, and a folded note. Meg opened it, read it, then passed it on to me. It said:

If you're reading this, then they've gotten me.
The tapes tell the story. They knew I had the tapes.
They just didn't know where. And because I had opened

the fund account for them here, they were certain that I must have been stashing them elsewhere. After all, why keep them right under their noses?

This seemed like a legitimate enough proposition when I first got into it. But then, at Grand Cayman, I was told the truth—even though, deep down, I really knew the truth all along.

My last word: I thought I was a true asshole . . . until I met Jerry Schubert.

Edward Peterson

I passed the letter on to MacGuire. When he finished reading it, Meg said, "That son of a bitch. With what he had banked here, he could have cleared our debts in a minute. This really *was* his 'running away' account."

"But why didn't he disappear if he was worried that Jerry might get him?" I asked.

"I think we should listen to the tapes," Meg said.

It took us well over three hours to work our way through all of the ten-minute microcassettes. It took us well over three hours to make copies of the twenty microcassettes, using MacGuire's own Dictaphone machine (and twenty spare blank cassettes he managed to unearth in the bank's storage room). Then there was an hour's wait while MacGuire drove us off into the night to the house of a lawyer friend named Caryl Jenkins, who was also a notary public and formally witnessed Meg's signature on a letter authorizing the bank to dispatch these tapes to the Federal Bureau of Investigation (Manhattan branch) in the event of either of our deaths. Then it was back to the bank, where the original tapes were transferred out of Peterson's safety deposit box and into a new box, now registered in the name of Megan Peterson.

Suddenly it was 7:00 A.M., the sun was rising—and Oliver MacGuire insisted on driving us to the airport.

"Do not worry about Caryl Jenkins saying anything to the fund's lawyer, Mr. Parkhill, regarding your business here tonight. I chose Caryl because I know he can't stand Parkhill."

"I cannot thank you enough," Meg said, touching MacGuire's arm.

"It has been a most *instructive* night," he said. "And do get the court order sent to me as soon as possible. Once it arrives I can transfer the account into your name, and you can have immediate access to its funds."

At the airport, I pumped MacGuire's hand, and asked him, "Why did you let me get away with the stamp and the deposit book?"

"Because I figured that whatever you did with them wouldn't bring the bank into disrepute."

"How could you be so sure?"

He shrugged. "Instinct. Trust. And sympathy. Especially for someone in way over his head."

"You helped. A lot."

He adopted a mock formal tone. "As long as I am not asked to break any laws, I am always happy to assist our customers in any way I can. Everything you requested me to do was basically legal, so . . ."

"You're still a friend."

He smiled. "Yes, but I'm also a banker."

Inside the terminal building, I didn't like the look of the ancient X-ray machine they had for hand luggage, fearing that it might wipe the tapes clean. So I asked the security officer on duty to inspect the bag by hand.

"What's inside the bag?" he asked before opening it.

I glanced at Meg Peterson. And stopped myself from saying, "Dynamite."

SEVEN

As soon as we stepped off the plane in Miami my phone rang.

"Ned, it's Oliver here at the bank."

"Didn't I just say good-bye to you?"

"I would have called you half an hour ago, but you were in the air at the time."

He sounded uncharacteristically tense.

"Is something wrong?"

"Remember when you asked me to ring you if Excalibur's lawyer ever called me to check on the balance of the fund?"

"Oh, Jesus . . ."

"I'm sorry, Ned. But he phoned as soon as I arrived back at the bank. And I had no choice but to give him the official balance. He does represent the account, after all."

"Okay, Oliver—thanks for warning me."

"Watch yourself."

I turned to Meg and told her what had just transpired.

"So the lawyer will report to Schubert that the account is a million dollars short?" she asked.

"That's right. And he'll think I've embezzled it myself. . . ."

The phone rang again.

"Ned."

It was Lizzie. She didn't sound relaxed.

"Don't go home," she said.

"What?"

"Don't go back to the loft. They're waiting for you."

"Who's 'they'?"

"Jerry's goons. They know exactly who you're with and where you've been, and they're after whatever it is you've got. And tell Mrs. Peterson not to go home, either. There are people waiting there for her as well."

"How do you know this?"

"Jerry told me."

"Did he sleep over?" I said, immediately regretting it.

"You are a total jerk."

"Sorry."

"Now listen to me, *please*. Jerry arrived unannounced to tell me that he'd just heard some news: The Connecticut cops have a witness who will finger you as the man who killed Peterson."

Oh Christ. It was Jerry who sent them the reception photos.

"Now it was pretty clear why he showed up on my doorstep to tell me this news—he was hoping, in his own dumb-shit, high-school-jock-romantic way, that I'd suddenly drop you and fall into his arms. But I have never given up on you, Ned. *Never*. Even though, Christ knows, I've wanted to. . . .

"Anyway, I played along, acted like I was almost relieved you were going to be busted, flirted with the jerk, but pulled the 'time-of-the-month' routine when he started to think it was his lucky night. And I would have called you back as soon as he left if I knew where you were, or if your cellphone had been on. I was absolutely frantic. Especially when he called me last night to say you'd disappeared with Peterson's wife, and fed me some lie about how the Connecticut cops had men posted at the loft and Mrs. Peterson's house, waiting to pick you up. And how I should call him immediately if you showed up here . . ."

"Calm down, Lizzie. Calm down."

"I can't calm down—they're going to kill you."

"Here's what you do. Call Jerry back, say you heard from me, and that I've decided to lay low in Miami for a few days. Tell him I've checked into the Delano. Let him send a search party down here. . . ."

"Okay, okay . . . what are you going to do?"

"Get to New York and sell my way out of this corner."

"Don't get hurt."

I hit the "off" button. Meg Peterson was looking at me, worried.

"Are your kids definitely at your sister's?" I asked.

She turned white. "Oh Christ, don't tell me . . ."

"Jerry has posted a 'welcome-home' party outside your house. So get on the phone to your sister and tell her not to go near your place . . . and suggest she take a drive out of town with the kids today."

Meg scrambled inside her bag for her cellphone.

"A land line, Meg," I said, pointing to the pay phone on the wall of the transit lounge.

"I read you."

Our flight to La Guardia was called. Meg was still on the phone when the final boarding announcement was given. A flight attendant approached us.

"Sir, ma'am, *please*—you must board now."

Meg ended her call and we were hustled aboard the plane.

"They're fine, thank God," she said as we walked down the jetway. "And they're all heading off to see a cousin of ours in Milford for the day. Oh—I have to tell you: The local papers have been saying that the police plan to arrest someone for Ted's murder by tomorrow."

"You mean, as soon as Mr. Hyatt Regency I.D.'s me."

We found our seats at the extreme rear of the plane. Almost immediately we pushed back from the gate and began to taxi toward the runway. My phone rang.

"*Here's what you do. Call Jerry back, say you heard from me, and that I've decided to lay low in Miami for a few days*."

I felt a deep chill run right through me as I heard Jerry mimic, verbatim, my conversation of five minutes earlier.

"What did I tell you about cellular phones, Allen? I mean, if someone can listen in on Prince Charles's cellphone, you don't think they can tap yours? Not that you need to worry about stuff like phones anymore. Because you're dead. As in D—E—A—D. And as for that duplicitous bitch you call a wife . . ."

A stewardess came running up the aisle.

"Sir, turn that cellphone off *now*. They interfere with navigational instruments."

I did as ordered. And whispered to Meg:

"We need to get off this plane before it takes off."

"What?"

"That was Jerry Schubert. He's been listening in. And I promise you, he's going to have a greeting committee at La Guardia. So we've got to . . ."

Suddenly the plane turned a corner and, without hesitation, shot down the runway.

"Forget that idea," Meg said.

I noticed a credit card phone in the arm of my seat. I turned around to where the air hostess was strapped into a jump seat.

"Can I use this?" I said, frantically pulling the receiver out of the armrest.

She nodded her approval. I whipped out a credit card and slid it through the little groove on the edge of the receiver. Nothing happened. I slid it through again. A message appeared in the little window on the receiver: INSUFFICIENT FUNDS.

"Shit, shit, shit," I muttered. Meg Peterson tapped me on the shoulder with her AMEX card.

"This might just work."

It did—and I reached Lizzie at her apartment.

"Get out of there *now,*" I said. "He's been listening in. He knows you've been leaking everything he's said to me. And he's really pissed off."

"Oh, Jesus . . ."

"Don't go to the office. Don't go anywhere he might think of looking for you. Just get out of there. And don't call me again. Go somewhere safe. . . . a museum."

"Remember that benefit we were at in October?"

"Gotcha."

My next call was to Phil Sirio.

"You in a plane, boss?" he asked.

"I'm in deeper than deep shit."

"Tell me how I can help."

I explained the problem. He had an instant solution. He'd grab his brother and his brother's car and meet us at La Guardia—whereupon they'd whisk us off to the safety of Ozone Park for as long as necessary.

"You can whisk Mrs. Peterson off. I've got some business in the city."

"Whatever," Phil said. "When do you land?"

"Just before eleven. We're on American flight eleven-thirty-two."

"We'll be there, boss."

I turned to Meg and informed her that we now had protection in the shape of Phil Sirio and his brother. Then, talking in a near whisper, I took her through the scenario I was going to enact as soon as I reached Manhattan—and how I would call her when she was needed. She scribbled down her number in my notebook. Then we lapsed into tense silence. And stayed that way until we touched down at La Guardia.

We were last off the plane. Phil and his brother Vinnie (a squat bear of a guy, with a silk open-neck shirt and several gold chains) were waiting for us at the gate. As we waved in acknowledgment, I saw I'm From Upstairs walking rapidly toward us. Just as he was about to grab my arm, Vinnie tapped him on the shoulder. I'm From Upstairs pivoted and instantly encountered Vinnie's fist. The blow landed between his eyes, and he landed on the floor. People scattered. Vinnie then quickly rammed his boot between the guy's legs, just to make certain he really wasn't going to pursue us. And the four of us ran for the street.

"Our car's just over there," Phil said, pointing to a gold Olds, illegally parked near the taxi stand. "We can run you into Manhattan."

"Just get Meg somewhere safe. I'll call you when I need you. And Vinnie . . ."

"Yo."

"Nice meeting you."

I jumped into a cab.

"Forty-fifth and Lexington."

I collapsed across the backseat. I momentarily closed my eyes. When I opened them again, we were in midtown Manhattan. It took a moment for me to get my bearings. I paid off the cabbie. I entered the stationery shop in which I had rented a mailbox. I dug out the key, opened the box, and removed the envelope stuffed with Bahamian bank receipts and the deposit stamp. Dropping everything into my briefcase, I ran out to the street again, hailed another cab, and asked to be dropped on Madison between 53rd and 54th.

I feared that Jerry might have a goon squad on the lookout for me in the downstairs lobby—but the usual security guard was the only person on duty, and he gave me a curt nod of hello. I rode the elevator up to the eighteenth floor, expecting tough guys in the reception area of Ballantine Industries. However, there was just a secretary. She looked up at me through the glass security door, figured me to be a well-dressed (if somewhat disheveled) executive, and buzzed me in.

"Can I help you?"

"Not really," I replied, passing her. She yelled after me—but I was now running, my eyes focused on the door at the end of the corridor. Made of massive mahogany, it screamed executive self-importance, and could only belong to one man in this organization. I heard footsteps racing behind me, but I knew I was going to reach this door first. And throwing my weight against it, I spilled right into the office of Jack Ballantine.

He was seated behind a huge Oval Office–style desk. But as soon as I made my crash landing he was on his feet. So was Jerry Schubert, who had apparently been seated in the chair opposite the desk. Jerry dived for the phone.

"Jenny, get me Security. . . ."

But Security was already here—in the form of Thug Number Two, of Hyatt Regency parking lot fame. He had me in a half nelson. Ballantine approached me, shaking his head.

"You disappoint me, Ned. Here I was, thinking you were a guy ready to play pro ball. But, as it turns out, you're junior varsity—and way out of your league."

"Get him into my office," Jerry ordered the thug.

"You made a classic mistake, Ned," Ballantine said. "You forgot that non-team players always get trampled."

I reached into my jacket pocket with my free hand and pulled out a microcassette recorder.

"Before you start trampling me, I think you should hear this first," I said, pressing the "play" button, and spinning the volume dial up to maximum.

"You're telling me that Jack Ballantine's behind this fund?"

"That's exactly what I'm telling you. Which is why, if you don't play ball with us, you and your family are heading for harm. Because

Jack Ballantine is like an Old Testament god. Cross him and he smites your ass. Permanently."

Jerry was heading toward me. "Give me that fucking tape," he ordered.

"Not so fast," Ballantine said, approaching me. "Play it again."

I hit the "rewind" button and then pressed "play."

Ballantine listened again. Jerry made another grab for the cassette recorder. But Ballantine blocked his attempted swipe, seizing him by the shirt.

"Back off, son," he said calmly, "or you might get hurt."

He pushed Jerry into a chair, then turned to me.

"Who's the other guy on the tape?" he asked.

"The late Ted Peterson. And if you look in my briefcase there, you'll see there are twenty other tapes—all containing recorded conversations between Mr. Peterson and Mr. Schubert, and all of a highly incriminating nature."

Ballantine bent down, picked up the briefcase, and peered inside. I continued talking.

"And I must inform you, Mr. Ballantine, that my associates are expecting a phone call from me in just under fifteen minutes. If they do not hear from me, they will presume the worst—and they will deliver the originals of these tapes to the FBI."

"This is bullshit, Mr. B.," Jerry yelled.

I ignored Jerry and stared directly at Ballantine.

"I would advise you to take this situation seriously, sir. And I would also ask you to get this fucking gorilla off me right now."

After a moment's consideration, Ballantine flicked his hand toward Thug Number Two. He released me and stood guard by the door.

"May I now tell you a story?" I asked.

"This guy is a fucking blackmailer!" screamed Jerry.

"Jerry," Ballantine said, "I'll say this just once: *Shut up*."

He then nodded toward me. "Okay, Allen. Talk."

"I'm not here to blackmail you, Mr. Ballantine. I'm here to sell you an idea. 'All salesmanship is storytelling.' Didn't you write that in *The Success Zone*? Well, here's the story.

"Ted Peterson, GBS executive, asshole supreme, meets Jerry Schubert just over a year ago at some cocktail party. Jerry gets talking about this private equity fund idea he's cooking up, Ted gets interested—because, though he's a high-flying executive, the guy's also a jerk when it comes to managing his money, and he's a couple of hundred grand in debt. They both see a mutual opportunity for fun and profit—especially since Ted is a member of a highly confidential GBS committee in which all the research and development people sit around and talk about products they're considering buying from small software companies that are about to go public.

"Before you can say 'insider information,' Jerry's paying Ted five grand a month for this highly confidential corporate info, which he then disseminates among your wide circle of wealthy friends—who, in turn, buy stock in these emerging companies, and turn a nice profit.

"So far so good. But, of course, Jerry has ambitions beyond mere insider trading. He knows that your wealthy friends, Mr. Ballantine, are looking for intriguing investment opportunities—and a way of washing clean a lot of dirty money. So he sets up a private equity fund called Excalibur and asks Ted if he'd like to be the chief talent spotter for the fund. Ted is delighted—the five percent commission could turn out to be a very lucrative sideline for him. And as an additional bonus, Jerry asks Ted to fly around the country on a couple of weekends and meet some of the well-heeled investors Jerry's bringing into the fund. And much to Ted's surprise, these guys start handing him briefcases full of money. He calls Jerry. 'What do I do with all this cash?' he asks. 'We've opened a fund account in Grand Cayman,' Jerry says. 'Hop a plane and deposit it there.'

"Ted agrees. And every weekend for a month, he does these little trips around the country to rich friends of Jack Ballantine—who love his private equity sales pitch so much they keep handing him suitcases of money. And before jetting back to the bosom of his family on Sunday night, Ted makes a quick stopover at a Grand Cayman bank, which happily accepts deposits seven days a week.

"The fund grows to fifteen million in a matter of weeks. But then Jerry drops a little bombshell on Ted. He doesn't plan to invest all this money in new emerging companies—because the Excalibur Fund is completely bogus. Instead, he wants him to work out a way of *laundering* the money . . . because all the cash he's been handling is dirty. Drug money dirty. Arms money dirty. Child pornography dirty. Excuse the editorial aside, Mr. Ballantine, but you know some very *interesting* entrepreneurs. . . ."

"Get back to the story, Allen."

"With pleasure. Ted freaks—because he's now being asked to engage in some serious criminal activity. I mean, compared to laundering drug and porn money, trading a little insider information is Boy Scout stuff. So Ted says he wants out. But Jerry threatens to expose his insider dealing stunts at GBS. Ted buys a tape recorder and begins to record all his business discussions with Jerry. Eventually, after multiple threats—like the one involving your name, Mr. Ballantine—Ted capitulates. And, after a bit of research, he creates a bogus software company in Budapest called Micromagna. They're allegedly selling word processing programs to other countries in the Eastern Bloc. What they're actually doing is sending empty boxes of disks to nonexistent, one-man-in-a-phone-booth companies in Warsaw, Bucharest, Bratislava—who, in turn, pay for these bogus goods with cash they've received from the Excalibur Fund. It's the perfect money-laundering scheme—dirty money gets used for alleged legitimate business deals. Nobody actually pockets a penny. The money comes out smelling clean.

"The scheme works brilliantly—but alas, Ted is unhappy with the measly twenty-thousand-dollar payoff he gets for all his hard work. Jerry promises more the next time around—and sends Ted to collect a whopping six point five million from a consortium of your entrepreneur friends down Mexico way. This time they decide to try the banking facilities of the Bahamas. Ted docks in Nassau with the six point five. He engages the services of a local lawyer. The lawyer makes a call to the Bahamian Bank of Commerce. Ted pays the bank a visit and opens an Excalibur account. While he's there, the bank manager suggests he also open a personal account for any commissions he gets from the fund. On the spot, Ted decides he deserves a healthy commission this time, and tells the banker to shove five point five million into the Excalibur account, and a million into his own personal account.

"Well, Jerry gets a little perturbed when he hears about Ted's commission, and threatens him and his family with grievous bodily harm unless the money is returned. At this point, Ted plays his trump card. He's got this extensive library of Ted and Jerry chats—which he will make public unless he gets to keep the million. What's more, he wants a retainer of fifteen thousand a month just to keep him sweet.

"You should listen to these guys intimidate each other, Mr. Ballantine. They just can't help but trade threats and counterthreats. And, I've got to tell you, I couldn't figure out why Ted didn't just take the money and run—until, of course, I heard the tape in which Jerry assured Ted that he'd do unspeakable stuff to his kids if he suddenly vanished. Even an immoral scumbag like Ted Peterson had to give in to that threat, and stay put in Old Greenwich."

Jerry was about to yell some disclaimer, but Ballantine silenced him with a dangerous glare.

"So now Ted's got this big problem. Personally, he's still six hundred grand in debt. And though he's got a million in this offshore account, he knows that Jerry will kill him if he touches the cash. And Jerry, too, has a big problem, as the million that Ted has embezzled belongs to his so-called investors—and they are not the kind of gentlemen who like to be stolen from.

"But then I show up on the scene, and Jerry sees a way of eliminating the entire Ted crisis. Before you can say *choo-choo*, Ted is under that train, I am Jerry's new delivery boy, and Peterson's house is twice turned upside down by Jerry's stooges in search of the tapes—which, as you now know, were kept elsewhere all the time."

I sat down.

"So that's the story, Mr. Ballantine—and one which is completely corroborated by all twenty tapes in that briefcase. They really make interesting listening, especially if you're a Fed. . . ."

Jerry was on his feet. "I want to say something here," he barked.

"I don't want to hear it," Ballantine said.

"Well, I'm going to fucking say it whether—"

Ballantine's face turned malevolent, but his voice remained hushed.

"No, you're not going to say anything. Now sit down."

Jerry looked at the door as if he was thinking about making a break for it. Thug Number Two shook his head as if to say *Don't even try*. So he sank back into his chair. Ballantine faced me again.

"So that's the *entire* story, Mr. Allen?"

I inadvertently smiled at his sudden, respectful inclusion of "Mr." before my name.

"No, sir. As you yourself said in *The 'You' Defense,* 'In business there is never one *actual* story. There are *many* stories.' Now, were those tapes to find their way to the police or the media, the story would emerge as I have described it—with disastrous personal consequences for you.

"However, there is a way of tailoring the story to avoid such a 'negative' outcome. And that is to cast Jerry here as the villain of the piece. After all, there's no documentation linking Ballantine Industries to either Excalibur or any of the offshore accounts. So here's how you spin it. Jerry set up the Excalibur Fund himself. He brought Ted on board. They opened the account in Grand Cayman. They used Micromagna to launder the money. They had an ongoing dispute about money. Jerry threw Ted under a train. End of story."

Once again, Jerry was on his feet. Ballantine simply pointed his finger at him, and he sat back down.

"It's an interesting scenario," Ballantine said, "but won't the investors in the Grand Cayman fund be exposed?"

"Why should they be? The money's laundered, there's no record of any of their individual contributions, and even if Jerry here names names, what proof does he have?"

"I like that," Ballantine said. "But what about the current fund?"

"Now that presents you with a wholly different set of problems, all of which are easily resolved. You go back to your investors and announce that you are returning their money with ten percent interest, because you have discovered that Jerry Schubert, your right-hand man, the guy you treated like a son, has been embezzling a significant chunk of the cash."

"That is such total bullshit," roared Jerry. "Allen's the embezzler. And I have proof right here."

He stood up, dug into the inside pocket of his jacket, and pulled out a sheet of paper, which he waved in front of Ballantine with maniacal desperation.

"It's a fax from our lawyer in Nassau, showing that over one million dollars of the money Allen was handling has disappeared from the Excalibur account."

Ballantine grabbed the fax from Jerry's hand. After scanning it, he turned to me and said:

"Is this true? One million?"

"Yes, sir—it's absolutely true. One million is missing from the Excalibur account . . . but not unaccounted for, as it's all lodged in a personal account in the name of Jerry Schubert."

Jerry lunged for me. But Thug Number Two got between us and quickly had him restrained.

"Mr. B.—*Jack*—he's fucking lying, I never, *never* would dream of stealing from you."

I reached into the briefcase and pulled out the envelope brimming with deposit slips.

"Mr. Ballantine, he asked me to open the account in his name. . . ."

"You piece of shit!" Jerry screamed.

"Inside here you'll find his bank account book, and copies of deposit slips for everything he asked me to stash in his own personal account. Just for the record, it was twenty percent of all funds. The good news, however, is that I kept careful records of everything that your investors paid in—every time I made a deposit, I ensured that the investor's name was on the deposit slip. So you won't find it difficult to refund their money. Just add twenty percent to everything they're owed . . . as well as the interest you're going to pay them, of course."

"And what am I going to pay you, Mr. Allen?"

"We'll come to me in a moment. First there's the matter of Mrs. Peterson. She's asked me to negotiate with you on her behalf. Now, as you can appreciate, her life has suffered a considerable amount of distress recently. The sole breadwinner in the family thrown under a train. Her house torn apart twice. Nasty men prowling around her kids. And, of course, she is in possession of evidence that could end your freedom forever, sir.

"But take my word for it: All she wants is a quiet life. And a certain amount of compensation for her losses. So here's the math—and I must say it strikes me as quite reasonable. She gets to keep the million in Peterson's offshore account—which will essentially get her family out of the debt Peterson left them in and pay the first mortgage still remaining on the house. Then she would also like an additional one million, which she plans to invest in nice safe unit trusts and mutual funds, to provide a reasonable annual income for herself and her two children."

"And what about the tapes?" Ballantine asked.

"You get to keep this set. The originals stay locked away in a secure place—with instructions to ship them to the Feds should either Mrs. Peterson or myself meet a sinister end. But that's not going to happen, is it?"

"How do I know you're never going to use those tapes as a bargaining chip against me again?"

"Because, with all due respect, after today I never want to see you again. And Mrs. Peterson simply never wants to meet you. So . . ." I pulled out my cellphone. "Do we have a deal?"

"It's not cheap."

"Altogether, you're going to have to find around three million to cover Mrs. Peterson's settlement and make up the shortfall to your investors. But, hey, it's a small price to pay for your freedom, your *life*. And anyway, what's three million to Jack Ballantine?"

He shook his head wearily. "Give me the phone," he said.

"The number's already programmed in. You just have to press 'send.' "

He did as instructed. "Mrs. Peterson? Jack Ballantine here. I have been in extensive talks with your negotiator, Mr. Allen. And I'm pleased to say that I agree to your terms. I'll pass you over to Mr. Allen now."

He handed me back the phone.

"Hi, Meg."

She sounded dazed. "He really agreed to everything?"

I looked over at him. "He is a man of his word."

"You must be amazingly persuasive, Ned."

"I can only play with the cards I'm dealt. And you gave me four aces. How are Phil and Vinnie treating you?"

"Great—but they're playing me old Al Martino albums."

"Well, there's a price for everything."

"I think they deserve a reward from my windfall. Would they accept ten grand?"

"I doubt it—Phil's more ethical than he cares to admit. Listen, I've got to go."

I turned the phone off.

"She's very pleased," I said.

"I'm sure she is," Ballantine said dryly. "And now, sir—how can I please *you*? A million? A new job? Both? What's the price?"

"I want just two things from you. The first is this: At nine tomorrow morning, I'm due to present myself at the Greenwich police station to take part in a lineup, where the maître d' of the Hyatt Regency restaurant—a Mr. Martin Algar—is certain to finger me as the guy last seen with Peterson. I want you to persuade Mr. Algar—with some cold, hard cash—to finger Schubert here instead."

Jerry tried to express his objection to my idea, but Thug Number Two simply bent his arms further up his back.

"Schubert ordered Peterson's death," I said. "Schubert killed Peterson by proxy. Schubert should take the fall."

"Done," Ballantine said.

Suddenly Jerry slammed his heel down hard on Thug Number Two's left foot and broke free of his grip.

"I am not taking any fucking fall," he yelled and raced out the door. Thug Number Two was about to pursue him, but Ballantine said, "Call Security, let them find him."

Thug Number Two lifted the phone. I asked Ballantine, "Aren't you worried he might get away?"

"Believe me, he'll never leave the building," he said matter of factly. "Now where were we, Mr. Allen?"

"We were about to discuss my final request," I said.

"Which is . . . ?"

"I walk out of here, and you never come near me again."

"That's it?" Ballantine asked.

"Yes, that's it."

"And my offer of a million?"

"Is it legitimate?"

"As you yourself said, I *am* a man of my word. And in addition to the money, I am now in the market for a new right-hand man. Two hundred grand a year—and, needless to say, a lot of perks. All yours, Mr. Allen."

"No thanks," I finally said.

"Don't tell me you're not even tempted."

"Of course I'm tempted."

"One million dollars and an impressive new job would solve a lot of problems."

"And create some very large new ones. I cannot compete in your league, Mr. Ballantine. I'm not enough of an asshole."

He smiled thinly. "That's a real pity, Ned," he said. "Because assholes always win. Anyway . . . it's your life."

"That's right. It is. And I'd like it back."

"Fine by me. What was the name of that maître d' again?"

"Martin Algar. The Hyatt Regency Hotel, Old Greenwich."

"Did you get all that?" he asked Thug Number Two.

"I did."

"Offer him twenty-five grand, no more," Ballantine said. "And find a picture of Schubert to bring with you. I'm sure you'll have no problems with the guy."

"Piece of cake," Thug Number Two said, and left.

"So . . . ," Ballantine said, stretching his arms out in front of him, "game, set, and match. A very impressive performance, Ned."

"Thank you. May I ask a question?"

"Shoot."

"Are you really going to be turning Jerry over to the cops?"

"What do you think?"

"So what will you do with him?"

"It won't be pleasant. But it will look accidental."

"Is that really necessary?"

"I'm an asshole, remember?"

"You're going to get hit with some very ugly publicity . . ."

He cut me off. "I'll survive it. I always do."

"I know that, Mr. Ballantine. In fact, *everybody* knows that."

He proffered his hand. I didn't take it. He shrugged, as if to say *I can live with your disapproval.*

"So what next, Ned?"

"A walk."

"I mean, after that."

"I'm just thinking about the walk, Mr. Ballantine."

"Watch yourself," he said. I met his stare.

"You watch yourself, too."

I rode the elevator down to the first floor and stepped outside. When I hit the street, I found a cab and asked the driver to take me to Seventy-seventh Street between Central Park West and Columbus.

"Remember that benefit we were at in October?"

I did. It was a black-tie charity thing, held in the dinosaur hall of the Museum of Natural History.

When the cab pulled up in front of the museum, I ran inside, paid the admission fee, then headed up the stairs to the dinosaur hall on the fourth floor. But when I reached the entrance—and spotted Lizzie from behind, standing near the Tyrannosaurus rex—I slammed on the brakes.

Careful now. Don't overplay your hand.

I stepped out of the hall. Pulling a notebook and a pen out of my pocket, I scribbled

> *Lizzie:*
>
> *It was an eventful morning, but it looks like the coast is clear.*
>
> *I have to run an errand now—but I'm planning to have a cup of coffee at Nick's Burger Joint (76th and Broadway) in around half an hour. It would be nice to see you. If, however, you don't show up, I will understand.*
>
> *Love,*

I scrawled my name at the bottom of the note, then tore the page out of the book and found a museum guard standing nearby.

"Could you do me a favor?" I asked him.

"Depends," he said.

"See that woman standing over there by the T. rex? Would you mind giving her this note?"

He looked at the note warily, as if it might be obscene.

"Read it if you like," I said. "Anyway, I'm her husband."

"Sure you are, pal," he said, snatching the note out of my hand.

I watched as he walked over to where Lizzie was standing. As he handed her the scrap of paper, I slipped away down the stairs and headed toward the main entrance.

I turned west on Seventy-seventh Street, then north on Amsterdam, stopping at a stationery shop near the corner of Seventy-ninth Street.

"Do you sell padded envelopes?" I asked the woman behind the counter.

"Sure," she said. "How big?"

I reached into my jacket pocket and removed the Bahamian Bank of Commerce stamp.

"Big enough to fit this," I said.

She reached below the counter and handed me an eight-by-ten padded envelope. I wrote Oliver MacGuire's name and address on its front, then pulled out my notebook again and scribbled eight words:

Oliver:
I closed.
I owe you one.

Ned

I tore out the note and placed it with the bank stamp inside the envelope.

"You want, we can sell you the stamps and mail that for you," the woman said.

"That would be great," I said, handing her some cash.

"The Bahamas, huh?" she said, staring at the address. "I'll need to put a customs sticker on the front. How should I describe the contents?"

I thought about this for a moment, then said, "A souvenir."

She looked at me with amusement. "Of what, if you don't mind my asking?"

"Things past."

I stepped back outside. I started walking west. On my way, I hoped, to a cup of coffee with the woman who might—or might not—still be my wife. I tried not to think about what to say (if, indeed, she did show up), or how to react, or what strategic pose to adopt. This wasn't a pitch meeting. This was a cup of coffee. Nothing more. It might be a pleasant cup of coffee. It might be a disastrous cup of coffee. It would be what it would be—and I would deal with the outcome.

That's what selling teaches you: This is never an easy ride, and we spend most of our lives scrambling. But once in a while, you *can* sit down with somebody and have a cup of coffee.

And when you sit down with somebody over a cup of coffee . . . well, it's always a beginning.